MARY HAMER

Mary Hamer travels widely and has lectured in many countries. Her work has appeared in *The Economist, The Guardian* and *The Independent*. She has contributed to television and radio programmes, such as *In Search of Cleopatra, Women's Hour* and *Night Waves*.

Mary began her career teaching at Cambridge University but soon found that research was her real passion. Ever since Rudyard Kipling lit her imagination as a child, Mary had wanted to write about him. Later, she realised that the story of his sister, Trix, was just as compelling.

To explore the impact of their daunting early experience on their lives and work as adults, she set out to research the facts in libraries and archives. But it was visiting the places where they lived, from Mumbai to Cape Town, that brought them closer to her. In Naulakha, the house Kipling built in Vermont, Mary slept in his bedroom and soaked in his own bath. For the intimate story she had to tell, she decided it had to be fiction.

Kipling & Trix is her fifth book and first novel.

First published in the UK in 2012 by
Aurora Metro Books
67 Grove Avenue, Twickenham, TW1 4HX
www.aurorametro.com
info@aurorametro.com

Kipling & Trix © 2012 Mary Hamer

With thanks to: Lesley Mackay, Ziallo Gogui, Neil Gregory, Simon Smith,
Jack Timney, Richard Turk, Alex Chambers.
10 9 8 7 6 5 4 3 2 1

 We are grateful for the sponsorhip of
The Virginia Prize to ea Consulting Group
www.eacg.co.uk

Cover design: Alice Marwick/www.alice-marwick.co.uk

Printed by Ashford, Gosport, Hants UK
ISBN: 9781906582340

KIPLING
&
TRIX

Mary Hamer

AURORA METRO BOOKS

Acknowledgements

I couldn't have written this book without the generous support of many individuals and institutions around the world. Not all of them can be named here but I particularly want to thank Henry Louis Gates Jnr. for keeping a welcome for me in Harvard and David Page, John Radcliffe and John Walker for giving me a home in the Kipling Society.

The staff in the Houghton Library and in Widener, like the keepers of Sussex University's Kipling Archive, have been unfailingly helpful. I shall always be in debt to Tanya Barben of the University of Cape Town, for sharing her exhaustive knowledge of Kipling's time in South Africa and to Barbara Fisher, for allowing me access to her own research on Trix Kipling.

I owe the Clink Street Writers' Group for astute feedback and for the constant friendship that kept me on track as I was writing.

Most of all I am grateful to my husband, Nick Cumpsty, for his backing.

Note about the book

The story I'm telling in *Kiping & Trix* follows the historical facts very closely. But in bringing it to life, I had to draw on imagination for scenes and conversations and to explore the inner thoughts of my characters. It was because I wanted to make emotional sense of these lives that I chose fiction rather than biography.

This book is for my brothers

Christopher and John

and in memory of Michael, 1947-2011

Song of the Wise Children

BY RUDYARD KIPLING

WHEN the darkened Fifties dip to the North,
And frost and the fog divide the air,
And the day is dead at his breaking-forth,
Sirs, it is bitter beneath the Bear!

Far to Southward they wheel and glance,
The million molten spears of morn—
The spears of our deliverance
That shine on the house where we were born.

Flying-fish about our bows,
Flying sea-fires in our wake:
This is the road to our Father's House,
Whither we go for our souls' sake!

We have forfeited our birthright,
We have forsaken. all things meet;
We have forgotten the look of light,
We have forgotten the scent of heat.

We shall go back by the boltless doors,
To the life unaltered our childhood knew—
To the naked feet on the cool, dark floors,
And the high-celled rooms that the Trade blows through:

To the trumpet-flowers and the moon beyond,
And the tree-toad's chorus drowning all—
And the lisp of the split banana-frond
That talked us to sleep when we were small.

The wayside magic, the threshold spells,
Shall soon undo what the North has done—
Because of the sights and the sounds and the smells
That ran with our youth in the eye of the sun.

And Earth accepting shall ask no vows,
Nor the Sea our love, nor our lover the Sky.
When we return to our Father's House
Only the English shall wonder why!

The Times January 18th, 1936

MR. RUDYARD KIPLING

STORY-TELLER AND POET

AN INTERPRETER OF EMPIRE

One of the most forcible minds of our time has ceased to work with the death early this morning of Rudyard Kipling.

Whether the mind of Rudyard Kipling was a great mind; whether he could be called a great man; whether he lacked in width of vision what he had in intensity; whether his achievement in self-expression will tend in the future towards the good which he ardently, single-heartedly, desired for the world – all these are questions which it is impossible to consider under the blow of a great loss.

PROLOGUE

Carrie Kipling ran her fingers over the page where she had pasted in her husband's obituary. This was one scrapbook that Rud would never take down from the shelf. She looked up at the row of tall green volumes that housed his newspaper archive, then round at the packed bookcases, the bare plain of the desk. His briefcase appeared absurdly small, like a child's toy, propped against the vacant chair.

Two years on, she was almost used to missing him. But today, as January 18th came round again, she'd had Rud in her thoughts ever since waking. It was the anniversary of their wedding, as well as the day of his death.

They'd lived together forty-four years.

Reading the column from *The Times* once more, she felt a gathering indignation.

'*A great mind? A great man?*'

'*Impossible to tell under the blow of a great loss.*'

She let out a scornful laugh.

How could they know anything, these men who only took account of scenes played out on the public stage? The world's honours, even the Nobel Prize, had meant little to Rud. 'What does it matter, what does it all matter?', he used to say.

She shifted in her chair, under the weight of his sadness.

For Rud, children were always the thing. And childhood. If they wanted to ask about minds, surely, childhood was the time when minds were formed? Or deformed. That certainly was the case for Trix. At the thought of her difficult sister-in-law, Carrie sniffed.

She turned back to Rud's obituary.

They were not asking the right questions.

'"Loss" is the word that really applies,' her voice was harsh in the empty room. 'Why don't they ask what Rud himself had lost?'

It was only after they lost Josephine that Rud changed.

Remembering, Carrie's breath came short, she flinched, hearing the echo of that high child's voice, gasping through fever.

'Give my love to Daddy and all.'

And what had it done to Rud to receive that message, to learn those words were all that was left of Jo?

She could do no more than guess. Too frightened of giving way completely, of a weeping that would never end, they'd clung together wordlessly. Later, when John was killed out in France – her eyes closed for a long moment – they'd been able to talk about him. But through all the years after Jo died, she was never mentioned between them.

Such a terrible mistake. Rud must have longed, as she did, to hear Jo's name spoken.

Forty years on, Carrie could look back on those dreadful months of 1899 with a measure of calm. She also thought she could understand more about Rud himself. His whole character seemed to alter that year.

The war in South Africa had come at just the wrong time. She was certain Rud would never have taken up with Mr. Rhodes otherwise, never have been so angry and so blind.

She found herself speaking aloud, her right hand with its swollen knuckles beating the table.

'If you want to make out what kind of man Rud was, why he acted as he did, try looking at all that he lost.'

Set it out, year by year, as in these scrapbooks, she thought fiercely. See the pattern.

Begin with his childhood, when he left behind in Bombay a whole world that loved him...

The light was going. She switched on the lamp.

* * *

Ruddy was crooning to himself as he laid out the stones. Two by two he set them down, smooth and dark on the dulled figures of the Turkey carpet in the Bewdley dining room. He liked the freckles on the stones. The game changed. There was a stone with an empty face. Still on his knees, he moved over to the door which he had pushed shut earlier and set that stone down there on its own. His singing grew more urgent. He was standing over the stone now with his hands stretched out, so intent that when the door opened sharply the brass knob landed a punch against his temple, knocking him off balance.

His grandmother let out a scream that was cut off as the domino cracked beneath her black kid boot.

'You naughty, naughty boy. Who said you could come in here? These dominoes aren't toys to throw about on the floor. Come here.'

The strange white woman in the cold apron who was looking after him instead of Ayah came hurrying down the stairs. Grandmother's house had stairs, it was made of boxes stacked up on each other, boxes that were dark inside and smelled cold. In spite of the stiff new jacket that tied up his arms, Ruddy was not safe from the thin airs that blew around every corner.

'It's bedtime anyway, Master Rud,' the apron woman told him. But he was sobbing so hard he didn't hear. Even when his mother finally came to find him, scrubbed and dressed in his nightclothes, tears were still running down his cheeks.

'I can't do anything with him, Mum,' the nurse confessed.

Alice Kipling offered her an appeasing smile before taking a seat on the chair by the gloomy high mahogany bed.

'Now Ruddy, there, there, whatever's the matter?'

In his head he saw the baby. Mama liked the baby. She went away and left him in this cold house. She held the baby in her arms.

Her little boy, in his flannel nightshirt: Alice yearned towards the solid little body in its warm wrapping. She would have taken him on her knee but he arched away.

Biting her lip, his mother stroked his hair. She hadn't thought of this, when the plans were made for her coming home to England for her second confinement. After what she went through with Ruddy, she couldn't contemplate another long labour without reliable medical attention. It'd seemed such a good idea to leave Ruddy with her mother here in Bewdley.

How much she had still to learn about him, though he was only two. His temper was frightful. He'd been spending too much time with those Indian servants. She'd change all that once they were back in Bombay. It was absurd to say it but, now, face-to-face with him, he seemed almost a stranger.

'Would you like me to sing to you, darling, while you go to sleep?' Alice was known for her pretty voice. He nodded at once, apparently relieved, sliding down under the bedclothes and dragging the pillow just so around his shoulders. Did he do this every night, she wondered, as she bent to kiss his forehead? Leaning back with a slight effort – how tired she still was – Alice began softly with one of her favourite pieces:

'Twas the last rose of summer, left blooming alone,
All her lovely companions –'

A howl of rage and dismay interrupted her.

'Not *Angrezi*, not *Angrezi*,' the child cried, followed by a burst of sound which she could not follow, though her ear did pick up the rhythms of Hindustani on her son's voice. The child turned his face away from her to the wall.

Hesitantly, she whispered, 'Ruddy, please turn round,' and though the head remained averted, a small hand appeared from under the blankets and reached back towards her.

* * *

Tiny striped squirrels darted across the paths in the gardens of the Sir Jamsetjee Jejeebhoy School of Art. From her post close by the back gate of the compound, Ayah was admiring the ships, more than she could count, as they stood out at anchor in the flashing sea.

Now and then she cast an eye over at the perambulator, standing in the shade of the great neem tree. All springs and tall wheels, shining red and green, it was almost a carriage, as Ayah boasted to her sister-in-law who saw nothing of life outside the house. Closed off there behind a muslin screen, her Baba, the baby girl the Sahib said was to be called 'Trick-see', lay sleeping.

'She's such a tricksy little baby,' he told them.

Ayah snuffed up the scent of frying spices, *methi, zeera*, wafting over from the servants' quarters across the way. It mingled with the smell of earth. The garden was damp from the early watering.

The house itself was still, for Ruddy Baba, so proud that he was four years old now, had been allowed to set off with the Sahib that morning. Each day after breakfast, Kipling Sahib left to walk across to the new government college, where they did not sit to read and write at desks but worked in clay like poor village potters. What could be the gain? There the Sahib would remain all day, making drawings and other playthings, like a child.

But soon, soon Ruddy Baba would be back, holding the hand of his friend, Vaz, the tall gardener. He would come pounding clatter-clatter up the steps towards her on those small pink legs, sailor collar all anyhow, full of his adventures, all 'Listen, Ayah, listen!'.

For the moment though, she was free. Fanning herself with the end of her sari, drinking in the breeze coming off the sea, she smiled at Prem, the young bearer, as he came round the corner of the house.

'I knew it would not be long before you found me. It is the tailoring you are wanting, no?' Prem looked abashed but she laughed at him, patting the floor beside her, 'Sit, sit. Madam Sahib has gone out for the morning.' She handed back the *kurta* she had offered to mend the day before.

Prem squatted beside her. After a few words of thanks, he fell silent. Usually he was eager to share the news he'd picked up around the butchers' stalls. To report what the vegetable-sellers in Crawford Market had the impudence to charge today for chillies.

'Is true what they are telling me in kitchen? Cook is telling me all British children are leaving us, going over the Black Water, when they are small, small?'

Ayah felt herself grow still but she nodded, silently.

'Why are they doing this, Ayah? Why?' In his haste, he forgot to insist on her home name, which he alone in the household knew. 'They are tearing them away from those who take care of them while they are still nestlings, no wings of their own to fly, just helpless, so…' He cupped his hands, as if cradling a warm ball of new life. Ayah nodded for a second time but her throat was tight and she could not speak.

After a few moments she ventured, 'It is the fevers, they say. They fear the fevers. There are too many Babas in their burying-ground.'

Prem turned aside from her to spit in disgust over the wooden rail of the verandah, making a dark star on the red dust of the path.

'A child can die because they are alone, without need of any fever. Do they not know this?'

'That I have never heard talk of.' Ayah braced herself against the doorpost. Looking straight before her she went on: 'It will be so, with Ruddy Baba and with Baby. Also with that other Baba, which is to come.' All the servants knew that Alice was pregnant again, though she had barely admitted it to herself.

'It is that of which we speak, no?'

'Do they not know? Have they no old ones to teach them?' Meeta could not give up so easily.

'No. They do not know. And they will not care for anyone who tells them to do other than their kind. They will do as the other British.' She held the end of her sari before her face, while Prem stared out over the flower beds towards the bright colours of the perambulator where it lay beneath its muslin shroud.

* * *

Alice Kipling's hands were cold in her husband's, as he sat beside her bed in the stifling room. Although a whitewashed *punkah* was creaking regularly as it rose and fell, the air lay heavy, stagnant.

'I shouldn't have let Ayah touch him. I know I shouldn't. But I was desperate. I hadn't been able to sleep, I was so afraid. I knew that the doctor thought Baby John wasn't strong. I could see it in his face.' As she spoke she drew her hand away to pull again at a lawn wrap thrown about her shoulders.

Lockwood Kipling waited then once more began stroking the cold hands. He made another attempt to break through her refrain.

'Darling girl,' he repeated, 'do believe me, no-one is blaming you.'

'Ayah brought him in to me. It can't have been more than an hour or so later. When I looked I thought he was just asleep. If I'd realised he wasn't breathing I might have been in time. I might…'

'Alice, Alice, there was nothing you could have done.' Lockwood's eyes were rimmed with red but he kept his voice steady. 'The doctor warned me from the start that little John might not live.' That was a fact. Doctor Mackintosh had shaken his head over the child, though there was every chance for the mother, if she could be kept calm and quiet. 'There's no question of any fault on your part,' Lockwood went on.

'I was his mother,' the stricken voice continued without pause. 'I should have known – '

'Ayah says –'

'Ayah! What are we doing trying to bring up children in this dreadful country, with only black servants and their filthy ways?'

He flinched at her language. Then his heart turned over. What if she were to refuse to remain here with him in India? Fending off that thought, he paused to gather himself.

'Come, come, dearest. Ruddy's already getting on for five. He

and Trix will be out of Ayah's way and safe back at Home with
your mother in Bewdley before they are –'

Oh no. Beating the air with both hands, Alice was sobbing.

'Never. You have no idea. She said terrible things, things about
Ruddy. How bad he was. And me. That I wasn't a proper mother.'

Lockwood was silenced. He'd heard nothing of this at the time.
She must have been too angry and ashamed to speak of it, even to
him. He edged his chair closer.

'I would never let them go to her, after that.' She turned to him,
piteous now.

This was no moment to reason with her.

'Dearest one, of course not. I won't have you made unhappy.'

The words were firm enough but his mind was racing. If not her
mother, what choices were left to them? There was no question,
the matter had to be resolved. It was no good thinking that Ruddy
and Trix could go to her sister, Georgie. He was not at all sure
that her marriage was going to last: the household at The Grange
could well break up. Ned Burne-Jones, always susceptible, had
made an absolute fool of himself over Maria Zambaco, the Greek
beauty. Tried to run off with her last year and funked it in the end.
A shambles.

Georgie'd been heroic in her efforts to keep the family together
– but standing by as her husband's mistress visited him in his
studio 'to be painted' must have been torture. In her own home,
too. *Just passing by that door, so firmly closed, caused my heart to shrivel,'*
she'd written. The affair was supposed to be over but Ned was still
seen around town in her company. No, Ned and Georgie were out
of the question. There was one other married sister with a child.
Stan would have been company for Ruddy. But the health of his
mother, Louie Baldwin, wasn't up to it.

Then, even as he bit his lip, his mind cleared. He and Alice
weren't the only parents sending their small children back to
England and needing to find them a home. There must be people
who took children in for a living. He remembered advertisements
he'd skipped over, as he scanned the paper for news of travellers

who might have carried embroideries or carvings from beyond the Khyber to sell. Time for a closer look.

'You mustn't worry about this anymore, Alice,' he said. She was lying back now, flushed and breathless.

'I think there may be an alternative but you need to rest.' He reached for the sleeping draught the doctor had left. Alice sipped at it slowly, as though she could barely muster the energy to swallow.

'That's the way, my lovely girl.' Lockwood held the glass to her lips till only a chalky residue remained.

Alice gave a tiny smile in reply. Sitting on by the bed, he waited till her eyes reluctantly closed.

Then he went off to find the most up-to-date copy of *The Times* and that week's *Pioneer*. Between them he'd surely find a lead.

HOW FEAR CAME

1871–1877

'Rudyard, I'm not going to tell you again. Let go of Trixie's hand. Come and sit in your own place and eat up your tea.'

He stared back at the strange woman who wanted him to call her 'Auntie Sarah' and said he must forget about India.

At the other side of the table, Harry, the big boy who called the woman 'Mother', stuck out his tongue.

'You live in Southsea now and that's where you're staying. And you're lucky to be away from those heathens,' she kept telling him. He didn't believe her. Not staying for years and years. Not till he was nine or ten and grown up.

Trix was crying again.

She wasn't eating that bread and butter either, even though for Trix, Auntie had put sugar on it. He patted Trix's head, like Ayah did when they hurt themselves. He was big, nearly six, he had to look after Trix. Three was very little.

'Trix, Trix, don't cry. Mama and Papa are going to come back. Soon. They'll come back soon.'

He could feel the strange woman waiting, her eyes on him.

He shook his head.

Losing patience, Sarah Holloway swept round the table and dragged him back to his chair, where he sat, not eating, glaring defiance.

'Do you know what happens to bad children?' she asked.

'No, what?' In spite of his misery he couldn't help asking.

'God sees what they do and he marks them down for punishment. He watches them all the time and when they die he sends them to burn forever in Hell.'

The children were glazed with shock.

'We have different gods in India,' he attempted boldness. Then, quavering, 'Mama wouldn't let him. Ayah –'

'It was because you're so bad and wicked that Mama left you. And anyway your Mama has to do what God tells her.'

Struck silent, he gazed trembling at the new world that she had revealed, while Trix sucked frantically at her thumb.

* * *

'How does it work?' Ruddy's words came out with difficulty. His chin rubbed against the stiff, thick collar of the new jacket when he tried to talk. He pulled again on the old man's hand.

The broad figure of Sarah Holloway's husband, Pryse Agar Holloway, turned, responding to the tugging away down on his left. Inclining slightly, he pointed above their heads to the whistling rigging.

'See those ropes going upwards to the top of the mast, Ruddy? The proper name for them is the shrouds. And the little ropes that look like a ladder, they're called ratlines – I can't see those too well myself, can't make out things as I used to – Well, that's exactly what the ratlines are used for, so that the sailors can climb up to that platform at the top of the mast.'

Shrouds. Ratlines. Ruddy tasted the words. But he still wasn't sure – what happened when you got to the top of the shrouds?

How did you get onto the top of the mast? He peered upwards through the foggy air. But he didn't want to disappoint Uncle Pryse.

'Yes,' he said firmly, 'I see.'

'That hand of yours seems a bit cold. We'll have to go home soon.'

There was a moment's silence, a shared hesitation. The winter afternoon darkened.

'I'll tell you what, Ruddy, let's see if you can remember the list of all the ships I sailed in, in the right order. You can sing them out to me as we go along.'

Hand in hand the two trudged off into the gathering dusk, while snatches of a treble chant – 'the Brisk, the Stormrider, the Apart' – flew away into the wind.

* * *

'Lorne Lodge, Havelock Park, Southsea.'

Trix was practising as she stood muffled up in the hall, waiting. That was what you had to tell a policeman if you were lost. Trix did not want to get lost. To be left behind, all forgotten, like that little dog who wandered up and down outside their house. She'd had to hold her hands over her ears to keep out his crying.

Auntie says this house is five years old. I'm going to be five. In the summer.

'Why is it called Southsea?' Trix asked.

Auntie was sticking a long pin into her hat in front of the looking-glass. There was another one sticking out from her mouth.

Trix had to wait till Auntie had taken it out.

'Because it's by the sea, of course, dear.'

'But you have to walk a lot to get there.'

Auntie didn't reply. Once they were out on the street, she closed the metal gate behind them with a clang.

'I don't say it's convenient but it is very select here. '

Slekt? Ruddy would know.

Auntie took Trix out with her every day.

'Watch where you're stepping dear. The amount of sand and grit that the builders spill everywhere is just shocking. I wonder they don't mind the waste. But we don't want it on our shoes and treading into the house, do we Trixie?'

Trix didn't like it, seeing the earth all bare and torn up, with nothing growing any more. There were only wide brown puddles. If you slipped into them you would drown.

She stopped looking. She smiled back up at Auntie, clutching tight at her hand.

Most days they turned towards the place where Auntie did her shopping. Trix had to wait outside the butcher's after the day when she was sick onto the sawdust floor. But she didn't mind the grocer's. She enjoyed watching Mr. Taylor's clean pink fingers as they twisted the sugar up into a blue paper bag with little ears.

On days when Auntie was going to visit her friend, Mrs. Possiter, they went the other way up the road. Just a little way along, enough to count up to twenty going slowly, they came to the place where the men were building the new houses. There were heaps of pebbles and muddy pools and pieces of string pulled tight with little pegs.

'No, don't touch, you'll get all muddy,' Auntie told her. 'They're to mark out the spaces for the new houses, more houses like Lorne Lodge. Though not so exclusive. There's going to be street after street of them, more's the pity. It'll be going on for years.'

In really bad moments, Ruddy tried to make himself brave enough to carry on for years and years, even forever, on his own. He was never sure what he'd find when he woke up in this place. Trix might go away and leave him too. Sometimes he did wonder whether she actually liked crying and making the Woman come. That in a way she didn't mind getting him into trouble.

Thinking this was so bad it made his head feel queer, so that he had to sing the chant he had invented. Over and over he sang, till his head felt better. There were just names in the chant, Indian names, the names of the servants who still lived in the house in Bombay. That was the place the people he used to call Mama and Papa had gone back to.

'Why did they leave us here? Why didn't they explain?' he would ask Trix.

'Auntie said –'

'No, Trix, that's not true, what Auntie says. I'm sure. I mean I think –'

Trix kept looking doubtful, even though she would nod in the end and seem to agree.

At night before he went to sleep, Ruddy started going through the list of his old companions one by one, starting with Kamal, the new little kitchen boy, who made faces behind the back of the fat cook. Through Chowkidar standing up tall, wooden *lathi* in his hand to beat off burglars, Mali out in the garden doing the watering, Sais standing at the head of his pony after breakfast, right up to Meeta, the bearer, he would sing, rocking himself. The chant finished in triumph with 'Ayah, Ayah, Ayah!'

He had to share Harry's bedroom. One night the horrible boy heard him, even though he was whispering it into the bedclothes.

'Cry baby, cry baby!' Harry jeered. Harry was twelve, a whole five years older than him.

He wasn't crying. The stupid boy just couldn't recognise the sounds, he didn't know Hindustani. No-one here knew Hindustani, except him and Trix. But at night, in his dreams, he heard it all about him.

But those dreams were fading. The colour seemed to be leaking out of everything that he knew. Ayah's strong, warm, brown hand pulling him along, when the tall coconut palms along the beach banged together in the wind. Fat red mangoes in Crawford Market. The man with the flute and the green turban who made snakes dance, the day he was four. Marigold petals in the dust near the temple. He made up new games, new magic to bring the colour back, to keep alive the Hindustani voices in his head. They might keep out the ugly Woman and her screech.

Now that he could read, that helped, but it was not enough to stay deep inside books. She kept taking them away, for one thing.

'You mustn't strain your eyes,' she repeated.

He didn't believe her. She just wanted an excuse. So it frightened him one day to realise that he could no longer see the blackboard at school, even if he sat in the very front row.

She might be right about other things. About God and Hell. That might be true. However was he going to tell?

He shivered when he was going to bed that night, though his head felt hot.

* * *

'Never mind, Trix', Ruddy relented, seeing her lip begin to quiver. She nearly always got sad when it was close to bedtime. It was different for him. He was eight and a boy. 'I've got an even better story today. But you have to pay attention.'

So long as Trix was listening he could go on forever, the stories spilling out of him. His words turned into pictures that heaped and piled around them where they sat on the dust-coloured drugget, like the silks that man spread out over the verandah for them to buy. The trouble was, Trix would fall asleep and then it didn't work. His voice seemed to dry up to just a whisper. That made him frightened. It was Trix listening that he needed, her eyes that went round at the specially exciting bits and the giggles that she pressed back into her mouth with her fists. No-one must overhear them.

That Woman caught them at it one day.

'What nasty stuff are you filling her head with? Trixie, come away at once.'

And Trix was kept close to Auntie's side for a long fortnight of mourning.

Alone in the musty basement they'd been given for a playroom, Ruddy valiantly kept up with his own private magic. He piled up the sacred wall, the bastion that kept everything out, and crouched behind it, humming. Yet though at first he was able to summon the stories in his head and to step inside them, by the end of the first week, those that came to him slithered away and would not let him in. Then he found that sounds made deep in his throat while he rocked himself were better than keeping silence. He could hear something. He could hear himself.

The day Trix was allowed back, she came peeping round the yellow pine door, then ran to throw her arms round him. He did not dare to feel glad. Now he knew what would happen. When there was no-one to listen a trap closed its teeth on him. He was afraid he might die.

'Iyam, Iyam paying attention, Ruddy,' Trix insisted, struggling.

If he wasn't quick she'd be making enough noise to bring That Woman running. He refused to call her Auntie Sarah, not inside his own head, whatever she made him do in front of her. He was sorry for Trix. She was still a baby, not even six yet. But he wished she would be more careful about keeping their secrets. Not telling everything to That Woman.

'Sit up then, and stop sucking your thumb.'

At her look of hurt surprise, he felt a stab of misery.

'Come on now, this is a really special one.'

And he moved, though he had not meant to when he started, to telling the tale of the Djinn who helped the Sultan with the thirteen beautiful daughters. Each more beautiful than the moon – but none more beautiful than Princess Trix, 'who was the best beloved of them all'. Chanting this chorus, eyes sparkling, Trix sat bolt upright till the storyteller's voice softened to a close.

'I do love you, Ruddy,' she breathed into the silence. Her brother reached over and patted the curls out of her eyes as he had seen Ayah do.

'There. You can kiss me if you like before you go to bed.'

But when he felt her arms closing round his neck he went stiff. Turning his head away, he felt the tickle of her kiss against his ear.

* * *

Trix could hear the tap of Auntie's heels as she came hastening down the passage. Ruddy was right, she looked like a big black beetle scuttling along. Monday. Soon the horrible boiling smell would start. Auntie would be cross this morning. She always shouted, especially at Janey, on washing-day. It wasn't fair. How could Janey do out the grates if the copper was to be lit first thing? But Janey just winked at Trix and went on with what she was doing. 'Maid of all work? I should say so,' she would joke, in the safety of the scullery, while Trix watched her cleaning the knives with a special powder.

Something had distracted Auntie. The footsteps paused. Was anything wrong? It couldn't be Ruddy, this time, he'd already left. Lucky Ruddy, going out to a proper school. What else could have made her stop? Trix felt quickly for her hair ribbon. No, that was still tied.

She wrinkled her nose as Auntie hurried into the breakfast room and took a chair beside her. That black dress had such a funny smell. But she'd been wrong. Today Auntie was in quite a good mood.

On Mondays, lessons started with yesterday's Collect. Auntie didn't seem to know how easy it was for Ruddy and Trix to learn them. Easy peasy, even though she was so much younger. That stupid Harry didn't want to learn things even though he was more than thirteen and really big now.

'You'll never get anyone to employ you with marks like that,' she'd heard Uncle Pryse tell him in an angry voice.

Trix got to the end of the verses without a single mistake.

She relaxed.

'What a good girl you are, Trixie,' Auntie was smiling.

It was like the sun coming out.

*

'Go on, Trix, try, you can't really have forgotten Bombay,' Ruddy coaxed.

It was late afternoon and they were sprawling outside on the grass in the narrow back garden. Where it touched the bare skin on their wrists, the juicy green tickled.

'Wouldn't you like to be out in the sunshine?' Uncle Pryse had asked, dragging back the heavy bolt on the back door. 'I'm a bit tired today, or I'd join you myself,' he added, shuffling back to his chair.

If Harry had been at home, it wouldn't have been so quiet and friendly in the garden. But Harry wasn't expected back before dark.

'I don't care if Father wants me to practise my arithmetic before I go out. Fred's bringing his terrier and we're going ratting,' Trix heard him tell Auntie Sarah. She never really tried to make him do what she said.

There was nothing to worry about. Trix knew that Auntie never got back from her Missionary afternoons before five.

'Think of green, green that's fuzzy. Green netting stretching in front of you. Close your eyes. You're in the big red perambulator, inside the net to keep snakes out. Bouncing a bit because of the stones in the path. I'm running along beside you, holding out a flower for you.'

Trix looked uncertain. She could see this picture but she didn't feel she was inside it.

'Once I brought you a little green frog but Ayah made me put it back under some big leaves,' he went on, encouraging.

'Was she cross?' She couldn't remember it at all.

'Ayah just laughed and said' – he paused and screwed up his eyes – 'she said "Ruddy Baba, sweetness, better a kiss for Baby than a frog to eat. And not even cooked."'

Trix wanted Ruddy to stop. It made him happy, talking about India but she just couldn't. She didn't like it, when he spoke of Ayah and Bombay and tried to make her remember too. Like pushing her up against something hard.

'Come on, Trix. I don't believe you can't remember. When I was your age I used to dream about India every night.'

Your age! He was only two years older. Well, two and a half. She turned on him, pink with anger.

'I have dreams too. I dream about fire.'

* * *

'Rudyard, give me that book. You've had your nose in it ever since you came home. That's quite enough of that selfish reading for one day. There's your sweet little sister, longing for you to pay her some attention. It's time to play with Trix now, until bedtime.'

Sarah Holloway caught a look of fury before he turned away.

She could not take to this Rudyard with his heathen Indian name. If he'd been as mild and biddable as Trixie, they could have had such happy times together, the three of them singing those sweet hymns from Sunday school.

But Rudyard pursed up his lips when it came to singing. When he explained that 'he couldn't 'cos the words were just stupid' she'd had to forbid him all books for a week. The idea, that he, child as he was, could presume to sit in judgement. He did consent to learn the Collect and the chapters that she gave him as punishments but outside the Bible he just would not go.

Trix, on the other hand was good as gold, all that she could ask. Always ready to lift her cheek to a kiss. As good as having a daughter of her own.

'Trixie is such a sweet little pet, I'm thinking of asking her to call me "Mother", she observed one evening to her husband. It was May but they really needed the fire, though she grudged the coals.

'Heavens above, woman. You'll do no such thing. What do you think the child's family would make of it? And what about Ruddy? There's an affectionate little chap and really intelligent.'

The animation in his voice put her out.

'You never took such interest in Harry, your own son.'

The heavy eyebrows lifted and Pryse Holloway raised his head. 'That is a dreadful thing to say, Sarah.'

A pause. She began to justify herself. 'Well, I'm sure everyone notices. Mother and Aunt often say things.'

Pryse Holloway looked drawn. It was clear he had no desire for this conversation. He waited.

'Harry feels it, you know. More than once he's said to me that it upsets him. And after he's been so unselfish, sharing his own room with Rudyard all this time –'

'Why hasn't Harry spoken to me directly?' He didn't hide his distaste. 'Sarah, what have you made of him, with your tracts and ministers and pleasure in finding fault –' His face was dark with blood but he kept on.

She was frightened but excited too, 'Harry's a good boy. Just because he loves his mother –'

The gnarled hand came down heavily on the table, though no further word was spoken.

She drew back but soon could not prevent herself.

'That Rudyard is a little schemer. You can see he's watching and scheming to get his own way every waking moment. Just look at him. Behind that forehead that you admire so much' – Pryse had once remarked on the boy's open brow – 'there's wilfulness, there's wicked pride. It would be sinful to let them go unchecked.'

The old man sagged in his chair. 'Have it your own way, Sarah. Harry's an angel. Little Rud's the other thing. But mark my words,' – here he looked at her straight, till her gaze wavered and fell – 'mark my words, if I find Harry tormenting the child again, I shall send Ruddy away.'

'You can't. You know we couldn't manage without the money. Even if Harry brought something in. What are you saying?' She was struggling for breath.

'Believe me, I mean it.'

Slowly, leaning on the furniture, her husband got to his feet and left the room.

He wasn't well, she told herself. None of it meant anything. That his health wasn't good was quite true. Before the leaves had begun to turn at the end of summer, her husband was dead.

* * *

Ruddy was not going to look at Harry this time. Not directly into his face. He was strong, hating Harry and despising him. It didn't matter that Harry was fourteen and he was only nine. It didn't matter. However big he was, Harry was stupid.

If only they didn't have to share this bedroom. Ruddy tried not to think of the nursery in Bombay, where Ayah moved quietly in the warm dark and he could hear Trix as she stirred in her own white cot across the room.

He was Harry's prisoner.

He and Trix had a special name for Harry. They called him The Odious Boy. Ruddy squeezed his stomach right in and the pain went away again. He was not afraid.

The Odious Boy held out the book. Ruddy waited to see if it would be snatched away. After a pause, he reached out and took it into his hands. He stroked the raised patterns on the cover, knowing Harry was waiting. But he wasn't going to say anything this time.

'You don't seem very pleased to have your book back,' Harry mocked.

It was much better to keep quiet. To stay still and pretend that Harry wasn't real. Otherwise that horrible game would start over again, the game Harry had played after he hid the Hero of the Mutiny, the lead soldier that was always placed first in the charge across the floor of their basement playroom. It had arrived with others in a box from a big shop in London. Harry kicked that box, with its shiny label on the lid, whenever he got the chance.

But one long wet Sunday afternoon he went further. The Hero could not be found, though Ruddy turned over every toy in the cupboard and Trix stuck exploring fingers under the edge of the carpets upstairs. Now she was older, she was often quite sensible.

'What if I could find it for you? Want me to look too? Suppose you dropped it in the bedroom?' Harry offered, appearing unexpectedly in the basement.

'Oh Harry, thank you!' Trix looked happy again.

But he was back far too soon.

'You must've left it under your pillow,' he said.

Ruddy flew at him, kicking.

Harry had no difficulty in holding him at arms' length, while he grinned over at Trix.

'He don't really deserve to have it back, after all, eh, Trixie?'

Remembering that day, the hot tears, at last the begging, Ruddy did not speak. Instead he stepped aside, leaving Harry to sit smirking on Rud's own bed. The Odious Boy knew he didn't like him doing that.

Papa had sent him that book. Still stroking the board cover, Ruddy turned towards the chest of drawers against the far wall and sat down on the floor, his back against it. There was enough light there to look at the pictures. He'd wait for Harry to get bored and leave.

He betrayed himself with a gasp that he could not suppress. What he held in his hand was no longer a picture book. It flapped idly open on his knee as he looked up, in question.

Harry was ready.

'Choice, ain't they? Father always used to be on at me to improve my mind. I thought I should give myself something uplifting to look at since I've done with school lessons now.'

Harry went out to work these days.

'We can't afford for you to lose this job, get up this minute,' his mother insisted, shaking him every morning.

Following Harry's gaze, for the first time Ruddy observed the crooked line of torn pages stuck with pins that marched along the wall over Harry's bed.

He knew he was beaten. Uncle Pryse would have been angry. But Uncle Pryse was dead.

This time though, whatever happened, he wasn't going to cry.

*

When they first came to Lorne Lodge it had been easy to fit under the table and more cheerful than the cold playroom down in the basement.

'We're going to have this as our secret place. We'll call it "The Even Threshholds,"' Ruddy instructed. 'Mama used to say. "Children, be careful, don't run. You'll trip on that uneven threshold."'

He said the words again. He could hear his mother's voice.

He frowned. It'd sometimes used to sound as though she didn't like Bombay, which couldn't be right.

But all that was years and years ago. Now they were so much taller, the struts of wood between the legs rather got in the way. Still, once in a while, Ruddy would hold up a fold of the furry table-covering invitingly and Trix would slip, with a giggle, under his arm. Their noses wrinkled at the dust and the heavy smell of food that enfolded them once the door of their tent was let fall but as they settled themselves among the crumbs that Janey had missed, they were smiling at each other.

'We're almost too big to fit under here, you know, Ruddy.' Trix couldn't find a place to put her legs without kicking him.

'Don't *say* that. Trix, it's our own place that we've made. It's ours.'

Picking up her brother's agitation, Trix fell silent. After a pause she began again timidly, 'We can't stay down here too long anyway this afternoon. Auntie wants to take me out with her at three o'clock. We're going to visit Mrs. Chippington from the church.'

'You go then, go now, if you like her so much, her and her horrible friends in their stinky old black dresses. I can tell myself stories. I don't need you to be here.'

Trix felt her eyes fill with tears. Her chin was wobbling so much it made her mouth twist as if wires were pulling it. 'Oh Ruddy, don't be angry with me. She's not so bad.'

'Not so bad? I hate her bloody to hell.'

His ferocity entered Trix like a knife. She couldn't bear it. Shrinking, she whispered, 'Don't. Please don't be angry with me.'

'I'm not angry with you. Yes I am.' With a great effort: 'I want you to stay with me, not go with her.'

Trix was crying soundlessly into the fists she had bunched up against her face. 'I don't know what to do,' she heaved out between her sobs.

'Well, you said we were getting too big for this. Perhaps you're right. I don't think I like it under here any more,' and he was crawling away from her out into the drab light of the dining room.

Ruddy looked slightly ashamed of himself as Trix emerged but he couldn't resist inspecting his sister's face, to see how his rejection had registered. The little girl turned to adjust the fold of chenille, brushing them back into place.

Ruddy's face hardened.

'You'd better go and wash your face if you don't want her noticing and asking questions. But perhaps you'd like a chance to tell tales about me like her disgusting son.'

Trix took the blow in silence.

Ruddy would be cross with her all afternoon. She could always go and help Auntie Sarah though. It was no good fighting her. Trix could see that, why couldn't Ruddy? When they first came to live here, when she was tiny, his hugs made her feel safe. He was older, he knew what to do.

But now she sometimes felt like the older one. She could see that Auntie Sarah would always win. And though Ruddy often talked about Mama and wondered why she had sent them to live with Auntie, there really didn't seem to be any feelings about Mama, or any picture of her, left inside Trix.

Leaving the room, she turned back towards Ruddy hoping to be friends again, but he would not raise his eyes to hers.

That night the fire dream came back again. Trix was sitting at a table. But she seemed to have shrunk. She could barely see over it. There was something soft under her, like a cushion. And there was a fire, a huge fire, right there inside the house.

A fire that stretched out its arms for her.

However much she tried, she couldn't make a sound. Always,

when she tried to get down and run away, in the dream, Auntie stopped her, shouting, 'Be good or I'll give you a kiss and send you to Hell!' Now Trix fought with all her strength, fists pounding.

'Child, child, whatever's the matter?' Auntie was sitting bolt upright, wide awake beside her. 'You're thrashing about enough to wake the dead.'

'I'm going to get burned. Let me go,' Trix gasped.

Auntie Sarah's shadow, hair twisted up in spikes all round the head, reared up on the bedroom wall as the candle she had hastily lit spluttered.

'It's only a dream, Trixie. Go back to sleep.'

Trix shuddered as Auntie reached over to pat her before rolling onto her side.

'There now, settle down, do.'

Trix wanted to keep herself awake but her eyes insisted on closing.

The minute she woke up next morning, Trix could hear the thrush singing out in the pear tree. She wanted to run straight out into the garden and join him. The song kept on all the time she was washing her face and hands and pulling on her clothes.

Auntie called her to stand in front of the looking-glass to have her hair brushed. When she'd finished tying the dark blue ribbon for weekdays Auntie remained, winding Trix's curls into ringlets around her finger while she spoke.

'Always remember, Trixie, that it's the Lord who is made angry by sin and it's only His anger we have to fear. The wicked will have to live in the flames of Hell but so long as you keep on as a good girl, you've nothing to worry about. That's what I've always taught you, right from when you were small, you silly girl.'

Trix smiled politely. If she just smiled and didn't say anything, Auntie might talk about something else.

* * *

Month after month, every week had the same pattern but Trix didn't mind that. She liked knowing that there would be lessons with Auntie Sarah every morning in the dining room. That Auntie's friend, Mrs. Possiter, would visit on Tuesdays and that on certain afternoons Auntie would go out to join other ladies busy at the church. The Missionary Society had so many bazaars, the ladies always seemed to be sewing horrid fussy things, to sell at them.

Time spent with Ruddy was different. Then it was safe to come alive. Trix loved the dark late winter afternoons together in the basement. Once the gas was lit, the room no longer seemed so dull and dingy. It felt almost snug.

She could hardly wait to talk to him. Yet glimpsing the evening star, brilliant and lonely in the darkening sky, she caught her breath.

Flat on his stomach, Ruddy was training two black beetles to climb over the mountain trail he had built. His nose was almost touching them.

'Do look, Ruddy. Out of the window. The star.'

He didn't give any sign that he'd heard.

'What's the matter? Why don't you come and look?'

'No point. You know I won't be able to see it. Stop making a fuss.'

She remembered too late. It wasn't the first time she'd found Ruddy couldn't see what she could. Would he have to wear spectacles when he was grown up, she wondered. For now though, he didn't like talking about it. He just got angry.

Trix waited. She wanted him in a good mood, ready to listen.

'Remember, it's my turn today. Come on, do sit up and listen,' she finally burst out.

He waved a booted foot in her direction.

'You are a beast, Ruddy. I'm telling you something really interesting.'

'No, come on. Sit up. It's my turn, be fair. I heard Auntie's friend telling her this story today, after the Ladies' Meeting at church. About a girl who wanted to get married –'

She broke off as Ruddy rolled over. He sat up and looked at her.

'Girls aren't interesting,' he put out his hand before she could launch herself at him. 'I don't mean you, Trix, I mean stories about girls.'

'It is a good story. I know it is. All right, I won't tell it to you. But when I'm older, you'll see. Everyone will read my stories because they're real and true, not just made up ones like yours.'

But she could tell he didn't want to have a quarrel.

'Let's do "planning the house we're going to have when we go home to Bombay,"' he offered.

That winter it was their best game. It didn't matter any more that she couldn't remember.

'My bedroom will have white muslin curtains with flowers and flowers in all the vases, not like those dead twigs in front of the fireplace upstairs, and I'll have a special room to make my stories up and do my writing in,' she began.

'And my study will be at the other end of the house and we'll meet in the middle to read our stories together. My faithful servant will sleep across my doorway and I'll have a desk as big, as big as – as the altar in church,' he finished grinning.

'Mine will be made of rosewood.'

Trix wasn't going to be floored.

'If we're reading out poems, we shall lie on couches, but for stories we'll sit in carved armchairs, old carved chairs, like Aunt Georgie's.'

'We'll walk up and down the whole house, talking really loudly.'

'It will be the biggest most beautiful house in the whole of India.'

'And Janey will come with us and be in charge of all the other servants but never have to do anything herself.'

*

Every Christmas a man came for Ruddy and took him to London.

'It's all very well for the grand Mrs. Burne-Jones to send for Rudyard. She is your mother's sister, I suppose. And he's a boy and older. But I always tell her you'd rather stay here with me. That's right, isn't it Trixie?'

Trix nodded dumbly. She didn't want Ruddy to go and leave her. But she knew that she didn't at all want to go to London herself, to stay with a strange aunt and uncle.

This year, though, there was no escape.

'I suppose it's all your idea, Miss Trix. Not good enough for you here in Lorne Lodge. Oh no, you both want to be off with your grand relations in London.'

Trix flinched but her face remained blank. She looked across at Ruddy.

Auntie followed her gaze.

'I see, it's you we have to thank, Master Kipling, for upsetting us all. You've been putting ideas into your aunt's head, with your letters.'

Ruddy could only stare.

'I've had a letter from Mrs. Burne-Jones myself.' She shook the stiff criss-crossed sheet at them. 'Not that I don't expect one, at Christmas, to thank me for all I do for you.'

Both children remained silent and alert.

'She's sending her man to collect Rudyard for his Christmas visit again. But she wants Trix too this time. *If necessary I will come myself for Trix,*' that's what she says. No thought of what it means to anyone else. You won't enjoy being away from home, Trixie, but she doesn't think of that.'

'Aunt Georgie is the kindest person in the world,' Ruddy shouted, interrupting her. 'Trix will love her and love staying at The Grange.'

'That's enough from you, Rudyard. No-one asked for your opinion.'

Ruddy seemed to fold into himself. His fists were clenched as he turned and made for the door. In a moment they could hear his boots clattering up the stairs.

Down in the breakfast room Trix was sidling towards Auntie.

'I won't have to be away for very long, will I?' she asked.

'There now, that's considerate. Not like some. You'll miss me, won't you, darling?'

Shivering, Trix replied, 'Yes Auntie. Auntie, do I have to go?'

Auntie looked pleased, though she repeated mournfully, 'It's not for us to argue with the likes of Mrs. Burne-Jones.'

Trix couldn't help noticing that Auntie told all her friends about 'my letter from Mrs. Burne-Jones in London,' but in a pleased voice, as though it had made her happy. Not angry at all.

She pushed that away and with it the thought of Christmas.

In early December, under the wing of Aunt Georgie's outside man, the children took the train for London. They were going to stay at Aunt Georgie's until after Ruddy's birthday on December 30th.

Trix did wish that she was going to be ten like Ruddy.

He had told her about the big bell-pull.

'Feeling it in my hand's the first sign. I'm back at The Grange, with Aunt Georgie and Uncle Ned. I've got there. Everything's going to be happy for days and days.'

'You can pull it, Trix, because it's your first time,' he offered, as they climbed down from the hansom onto North End Road, where they stood stamping their cold feet as their bags were passed down and the driver was paid.

Trix hadn't expected The Grange to be so big.

She would have trailed behind Ruddy but he took her hand and dragged her towards the tall front door where light gleamed behind the curved glass at the top.

Up the stone steps and though he wasn't really much bigger, he was putting his arms round her to heave so that she could reach the iron handle. Even through her woolly winter gloves it was cold.

'You go ahead, Master Rud, you're getting to be a real strong 'un', old John applauded.

The peal was still sounding when the wide panelled door flew open and a tiny dark-haired lady, not much taller than Ruddy, stood in the doorway holding out her arms.

'My darlings, how lovely! Ruddy, dearest, and this must be Trix. How like your mother you are, darling.'

Aunt Georgie smelled of lilacs. Trix was kissed, she melted into the warm arching space of the hall and stood silent as unfamiliar hands unwrapped her scarf and deftly unbuttoned her overcoat. She hoped Aunt Georgie wouldn't notice it was too short.

Her nose began to tickle.

'What's that, Ruddy?' she whispered.

'The tree, silly.'

And there in the drawing room stood a fir tree, high as a house. Little silver bells and golden chains hung on it, glittering and tinkling in the draught every time the door was opened. 'Soup and chicken sandwiches first, don't you think my dears? Why don't you sit here by the fire and have a picnic?'

Trix felt her throat close and she shuddered. Auntie Sarah used a whole sheep's head when she was making soup. Trix had seen one lying bloody and empty-eyed on the draining board, waiting to go in the big saucepan. She'd never been able to swallow the greasy grey porridge it turned into. Ruddy called it 'dead dog in a puddle'. But when she looked across at him now in appeal, to her surprise she saw that he was beaming.

Then the tray was placed on a small inlaid table in front of her.

Was this clear golden liquid called soup too? She sipped. Perhaps Ruddy was right and she was going to like being here.

Before they went to bed, Uncle Ned, who was so tall he could reach all the red candles standing out on the branches, lit them and they sat in the fluttering light while Aunt Georgie read to them out of the Arabian Nights.

They were to sleep in the old night nursery.

'You know where it is Ruddy. Go on, lead the way,' Aunt Georgie said.

But when Trix entered the wide low room at the top of the house, she saw there were four beds tucked up under bright patterned coverlets, not two. Aunt Georgie noticed how surprised Trix was.

'I thought you and your cousins would probably all like to sleep in the same room,' she explained. 'If I just put Ruddy in with Phil and you, Trix, in with Margaret, everyone would feel they were missing something. This way no-one's left out.'

Trix quivered, not sure whether it would have been worse to have to share with this unknown Margaret or to be apart from Ruddy.

But Aunt Georgie was still speaking.

'Margaret and Phil will be home tomorrow. But I thought Trix's first evening with us should be a quiet one.'

'Margaret and Phil? Oh hooray!' Ruddy was bouncing on a field of scarlet and gold.

Aunt Georgie left a night-light burning on the table between them when she went downstairs.

'D'you like it, Trix? It is just like I said, isn't it?'

'Mmm,' Trix murmured, closing her eyes. It was all too strange. But she couldn't say so, couldn't say she wanted to go home.

Instead, she lay listening to Ruddy's slow breathing, his little snorts. It seemed to remind her of something she almost knew, something that was happy. She wished they could always share a room.

Her new cousins seemed very noisy. Speaking both at once as they tumbled into the drawing room the next day, they flung themselves on Ruddy but did not cast a glance her way.

'Children, children, aren't you going to make cousin Trix welcome too?' Aunt Georgie asked. 'Come on now, Margaret.'

Close to panic, Trix realised that she didn't know how girls talked to each other. Margaret was chattering at her nineteen to the dozen, as Auntie would say. Auntie Sarah wouldn't like Margaret at all. Full of herself, that's how Auntie Sarah would put it.

'What's your favourite instrument? And do you like skating?' Margaret rattled off without a pause.

She didn't wait for Trix to reply but shot off more questions. Worst of all, Ruddy seemed to like all that gabble and to like Margaret too. He was spluttering in excitement, talking just as fast, changing into a different Ruddy as she watched.

But Ruddy was really the only boy she knew. You couldn't count Harry. How was she ever going to know what to say to big cousin Phil, who looked so grown-up in that striped waistcoat?

Trix regarded the three of them in silence, observing but feeling invisible, as though she was stuck behind a screen.

The Grange itself was unlike any other house Trix had ever seen. 'Except it does remind me of the illustrations in my best storybooks,' she decided. It was the high arches and the pillars, the feeling you were looking through rooms and rooms without coming to an end. Dark shining doors swung silently open at her touch. It was like the house in *Beauty and the Beast*. And perhaps a house could have too much space. There were days when she felt that her feet might not hold her to the floor and she would float helpless, weightless, up to the high wide ceilings.

There were flowers and leaves everywhere and not just in vases. This was something to do with Uncle Ned and his work.

'He designed it all,' Ruddy told her, with a grand gesture that took in the patterned paper covering every wall and the carpet that she'd been gazing at in wonder. 'At least his friend, that fat one we call Uncle Topsy, has a company called Morris and Co. that makes beautiful things.'

Trix looked at him sceptically.

'Uncle Ned does make designs as well as paintings,' he added defensively. 'Up in the studio, I've seen designs for stained glass.'

Trix shrugged and went back to studying the carpet. Such bright colours, pink, blue, green, all at once together and at the same time so – so carefully arranged. Like the curling, complicated willow leaves on the walls, they made her think of summer in a garden far away.

But here she was, in Fulham, with all these people she didn't know. Uncle Ned was so dreadfully unlike anyone she'd ever met. Apart from the Reverend Mr. Sharpe at church, all Auntie Sarah's friends were ladies. There were the men who stood behind counters and served Auntie in the shops, too. But Uncle Ned wasn't at all like them.

The first time Trix heard Uncle Ned shout 'It's no good the light's gone,' as he burst into the drawing room, she shrank back. Trix looked quickly at Aunt Georgie. She was still smiling, but she did sound rather sharp when she spoke at first.

'Ned, you're frightening Trix. Do calm down.' She turned towards Trix. 'Uncle Ned's come down from his studio because he's had to stop painting for the day,' she explained. 'In order to paint he needs daylight. At this time of year he has to stop before he really wants to.'

It was a surprise, hearing Uncle Ned scolded, like a child, but after that she was less shy of him.

He sat down with them all and began drawing.

Trix had never seen an artist making something before. She had been deep in *The Frog Prince,* her new storybook, sent from India with Mama's name in it. Trix had been dreaming over the picture of the Princess amazed to find the hopeful little frog at her door, but she laid it down. From across the room she watched the feathery beard bobbing and jerking as Uncle Ned turned first to look, then to draw.

'Would he mind if I crept behind him?' she wondered. It was his hand with the pencil, moving so surely over the paper, that she wanted to see.

No-one seemed to notice when she left her chair. Sliding behind the big Knole sofa, she side-stepped a low table piled with books and papers and came up behind him.

'Hello, little bird,' he murmured without pausing, 'if you want to watch, fetch that stool and you'll be more comfortable.'

After that, she sat herself down close to Uncle Ned whenever he came in to draw.

The day he took them up into his studio was the best. New smells, clean and sharp, that she'd picked up a whiff of downstairs, hit her as soon as the door ahead was opened. Like the smell of that gum on the pine tree in Auntie Sarah's garden. She almost tripped, she was in such a hurry to see inside.

It was after tea, so Trix knew it was dark outside, but the spread of shining black glass at the end of the high room took her by surprise. No curtains. In the drawing room they'd just left, heavy folds of velvet were pulled close. But of course, when he was painting, during the day, Uncle Ned didn't want to lose a scrap of light. Pieces of cloth, much bigger than any blanket, hung along the far wall. They seemed to be pictures of ladies and knights, made out of sewing or embroidery. Trix had just learned cross-stitch. She could see that these pictures must have taken somebody months and months, sewing all day.

While she stood taking in the place where Uncle Ned came to work, the others had rushed over to a long scarred table, littered with pieces of string, torn wrappings, brushes, cups and glasses that needed washing and tubes of what must be paint.

Uncle Ned noticed Trix staring at all the mess.

'No-one's allowed to clear up in here, not even your Aunt,' he told her.

Margaret and the boys were already fingering the tubes of paint, choosing the ones they hoped they'd be allowed to use. Trix shook her head when Uncle Ned held out a brush invitingly. She was more interested in looking. It was the large paintings, stacked against the walls that attracted her. Some appeared finished, others were just faint outlines, like the idea for a new game. There were so many of them. So many beautiful ladies – such blues, such golds. Sinking to the floor, she sat back on her heels, so she could gaze more closely.

'More exciting than those pencil sketches you've seen me make, eh?' Uncle Ned's voice came from across the room. 'Is it the colours?' he asked.

Trix scrambled up, with a nod. 'But it's the stories in the paintings, too. They're all stories. This one here, it's the Sleeping Beauty isn't it? You can see all those girls asleep too, lying round her, they must be her maids. And the roses and briars, they're growing in through the window and all over the furniture.'

Uncle Ned seemed pleased. He was laughing.

'Quite right. Not everyone observes so closely, Trix, you'd be surprised. Come and look, I've got something over here to show you,' he beckoned.

'My friend Mr. William de Morgan makes these tiles,' he said, lifting heavy shining squares one by one out of a stout wooden case. 'What about these for colour? He's been experimenting and wants to know what I think. What shall we tell him, little bird?'

Trix found her voice as she traced the different patterns, smooth and cold under her finger.

'This one's the best, Uncle Ned,' she decided. 'There's something too smudgy about the one in green.'

Trix never knew how solemnly Ned Burne-Jones relayed her views to William de Morgan, when they sat taking tea in the drawing room later that week. The children were clustered on the sofa around Aunt Georgie, who was reading aloud.

'Don't look straight at the child, you'll embarrass her. She's the one over there leaning against Ruddy. I tell you, Will, she has the beginnings of an eye. It's a thousand pities we can't keep her here and bring her on.'

'A thousand pities indeed,' repeated de Morgan rather grimly, eyeing his friend. It was widely known that Ned had never really given up his devotion to Maria Zambaco, despite developing other romantic attachments along the way. Georgie's nerves probably couldn't bear the strain of two more children.

Apparently oblivious, Ned met his gaze.

'Yes. Life must be more stimulating for them here, of course. But it would be quite wrong to disturb the Southsea arrangement.'

He paused to squint at his drawing pad, holding it out at arms' length.

'The two of them seem very happy and settled with Mrs. Holloway – she obviously feeds them well – look at him, Rud's really quite plump – and Georgie says you never hear a word from them against her.'

* * *

Watching Margaret and Phil as they leaned close to Aunt Georgie while she read to them in the evenings made her uncomfortable. She shouldn't be here, she didn't belong. Even when Aunt Georgie put an arm round her, Trix couldn't feel at ease. She was used to Auntie, at home in Southsea, she belonged there, not with these people. She longed for some time alone with Ruddy. But he seemed to like rampaging around with the cousins more than talking to her.

Trix was counting the days till she and Rud could go home. When at last the holiday was over and it was time for John to take them back to the train her eyes were bright.

'Ruddy never says much about Southsea. Dear child, he shuts up like a clam, in fact, if you ask him. It's no easier to tell with Trix. I wish she wasn't quite so withdrawn. But you can see she really does care for that woman, she's so happy to be going back,' reflected Aunt Georgie, as the wheels of the departing hansom kicked up spray from the slush.

* * *

Summer was coming, when very quietly, one Wednesday morning, Trix got off the bed she shared with Auntie Sarah. She didn't put her shoes back on, even though Auntie had gone out. Ruddy was at school. Down in the scullery Janey was banging about.

She hadn't really got a headache. But it was the only way to get Auntie to leave her behind.

'You won't be alone,' Auntie said. 'There's Janey in the house.'

Trix knew that Auntie didn't want to miss the Ladies' Sewing Circle at the church. That's why Wednesday was the day to do it.

She crept to the door. Out on the landing the lino was cold to her stockinged feet and more slippery than she'd expected.

Going down the stairs she clutched the shiny ridges of the banisters. Falling would make such a noise.

At last she reached the door of the breakfast room and leaned against it, trying to breathe more quietly, as she took the chill metal of the knob between her hands. Twisting slowly and steadily she eased the lock till it clicked, quietly as a cricket.

The canary was looking straight at her from its cage hung by the window. It seemed to be expecting her. She knew what to do. Every morning after breakfast she watched as Auntie reached up opened the neat little door and held a finger inside the cage.

'Who's a pretty little thing then?' Auntie would coo, travelling over to the table, the bird perched on her outstretched hand.

'Ugh,' Ruddy said when they were alone, 'to see the horrid mangy thing pecking at the crumbs and bits on the tablecloth. It's revolting.'

Trix shuddered too. But it wasn't Jacky's fault. Jacky hadn't asked to live in Lorne Lodge. She had to drag across a chair to stand on to reach his cage. It was heavier than she'd expected and kept catching on the carpet but she managed. Climbing on the furniture and stepping on the upholstery, both absolutely forbidden, Trix knew she could win. Auntie would never know.

Once she was level with it she could see that the bird was frightened. It wasn't used to her coming so close. She hadn't thought of that. The fluffy yellow creature shrank back on its perch.

'Who's a pretty little thing?' she asked softly. If she sounded like Auntie it might make him feel safe.

Jacky only quivered.

Hearing a step on the stairs from the basement, Trix paused. But Janey passed on along the hall and up to the top of the house.

There was no time to lose. The cage bucked and swung as she grabbed but her hand was tight around the frantic feathery ball.

'Don't fight me,' she whispered. 'Jacky, you're going to be free.'

The most difficult part came now, when she had to get down from the chair with him in her hand. She never thought the wings would be so strong as they tried to beat.

She could just reach the metal catch on the window with her free hand. It was dreadfully stiff. Tugging had no effect. Her fingers felt bruised. She couldn't do it.

She did want to set Jacky free. But she was starting to hate the frenzied thing that she held so tightly.

She'd have to put it back.

Trix took a deep breath.

She would shut him up again, so she could use both hands to work the catch. If she let go he'd just fly and perch on the looking-glass over the fireplace. She'd never be able to catch him or let him out. Auntie would find Jacky there when she came home or Janey would. That would be almost as bad. He'd never escape.

It wasn't easy climbing back up again with only one hand free but she did it.

The cage hung steady, the door open. She was reaching up, her hand inside still firmly clasped around the demented wings, when she leaned too far.

The cage swung away.

Her grip tightened, she lurched forward, grabbing wildly, as the chair toppled with her, and banged her head as she came crashing down among the chair legs.

'I'm sorry, Jacky, oh Jacky, I didn't mean to,' she wept over the crushed yellow handful, sticky in her palm.

'There's no keeping this from the missis,' Janey warned. 'But we can give him a bit of a funeral under the holly. I'll dig it up with the coal shovel.'

She splashed Trix's face with cold water afterwards.

But she forgot to sweep up the little trail of coal dust in the hall. The moment Auntie got through the front door she asked what had happened.

Trix sobbed again as she faltered out her story.

'I know you wouldn't have meant any harm, Trixie, *you're* not full of spite, unlike that brother of yours.' Auntie's kindness took her by surprise.

*

'It's my duty. You can't be allowed to continue in falsehood, Rudyard.'

'But I'm not. I didn't mean –' the boy faltered.

'The plain truth is that you threw that book away. That beautiful book of prayers and stories from Scripture that I sent to school with you. Making sure Mr. Vickery knew you came from a good home.'

'Truly I didn't. I didn't throw it away.'

'But you've already told me that you did. "I put it down on the wall when I was pulling up my stockings." That's what you said.'

'But I only forgot it, I was going to –'

'And then you left it there. You left it, hoping that I wouldn't find out. But the Lord has his ways.'

'I didn't think – '

'Oh yes, Mrs. Possiter saw it all, living opposite, and she rescued it for me. I've had that book since I was a girl. As soon as you came into the house I saw you hadn't got it with you. All those years I've treasured it and then you have to – and when I asked you where it was – as soon as I ask you, you say, "It's up in my bedroom".'

'I only forgot. I thought –'

'I'll give you forgot, I'll give you thought, you little liar. It's not as if it was the first time. What about that school report that disappeared? The one you "never had"? You threw that away, you've admitted it.'

Rud hung his head.

'But if it hadn't been for Harry – he's got a head on his shoulders, *he* wouldn't let you get away with it – I'd never have got to the bottom of that business. But I'm going to teach you to love the truth, like Harry. Now I want you to take this Holy Bible, in your hands and swear in the hearing of the Lord that from now on you will only tell the truth –'

He pushed it away.

'I do love the truth. But you don't. You're always saying how good and clever Harry is.'

A gleam of satisfied outrage lit her face.

'Right. You're going to wear the name of "liar" on your back till you've learned the meaning of truthfulness. And respect.'

At least she was not going to hit him, again, with that cane that made him crouch and hide himself, like a dog. His head seemed to be watching all by itself as she bustled about, dragging drawers open, looking for the scissors, then going rooting in the cupboard. When she turned round she was holding a piece of white card. Even when she had found the dusty bottle of ink and was inscribing a large square of card with the word 'LIAR', he could not believe it was real. That the next morning he would have to go through the streets with the placard pinned to the back of his coat.

He set off white-faced, his shoulders hunched, waiting for the jeers of errand boys and old ladies' clucking disapproval. Yet he had only gone a few yards when a sobbing Trix burst out into the street after him and tore the placard from his back. She took up her stand, small hands held up curved before her, frail claws raised against all comers.

The following day, Ruddy fainted when he got out of bed. After that, he wasn't sure any more where he was. The sounds from outside his bedroom made him uneasy. They came and went. Sometimes he seemed to know what they meant while at others he registered with a start that he had been making up a dream, making it up out of the noises which were near at hand but which he could not quite make sense of.

Harry's bed seemed to have gone. Perhaps the men in his dream were real. Maybe they took it away.

At times the doctor came.

He was sure of that because on each occasion the same procedure was followed. There was none of the exhausting unpredictable extravagance of his dreams.

The old man would come in through the door, opening it wide, unlike That Woman, who slipped through the merest crack. The doctor would put down his bag near the foot of the bed. Then the doctor would bend over him. Once his face was quite close, Rud could make out the features clearly: the brilliant eyes behind thick spectacles, the wiry grizzled eyebrows.

'Feeling a little better today, hey?' But the touch of the hand that rested on his forehead was gentle, the grip that took hold of his wrist, feeling for the pulse, made him feel safe.

The visits repeated themselves. He did not know how often. Then, one afternoon, when he had been allowed to sit up – and very dazed and uncertain it made him feel, his head so far above the ground – instead of going away, the doctor drew up a chair and sat down.

'Young fellow,' he said, 'you're doing famously. I think I shall be able to leave you in the care of Mrs. Holloway in another week.'

The doctor was not altogether surprised by the effect of his words, or by the sobs and agitated gestures. In his experience, children did not start hallucinating unless they had a high fever or had been under intolerable stress. The child's temperature had never been sufficient to account for the derangement in which the doctor had found him.

On the other hand, the Holloway woman gave him pause for thought. She had almost seemed to be expecting him to attack her. He was hardly through the front door the first day before she was telling him what good care she took of the children and how much they meant to her. A rather wan little girl, whom he had not seen again, had been clinging to the slick black folds of the woman's skirt.

'Tell the doctor, Trixie, tell him how you love me.'

'Not just now,' and he had escaped to his patient. It was a grim sort of house but clean, very clean though it was so bare. The liver-coloured tiles in the hall gleamed, the brass doorknobs were icy to the touch but they glittered. Biblical texts worked painstakingly in wool hung over every doorway. The boy had been slow to make progress; a finely wrought constitution, everything told on it, the doctor feared.

He laid a soothing hand on the child's arm and the sobs began to die down.

'Is there something you would like to tell me?' he asked quietly. The child merely stared, then shook his head. 'Are you afraid of something?'

A long pause.

'Please. I can't read.'

'You can't read? You mean you're in trouble at school?' With a child anything was possible. But no. With painful slowness came the admission:

'I don't seem to be able, to be able to see things properly. They're there and then they're not there.'

The old man sat back, surveying him thoughtfully. Spectacles alone, he thought, would not put this problem to rest.

* * *

Georgie had persuaded Trix to come back the following year for another Christmas with her cousins. Now the festivities were almost at an end, however, Georgie was relieved. The big drawing room of the house in Fulham presented a dispiriting sight. In broad daylight the after-Christmas wreck was painfully evident.

'That tree's no longer a joy to the eye,' she said aloud. 'But I don't have to tell you that, Marjorie,' she added to the housemaid, in her brown morning uniform, who was on her knees brushing up the dropped pine needles. 'Do be careful, I can see broken glass. Some of those baubles fell off when the children were racketing about last night during the party. Master Ruddy's party always signals the end of Christmas and just as well. There's always damage.'

They were all growing up fast: Ruddy turned eleven and her own Margaret ten. It didn't seem possible. Even shy little Trix must be eight. Georgie'd left her fast asleep, hoping a day in bed would get rid of Trix's cold. She felt glad that Phil was young for sixteen and still needed her.

The holidays were almost over. Phil would be going back to Marlborough next week. Ruddy and Trix were leaving this Friday. The tree could come down later that day. She must get back to her correspondence. It was the greater part of a year since her mother had died but letters of condolence were still trickling in and must be acknowledged.

Georgie was busy writing, at the little walnut *escritoire*, when Phil and Margaret found her. They'd rushed in straight from the garden leaving muddy footprints on her favourite Persian rug. She gave a sigh of exasperation.

Even before they began to speak she could see that they were disturbed. Margaret was clutching her brother's hand.

'Mother, it's Ruddy. He's being awfully strange. I think you ought to come,' Margaret stammered.

'I thought you were all such friends, darlings. Do you mean you've had a quarrel?'

'No Mater, honestly. Nothing like that,' Phil replied. 'He keeps saying all these strange things. But it's not us he's talking to. He just stares. And he won't answer. When we ask what the matter is, he just keeps jabbering.'

'I don't like it, Mother. Make him stop,' Margaret burst out with a sob.

Georgie was already on her feet.

'Margaret, darling, why don't you go down to the kitchen and ask Cook if you may have some milk and a biscuit. Tell her I'd like you to stay with her till I come back.'

The warm cave below stairs was a haven for all the children.

'Now, Phil. You'd better take me to see Ruddy.'

He was already a good head taller than herself but she put her arm round his shoulders anyway. The cold air from outside still clung to the wool of his jacket.

'I'm sure it's just a silly game and he didn't mean to upset you.'

She caught up a heavy shawl from a hook as they passed out by the door into the garden.

The sun was making a dazzle on the melting frost. Georgie shielded her eyes. Looking right down, beyond the lawns and flower beds, near the orchard, she made out a stocky figure in movement.

Ruddy appeared to be brandishing a fallen branch. The gardener kept a pile of dead wood at the end of the garden, ready for his bonfires.

She crunched over the stiff grass, aware that Phil, nervous as ever, was dropping behind.

'Ruddy my dear, is something the matter?' Her voice faltered.

Ruddy wasn't looking at her.

He hadn't heard.

'I know you're dead, you're only a ghost,' he panted, thrashing out at an ancient apple tree.

Georgie drew in her breath. With a single look she sent Phil heading back inside.

'Treat this like sleepwalking,' she decided, moving slowly towards her nephew. Standing behind him she laid both hands firmly on his shoulders.

Ruddy continued with his flailing.

Then he appeared to register her presence.

Pausing, he stood irresolute.

Long moments passed before the branch fell from his hand. He slumped and might have fallen if she hadn't moved to clasp him against her, arms meeting round his solid chest. The sudden weight made her gasp.

'Ruddy, dearest,' she managed to speak steadily, 'It's all right. Aunt Georgie's here. It's all right. We're going back now into the house where it's warm.'

'When you're ready, darling, you can tell me all about it,' Georgie said some time later.

'But first try to eat some of this toast.'

Ruddy was stretched on the *chaise longue* in her bedroom, under an afghan blanket. He had slept for a while.

'I thought the tree was Grandma,' he said slowly.

'I mean I *had* to hit it. I was making sure.'

By the end of the day Ruddy was fit enough to join his cousins for a quiet game of Happy Families. They viewed him with cautious interest but he seemed to have returned to his normal self.

Once the children had trooped upstairs for the night, however, Georgie turned to her husband. 'Do put down that pencil, Ned and pay attention. I'm concerned about Ruddy.'

Reluctantly the sketchbook was set aside.

'I can't begin to understand it,' she finished after describing the scene in the garden.

'Thinking the tree was your mother's ghost? Bashing it? Quite extraordinary. What could Ruddy possibly have against his grandmother? She always struck me as harmless enough, poor old thing, if a bit preachy.'

Georgie chose to ignore the tone of disrespect.

She considered.

'I don't think Ruddy ever had much to do with Mother. Of course she was critical of his behaviour when he was really tiny. Remember, they came, back from India when Trix was born, but that's all. She was fond of him in her own way.'

'I remember now,' she added thoughtfully. 'Mother did visit the children at Southsea, soon after they first arrived. Ruddy must have been six at the time. She and Ruddy spent a morning together. She always said how much she loved that morning, teaching him hymns and reading to him out of the Bible, some of her favourite –'

'I don't suppose he loved it, though, do you?' Ned interrupted.

Georgie, who secretly shared this scepticism, was too deep in thought to respond. After a pause 'I think we'd better keep Ruddy here a while longer, till he's had a chance to settle down. There's something terribly wrong, I'm sure, though I can't put my finger on it.'

'Better get his eyes tested if he can't tell a tree from a ghost,' Ned offered, picking up his pencil.

'I can certainly arrange that. But first I'm going to sit down and write to his mother. Alice should know about this.'

WE BE OF ONE BLOOD, YE AND I

1877–1891

Georgie wasn't the only one who wrote to alert her. An elderly friend was prosaically concerned about Ruddy's poor sight. Both had their effect: Alice swept the children up and away from Southsea in scarcely more than a day.

Such absurd clothes solemn little Trix was wearing – was that a bustle? – and Ruddy flinched when she first went to kiss him. But he didn't resist for long. She'd known it wouldn't be difficult to win him round.

Her heart did misgive her when she first saw them. They were such waifs.

Better to look forward.

They were quite different already. Thank God, it hadn't been her choice to leave them so long in that place. How could she have guessed it would turn out badly? When the news had come through two years ago that 'Mr. John Lockwood Kipling was appointed Principal of the Mayo School of Art and Curator of the Lahore Museum', at first she'd felt only relief. A higher salary was the least of it. Jack was much too good for his ancillary place at the School of Art in Bombay. Their whole standing out here would be transformed. But it did come at a price.

'It means no Ruddy and Trix for me this year and I've waited so long,' she had written to Georgie at the time.

'I can hardly bear it. But we'll be leaving Bombay and it will be up to me to oversee the move and establish a new home. If I left it to Jack we'd be camping on the Maidan.

It is a wonderful promotion but I do dread the Lahore climate, hundreds of miles from the coast. Bombay at least had the sea breezes. And Lahore's little more than a frontier town, still given over to the natives (Jack makes me use that word but plenty of people call them niggers). There'll be nothing in Lahore to compare with the Sassoon Library, or the Asiatic Society of Bombay. Jack may be in raptures about their mosques and monuments but I for one rejoice that our people all live quite separately, well outside the city walls.'

At long last, here, now, she was back in England. Able to hold her children warm in her arms, not just brood over photographs, trying to read their faces. Instead of letters, living voices. Eager as she was to remove them from Lorne Lodge she'd been careful to remain diplomatic. You never knew.

'We all need some good English country air, Mrs. Holloway.'

She had to insist before Ruddy would turn round to wave good bye.

The three of them were going to spend the whole summer together at Mr. Emplins' farm on the edge of Epping Forest.

*

Now Ruddy stood before her unabashed, dripping muddy water and pondweed onto the tiles that Mrs. Emplins had carefully strewn with sand only that morning.

'I do believe you are the naughtiest children that ever –' Alice began but she could not go on for laughing.

'Trix's hat blew off and I was rescuing it from the duck pond,' Ruddy explained with a holy look.

'Ooh, Ruddy, you know you tried to make it sail back to me on the water. It wasn't a rescue at all!' Trix gave him a shove. She used to keep that straw hat with its cornflowers round the brim in a place where she could see it from her bed at night.

Alice only laughed the longer.

'Never mind, Trix, you shall have a new one. We'll choose it together on Thursday. Mr. Emplins will let us ride with him when he takes the cart into market.'

Day by day, the children were compiling their observations, assessing their mother, though they did not speak even to each other of all they learned. Wordlessly they appreciated the way Mama didn't make them go to their bedroom or put a stop to their games of battledore out on the rough grass of the shorn meadow. Every evening, right on into the time Mama called 'the gloaming', when you could hardly see the shuttlecock, they all played.

'I do like to see her – don't you, Trix? – Mama with her skirts caught up and all her pretty hair coming down,' Rud murmured across their little whitewashed bedroom just before he fell asleep.

But even as she whispered, 'Yes, I like it too, Ruddy. And all the games,' Trix wished Ruddy hadn't said that. He never used to like anyone but herself.

Summer was long past and winter approaching, when they left the farm for London and rented rooms on the Brompton Road. Their father, Lockwood, was to join them there after Christmas.

When she first saw Papa, Trix was disappointed. She hadn't expected him to be fat. And he wasn't very tall. She didn't know what to say to him at first, just tried to look polite and interested. Then she realised that he was rather like Uncle Ned. Even when Mama was trying to have a conversation with him, he kept on making drawings.

He seemed to understand that Trix liked watching him as he sketched.

'Would you like me to draw the garden you and Ruddy used to play in?' he asked.

'There was a well in that garden you know, Trix, and a water-wheel. Two big white bullocks walked round and round to turn the wheel and bring the water up. They had to wear blindfolds, to stop them getting dizzy. See, like this.'

His pencil flickered across the page. Trix edged closer.

Papa didn't look at her but went on speaking.

'Here's the place where Ayah used to stand your perambulator, in the shade of a big tree. And now, this is what Ayah used to look like –'

'There were red flowers. They were roses.'

It was her own voice speaking but it startled her. It was so loud.

Papa looked up. He took out a clean handkerchief and stood there holding it. He didn't seem to know what to do. 'Don't cry, my pet. There's nothing to cry about. It was sad leaving it all but that's over,' he said at last.

She didn't know that she was crying. But the gasping wouldn't stop.

Her chest was still heaving when Papa stroked her wet cheek. 'We can't go back to that garden. But in a few years you'll come out to us in India again, to Lahore this time, and then you shall have a pony all of your very own to ride.'

*

'Trix, lovey, would you like to make a drawing yourself?' Papa asked, one afternoon Trix accepted the stalk of charcoal gingerly. She wanted to make something beautiful for Papa, wanted it so much that she could scarcely breathe. The black stick was cool in her hand as she drew it across the paper. But the picture in her head, the bird with its beak open, singing in the tree, wouldn't come out.

The marks she made on the big white sheet were dark and ragged. Not beautiful at all. The more she tried to make them look like a bird, the more of a scrawl it grew. She threw the charcoal down with a sob then looked across at Papa, scared.

'It's all right, Trix. We all get cross when we can't do things first go'.

He ruffled her hair and picked up the gritty bits of charcoal.

But one day Papa went back to India. He didn't even wait to have one Christmas with them.

'I was only here on special leave,' he explained.

Anyway, Papa liked Ruddy best.

'What d'you say to coming with me to Paris, young man?' she'd heard him ask. 'There's a rather grand show I have to prepare for the Paris Exhibition. That's the only reason I could get away on leave.'

Papa had not come back just to see them, after all. Trix waited but he didn't invite her to go to Paris or to see his grand exhibition. They could all have gone together. He didn't think of that. He just took Ruddy.

'The Pater had his work cut out, in charge of all the exhibits from India, so he gave me money to buy my own lunch. He let me go exploring all day by myself,' Ruddy boasted on his return.

Sometimes she hated Ruddy.

July was chill and wet, not at all like last summer. Mama took Ruddy out to the shops almost every day, leaving Trix behind in their lodgings. The landlady put her head round the door, occasionally, to make sure Trix wasn't playing with matches and sometimes she gave her a piece of cake, but she was still lonely.

'These aren't pleasure trips, you know, Trix,' Mama told her. 'Ruddy's new school has sent me a simply endless list of things Ruddy's going to need. *Four* pairs of flannel pyjamas if you please.'

Pyjamas? Ruddy was going to sleep at his new school, not at home? Slowly it came over Trix. They were going to be separated.

It wasn't really news to her but only now did she begin to feel what that meant.

'Of course you can't possibly go to the same school as Ruddy, Trix, darling,' Mama said. 'Don't be silly. They only take boys at the United Services College. Cousin Margaret loves Notting Hill High School and so will you.'

At first Trix thought that if she could just explain, Mama would find a way for her to stay with Ruddy. She'd understand. But when she tried again, the next day, Mama became angry. She replaced her sewing on the table, among the pile of shirts and underclothing still waiting for name-tapes. She turned.

'I hope you're not going to be tiresome about this, Trix. It's all settled. Ruddy is going off to school in Devon and you're going to live in Warwick Gardens with Miss Craik and her sister. You'll be starting at the High School in September.'

'Staying with Miss Craik?' Trix faltered.

'And her sister. That's right. And of course there's Miss Winnard too. Until you're old enough to come out to us in Lahore, your home will be with them in Warwick Gardens. And while I remember, darling, they've very kindly agreed to have you to stay with them next month. Ruddy will be going to the Baldwins, to stay with Cousin Stan. There are visits I have to make while I'm here at Home.'

'But I don't really know Miss Craik and – and the others.'

Her breath was coming quickly. Before she had time to lose heart, Trix spoke up.

'Please, Mama, can't I go back to Auntie? I could stay with her. I know she'd have me.'

Mama stared. 'You really want to go back to that –' she broke off.

'Let me, Mama. Please. I do know Auntie Sarah and I don't know those other people.'

Mama continued to look doubtful but she resumed her sewing.

At last, 'Very well, Trix. I'll write to Mrs. Holloway and enquire.'

'Just as well I did hold my peace,' Trix heard her add under her breath.

* * *

His first term at the United Services College almost over, Ruddy was slouching down the lane towards the village of Appledore with Nicholson the other new boy. It was Wednesday, their free afternoon. Some fellows, the really keen ones, got up games of footer but most, like himself, preferred to leave the school premises far behind. There were still rules. They had to wear their striped caps and school jackets but otherwise they were free, so long as they were back for prep at five.

A night of rain had left the lanes glistening and the air was sharp with the smell of hawthorn.

'D'you think they make us wear our caps so the villagers can sneak on us?' he asked Nicholson, the other new boy, as they tramped along. Between them they had scraped up one- and-sixpence and were planning to buy chocolate in the musty little shop on their way.

Nicholson paused, with a look of surprise. Without removing the grass stem he was chewing, 'Dunno…' he mumbled. 'Never thought about it, Giggers.'

That's what they were calling him here. 'Giggers', meaning 'giglamps', for the spectacles. He rather liked it. Poor Nicholson still didn't have a nickname. Ruddy pushed the glasses further up his nose. That was better, the earpieces stopped digging in. He went back to explaining about rabbits. Although it was broad daylight the creatures were skipping about in every field they'd passed.

'So you see,' he resumed, 'they get transfixed. It's fear. They're so exposed and the light blinds them so they can't find where the shadow is. That's where they'd rush off to hide, normally, in the shadows.'

Nicholson seemed quite impressed. He waited, boot poised above the large pebble he had been kicking along the path. 'But Giggers, have you seen this, actually seen it yourself? It's not just out of a book?'

'I tell you, it's true. I went out in the woods one night with the boy from the farm. We were looking for badgers. We borrowed the big kerosene lantern from the milking shed.'

He felt the excitement of it all over again. 'We never did see any badgers, though we found the sett all right. We ended up going for the rabbits: it's no end of fun to watch. Their eyes fix and they can't move, once you trap them with the light.'

Nicholson was smiling but he didn't seem very sure. He tried a sideways punt and the pebble shot away into the new growth of stinging nettles lining the track. After poking around after it with a stick, he gave up and returned.

'Do your people live on a farm? I thought that they were out in India,' he asked.

'Oh, the farm was just somewhere we were putting up last summer when the Mater came home to see my sister and me. The Pater used to be stationed in Bombay. That's where I was born, but now he's Director of the Museum in Lahore.'

Nicholson nodded, walking faster, now he'd given up on the pebble. 'Mine's up in Burmah. I didn't know you had a sister. I suppose you had to come back to live with your grandparents before you were old enough for the Coll.'

Ruddy let his face go blank, just as he had learned to do faced with Harry. His hands dug deep into his trouser pockets but came away again empty before he spoke.

'Not exactly. We were living with a poisonous woman in Southsea. That was why the Mater came back.'

Nicholson looked surprised. 'But why did she –' he checked himself. Ruddy could see him remembering that other chaps didn't always like to talk about their families. Beginning again, 'I suppose she came back as soon as you told her it was no go.'

Ruddy turned up his face consideringly towards the pale April sky.

'I think, actually, it might have been a friend of theirs, an old chap from Bengal. He came to visit Trix and me one day at Southsea when I was seedy and they kept asking me what I could see. That's when I got these,' he flicked a hand up at his spectacles.

'I think he told the Mater to come. Or it could have been my aunt, I suppose.' Seeing the confusion on his friend's face, he added quickly, 'I hadn't said anything, you see. I thought – I don't know – I think I believed she thought it was … that it was good for us. That she had chosen the woman deliberately.'

Nicholson nodded, looking wise. All the fellows here had fathers in the service. They knew that orders came through and you moved to your new posting. You didn't ask questions.

Ruddy didn't want to have to say any more.

'What about your people, Nicholson? Do you have a sister?' he asked.

'Two, worse luck. Always fussing.'

Ruddy stopped still and gazed at his new friend, with a frown.

'Girls are a bit strange. My sister says she wants to go back to Southsea to live with that foul woman in the holidays, once the Mater has gone back to Lahore.'

Nicholson struggled and gave up.

'But you said she was poisonous. My father's right. Women are a mystery.'

*

It was halfway through Christmas term at the Notting Hill High School. The smell of potpourri and beeswax that rose to meet Trix as she went through the door of 26, Warwick Gardens had become familiar over the past twelve months. Miss Craik had let her help to lay out the rose petals from the garden to dry and gave her the orris root to mix in later, when it was time to make the year's supply last June. Now the afternoons were turning dark early and the gutters Trix walked by on her way home were choked with sodden leaves.

Edna, the maid who had opened the door for her, smiled before turning back down to the basement. Trix stepped gingerly across the polished floor, trying to stop her shoes from squeaking. All three ladies meant to be kind. They just didn't know how difficult it was to live with people who were so quiet and polite all the time.

She did her best to slip through the house without leaving a trace of herself. That way she couldn't offend anyone without knowing. The ladies were all much too kind to hurt her feelings by saying anything. It meant she was never quite sure if she was doing the right things. With relief, she reached her bedroom unnoticed.

It was quite different at school, where the rules were clear. She was still surprised that the lessons were so interesting. As she began to spread her homework books out on the desk in her bedroom, Trix felt the return of a pleasant excitement. She was getting some of the highest marks in the class.

'I can see you're going to be a writer like Miss Craik and her sister,' her English teacher had said.

'Not like them!' Trix had only just held back from exclaiming. The ladies were so mild in their views it left her feeling stifled. Tonight, instead of kindness what she needed was to be on her own. She needed to think. And not to be interrupted.

Leaving her bedroom and the pile of homework half-unpacked – one of the ladies might look in to see if she needed any help with it – she slipped along the landing and let herself into the linen cupboard. The size of a small room, she'd discovered it during her first days there on her own. It was lined with shelves piled high with sheets and towels, blankets and counterpanes, all arranged in orderly folds, almost like a shop. That first time she'd crept in and curled up in a nest of blankets for comfort but today she remained on her feet, her back against the door.

She needed to understand just what exactly she was feeling. Something didn't quite make sense.

When Mama first told them they were going to spend all summer together in the country they had both been so happy.

'No lessons,' she and Ruddy capered.

'No housekeeping for me,' put in Mama, 'and no beastly Indian servants.'

Ruddy's face fell. Mama must have seen it too.

'Best of all, I'll have my favourite company in the whole world, my own darling, clever children,' she went on quickly.

Trix frowned, remembering.

Her darlings? Her favourite company?

But Mama had gone away again. Trix didn't want to think what that meant. Far away, first to visit other people, then back to India. To a place Trix only knew the name of: Lahore.

'I have to look after poor Papa,' she said.

That was such a weak excuse. Trix couldn't make it come out right. She felt as though she were sinking, wondering about Mama and struggling.

The chime of a handbell. The signal for Trix to join the ladies in the drawing room for tea. As she passed through the hall she glanced at the little table under the clock, where the post was left divided up into piles. Oh good, one for her today. From Auntie. Wanting to know when the end of term was and when she'd be arriving for the holidays. Would it be more rude to make herself late for tea by reading it here, at the foot of the stairs, or to read the letter in the drawing room, instead of paying attention? Sighing, she pocketed it. After tea would have to do.

'Now dear, you won't mind, there's a young lady going to be staying when you arrive. Her name's Miss Garrard and she's very well-connected. The Garrards, you know, the Crown Jewellers. I've put her in Harry's old room.'

Trix threw down the letter. She rather thought she did mind. She wanted everything to be the same as before. Apart from Harry. She didn't mind at all if he wasn't there. But just herself and Auntie. She didn't need another girl, especially one old enough to be called a young lady. There were enough senior girls at school giving themselves airs.

* * *

Fourteen now, and Ruddy was beginning to feel himself a man. Usually, travelling on his own like this, he'd have been light-hearted. But today he was taking the train for Portsmouth. Going back to Southsea. Even bagging a corner seat didn't lift his mood.

He swallowed. The jolting had never made him feel sick like

this before. There was sweat on his forehead and that wasn't just the heat.

The used, dusty smell of the upholstery offended him. He leaned away from the padded backrest. Finding the window at his side resisted, he got to his feet and tugged. It gave abruptly with a jerk that made him stagger.

The man with gold braid round his cuffs, who was seated across the carriage, looked up.

'Good for you, old chap,' he said kindly. 'Sound move.'

If it was up to him he'd never set eyes on That Woman again as long as he lived. She was death itself. Poison. How could Trix keep going back like this, every holiday?

Usually he managed to overlap with her for a few days in Warwick Gardens but this time, summer term at the Coll. had ended too late for that.

He could scarcely believe he'd agreed to make this visit. But he needed to see her. Just being with her calmed him down. And she was the one person he could trust to say something about his poems that was worth listening to, not just 'Ruddy, how clever'. She had an ear.

They were jolting over the points outside Guildford.

'This is horrible.'

He'd been on the verge of speaking aloud. He clamped his lips together. He hadn't realised he'd feel like this.

Think of The Study and the fellows. Remember boiling that bottle of red ink over the burner Beresford rigged up. Stoppering it had been his own idea. A fountain of blood. That'd been no end of a scheme. Worth all the scrubbing afterwards.

Stopping for Haslemere.

He revved at his imagination. Remember those fellows and their voices.

'Go to it, Giggers. We haven't a bean, it's time for you to write another set of sweet verses for the *Penzance Mail*.'

Five bob a poem, ten if it was over a dozen lines. Money for jam.

He couldn't see through his spectacles properly. Wiping them didn't seem to help.

He shut up his battered copy of *Uncle Remus*.

A shiver. Oh no, surely he wasn't actually going to vomit? A hand flew to cover his mouth. As the qualm passed he became aware again of the satisfying bristliness of his upper lip.

Trix'd be surprised to see his moustache. It really stood out now. He was the only man in the lower forms who unarguably needed to shave. Other fellows might be head and shoulders taller for all he cared. Now it didn't matter so much, either, that he was such a funk at games.

He stroked the moustache, appreciatively. What a head start it'd given him with the fisher-girls! He had been loitering with Nicholson behind the beach shacks, eyeing a knot of girls, who seemed determined not to look in their direction. Then that pretty dark one left her friends and came straight over to him, to him not Nicholson. His body surged at the memory. Her friends were good too. Lips, then tongues, those girls had plenty to teach. His hands no longer trembled as they slid inside an opened bodice.

Havant. Soon be there. Getting off at Fratton.

Fratton, one stop before Portsmouth, the nearest station to Havelock Park and the House of Desolation. Beresford, with his naval connections, had laughed when he solemnly explained to the Study, 'I don't actually go as far as Portsmouth. I usually get off at Fratton.'

The others just looked baffled, lost to understand his joke. He'd waited, relishing the moment. He was adding to the common store of significant information.

'Getting off at Fratton, it's what those matelots say for pulling out in time.'

By afternoon every boy in the school was sniggering at the name of Fratton.

Trix, soon. That'd better make it all worthwhile. At times he'd found something flat in the tone of her letters from Southsea. But this last one struck a note of excitement.

'You can't imagine, Ruddy, I've got a new friend here, her name's Flo, and she's an art student. A painter, awfully clever. It's made such a difference. She's older than us, sixteen. Auntie's so impressed, quite cowed, poor thing, but that's something you'll be pleased to hear, I know.'

In spite of all his misgivings he felt a stir of curiosity as he got down from the train, overnight bag in hand.

It was a surprise to find his sister waiting for him on the platform. Surely they didn't let little girls of twelve out on their own? And then he understood, as Trix gestured, blushing, towards a young woman standing over by the ticket office and keeping discreetly to the background. Flo. Her chaperone.

Astonishing, Trix had gone absolutely puce.

At first he took in only the brilliant cobalt blue of the other girl's long coat. She wasn't looking at them. A greyhound, elegantly stepping at the end of a scarlet leash, had absorbed her attention. As they watched, she fell to her knees, smoothing back its ears with little cries of admiration and pleasure. The owner, a portly man in tweeds, quite as gratified as his dog, was moving off by the time Ruddy and Trix came up to her.

The words of introduction passed over his head unheard as he stared into the exquisite oval of Flo Garrard's face. The line of that cheek. Grey eyes fringed with heavy dark lashes gazed steadily back. He blinked.

She was speaking. Something about being pleased. About Trix's brother. His poetry.

The languid drawl of her voice made his spine tingle.

He stuttered as he took the hand she held out, direct as another boy. It was cool and smooth. He didn't want to let go.

Trix was babbling away.

'It's just like you, Flo, to fall in love with that dog. She's mad about animals, aren't you Flo? Wait till you see Flo's pet goat, Ruddy. It's so funny. His name's Jeremiah. Auntie thinks it's a disgrace, the name of a prophet. Doesn't she, Flo?'

His sister was trotting along clinging to the new girl's arm with an adoring look. It disturbed him for a moment. Was this one of those 'pashes' that she said the girls at her school went in for? She did look stupid.

Then he too became absorbed in gazing at Flo.

The delightful turmoil carried him through the worst of arriving at Lorne Lodge and having to speak to That Woman. She was even uglier than he remembered. And he was going to have to sleep on that horsehair sofa.

'You don't mind, do you Rudyard? Miss Garrard's occupying your old room. It's ever so kind of her, she shares it with your sister.'

It gave him shivers to think of Flo sleeping there, where he used to sleep, perhaps in that same bed.

At once he felt shame. That rare, that exquisite creature, how could he? Keep those impulses for the Appledore fisher-girls.

He turned back to the conversation. The Woman was almost grovelling. Exchanging looks with Trix he understood. The glance she threw at Flo told him everything. It was Flo's presence that commanded this unlooked for courtesy.

'The old brute's terrified I'll leave. My people pay her more than she's used to, so I make sure to have things my way,' Flo explained simply, once they sat down to supper alone.

'There's never any question of her eating with us.'

What a woman! Ruddy was dazzled.

After supper, which was almost edible, compared with food at the Coll, they escaped.

'I think we'll make for the sea, don't you, little Kiplings? Tell me, when does a Kipling become a full Kip?' Flo teased.

Trix giggled but Ruddy wasn't sure whether to smile. Was she making fun of him? She was very tall for a girl. He tried not to show that he was struggling to keep up, she walked so fast on her long legs.

Next to Flo, Trix looked such a child, in that cap with a bow over her eye. Flo herself was wearing a loose dress of seagreen silk, belted at the waist with plaited thongs, under her blue coat. It was just the sort of thing Aunt Georgie would choose. No stupid frills. And such colours, like one of Uncle Ned's paintings. You could tell Flo was an artist.

Small waves were lapping quietly in the distance as they settled themselves in a line on the sea wall, one on either side of Flo. She was a good sport. Other girls who looked younger than her were titupping along the pavement or sitting with their feet together on the municipal benches, looking respectable. Not Flo. She'd swung herself up onto the wall without hesitation.

Trix was chattering. Ruddy sat staring out to sea, wondering what he could say to sound interesting, when he sensed Flo fumbling in her coat pocket. He turned to see her select a white cylinder from a slim silver case.

'I say, you don't smoke do you? I didn't know that girls smoked.' To his horror his voice was squeaky with surprise. He hadn't sounded like that for more than a year.

Trix looked up, 'They're called cigarettes. Flo buys them when she goes to Paris,' she explained, infuriatingly smug, replacing her head on Flo's shoulder.

What a baby she was.

'Of course I know what they're called, you infant. Don't forget I've been to Paris myself.'

Now Flo would think he was just a squabbling kid.

'Why did you choose to come here to Portsmouth to learn painting?' he asked.

That should get some conversation going.

Flo laughed but she didn't look happy. 'That's a long story', she replied 'and rather a gloomy one. Don't be taken in by my name. They're not terribly proud of my father at the crown jewellers. Let's just say Portsmouth was cheap enough to appeal to those who hold the purse strings. And it's a step on my way. I'm going to live in Paris and paint, one day.'

He was rapt. In this woman he picked up a conviction to match his own. He'd begun keeping a careful record of his poems in proper leather-bound notebooks marked 'Private'. Turning out verses for the local papers to earn a bob or two at need certainly wasn't the limit of his ambitions.

He stared with renewed admiration at the strings of carved wooden beads hung round the creamy neck. So much for the crown jewellers! Flo, like him, was having no truck with all that.

Next morning he woke up thinking about her. Not just a stunning girl but another artist. There must be a way to get to know her properly. To spend time together, without having to bother about his little sister.

He'd write to Flo just as soon as he was back in Warwick Gardens. Send some of his work too. Once he got back to his notebook with the fair copies, he'd make a choice and ask for her views.

That should get things started.

Drafting, then redrafting, his first letter absorbed his attention all through the journey back to London.

* * *

Over the next two years, in galleries and parks, in tearooms, when they could, Ruddy and Flo joined each other to talk about art and to argue. Flo shocked him with her 'Sorry, he may be your uncle, but Burne-Jones and his work are just old hat.' He wouldn't have taken it from anyone else.

Ruddy, now sixteen, was strolling through Kensington Gardens, the spring sunshine warm enough to make him loosen his scarf. Away from the clatter of the streets and the stink of horse piss, he could pick up a hint of newly cut grass. At his side Flo was laughing at the small dogs – excited to be out in the bright day – who yapped and lunged at the end of their leads.

Thank heavens Trix wasn't here too, mooning over Flo. That was one good thing about her passion for going back to Lorne Lodge. Today he had the clear field that he needed.

He must get on with it. Another week and Flo would have left for good. The pressure of his need to speak, to have things clear between Flo and himself, made the air seem thin. He gasped and she turned to him in alarm.

She really did care. He took courage.

Before he could summon himself, however, Flo began.

'I can't believe that another week and I'll be in Paris. You've been a brick, Ruddy,' she went on, 'without you I don't know what I'd have done.'

Hope blazed in him at this rare concession. Flo usually avoided anything that verged on the personal.

'Only another artist could understand. My wretched trustees! I thought they'd never stop. "How can you need more classes when you've just had a year at the Slade?" It was you made me step up the pressure on them. There's iron in you, Ruddy, when it comes to art.'

He glowed. She was stunning in that long mauve smock, her dark hair held back from the pallor of her face by an amber clip. Even the leather art satchel she was carrying added to that air of distinction.

'It's ripping, being able to send you my work, Flo.'

He was edging towards it, almost on the brink. They hadn't been able to meet anything like as often as he'd wanted but he'd been sending her poems almost every week. Meeting Flo, falling in love with her – such a flood. Of course, he'd been writing tons of poetry anyway but she'd brought out something special. And fear. That wasn't so good. The fear that she'd go away and he'd lose her – that he was losing her. He'd put a stop to that now.

'Other people are such idiots,' she smiled. 'One simply has to have other artists to talk to. Who else could one possibly live with?'

She was making it easy for him. She guessed. His heart bounded.

'I feel that too. You're the one person who understands. And you're so beautiful. I want to be always near you.'

There, it was out. She was smiling, her eyes half-shut, veiled.

'You are the most alive person I know, Ruddy. You keep me going. Most people are half dead.'

'I want to keep you going always.'

She smiled but did not reply.

They came to a stop before an empty bench. Before taking his place at her side, he looked enquiringly at her. Reverently he took her hand. The sensation sent thrills right up his arm. A distraction. This was spiritual, a meeting of minds.

'Do keep writing your poems – though I don't know why you dwell on all that hopeless love and failure. Pre-Raphaelite stuff. It's today's experiences we need to examine. I'm holding you to your resolve. Poetry or death!'

'Or life, I suppose,' he spoke a little wildly, dizzy with encouragement. No need to feel hopeless, she was telling him.

He still hadn't given her the poem. His own lines rang in his ears, pleading to be spoken:

'Let thy soul's perfect music interpret its harmonies –
The passion that is in a line, and whence that passion had rise,
For my heart is laid bare to thy heart, and my soul in thy hands' hold lies.'

Better though to let her read them first. Quietly, on her own.

'*For* life, I mean. Flo, I've written a poem for you. Just for you, that is. I –'

She broke in, 'Ruddy, we think alike. I've got something to show you too. The sketches are just here in my bag. Is that your poem? Let me take it so I can read it later, with proper attention. I'm thrilled,' she added, undoing the straps on her satchel, 'I've heard about the most extraordinary painting Edouard Manet's been working on, someone's taking me to his studio to see it next week. It shows a bar, with mirrors –' She slid his envelope into the pocket behind her pastel crayons.

He'd done it. His formal proposal was in her hands. And hadn't she as good as accepted?

*

It was late afternoon towards the end of the summer term. Rud leaned back in the wide Windsor armchair that stood across from the desk in the Head's library and removed his spectacles. He wiped them with great deliberation then returned, dismay mounting, to scanning his father's letter. He hadn't realised where it was all leading, when that man from Lahore – what was his name, Wheeler? – had summoned him to London and jawed away at him for half an hour. He'd imagined that it was just the Mater with her fussing, wanting to know how he was. Now he felt as though he'd been tricked.

He'd been pleased enough to get an exeat to go off on his own to meet the man. You feel stifled, always in the same company. It could be pretty average good fun all together in Number Five Study but he liked being on his own too. *Had* to be on his own. Best of all, like this, in the Head's library.

'If you're going to write, Rud, you'd better see as much of what's been done in that line as you can,' the Head had declared. And he certainly was going to write, couldn't stop himself, he'd already filled four notebooks with his poems. All fair-copied. Work done off his own bat. No need, really, for Flo to urge him to keep writing.

He'd gone over and over the memory of that walk in Kensington Gardens, when he'd told her of his feelings. Just remembering her smiles lifted him with rapture. She hadn't needed to say anything. The understanding between them was perfect. It was on a different plane from that stuff with those fisher-girls.

But now, he could scarcely take it in, this letter the Pater had sent to the Head, his old friend Cormell Price.

'As you know, there was never any question of the Varsity: the funds wouldn't stand it. So his mother and I are mightily relieved that Wheeler thinks he can make use of Rud on the CMG. He needs a European assistant and the boy made a good enough impression – as well he might, with all the care you've taken of him, Crom.'

Without a by-your-leave, they had obtained a position for him out in Lahore and now they were instructing him to leave England?

Leave Flo? It was out of the question. The letter had been handed to him with a broad smile, as though he should be overjoyed! A journalist, forsooth! Assistant editor on the *Civil and Military Gazette* or whatever the God-forsaken rag was called. They'd deceived him. He'd no notion of going out to India. His life was here in Europe, writing. With other artists, at Flo's side in Paris.

'I had not spoken of this to you earlier but it seems I must. I consider myself an engaged man and am not at liberty to leave the country,' he wrote to his parents.

His father's prompt reply filled him with chagrin.

'My dear boy, I don't believe you realise how fortunate you are, to have a position offered you at sixteen-and-a-half with no experience or qualifications. A position, moreover, that by and by will carry a very decent screw, considering your age and the fact that you'll be living at home without any expenses.'

The Head appeared to concur. His passage on the *Brindisi* had already been secured and he was to sail from Tilbury on 20th September, bound for Bombay. He was helpless

* * *

1883, a year on, and his sister was embarking on the same journey. Trix and her new friend Maud Marshall, both fifteen but wishing to appear older, were only a few days into the long voyage. Yet already they'd agreed to meet every morning straight after breakfast, to work on their poems and stories.

'I can't believe my luck, you're the first girl I've met who's thought of doing anything serious. A tinkle on the piano and a few pastels were enough for the rest of them,' Maud exulted.

'How awful for you. At least one of my old friends, Flo Garrard, is a very serious painter. It's a bit sad for me, actually. She's gone off to Paris. I haven't a scrap of talent for painting myself, though.'

Trix was careful not to say anything about Uncle Ned. When she heard Mama drop his name into conversation with new people they met on board, it made her uncomfortable.

'I do sing a bit,' Maud confessed, 'drawing room songs, for after dinner you know. Stuff to please Colonel Sahib, I mean Father. Nothing up-to-date, perish the thought, he'd hate it. And I'm not at all sure Mother likes it that I want to write.'

Trix laughed. How different peoples' lives were.

'In my family everyone writes,' she replied. 'Mama even does the "Notes from Simla" for the paper on top of all her poetry and Papa's always sending off learned articles. Even my brother Ruddy, who's not much older than I am, works on a newspaper.'

'Goodness, which one? And how dashing, a brother who writes.'

'It's the Punjab paper, the *CMG*,' Trix took pride in being able to sound like an old India hand. 'But don't get the wrong idea. Ruddy writes simply reams of poetry, but it's nothing to do with his job. That seems to be more about reading. Digging out facts from all the local papers for his editor to write about. Then proofing most of the pages before they go to press.'

Maud seemed taken aback. 'I don't believe I'd know where to begin with proof-reading and all that. I've only thought about the imagining part.'

They found a quiet corner of the deck and drew their long chairs together.

'It's funny, I simply love writing stories though I hated lessons, didn't you?' Maud asked, settling herself.

Trix laughed and nodded companionably. She wasn't going to intimidate Maud further by revealing that the Headmistress had wanted her to stay on at school.

Trix would make an excellent candidate for the new women's colleges in Cambridge,' Miss Morant Jones had written to Mama. *'The expense would of course be much less than for a son,'* she'd added discreetly.

It was exciting to think she might have the brains for it. But Cambridge would have meant waiting even longer without seeing Ruddy. Mama hadn't pushed her.

'I'd rather not have my pretty, clever daughter turned into one of those fearsome bluestockings. No man wants a girl who thinks she knows more than he does,' Mama had concluded.

'It's your turn to begin, Maud.'

'Oh dear, I can't lie back like this when we're working,' Maud wriggled and sat up.

'We could sit side saddle,' Trix offered, swivelling her legs round till her feet touched the deck. 'Like this?'

Maud's high pitched laugh was lost in the open air.

'Trix Kipling, it's perfectly clear *you've* never sat a horse.'

Pink in the face, Trix sprang to her feet.

'If you're going to just play about, Maud –'

'I didn't mean anything by it, Trix. Don't be cross. You forget that the one thing I really learned, out in India, was how to ride. I'm longing to get back to all that – almost as much as I'm longing to be a writer. And you already know so much about writing. Come on, do. I'm depending on you to show me.'

The invitation, the opportunity, were too much for her. Trix returned to her seat and prepared to listen.

Taking a small notebook from the pocket of her serge skirt, Maud began to read aloud. When she reached the close of her short story, where romantic love and daughterly defiance were heroically entwined, the voice of Trix was decisive.

'You know, I do think this new draft is an improvement. Making the girl say right out what she feels. And that whole scene with her mother is really daring. Much more convincing, too.'

Maud was flushed and grateful. 'I don't know how you do it, Trix, but you seem to hear exactly where a piece is going wrong.'

It was the turn of Trix to look gratified, before she reached for her own notebook.

'It's another parody,' she explained. 'I can't resist doing them. I'm making a collection of all the ones I've finished, to surprise my brother.'

Trix could see her friend growing anxious, so she added 'It's a poet I know you've read, Maud. I'll give you a clue. The title is 'Jane Smith'.

I journeyed on a winter's day
Across the lonely wold;

No bird did sing upon the spray
And it was very cold.'

Trix began with a straight face but by the third verse her composure was giving way.

'A little girl ran by the side
And she was pinched and thin
"Oh please sir do give me a ride
I'm fetching mother's gin."'

'Wordsworth, Wordsworth,' Maud applauded in triumph. 'Do go on. His real poems bore me to tears, but this is such fun!'

* * *

All four Kiplings, 'the family square' that felt complete again, were now reunited in Lahore. Alice and Lockwood had chosen to live on the Mozung Road, in the quarter built by the British. Situated between the Upper and the Lower Mall their home stood well outside the ancient walls of Lahore. It was a handsome Punjab bungalow, with a verandah on all sides, opening through pointed arches supported on double columns. Inside, the rooms opened out from each other, separated only by curtains as often as doors.

Trix hesitated, standing out in the passageway, wondering whether Ruddy was busy but he'd picked up her rapid footfall.

'No need to hang about, Infant, I'm at liberty. Take a pew.'
She slipped through the fall of printed cotton at the entrance to his workroom, the words tumbling out.

'I'm so excited, Ruddy. You know Mama's decided I'm too young for the fleshpots of Simla and we're to spend the Hot Weather at Dalhousie? Well, I've just had a letter back from Maud and she's going to be there at the same time. It will make such a difference.'

'I suppose that means you'll sit and giggle together and there'll be no getting a sensible word out of you,' he growled.

'You don't understand, Maud's really serious about her writing.'

Rud didn't look convinced but she wasn't going to argue.

Glancing from the wide solid table to the shelves put up by the local carpenter, following her brother's design, Trix broke out, 'You are so lucky, having a study. I know it doesn't feel like a separate room,' she added, 'just a bit of the hall Mama's curtained off for you, but it's still a proper place for you to work.'

'You can come in here as much as you like when I'm at the office. Just don't touch anything or move the papers.' Rud was quick with his offer.

Trix laughed. The surface of the table was covered layers deep in loose sheets.

'I hope you number your pages,' she observed.

'Away with that housekeeping eye, O Maiden, and let's get down to it,' with her he still revelled in all the flourishes of the storyteller. 'Now I've got you here I intend we should pull together and that we should both enjoy the advantages of my position. That's one thing your friend Maud can't offer you: if we use the office printshop it won't cost us a penny to publish our book of verse. Your parodies and mine together – all we need to do now is agree on the order.'

Trix's smile was gone.

'Oh Ruddy, I don't think Mama's going to let me.'

'What?' He looked black.

'I mean, I can put in some of my poems. But the really good ones, the ones that made you laugh, Mama thinks are not suitable. I must think of my reputation.'

'Your reputation? How are you going to get a reputation if you can't publish your best work?'

'I don't think she has that kind of reputation in mind. It's men. "Men don't like girls who are too critical," that's what she says.'

'That's rich, coming from the Mater. As sharp a tongue as was ever heard throughout all Hind.'

Trix could tell that this was a phrase picked up from the vernacular. She saw his temper was rising. But she could break the spell, with her talent for mimicry.

"'My dear child, it's no use thinking you can write just anything you fancy, like Ruddy. Your case is completely different." That's what she said. "Yes, we can publish our little volumes easily enough out here. But it's like shopping in the bazaar. Cheap. As women we have to learn to be our own first editors. You see, you'll be judged on it. I couldn't bear you to spoil your own chances."'

He was laughing long before she'd finished. But they both knew that this was one of the occasions when resistance was barred. Any argument on their part would provoke scenes of a kind not to be endured. Their father, too, had learned, and that early in his marriage, that when she was crossed Alice was without compunction. She would wear her opponents to rags.

'*Nil desperandum*, Trix,' her brother said at last. 'You're sixteen, for heaven's sake. She doesn't begin to realise you have a mind of your own now. When I came out here at sixteen, I found she'd taken some of the poems I'd sent her in letters and had them published. No thought of asking me. "Schoolboy Lyrics" indeed: "Mother's Epic Cheek" would have been more like it.'

'Was that the time of the great Three-Day-Sulk that Father makes jokes about?'

'I prefer, O Maiden, to reserve my dignity; Let us call it the Period of Superb Withdrawal.'

'Come along,' his arm swept a space on his desk. 'Sit here beside me. We'll find a way to arrange the mortal remains to make a decent showing. Plus, we must think of a really good title. I confess, for the moment I'm stumped.'

'Do you think "Echoes" would be any good? I was wondering. You know, the after-effects of hearing, when the sense seems to change …' her voice was beginning to trail uncertainly but seeing her brother's look of pleasure, Trix sat straight again.

'I had an idea too about which of yours should lead,' she said, reaching for the worn brown envelope marked 'Trix and Self'.

* * *

'Feeling abominably seedy,' Rud wrote and laid the pen down by his diary. It was now his third year in Lahore at the *Civil and Military Gazette*. The clatter of machinery seemed to have got inside his head so that his thoughts jerked and rattled to the rhythm of the presses. Usually he could absorb their throbbing and ignore it but not today. In the gloom that opened beyond his tiny office, lean, turbaned figures moved languidly among the swing of the machines. When would he be free to go home? Not for an age: there was still a full set of proofs to be gone through and he wouldn't be getting them just yet, not for at least another hour. Across the way he could see Stephen Wheeler, his Chief, sitting in his office, head on hand, reading intently.

It was a week now since he'd presented himself at the hospital for tests. What was he going to do if the results showed he was infected? Tarleton Young had been soothing and as a Medical Officer of experience the man ought to know. Not every chap in the army picked up disease, only one in three, he reminded himself. At least that's what they claimed, the men he bought beer for in the Infantry barracks over at Mian Mir. He learned a lot from them. He looked up at the moon-faced clock high on the end wall. He might just catch Young before he set out on his afternoon tour of inspection.

'O Ram Dass,' he called to his friend the foreman, 'keep these donkeys at their work unceasingly till my return.' It was an old joke between them all, with its half-veiled reference to an obscene folk-tale: voices rose in appreciative laughter even as the foreman replied that the word of the *Chota Sahib* would be obeyed. *Kipling minor*: it had almost ceased to irk him. Here in India you were known as the son of your father.

The presses were thrashing away at an outside order: no good letting the men slack off or the job would be delayed. Printing the *CMG* took priority and had to begin on time but they couldn't afford to be late with the outside work. The *Civil and Military Gazette* might be India's most influential newspaper after the *Allahabad Pioneer* but it could never pay its way on sales alone. Putting the diary back in the drawer, he took his coat from where it hung on the broken hook by the door and picked up his hat, the solar topee that gave him the air of a walking mushroom. The light hammered at him as he left the building.

Jeyes Fluid, 'the sweet and wholesome fragrance of British India', he observed in passing, teased his nostrils once he entered the hospital quarters. At least, thanks to his job as a journalist, he was unquestioned in his comings and goings. Behind the Medical Officer's desk, Tarleton Young looked steadily at young Rud Kipling.

'There's no question, you're taking your life in your hands if you go on these forays alone, Rud.'

Another new name. A man's one. About time, he wasn't a kid. Out here, only his family persisted in calling him Ruddy.

'Look, Young, I didn't come here to be preached at.'

'I'm not preaching. I'm trying to keep you alive: a little dose of clap would be nothing compared to the knife-wounds I've seen on men who thought they knew what they were doing and got mixed up in bazaar affairs. It's knives out there before you know it.'

'I'm not "mixed up" in anything, as you put it. I think I love her.'

'Just as you think she gave you the clap?'

'It might not have been Almitra.'

'Good God, man, do you know what you're doing? A girl brought up to that trade by her own mother – you know nothing about her.'

Rud got to his feet.

'Anyway, you think that I'm probably in the clear – I'm much obliged to you.'

'Till the next time, Rud. I'll see you this evening perhaps at the Club?' But the door had already closed behind Tarleton Young's patient.

Rud was almost glad to have spoken out about Almitra. He would have liked to open his heart to someone more congenial than Young, but where to turn? He was determined never again to let the Mater see into his soul, even if he'd thought she were up to hearing that her son wanted to marry his fourteen-year-old Parsee mistress. He blushed to remember how recently he too had despised all non-Europeans. Still, a man could learn.

He felt more torn in the case of his father. He was fairly sure that the Pater wouldn't turn a hair at the fact of the mistress. Yet he knew that he did not want to risk opening his life to his father's scrutiny. He was afraid it would begin to look different, to make him feel bad, once he saw his own life through his father's eyes. For a moment he felt utter rage merely imagining that calm gaze.

Reminding himself that it wanted only two nights till Thursday, when he would see Almitra, hold her in his arms again, he reined in his imagination and turned his steps towards the offices of the *CMG*. Later, he might drive over to Mian Mir. He would not, he absolutely must not allow himself to dwell during office hours on the touch of that slim body, in its folds of rustling rose-scented silk.

It was still hard for him to believe his luck: the old woman had followed him after an unsatisfactory evening session with one of the Eurasian girls who hung about the Shalimar Gardens. When she'd laid her hand on his shoulder, his first impulse had been to shake it off. But all that her hoarse whisper had boasted of her daughter, Almitra, had proved true, and more besides. Almitra was indeed beautiful. She threw all white women into the shade. What he hadn't expected was her tenderness, her sympathy.

All that Flo had once seemed to promise. Had Flo really meant to get rid of him? '*We must forget each other*,' she'd written when he went away. Her image still haunted him, at night on the edge of sleep. At times he still cherished hope.

Hope against hope. But he was not going to invite that black mood.

How trustfully Almitra had taken his hand, at her mother's bidding. 'And are you white inside, under all those clothes, Sahib?' she had murmured when he pressed her to talk with him. He had laughed aloud, pulling his shirt right open, till his smooth chest was exposed to her exploring hands.

There was a whisper of freshness in the air on Thursday night, when he slipped through the great archway that marked the entrance to the bazaar. It must have come from the river, Rud thought, breathing with pleasure air that was all of a sudden grassy and sharp. Determined to preserve his secret, he never left the club early on these Thursday evenings, though it played havoc with his nerves to sit listening apparently placidly to the dull men round him exchanging their familiar platitudes. As he held to the shadows beneath the high uneven walls, there were few to mark him even in the old city.

Once inside the bazaar he went warily, eyes on the ground to keep his feet from the heaps of nameless refuse casually piled by carved doorways, navigating chiefly by his nose. Just past the *serai*, where the reek of camels was unmistakable, a trail of scented smoke beckoned to him. Any other night he might have tried to follow where it led, to a hidden temple, perhaps. Or maybe to a party of men sitting smoking round an upstairs room, their eyes brimming with tears as the words of the Persian Hafiz were sung.

His heart was drumming in his chest, his breath came hard as he drew near to the alley which led to the old Jain pillar by the last turning. Ahead lay the ancient door daubed with blue and jagged with rot at the base. The squat negro sat by it as usual, sharpening his long knife. Taking command of himself, Rud greeted him pleasantly, using the vernacular. Almitra had taught him more in a couple of months than a year of private tutoring from a *munshi*. He slipped through into the courtyard, hearing behind him the scrape of the door as the guard dragged it back into place.

But where was she? On many occasions that sound had been the cue for soft cries of excitement, as Almitra ran out from the lighted room across the dark courtyard, calling his name. Instead, tonight the lit doorway was empty, though shadows were moving inside. Still unsuspecting, he was in the room in two strides, only to find it empty apart from the old mother. At the sight of him, she scuttled off and he could hear her voice raised in argument, though he could not follow the exact words, before Almitra stepped into view.

With half his mind he'd noted the demurely covered head but he was still taken aback by the formality of her greeting. His arm went round her, releasing a waft of fragrance from the violet folds of her shawl, as he asked, 'Heart of my heart, why so many strange happenings?'

She disengaged herself sinuously, and before he could protest, Almitra began what was evidently a prepared speech. She was going to be married. They had been very happy together but now it must come to an end.

He simply could not take the words in. Yet at the same time, something deep within him understood what he was hearing only too clearly, loosening streams that poured down his cheeks almost impersonally, as if from melting snows.

Almitra's voice changed. 'Ruddi, *chota*, sweet one. Be wise. Yes, of course, I love you very, very much. But it is time for me to marry. No, no, no'– she put his promises aside with a gesture of both hands –'my mother is never allowing. My uncle has found me very good husband, very rich merchant in Peshawur. I am lucky, lucky girl.'

She was dry-eyed, he could see that, and positively agog with excitement, immune to his protests, not listening to a word he'd said. Meanwhile, gasping for air, his whole body registered the shock. Even so, a sceptical voice inside his head was already raised in question. If the merchant did indeed exist, what lies had he been told? Rud caught his breath and spat, full in her face. Her eyes were blank as she reached and mechanically wiped her scarf across her cheek, retreating as she did so, while her mother hurried forward into the room. Before the mother's voice could be raised to call for help, Rud was gone. Afterwards he could not remember how he got out into the harsh moonlight.

The devil of it was that he did still love her, even while his mouth was acrid with hate. The games they had invented together, in that low-lit room, haunted by the scent of jasmine. Once Almitra had tried to get him to copy her as she danced, head angled, bells tinkling at her narrow ankles. Children again, they were abandoned to laughter, yet when he was with Almitra, laughter soon gave way to a passion that yielded in turn to a lingering tenderness.

Never again would he lie, his head in her lap, as she crooned the old songs from her grandmother's village.

He feared for her, for what they would make of her.

Sleeplessness was nothing new to him. He spent the rest of the night seated at the small table in his bedroom in his parents' home. 'Bikaner House' as friends named it, comparing it with the barren wilds of Rajasthan. It seemed as though hours passed while he remained staring, staring out over the bleak expanse of garden. For fear of snakes it was stripped as bare of growth as the desert sands.

Towards morning he struck his clenched fist once more against his aching forehead only to find that, beyond his choosing, his body was taking up a beat, a beat that was familiar, though he couldn't place it at once. Then he knew. It was a line from the *Arabian Nights*, from a love-song:

'If my feet fail me, O heart of my heart, am I to blame, being blinded by the glimpse of your beauty?'

He let himself chant the words aloud, soothing himself with each repetition. Imperceptibly, though, he found his drumming fingers shift their rhythm, as if to find an answering voice:

'Come back to me, beloved or I die,'

he sang under his breath.

'By Jove,' he said slowly, after a while, digging around in his pockets to find his usual pen. There is a story here and I'm going to find it.' His guts contracted as what he knew, what he had known, came back to him in force.

'A man should, whatever happens, keep to his own caste, race, and breed. Let the White go to the White and the Black to the Black. Then, whatever trouble falls is in the ordinary course of things – neither sudden, alien, nor unexpected.'

This is the story of a man who wilfully stepped beyond the safe limits of decent everyday society, and paid for it heavily.

He knew too much in the first instance; and he saw too much in the second.
He took too deep an interest in native life; but he will never do so again.
    'Deep away in the heart of the city…'

                              * * *

Another year, another blistering Hot Weather and Rud was sent up to Simla to recuperate. Everything always seemed much more straightforward, once he left the frying pan of the plains and got up into the hills. For one thing, Trix awaited him there. Ever since Trix had come out to India to join them he'd been feeling happier. Why, he scarcely ever thought about Flo now.

He couldn't help being a little anxious, however, about Trix. She was so evidently delightful. He'd already been obliged to see off more than one lovesick swain.

'It's much too soon for you to think of marrying, you know, Trix. We should all remain together as long as we can.'

They were taking a walk together round Jakko hill, waving and smiling as others trotted by on horseback but unwilling to be interrupted.

'You underestimate Mama,' she replied, pausing to brush a small caterpillar from his jacket. 'And romances of the peerage tempt me daily, you know, Ruddy.'

She was laughing as she said it but would she succumb?

He turned to face her.

'It's true, then, what I hear about attentions from Clandeboye? I can see the Mater would find that hard to resist, an offer from the son of the Viceroy.'

'I've resisted Arch Clandeboye for myself, thank you. He doesn't really appeal and I don't see myself in a tiara. But there've been consequences.'

She looked back at him teasing, waiting for him to ask.

'Wretched girl, go on.'

She waited till they had settled themselves on a small wooden bench, placed to offer a view over the town.

'It might come as a surprise, but his mother, Lady Dufferin's very put out.

''If my splendid Arch is not good enough for Miss Kipling, I altogether give her up. I simply can't understand what he sees in the girl.''

Trix took off Lady Dufferin to a T. He was rocking with laughter.

'That's what she told Mrs. Hetheringham. And so it's all round Simla. But that's not the end of it. She decided they must protect her darling Arch. The Viceroy was instructed to tell Mama I should be sent home.'

'No!' his voice was louder than he meant. A passing rider pulled at the reins as his mount tried to shy, whinnying.

'I told you not to underestimate Mama. She thinks Simla's my best chance of finding a husband. She wasn't going to be so easily cowed.'

They exchanged wry smiles.

'Mama was rather splendid. This is what she said: "Perhaps it is Lord Clandeboye who would profit from a change of scene?"'

He enjoyed that. One up to the Mater.

Shifting his weight on the bench, however, he was distracted. He wriggled. Was he sitting on something sticky? Once on his feet he brushed furiously at his trousers.

'It's only resin from the pines, it will come off,' Trix soothed him.

'I do wish the Mater'd give you more time –' he wanted to slow it down, all this talk of Trix and husbands.

'I know, Ruddy I know, but what else am I to do out here? Afternoon calls and tennis at the club aren't enough for me. I did take those classes in nursing but I'm not made of the right stuff for that. At least a home of my own to run would make me feel as if I had a position in the world. Some authority. Wasn't a child.'

He came to a halt, heart pounding, blocking the path.

'But what about writing? You're not thinking of giving that up? Giving up on me ?'

Immediately he felt foolish. He blew his nose.

'Never. How could you even think that? But unless I'm to live as Mama's daughter under her roof –'

And under her sway. He allowed the words to remain unspoken.

Rud had never relished the thought of Trix having suitors. But now that she seemed to be making a choice among them, favouring one, as the season wore on, he was positively alarmed. Her judgment was so poor. He'd have expected better of eighteen.

'I cannot conceive of the attraction of Jack Fleming. The man is tedious beyond words, my Infant. What appears to you like silent strength is mere bone – solid bone filling up the cavities of the skull, where other mortals like ourselves keep our brains. He may share a name with the Pater but that's all they have in common.'

Trix looked up from her magazine, taken by surprise. A wet afternoon and they'd been sitting reading, more or less in comfort, though the fire in their little sitting room was smoking.

'I am not your infant, Rud. Would you prefer it if I accepted Archie Clandeboye after all? Became daughter-in-law to the Viceroy? Archie's still asking me. Scarcely a week goes by.'

This was new. She never used to take a sharp tone with him.

'You know very well I've no wish to see you married to Clandeboye or any other knuckle-headed grandee,' he snapped. 'And let's keep snobbery out of this. We can leave that to the Mater.'

The smoke was making him cough. He leaned across the writing table to open a window.

Trix was tight lipped.

'You have no idea what it's like. All these men. All *wanting* something.'

Palms upraised, she seemed trying to push the air away.

'Every word you utter convinces me more deeply. You're simply not ready for marriage. You can't make a proper choice if you really have no idea what these fellows want from you.'

He waited but there was no response, no blush. Her face remained blank. He tried again.

'It's not just poetry and roses, you know. My dear girl, why do you think people here in Simla are calling you the Ice Maiden?'

That was new to her, he'd not intended the shock. White-faced, all too evidently pierced to the heart, she turned and walked out of the room.

Next week he would be going back down to the plains. Sitting up in bed, sipping the tea his mother had carried in with her own hands, Rud looked across at her and smiled.

'That's better, my dear. You looked like a ghost when you first arrived,' Alice surveyed her son critically. 'You can't afford to let your health get broken down, Ruddy. This country's treacherous. I don't like to think of you exposed to all manner of horrors. Appalling sights. I still don't believe it was necessary for you to visit that school where the roof fell in, before they'd removed the bodies.'

'Really, Mater, you don't need to warn me about the dangers. I've lost too many friends at what I've come to see as the regulation age of twenty-two.'

'Well then, take heed. I know you're very attached to Kadir Baksh but I wonder if perhaps you should get an older servant, one with more sense of responsibility. If any of them have. You don't look as though you're properly cared for.'

He stared, the cup still in his raised hand. She'd done it again. It was hopeless, she never could see what was in front of her.

'Whatever faults you find with my appearance, Mother of mine, they can't be laid at the door of Kadir Baksh. Don't you remember? I told you that he nursed me through that terrible attack in the Hot Weather of '84, when those of us still in Lahore were all going down with typhoid. I was rolling on the ground in agony –'

Cared for, indeed! He thought with gratitude of the calm morning wakenings, the low voice of his servant murmuring, 'It is finished Kipling Sahib, the shaving is completed and the *chota hazri* awaits.' Beside him, as he opened his eyes at that soft invitation, the tray of tea would be standing ready to his hand. Over by the *almirah* Baksh would already be storing away the long cut throat razor, scrupulously rinsed and dried, in its travelling case.

'That tumbler of hot milk laced with opium stopped the typhoid in its tracks. And it wasn't the only time Baksh has stood between me and death.'

He meant to impress her but his mother merely looked quizzical. She'd better hear the whole story.

'Very well, Mater, listen to this. A native ruler in Patiala tried to bribe me, to get the *CMG* to come out in his favour. I thought it would be poetic to send the cash back by the hand of a sweeper – show what I thought of him and his offer.'

She'd picked up the teaspoon and was turning it in her hands. He couldn't read her face. Was she paying attention? He pressed on.

'It was pretty foolhardy, I can see that now. Though it did have style. When he realised what I'd done, Baksh was appalled. Protecting me from revenge was his first thought. "Kipling, Sahib, eat only food I have tasted first, from this day." And he made me stick to that.'

'Ruddy, that does sound awfully like one of your stories for the *CMG*.'

Winded, he fell silent.

His mother went on. 'As for letting Kadir Baksh dose you – and with opium! You were lucky to escape with your life, in my opinion. I simply cannot credit that you allowed it. Really, dearest, what *shall* we do with you? Writing about this place is one thing but sinking into it –' Her head tilted, she smiled charmingly but there was steel in her voice.

'Well, you may take comfort from the knowledge that I'm not resigned to making my life out here as you have. I'm beginning to think of London.' His own words took him by surprise. It was nothing less than shock that he saw blanking his mother's face. 'Too bad,' he thought. 'She's asked for it.'

Alice did not allow the pause to lengthen.

'Don't let your head get swollen, will you, Ruddy? People may find your new little *Departmental Ditties* awfully amusing with its skit on officials and their documents. But are you sure you could write for an audience somewhat less parochial?'

'My proprietor seems to think so. He wants me down in Allahabad before many moons have passed, working on the *Pi*.' But she already knew that there had been talk of promoting him to the staff of the senior paper, the *Pioneer*. She was gone. His rejoinder fell upon empty air.

* * *

Yet another Hot Weather blasting the Punjab, with the thermometer still at 100 well after midnight all week. Leaning over his desk, for it was cooler than sitting, with a grunt of relief Rud finished proofing the advertisements for saddles and lamp oil. The waiting figure wiped his hands against his grimy *dhoti* before accepting them and carrying them away.

No longer concentrating on work, Rud was aware once more of his own mood. He didn't like what he'd overheard.

'The boy's pocket money.' So that's what his father thought of his employment – and of what it paid him. Rud set his teeth, remembering the weary hours he'd spent the previous day in grinding out digests of official reports for the paper. The Pater had no conception of how a day with the indigo crops and the prospects for jute followed up by the *Novoe Vremya* used a man up. He'd show them. That night he ate his dinner at the Club.

'But you know, Ruddy, we're not invited anywhere this evening. We could all dine together,' his mother had objected. At the time he had made no reply, letting them think what they would but in the afternoon he relented and sent a chit home.

At the Club, the usual crowd caught each other's eyes as they rose from the table, coffee –'filthy stuff'– left untouched. Forbes came clattering down the steps outside with Davis and Harrison to where Rud was waiting.

The drivers attending in their *tikka gharries* grinned at them:

'Old City, Sahib?'

'Double quick, *juldee jao*, jump to it,' Forbes took the lead once they had passed through the Lohari Gate. Tonight, he said, he was going to show them something different. But first they would smoke a pipe. There was still a novelty to Forbes in the opium houses. Shouldering aside the reeking curtain at the inner door, Rud felt its folds drag unpleasantly against his jacket. It was early in the night for the place but the figures stretched upon the slatted bunks looked as though they had not moved for hours. Maybe not for days. On his first visit the Chinaman who kept the house had pointed to more than one sunken-eyed figure that no longer left its mat but had a little food brought in now and then. Rud and his friends were not going down that road – too fly by half – but a pipe of the Chinaman's finest would give a fillip to the evening's adventures.

Inhaling deeply, as he lay stretched out on the frayed and blotchy cushions Rud felt his soul expand and open. From all the lives in the ancient city that lay about him, tremors played against his nerves. The steps of the young men were slowed when they left, their eyes brighter, as they half stumbled into the street.

'What now?' All turned expectantly to Forbes.

'I'm going to show you something that even our friend Kipling here hasn't ferreted out yet. We're going to a new whorehouse tonight, gentlemen.'

A let down: he'd imagined magicians, sorcery. He didn't need Forbes to find him women. Disappointed, Rud gave his attention to the cloud streaked brilliance of the night sky, and to the domes and minarets of the far Mosque of Wazir Khan that reared themselves in silhouette against it.

In fact, he was already acquainted, if only slightly, with the *mohalla* they found themselves in, having marked it as he wandered through one midnight weeks before. There were lamps on the ground in the courtyard they entered and men sitting about smoking, the coals in the hubble-bubble pulsing bright.

'Are you ready for this, you fellows?' Forbes demanded as a tall woman stepped forward, ushering them inside. Blinking, his eyes watering in the smoky lamplight, Rud was still able to observe that she was thickly made up and that her bones were too heavy for a woman. He would have turned full face to make sure but he picked up a sudden rigidity in his companions. Following their arrested gaze his own fell on half a dozen painted boys, slim as reeds, doe-eyed, reclining on bolsters of peacock silk.

'Ohhh...' the newcomers stood foolish with surprise; all but Forbes, who looked pleased with himself. One of the children, he could not have been more than ten, tripped forward coquettishly with downcast eyes, to welcome them.

'We have friends for all of you sirs, many friends,' he offered. 'You have only to choose among us. We are many here tonight.' There was a pause. The men didn't look at each other. Forbes was first to move, beckoning a dark-skinned youth who ran up and flung a graceful arm around his neck. They left the room together. Rud took off his spectacles, wiped them and put them back. He was not in doubt of what he wanted. No room for uncertainty there. But at the same time everything that he'd ever learned told him to hold back. To his relief, he saw that Harrison was swaying and looking distinctly the worse for wear.

'Shall I take you into the air, old man?' he offered. Holding the other's head as Harrison vomited against a wall of crumbling damp-rotted brick, Rud experienced only gratitude for his escape.

* * *

The season for moving up to Simla had come round again. His fifth. And last, if he had anything to do with it.

The Mater was not so sure.

'Ruddy darling, all in good time,' she responded when he announced that he planned to leave India in the New Year.

'The moment's come to try my luck in London,' he insisted but she shook her head at him, smiling.

Though he'd been longing for the scent of pines and the whispering freshness of the hills, Rud was already beginning to feel trapped. With the Viceroy and the Administration in residence, came all the petty rivalries of a court. A British community seven hundred strong, ten times the size of the one in Lahore, should have offered more variety. Yet its feverish tone, its liaisons, its gossip, its all too legible adulteries and romances had become deadly predictable from year to year.

And now all that falseness had infected Trix. Constant scenes of stagey emotion over Fleming. Rud couldn't abide them.

'Hasn't that fellow gone yet?' he growled, from the narrow hall.

In common with most of the cottages available for rent in Simla, the walls were woefully thin but Rud was not troubling to lower his voice.

But Trix was beyond embarrassment. Stifling her sobs, 'Really Jack, I do mean it this time. It's too soon. I mean, I want –'

Jack Fleming did not let go of her hand but stood so close, she could see every hair in his moustache. He was so much taller than her, she shrank back.

'I cannot understand you, Trix. I thought we'd got this settled once and for all. Plenty of girls get married at twenty.'

'I've tried and tried to make you see, Jack. I just feel I – that we should –'

He didn't wait.

'If you didn't mean to stick by me, why the dickens did you call me back? We've been going through the same scenes for months now but I thought this time you knew your own mind. I call it damned unfair.'

She saw that he coloured under the bronze.

'I beg your pardon,' he apologised, without changing his resentful tone. 'But Trix, I thought we were so happy. Only yesterday you were reading Mrs. Browning's sonnets to me out in the pinewoods. Now you're behaving like a regular hill-station jilt – off with one romance, on with the next.'

'How dare you, Jack, how dare you?' All at once her voice

cleared. 'Please go and don't try any more to make me change my mind.'

Fearing that he might attempt to put an arm round her, Trix stepped out of his reach and held the door open.

Baffled, Captain Fleming strode from the room, almost forgetting to pick up his hat from the rickety table by the front door.

Within a day or two Rud was reporting to Lockwood.

'As we feared, Pater. Trix spent the entire afternoon out in the woods with me, weeping. Says she can't bear it, now she's sent Jack away. Good riddance, I told her, but she won't hear a word against him.'

Lockwood Kipling's usual calm failed him.

'I'm at my wits' end with her; we all are. The whole circus will now start up again. Whatever's the matter with the girl?'

That afternoon Trix made an attempt to explain herself. Standing beside her father under the porch, watching the drips from the eaves and waiting for the shower to stop, she broke out.

'You've no idea of the strength of his will. I sometimes feel like a prisoner when I'm with him. Then I know I have to escape.'

Lockwood had never heard anything like this. As a daughter, Trix delighted him, she was so lovely and so quick. But she'd none of her mother's unyielding confidence. He'd done his best to encourage her, though who could guess what she needed? He had such limited experience of young women.

This last time she'd sent Fleming packing Lockwood had really thought Trix meant it. She'd looked positively relieved. Now he spoke with all his tact.

'Jack seems to make you so unhappy, dearest, I'm sure it's best if you've decided to break with him for good.'

The face she turned to him was haunted.

'I do wish I could. But it's not so easy. Jack's determined to marry me.'

'Not against your will, surely?' he was aghast.

'It's so hard to be sure what I really want. You see, however angry, however sure of myself I am when I tell him to go, it doesn't last. For a day or two I feel quite exultant, then those terrible feelings come back. It's already started.'

Trix looked away and began to stab the tip of her umbrella into the moist earth beyond the tiles of the porch.

'What feelings?'

He really didn't want to have to deal with this but neither did he want to cut her off.

Trix went on poking and stabbing with the umbrella.

'Darling Trix, hadn't you better explain?'

She dug harder, as though trying to get at something that was buried.

At last she raised her head and looked squarely at him.

'It's, it's Hell,' she stammered.

He tried not to show that her use of strong language shocked him. A good thing Alice wasn't there to hear.

'It's this simply dreadful feeling I get when I send him away. I know I've been wicked and that I'm going to be punished. I get so frightened. I'll be left with nothing and no-one. Then all I want is to go home to Southsea but I can't.'

It broke his heart to hear the misery in her voice. But her actual words left him baffled. Home to Southsea? Left with nothing and no-one? She sounded more like a three-year-old who'd got lost. But perhaps this was just a sign of hysteria? Unmarried girls did seem to get over-excited. He must do his best to steady her. Strengthen her resolve.

'Going to be punished? My dear girl, whatever makes you think that? You've a right, a duty, to make your choice of who to make your life with, you're not a child.

She looked sternly back at him.

'Aren't I Papa? Sometimes I feel that I shall never be properly grown up.'

'Nonsense, darling. You've worked yourself into a state of nerves over Jack, that's all.'

Her eyes dropped and she bit her lower lip, uncertainly. Before she could speak again, he took her arm.

'Come along now, it's clearing'.

She didn't seem to hear.

She made him wait while she finished smoothing over the place where her prodding had disturbed the earth.

* * *

Rud had few regrets on leaving the family home to take up his new position at the *Pioneer*. He scented a new freedom. In moving to Allahabad, six hundred miles to the south, he exchanged the cramped alleys of old Lahore for a place of open spaces: after the 1857 uprising the British had set fire to the native quarters then rebuilt the whole city on modern lines. When Rud arrived, its Muir College had just been incorporated as Allahabad University. The Professor of Physical Science, Alec Hill, and his wife, Edmonia, known as Ted, soon invited him into their own home, as a paying guest.

'Won't you have any breakfast at all?' Ted Hill was trying to keep her temper. She was almost beginning to wonder whether she and her husband Alec had been wise to invite Ruddy Kipling to share their home. It had served him for a while to live under his employer's roof when he moved down to work on the *Pioneer* but that arrangement couldn't go on forever.

Up to the present the arrangement had seemed most satisfactory.

'Really Rud, that's not very flattering.'

He was taken aback. 'Flattering?'

She gave up. He was standing by the sideboard, drumming his fingers while the lid of the coffee-pot jumped erratically in response. Following the direction of his gaze, where he stared unseeing at the wall, she noted that the damp marks which had appeared during the last monsoon seemed to be spreading.

'Do you know where you're planning to ride? Shall I tell the kitchen you'll be –'

A snarl, there was no other word for it, interrupted her.

'I don't know, I tell you. I don't know.'

She heard him clattering down the steps of the bungalow, calling the while, peremptorily, for his horse.

'Splendid,' she thought to herself. 'Spread misery through the household.' Her own morning ride would be shortened by the time she would have to spend in conversation with Govind the *sais*, restoring his self-esteem after what promised to be a bruising encounter with her house guest. It was true that the cook, Amal – she did prefer to use their given names – didn't strictly need to be given numbers. Rud knew that as well as she did. The awareness of having been seen through heightened her sense of frustration, lacing it with shame.

Nevertheless, Ted knew that she was doing her best. She had observed that it was not uncommon among the British here in Allahabad for a husband to speak to a wife in such a manner. No American woman would have tolerated it. By any account, though, this was truly extraordinary behaviour on the part of a guest. And Ruddy could be so thoughtful. It was the sweetness in him, as much as the cleverness which had moved them to offer their invitation.

He had touched them. She and Alec had agreed that Rud deserved something better than those miserable flimsy structures that passed for bachelors' quarters at the Club. He could come as their paying guest. The money wouldn't be unwelcome: Alec's stipend was modest. They'd all lived companionably together for weeks now and there was no question but his company and his conversation made them feel alive again, after the suffocating social observances of the other Britishers.

'I'm going to get you honorary American citizenship; you're way too adventurous for a Brit,' she'd teased.

That evening they were all sitting together after a rather silent dinner. Evenings had been like this all week. Coming home after work, Alec had picked up the atmosphere as soon as he entered the house, wordlessly raising his eyebrows, to show he guessed the source of trouble and being careful to say little. They felt like parents at times, though Rud wasn't really much younger than they were.

With a jerk he began to apologise.

'I know I'm behaving abominably.'

Fearing that her husband was about to dismiss the matter, Ted spoke first.

'That's so. Is it something you're writing?'

A look of startled gratitude from Rud warmed her.

'I thought it must be something serious. Fever never brings out the beast in you like this.'

He laughed, shamefaced. Alec threw his wife a look. He got to his feet.

'I've not completed the report on my tour of the Satpuras and it's due in very shortly. Forgive me.'

She waited for Alec's retreating footsteps to patter away into silence. Give Rud time.

'Would you feel like reading it to me, what you're working on?'

He so often did but today might easily be different. She braced herself yet there was no rebuff. Instead, Rud sprang up, to return within a few minutes, an untidy sheaf of papers in hand. He took a seat closer to the lamp. Looking up at her before he began, he appeared unusually shy.

'It's about two children, called Punch and Judy. I haven't finished it yet. This is only a draft.'

As she listened, there unfolded a story of two small children who found themselves abandoned among strangers in a foreign land. Cruelty followed, from a woman who spoke of God and from Harry, her well-instructed son. The little boy, who had been lord of an Indian household, now learned what it was to be beaten.

"'But I'm not an animal," he had stammered, shocked. But that was not the end of it: Harry entered and stood afar off, eyeing Punch, a dishevelled heap in the corner of the room, with disgust.

"You're a liar – a young liar," said Harry, with great unction, "and you're to have tea down here because you're not fit to speak to us. And you're not to speak to Judy again till Mother gives you leave. You'll corrupt her. You're only

fit to associate with the servants. Mother says so."

Having reduced Punch to a second agony of tears, Harry departed upstairs
with the news that Punch was still rebellious.'

The sweat stood out on the young man's forehead as he read.

'Of course it's me, it's about me. And Trix,' he added, as he laid
the last sheet down on top of the others.

Ted knew she needed to be careful. Leave Rud to himself and
the story was going to be just a hymn of hate. He would be left
horribly exposed, for it was obvious that his plan would be to
publish it in *The Week's News*. Why not? He was editor, no-one
would challenge his decision. She'd always thought he had a bit too
much freedom there. Readers would back away, they'd dismiss him
and his story, say he was crazy. It could break him.

She had known, vaguely, that he'd not been happy when he
was small and sent to England for his education but she'd never
imagined this. What a terrible race the English were, what they put
their children through! She knew he was waiting, without looking
at her, for her response.

'My dear,' she began very quietly, 'I think you are a miracle.' He
relaxed. He had not withdrawn. She could go on.

'This is an astonishing piece. But I was wondering, your people
as you call them, won't they –'

He looked not a bit embarrassed by the implied question but
genuinely surprised.

'They know what happened to me as a child; it's not new to
them. Those arrangements were made by them.'

'Well, yes,' she conceded, objecting silently, 'But can they
possibly have faced the bitterness of the adult?' Speaking aloud
again, 'Your sister, what does she think about it all now?'

'We don't speak of it. We never have.'

'What, never? Not to each other?'

'Well, in the first year or two, when we were small we used to.
We tried to work out why they'd done it, gone away. Left us in
Hell. Afterwards, when she came back, we were just so glad to see

our mother. Later on, I think we might have been afraid. I don't know. To be honest, until now I haven't wanted to face it and I imagine Trix has felt the same.'

'So the two of you didn't come right out and tell your parents what a dreadful mistake they'd made, the lasting impact –'

Looking affronted, he got to his feet and began to fiddle with his spectacles. He held them up to the light, then took out a crumpled handkerchief.

'Lasting? I consider we've made a good recovery. At least I have. Trix does seem to be at sea where men are concerned, that I admit.'

'I didn't mean to suggest there was anything exactly wrong with you, Rud.' Her own heart was thumping. Did she dare go on? 'I was just wondering, you must have been confused. How on earth could you be sure about anything? What to believe? Who to trust?'

She waited. Rud seemed sullen but he didn't explode.

'I mean – you might have been afraid to tackle your parents in case they took Mrs. Holloway's part –'

He was folding his arms.

'You're so desperately angry –'

The sense of being blocked brought her to a halt. Rud was taking it all as an attack on him, closing down before her eyes.

'What could we say? Face-to-face, it would have been too much.'

It was not clear to her who he'd wanted to spare, whose collapse, whose violence he had been anticipating. This business of parents and children, the relations between them, was just too complicated for her. It only confirmed the general principle she'd always suspected. She rather hoped she would get away without children of her own.

It was certainly not her job to protect his family. She must do what she could, though, to protect Rud from himself.

'There's only one suggestion I want to make. I think it might help the story as a whole if you could maybe heighten the contrasts. A word or two in there suggested to me that you rather liked the woman's husband. Tell me about him.'

To her carefully concealed delight, Rud sat forward, the tension melting from his face and began to talk.

Before he slept that night Rud had drafted the paragraphs which brought back to life the old man who had held his hand and taught him about the sea.

Rud lost no time in getting his new story into print.

In the Wonder House, as the Lahore Museum was known to the sellers of watermelon and *paan* who took advantage of the shade by the gate, Lockwood Kipling walked to and fro between the blandly smiling heads of stone. Ever since they had come under his care, these sculptures, part Greek part Buddhist, had drawn him to them.

'Ravishing, ravishing,' he murmured under his breath, running a hand along curves that lay chill and faintly gritty under his touch. He wanted to understand the people who had made these things. But he would have to get the day's letters out of the way before he could get back to his reading. That was the worst of being director, the endless official projects and the correspondence. Well, that was the price he paid. It gave him the authority to advance the ancient skills of Indian artists. To win them respect.

'Sahib, Sahib, Kipling Sahib –' He whirled round in alarm at the familiar voice of the *khitmutgar*, who should have been at home in the Mozung Road harassing the sweepers at that hour. Sandals flapping, a scuffle of white drapery and even before he got up to his employer Ali Beg was panting out, 'Memsahib say home now, now this minute, Memsahib say *now.*'

To his relief he found Alice not incapacitated but pacing the drawing room, irritably swerving as she was impeded by the crowded furniture.

'It's her own fault,' he found himself thinking irrelevantly, 'that's how she likes a room. Tables everywhere. Fuss.' He saw she couldn't contain herself. She would never expose herself to public gaze in that state, though, even to walk on the verandah. Till he saw how angry she was, he had been terrified that it was the children. That Trix had been thrown from her horse or that Ruddy had fallen ill again. The boy's health was always going to be a concern. While as for Trix, he shuddered to recall what she'd put them all through over the past year, with her engagement to that dreary fellow, Fleming. On, off, on again.

'It's not Trix?' Anything was possible.

Alice ignored his question. 'Have you seen this week's *News*? The Christmas number, I mean?' The newspaper was brandished at him like a weapon.

His first thought was of some undeserved promotion, an acquaintance who had been advanced beyond what she considered his due. But of course not, she surely wouldn't interrupt his morning for that.

'Read it, just read it. I've never been so mortified. I cannot believe that Rud would do this to us. That boy has changed dreadfully over the past year –'

With raised eyebrows, Lockwood took the paper and pushed up his spectacles for a closer look.

'*Baa Baa Black Sheep*? Is that the piece you mean?' As he scanned the first paragraphs, a weight of dread closed down on him. Looking up, 'I think I'd better sit down to concentrate on this. No, not now, no *chai*,' he dismissed the hovering, pleasurably agitated servant.

He forced himself to keep on reading, though as he went on he could hear what seemed the groaning of another man. When it was done he let the paper drop and covered his face.

'Well?' Alice was biting the twin thumbs of her clasped hands. 'Well, Jack, well?'

He slowly raised his head.

'Alice, don't press me. This is almost too much to bear.'

'Don't I know it. Can you imagine, the whole of India will have read this by tomorrow morning. Held up to them by my own son. And how are we to keep it from Trix? Oh, it could ruin her prospects!'

He waved at her impatiently. 'You shock me. Try to think more clearly. In the first place, do you think this will be news to Trix? She was *with* Ruddy in Southsea, she's *in* the story herself. See, Judy, the little girl.'

'I'm sure it's all exaggerated beyond recognition, like everything Ruddy writes.'

'I can only pray God that's indeed the case.' Without noticing, he'd fallen back on the language of that Methodist upbringing he had so adamantly rejected. 'If we have been responsible, even through ignorance, for putting them through anything approaching this, I can never again look my children in the eye.'

'You mean you'll tackle Ruddy?'

There was a lengthy silence.

'No, I'll not do that. Nor will you, Alice.' His raised hand preempted a rush of response. 'We are not going to speak of this with Ruddy, not going to discuss it with Trix. We are going to go on as a family, as before.' He saw that this exertion of authority had succeeded. He would have his way. Alice was subdued. Though she fidgeted under his gaze, she would abide by his decision.

That evening, however, he found he could not prevent himself. When Trix bent over to kiss him, as she entered all fresh in her white muslin before dinner, Jack Fleming's pearls at her throat, Lockwood covered the hand she had laid on his shoulder with his own.

'Trix, lovey, this new story of Ruddy's, about those two little children, it's all made up, isn't it?' he pleaded.

'Oh Papa,' she faltered, 'Papa, I don't –'

Alice joined in. 'Come along, daughter of mine. You know what Ruddy's imagination is. Why are you hesitating?'

Transfixed, Trix turned her head from one parent to the other but she made no sound.

At the sight of the single tear which began to glide down his daughter's cheek, Lockwood Kipling rose to put himself between the two women. 'Darling girl, really there's no need for this. No-one is angry with you. Just, that story makes us terribly distressed.

We'll say no more about it, at present.'

'You must be able to understand that at least,' Alice had softened her tone. 'I find it impossible to make sense of Ruddy's behaviour. He's setting out to hurt us, he must be, to ruin things for us out here, now he's set on leaving India.'

A hiccupping sob burst from Trix.

Now the moment she had been dreading was here, Trix found herself as though struck dumb. Ruddy'd warned her there would be a scene when they read his story but she'd never imagined this.

Darling Papa, how could she deny him comfort?

But why, why did they want to go on so, pressing her to deny how wretchedly unhappy she and Ruddy had been?

She felt a bolt of anger.

Could she really be certain, though, that life in Southsea had truly been as full of cruelty as Ruddy swore?

But if he was right, why did the thought of Auntie make her feel peaceful and safe?

None of it made sense and it was all her parents' doing. It was a shock to find she could hate them.

'Ruddy could've been here, within reach, for another year,' Alice insisted, as they waited for Trix to return from bathing her face. 'If only he hadn't written that silly poem accusing poor Sir Frederick Roberts of giving jobs to his friends. So naïve. What does he expect of a Commander-in-Chief? After that his employers had to make sure Ruddy left sooner rather than later. Couldn't he see that it was one thing to attack public policy on drains and quite another to turn on the top people?'

Lockwood chose not to challenge this. Surely Alice remembered Ruddy telling them months ago that he'd be leaving in the New Year.

'I still think that we should allow him to take the consequences of his own actions, Alice. There's nothing we can do about this latest poem about the Viceroy, for instance.'

'Oh, don't worry, Jack, darling I've seen to that. I couldn't rest, once it had been intimated to us how very deeply the Viceroy had been offended. It took me the whole morning to write it but I sent off a letter of apology to Lord Dufferin last week.'

'But you had done nothing, Alice, it was Ruddy's work.'

'I wrote on his behalf, of course. As his mother.'

She was fidgeting with her cuffs: always a sign she had something to hide.

'It's not that simple. It might have been my fault. I'm not sure.'

His eyes widened. He waited.

'You see, Lord Dufferin had told me things. In confidence. About his plan of publishing a book of his mother's poems. I may have mentioned it to Ruddy, I don't know.'

Lockwood recalled that Rud had written something about Dufferin's mother and her poems. The tone was perfectly respectful. He was baffled.

'Lord Dufferin accused Rud of invading his privacy.'

Her mouth was trembling.

'This is a bit of a storm in a teacup, dearest,' he said, putting his arms round her. Try to forget about it.'

He didn't care to imagine the pleading, the humiliation that his wife had put herself through. And to what end? Ruddy was twenty-three, he'd books out and selling well all over India, even being reviewed at Home. He was going to make his career in London. The Viceroy's favour was nothing to him. Was Alice under the impression that she was protecting their own place in this tight little world?

Dinner was subdued that night and quickly over. Neither of the women ate much and Lockwood was soon left alone with his pipe. As he drew away on it, however, he could not find satisfaction or peace of mind. The problem Ruddy posed to him could not be dismissed. The boy – he must stop calling him that – couldn't seem to resist attacking those who wished him well.

He'd been so full of joy, seemed to feel so honoured, that day in Simla when Fred Roberts asked him what mattered to the men in barracks. Then, almost the very next week, Ruddy published that really quite scurrilous attack on Roberts. Lockwood was not confident in his own mind that he knew how to account for his son's behaviour. Terms like 'integrity' or 'the duty of a journalist' did not quite seem to fit the case.

Six weeks later Rud himself showed up in Lahore without warning. He fairly burst into his parents' home, slinging his old tweed overcoat down before the bearer could take it from him. 'Revered elders, pray show yourselves to an unbeliever'– his cry had carried to Alice as she stood out on the verandah behind the house, cutting her to the heart. It was a farewell that he had come to take; his evident joy smote her. But he would only be with them for a few days. She had been sipping from a cup of tea and gazing out at the hesitant blades of fresher green here and there in the dusty garden as she waited for Trix to return from her morning ride: now, taking a firmer grip, she sang out to him in her most musical voice.

'Darling boy, at the back of the house: come and kiss your old mother.'

There had been so little notice. Of course, she'd known he planned to leave India – he'd put it to her brutally enough. But not yet. Between one mail and the next, it seemed to her, the plan had been fixed. It was true that Mrs. Hill, in whose house he had been living, had been desperately ill since before Christmas: four weeks or more really quite raving with malaria and heaven knew what else, according to Ruddy's letters, which had shown an almost excessive degree of distress. But the idea that Mrs. Hill should undertake a long voyage as a means of recovery quite so soon appeared strange. However, the Hills seemed perfectly set on it.

'We're all to travel together,' Rud repeated, eyes shining, over a late breakfast. 'We'll be taking the long route, Burmah, Japan and then across America; Ted wants to show me her country.' Eyes still fixed on his mother, he continued more gently: 'It's no good. I do have to go, you know. I can't stay here. If I'm going to do anything with my writing I need to leave India.'

Alice thought bleakly of how she had humbled herself in apologising to the Viceroy – *'no-one regrets his offences more keenly than do his parents…'* she had assured Lord Dufferin. And still that had not sufficed to keep Ruddy with her.

Her son did not appear to notice her silence. 'I have to take my chance – and now I've got them to bring out my stories in the new *Railway Library Series* I want to catch the tide –'

'In the affairs of men?' But the fizz had gone out of what had been a favourite game, capping quotations. 'My boy, my dear, dear boy, I can't bear to see you go,' broke from her. Mother and son sat staring, horrified, at each other.

Back in her own bedroom, swathed in the becoming folds of her morning wrapper, Alice Kipling gazed across at herself in the blotched looking-glass and saw that she was old. This was not what she had wanted. Rud, with his absurd moustache and his station slang, was her boy, her own.

This pretence that he was a man and living a life he had chosen was tolerable so long as he was at least living under her roof. When they had all been together, the four of them in Lahore, they had all been happy. She pushed away the memory of her son's black moods and Trix's awkwardness. Letting Rud go off to work on the *Pioneer*, in Allahabad so far away to the south had been a mistake. She'd always sensed it.

Alice had her own opinion of Edmonia Hill – an American, a woman who let herself be addressed as Ted, a woman who had never fitted in. It had been a bitter day for Alice when Rud had accepted the Hills' invitation to take up lodgings in their house. But she must make an effort. There was nothing for it but to make this Mrs. Hill into her friend too.

When the SS *Madura* set sail for Rangoon on 9th March, in Rud's pocket as he stood waving from the deck lay a charming note addressed to Edmonia Hill by his mother.

* * *

Another three months and Trix too was about to leave home.

Her twenty-first birthday and her wedding day.

'*You've beaten me by a length,*' Maud teased in her letter. Maud was going to have to wait a whole year before she could marry that nice man she was engaged to, Tom Driver. But she did sound happy. '*Of course you know better, my dear, but he thinks every word I write glitters with genius.*'

Now the day had come, if she'd allowed herself, Trix would have wondered whether she was sure about Jack after all. But the giddy triumph of winning through, of forcing, yes, forcing Mama's agreement had been so intoxicating it had carried her aloft until today. Once Mama was on her side, she had known Papa would not be able to hold out for long. Remembering that made her uncomfortable, almost guilty. She'd never liked the way he couldn't stand up to her. Surely Papa would come to appreciate Jack, in time. Not everyone was at their best in general company.

She didn't even want to think about Ruddy, not today. He had been so harsh.

Ruddy simply didn't understand. She and Jack had proved that they belonged together: the misery she'd suffered during their engagement surely made that obvious. Every time that they'd quarrelled and she'd sent him away she'd been utterly wretched. That first autumn when she broke off the engagement and they were apart for months and months it had reduced her to despair. What did it matter if Ruddy threw up his hands when she finally called Jack back to her?

But now, where was Ruddy on her wedding day? Across the world in San Francisco, travelling with friends. Time for him too to make a new life, he'd claimed, a life among other writers. Her wedding had already been fixed for June but he hadn't put off his departure.

These sad feelings were not ones to be entertaining today. Think of the future. An end to being edited by Mama. No more playing second fiddle. She danced a few steps, pointing the toes of the little scarlet slippers brought down from beyond the Frontier;

she'd pounced on them when she saw them in the bazaar. Of course she was going to be a good wife, manage the servants and all that – why, she'd already started collecting recipes and hints to copy into a commonplace book. She'd gone through Mama's, copying down all the dishes that she might have to teach her Indian cook, from beef stew to junket and rice pudding.

But it was the thought of a different kind of writing, writing that would be her own that made her thrill. She was going to escape from that horrid sense of being stifled.

As mistress in her own house, with Jack, who though undeniably rather silent was utterly devoted to her, she would be free.

Flies buzzed among the flower vases, loud in her ears as the gasping of the organ, when Trix paused on her father's arm. She felt sweat trickle at the back of her neck and wherever it could find a path beneath her tight bodice. Could her nose have gone shiny already? At least Mama had gone over it with *papier poudré* for her.

Kicking aside the folds of silk, where the toe of her white shoe had caught, Trix looked squarely past the congregation, with its fans and mopping handkerchiefs, to the altar.

How well Jack looked in his dress uniform.

So tall and straight with his best man, that fellow-officer, Joe Johnson, beside him.

Of course Papa and Ruddy couldn't help being short. But from now on she was going to belong with these splendid men. The Daughter of the Regiment – Ruddy would laugh at that.

As she hung there, her father's hand came round to cover her own.

With renewed courage, Trix stepped forward.

After this she and Jack would never be separated again.

September, and the June heat in which Trix had stepped up the aisle had eased. Who could have predicted that she'd be back in

Lahore within such a short space?

There was so much to get used to and none of it foreseen. She'd not expected it, the pushing and grunting. Mama made it sound as though a key turned in a lock. But nothing had seemed smooth or familiar about this being a wife.

And how strange to be back living at home in the Mozung Road.

'You'd better go to your parents while I'm off on this Burmah posting,' Jack had decided. She couldn't have imagined staying on alone in Calcutta.

Tonight there was that dinner party at the Osbornes'. She would have to play the part of a bride. Smile charmingly, accept her new precedence with a becoming grace, not let them see – at the very thought of the performance demanded of her she felt exhaustion. If she'd not made a great effort, she feared she might have felt rage.

It was disconcerting but Jack seemed to offer almost more of a barrier to the writing than Mama had. Living at home, Trix had quietly determined to keep her drafts to herself, all wrapped in a favourite scarf of coral silk. Not that she wasn't delighted too by the tucked lawns and the smooth folds of cashmere but these, she murmured fiercely, these were her real trousseau...

Heart racing, for Jack she unwrapped her treasure and put all her writing into his hands. When days passed without a word from him, she braced herself to ask.

'Oh, was I expected to read them? Pixie, you know you've married a soldier, not a damned bookworm.' The phrase 'like your own people' hung unspoken.

When she sobbed in confusion he went on, meaning to be kind, 'I know we used to read poetry to each other. That foolishness has no place when a couple takes on the duties of married life.'

He went further: 'I'm sure there'll be some other wife on the station to share your scribbling. I think I remember Fortescue's wife with an album people used to write in.'

* * *

When Jack wrote from Burmah to say he'd been taken ill there, at first Trix didn't understand what a piece of luck that was for her. Not that she liked to think of it in that way. Jack had been ordered Home Leave. It meant she would be with Ruddy once more.

By the time they reached London she was keyed up, longing to talk about her writing. The novel was close to being finished, she needed Ruddy and his advice. She was allowing herself to realise just how much she'd missed his company.

But his looks, when she ran him to earth in his lodgings in Villiers Street off the Strand, the puffy eyes and the pallor that even his dark skin couldn't hide put all that out of her mind.

'Don't stare at me like that, Trix. I'm just a bit out of sorts,' he insisted.

'Why don't you come back tomorrow, when I've finished this piece?'

She left him hunched over the battered Pembroke table, his papers cascading from the sofa with its trail of torn braid. It didn't look as if the room had been swept for some time.

Was this what success as a writer meant? On arriving in London, Ruddy appeared to be instantly famous, in demand everywhere, according to the newspapers. *The Times* had just compared him to Maupassant. Alongside her pleasure in Ruddy's success Trix sensed something else, feelings she didn't care to look at. He deserved it, she told herself firmly. All that hard work.

As the days passed and she saw a little more of him, her resentment was displaced by anxiety. He was so driven, he worked till he was exhausted and nerve-racked. Trix felt only alarm.

As for his incoherent involvements! Now she viewed them with increased dismay. No sooner out of India but he'd been looking for a wife. Before he even reached London, he'd engaged himself to the sister of that nice Mrs. Hill, Caroline Taylor, a girl he'd only known for a fortnight. Another month or two and that was all off again, which was no great wonder. Next thing, he was back in love with that girl she once knew, Flo Garrard, the one he'd fancied himself engaged to when he was a schoolboy. He even seemed to be planning a trip to Paris in pursuit of Flo.

Why, if it had been a young woman exhibiting such frantic emotions, such a desperate need to attach themselves, she'd have been written off as an hysteric.

Thank goodness their parents would soon be with them in London. It was no good talking to Jack about any of this. But she doubted whether they'd see those love affairs in terms of something profoundly amiss, as symptoms or signs of something deeper, as she did. They'd prefer to focus on the headaches, which everyone liked to believe were brought on by overwork and eye strain.

Jack was spending his mornings at the Royal Geographical Society, so she was free, that is, she was obliged to make her own plans until after lunch. She'd arranged that they should meet the de Morgans at the South Kensington Museum later on. It had been kind of Jack to agree. She hoped he would at least try to make a show of interest.

Meanwhile, shopping or art? She was moved by a desire for guilty pleasures. A compromise: Liberty's – that was almost as good as spending time in a gallery. As she stepped out of the hotel, still struggling with the fastening of her glove, out of the corner of her eye she noticed a rather seedy figure, lurking against the railings, who appeared to be trying to attract her attention. She kept her gaze turned away. It was painful to find so much want here at Home.

'Trix,' the urgent whisper clutched at her.

'Ruddy!' Her own voice was harsh with shock.

He was hatless, unshaven, a button dangling loose from the familiar overcoat.

'What's happened?' She took a step towards him. 'Are you ill? What are you doing here?'

Only yesterday she'd left him, in low spirits, true enough, but not looking like a tramp.

He said nothing.

'Why didn't you come into the hotel and ask for me?' Could this just be a dream? It felt horribly strange but also true at the same time.

At last, 'I like being outside.'

That was all she could get out of him.

'I don't know,' he repeated. 'I don't know.'

Trix gathered herself. He wouldn't come back into the hotel with her. He shook his head when she suggested a cab to take them to his rooms near Charing Cross. Very well, they would walk. Perhaps they could find him some coffee at the station. Meanwhile she would try to take this in and decide what to do.

'I like walking,' he offered, as they made their way down from Bloomsbury to find the Charing Cross Road. 'That's what I was doing. Couldn't sleep, so I walked.'

He was like one coming out of a trance, she thought, disturbed.

'All night? Was that really a good idea, Ruddy?' she asked gently, taking his arm.

She glanced at him as they went along, monitoring his progress.

As if in response to her attention, he passed his hand wearily over his face and looked up startled.

'I don't seem to have shaved.'

A good sign? She simply couldn't tell.

As they came in sight of St. Martin in the Fields a watery sun broke through.

Trix had seen enough of Ruddy's grim lodgings to prefer the station tearoom. With a pang she noticed that he had to use both hands to keep his cup from spilling.

'I couldn't sleep. Just couldn't. Too many stories. But not the right ones. I wanted something else in my head, or nothing at all. So I walked. I walked and walked. Down east, along the river, you know. I've done it before.'

'But isn't that dangerous? Is that where –' she threw a look at his overcoat, where it lay tossed over a chair and about to lose that button. Now she saw that the collar was ripped too.

'It was a gang of lascars. I was listening and they thought I had it in for them in some way so they went for me.'

'Asian seamen? You were looking for opium?' He'd told her he ranked it with tobacco and getting the dose wrong might explain everything. 'Surely there are easier ways –'

'Not at all.' He was impatient now. 'I wanted to hear their language. Other tongues. Hindustani perhaps, I thought there might be a chance –' his voice broke. Recovering, 'I'd gone east, back to the spice warehouses again. Did you ever smell anything like it, in London, Trix? The air round those warehouses, it's the bazaar. That's when I came across those lascars.'

'Dear Ruddy, you do take the most frightful chances. We'll go down there together and you can show me, but in the daytime. Come on, let's get you home.'

He consented to lie down on the shabby couch in his sitting room, while Trix, armed with the landlady's sewing basket, took a chair beside him, where she sat at work, mending the damaged coat.

She had time now to realise how angry she was. With herself, for giving up her plans for the morning. With Ruddy, for being so helpless. When was he going to grow up?

After another week, in which she sat with him every morning while he worked, he was looking better.

'Sleeping, actually sleeping, too, Trix, I promise you.'

Every day he sounded steadier in himself. It appeared that her company alone had done the trick. This left Trix anxious, tempted to believe that she was indispensable to him but also alarmed. Would he fall back into a state of disturbance once he found himself without loving support? That frantic writing of his, all in isolation, seemed to bring it on.

But now Rud was himself again, she could venture to ask about her own difficulties with writing. It was becoming so much less fun than it used to be. And yet it seemed impossible to give it up.

'Not writing makes me feel – oh I don't know, as if I'm

suspended. Not living. Dead inside. Or maybe brought to a halt.'

'No-one knows that better than I.' His face was sombre.

Reaching out, Trix stroked his hand. Turning his own hand palm upwards, Rud clasped her surprisingly cold fingers in his own.

'Look here, you know, have you managed to get anything at all finished?'

Needing no further encouragement, she offered to bring her work round to Villiers Street later that day. They would meet to talk it over the following afternoon, while Jack was having his teeth seen to.

'You know, Infant, I shall have to stop calling you by that name if you show such command of language.'

She couldn't speak for pleasure and relief.

'That image from the mind of the girl who has got engaged against her better judgment: *"It appeared to May that she was entering a dungeon worn by the steps of those who had passed before."* It's very strong. I've never been a girl but I've often thanked my stars that I didn't have to make that choice – find a man I could at least bear and who could keep me, so I could get away from home.'

'I haven't shown it to Mama.'

'I think that's wise. Let's wait till we have the publishing sorted out. Maybe wait till it's actually in print and we can put the book into her hands. Unless I'm very much mistaken, it would be just the thing for the Indian Railway Library. Set in Simla, intrigues among the wives and daughters –'

'You don't think it's too like what you've already published in the *Railway Series*? I don't mean as good,' she added, her face crimson.

'Heavens, no. People out there have an endless appetite for seeing their lives in print. Anyway, you've written a whole knitted-up novel – all right, a short one – not just collections of sketches, like me. Let me send this to my fellows when it's complete. You do have another copy, I hope? Always keep a second copy.'

Her technique wasn't what you could call finished, of course. If she'd asked him, he'd have got rid of that note of apology which occasionally crept into the narrator's voice. But she hadn't asked him. She was intent on keeping the work her own. You couldn't fault her for truthfulness, he had to admit. Such a level tone too, most of the time, as though everyone else could see all that she saw, all that secret inner life of feeling. Before he pushed the thought away, he wondered whether his own sparkling effects didn't sometimes verge on the meretricious.

He did ask himself what people would make of this story of a sensitive literary girl bound to a silent man blessed with all the imagination of a turnip. If only Trix had stuck to her guns when she kept sending Fleming away. But it seemed to reduce her to despair. Perhaps she simply couldn't bear hurting the fellow? Then the whole performance would start over again. Try as he would, and God knew he had done his best to listen to Trix, Rud could make neither head nor tail of her behaviour.

They could be confident at all accounts that Fleming himself wouldn't dream of reading any novel, even one that was written by his own wife. He'd never met a man with so little interest in books. But for those who knew Trix, would it not be read in terms of her own marriage? She might have depicted the heroine as struggling to be fair to her husband – but what about the fact that the novel killed him off at the end? That told a different story, one that was more troubling. And Trix had barely been married a year.

There was no question; they had better find a pseudonym. 'Beatrice', 'Beatrice Grange' sounded reassuringly composed. He savoured the dangerous sport of disguising Trix under the name of Beatrice; people had often imagined that Beatrice was her given name. Curious, though, he admitted, the fact that nobody ever used the name to which Trix had a legal right, Alice. It was the name she shared with her mother.

The Mother, two days back in London, was stitching steadily, very upright in the hotel chair. She appeared to hold herself away from its worn plush. Rud suspected that this rigour of deportment was only going to increase. She would be averse to taking on any appearance of age.

'So you see, Ruddy, why I'm asking. If you could make use of your connections on her behalf, it would mean a great deal to your sister. Poor love, she's had so many disappointments.'

He put up his hand to stop her. Any confidences concerning her life must come from Trix herself.

'You can't doubt that I'd move heaven and earth for Trix –'

'But here she is,' Alice interrupted, with a tight smile.

'Dearest girl, we were just talking about you and your writing. Ruddy's so anxious to see it, aren't you, my son?'

Conscious of her brother's suppressed irritation, Trix hesitated, blinking. Clearly, their mother had no idea that the two of them had been forging ahead without waiting for her.

Trix was relieved that Ruddy was staying on an even keel, though he suffered badly from headaches.

'My eyes aren't quite right, either,' he finally admitted.

As she'd anticipated, their parents readily agreed with the doctors. This was clearly a case of overwork. After all she'd seen, Trix couldn't help suspecting that something more was amiss, but she was sworn to silence and Ruddy was sent off to Italy for a holiday.

Not long after his return December brought news of other visitors from India.

'It really is quite too bad of you, Ruddy.'

'Do leave the boy alone, Alice.'

'Not so much of the *boy*, if you please, Pater.'

Startled, Lockwood gazed more keenly into the face of his son. Evidently Ruddy was still on a very short fuse. That trip – the doctors had been so sure it would set his nerves to rights – appeared to have banished the worst of Rud's symptoms but he was still a good deal strung up.

Alice was continuing, unabashed. 'Poor Mrs. Hill, losing her husband like that to typhoid, such a terrible shock. Her whole life to make over again. Packing up and leaving India – though some would call that a blessing in disguise. I cannot understand, Rud, why you're not planning to spend time with her when she passes through London on the way back to America. Don't you think you owe her some attention? I say nothing of Miss Taylor. You do know her sister's travelling with her?'

Lockwood spoke. 'Have a little imagination, my dear. There are reasons why Ruddy and Miss Taylor might prefer not to meet.'

That at any rate was safe to be mentioned. A brief engagement, hastily terminated, was sufficient to account for any disinclination for further encounters. He guessed, though, that that was not the whole story. Lockwood had never dared to share his speculations concerning his son's feelings for this Mrs. Edmonia Hill. He had half expected Rud to set off at once for India when the news of Professor Hill's death had reached them. But no. Instead of greeting the opportunity to be at the widow's side, of perhaps declaring himself after a decent interval, Ruddy had reacted to the news that she was free with a kind of nervous prostration. In his father's view, Ruddy had taken doctors' orders as a licence to flee. Italy was just a convenient bolt-hole.

'I really don't know what you mean, Pater.' His son's voice had an edge. 'I am on terms of the most perfect civility with both Miss Taylor and her sister.'

'Hadn't you better do the civil thing then, Ruddy? At least offer your services to them.' Alice had not given up.

'Services? They're experienced travellers, not helpless females adrift in the great world, you know.'

Alice threw up her hands. Her always competitive spirit was roused.

'Well, I at least shall make every effort to meet them. *I* can't forget how good Mrs. Hill has been to both my children. Not just to you, Rud, and that over months, I may say. She was kindness itself when Trix was passing through Allahabad earlier this year.'

Rud appeared relieved to have his own debt compared with that of Trix. 'Very well, where did her note say they were putting up? The Metropole? I suppose I could call on them one afternoon. And now I must leave you: I'm lunching at the Savile, with Gosse.

'Just so long as he doesn't see too much of that dreadful pushy little American girl, Carrie whatnot.' Her son was scarcely out of the room before Alice spoke.

'Balestier, Carrie Balestier,' Lockwood corrected. 'I thought she was a rather decent little thing myself.' Even as he appeared to be paying attention to his wife's plans for the rest of the day, Lockwood's mind was taken up with his son. He wished he could be more confident that the boy knew what he was doing. Ruddy liked to speak grandly, man to man, of his intention of 'marrying' but there was no evidence that he was equipped to choose a wife.

And in a matter of months they'd have to leave him alone in London once they returned to Lahore and Trix went back to Calcutta.

OLD COMRADES ON NEW SEAS

1891–1898

A pale flat light showed outside the windows without making its way into the room.

Though the breakfast table had been cleared for more than an hour, there was still a heavy reminder of food in the air. It was the time of day Rud most feared, alone face- to-face with the work that he *must* do if he was to make a life for himself here. On his own once more in London, he was struggling.

But at least he had a new project, a joint venture.

A brief knock and Wolcott Balestier was with him. With hardly a word they sat down together, one each side of the scarred mahogany table. It was not twelve hours since they had parted after one of those evenings at home with the Balestiers that he looked forward to. Wolcott's sister Carrie made a fellow feel at home, even if she did laugh at him.

'Why of course we'll set a place for you every night, Rud, if that's what pleases you. Lord knows you keep enough of your wardrobe here.'

He could stand feeling a bit sheepish.

'Your turn to start,' Rud nodded and Wolcott prepared to read aloud.

'I just had this idea for the fourth chapter, late last night: see what you think.'

Throwing himself back till his chair tilted under him, Rud gazed up at the ceiling as he listened. He took out his pipe and reached for tobacco, yet his whole attention was fixed on the other man. He felt himself expand in Wolcott's presence, become more intensely aware. The moment the reading came to a halt, he sat back up again.

'It's damned good, you know, we're getting on famously.'

Other people were more doubtful about this collaboration.

'I thought Mr. Balestier was an agent, not a writer,' Aunt Georgie, who was not uninformed about literary London, had objected.

More bluntly, 'What the devil is in this for young Kipling?' they had asked at the Savile Club: one or two, already trembling for Wilde in his recklessness, had hoped that whatever happened they would be discreet.

Rud was excited. He leaned over the table to lay a hand on the other's sleeve.

'You really think that McClure will give us a contract for the novel even before it's finished? And he likes the name? I wondered whether *The Naulahka* was too enigmatic but it seems you were right, it intrigues, even if people don't know what it means – it's always the way. A hint of the inscrutable, a pinch of the *Arabian Nights* but not too much.'

Wolcott turned his lazy smile on his friend. He found something quite intriguing in Rud himself, in that paradoxical combination: the still boyish mouth under that heavy moustache, the clipped English spoken out of a face that was almost dark enough for a native. He looked down at the hand as it lay on his sleeve then back up at Rud. There was a pause. He did not want it to be removed.

To his disappointment, Rud sprung to his feet, scattering tobacco, his face darkly flushed. 'That book I was telling you about – I found it last night; let me give it to you before I forget.'

Sighing, Wolcott prepared to leave: he must get to his office in Westminster Yard by twelve-thirty at least. Then he saw that the hand which held the battered volume out to him was trembling. Stepping forward, he laid his own hand lightly on the other's shoulder, up by the collar; he could feel the warmth of the skin he could not quite touch. 'My dear fellow,' he began but got no further than 'My dear' before he was leaning forward into an embrace. His lips brushed Rud's hair.

Rud shivered. All the fear he'd felt at the house of the boy whores thrilled in him, the rush to escape, the desire – Wolcott was his only real friend, all that mess of feelings could swamp everything. It was always the same, that sex thing ended in leaving him more alone.

He stepped aside, hands raised to fend Wolcott off.

He was shaking. 'You don't understand. There are terrible risks. I never want to go through it again.'

'As you wish, Rud, as you wish. But you must know how you make people feel. You're so open, you seem to invite, it makes –'

Once the battered door had closed behind Wolcott, Rud waited and then turned the key. How to retain this friend, this companiable presence which kept him writing? The thought of going back to working in isolation filled him with dread. In Lahore, working on the *CMG*, he'd been desperate to have time for his own work. He'd never realised that the demands and the pressure had been also a support. The truth was that he'd seemed to be falling apart in London, left to himself. He didn't want to go away on rest cures, he hated the fishing holidays recommended by doctors, he wanted to write.

It was after ten and the handsomely furnished space Wolcott kept for entertaining was clearing. The evening had gone well, thought Carrie Balestier. *As usual* she almost dared to tell herself. Her brother so wanted these occasions, their *salon*, as they giggled together, to be a success. His plan of campaign as a newcomer was based on making themselves the nerve centre of London letters. She guessed only a Yankee could be so brash and get away with it.

Bram Stoker had stayed on, having arrived late from the Lyceum but Henry James was clearly about to leave. Hat in hand he was beside her, smiling down gravely. They could always count on him to show up for their literary evenings.

'Carrie, my dear' he bent over her. A genuine Boston Brahmin! Those exquisite manners of his would have made her feel awkward if she hadn't been sure of his kind heart.

Yet she did hope he wouldn't linger. Rud Kipling was standing by the fireplace, absorbed, arguing with her brother and she longed to join them.

To her disappointment, Rud broke off as she watched and began to look about ineffectually for his things.

'I believe I ought – there's something. Do forgive me.'

With a smile and a touch of the hand, she turned from the older man.

'I see that I must let you go,' James laughed gently. She could feel his benevolent gaze on her as she crossed the room.

Earlier, as she grew warm in the crowded space, she'd been about to cast off her shawl when she caught sight of Rud's coat on the back of a sofa. She'd dropped her own garment to cover it, hardly knowing why. Now, coming up to Rud, with a showman's gesture she revealed his lost overcoat.

As he shrugged it on he mumbled apologetically.

'I'm just off to Gatti's, the music hall by my lodgings. Don't want to miss the late show. A song I wrote might be on the bill tonight.'

She could have just swallowed her regret. But no. Before she realised what she was doing, she heard her own voice asking,

'Won't you take me along with you to hear it?'

He paused in his struggle with a sleeve that was the wrong way out. Seeming startled but also pleased he looked straight at her.

'You'd come just with me? No chaperone? I know Wolcott isn't free to come with us, he's just told me he's working late.'

Delight. And a tremor. But what had she, Carrie Balestier, ever cared for the proprieties? She'd stuck out like a sore thumb back in Brattleboro: 'way too opinionated in her dress and conversation' they'd complained. Here in England, they didn't expect an American woman to match their notions of a lady. She meant to explore.

The man on the door was muffled in a heavy topcoat, though the month was June and the evening warm.

'Old soldier,' Rud hissed when she looked at him questioningly. 'Years in the tropics, feels the cold.'

When they arrived at the head of the queue, 'Evenin' sir, we're seeing you pretty regular these days and glad of same.'

'Likewise, Hobbs.' Then, with a gulp – was it embarrassment, could it possibly be pride? – 'This is my friend, Miss Balestier.'

Hobbs touched his hat and gave an awkward bow but Carrie held out her hand.

'I'm very pleased to make your acquaintance Mr. Hobbs,' which was no more than the truth. This was a new world, newer and more thrilling than that evening of decorous conversation they'd left behind.

Rud handed over a shilling and they were inside. Deafened at first by the roar of voices, they gasped in air thick with smoke.

'Take my arm,' he ordered 'I'll get us to a seat, just hang on to me.' With a thrill of pleasure she felt the warmth of his arm right through the sleeve. She shut her eyes wanting for that moment only to be aware of him.

When she looked about her once more, she saw that the audience, men and women mixed, were seated around a central ring. It brought back the trip she'd taken out West, with Wolcott. A boxing match she'd witnessed in a remote lumber camp. Far more women here, of course but the same energy. Something raw that made her tingle.

'A pint of porter comes with those sixpenny tickets. Can I leave you while I collect mine? I don't suppose you –'

'But I want to drink beer too. I'm going the whole hog this evening, Rud. Other women are drinking…'

'So you're going to join the four and eleven penny bonnets are you? Want "one of them glasses like a lidy"?

She frowned.

'Is that some kind of criticism? Of these women?'

Under the crude flare of the gas lamps she couldn't be sure but he seemed to flush.

'It's just a way – a way of describing them,' he said lamely.

'I'm sorry, Rud, to me it sounds downright snobbish. Hateful. I didn't think it of you.'

Silence fell between them, louder than the surrounding noise. Then she remembered Hobbs and Rud's lack of 'side', as the Brits called it. 'Swank' was good enough for her.

'Well, I guess we can't turn you into an American overnight, Wolcott and I. But Rud, I'll make a democrat out of you yet.'

'I think you might,' he answered quietly, as he rose to make his way over to the bar. Business was brisk: it was several minutes before he wriggled his way back through the crowd, a glass in one hand, a pewter mug in the other.

She took a sip of the dark porter. How bitter it was. Strange. After that awkward outburst she felt more at ease with him than before.

'Plenty of soldiers up in the gallery,' he pointed overhead. 'It's a good sign. They've heavy boots and when they stamp out the chorus, they take the whole house with them.'

The thinly padded bench hard beneath her, ears ringing, she laughed, feeling more alive than in weeks. A relief from books and writers. She settled to the show, with its tumbling sequence of acts. Queens of song followed comic vocalists, dancers capered in top boots. And then came a man dressed as a woman – very stylishly – who also warbled. She'd certainly heard of such things but this was the first time of seeing. A new world. But underneath her own pleasure, she knew that beside her there was tension, a waiting.

Then, 'That's my fellow, here he is,' Rud exclaimed.

A stocky figure, topped with a soldier's forage cap, had appeared. With a flourish, arms thrown wide, the Master of Ceremonies, in his white tie and tails announced 'The Great and Only Mr. James Fawn, Consort of the Muse.'

'He won't sing mine first, it's not quite so new now,' Rud told her, over the din as the orchestra broke into the Consort's first number. He had the audience in the palm of his hand at once. Just like Rud himself when he talked: he could hold a room spellbound.

He was clutching her wrist to get her attention. The intimacy of it. As though he was sure of her, knew he had a right. A flush was mounting her face, she could feel it: how glad she was to have come.

'Here he goes. This one's mine.'

'At the back of the Knightsbridge Barracks'

The crowd shrieked with joy at the familiar opening.

She would have missed the second line if the singer's timing hadn't been so good. He hung on till he could be heard again.

'When the fog was gatherin' dim
The Lifeguard talked to the Under-cook
An' the girl she talked to 'im.'

The audience, men and women together, yelled the chorus at the top of their voices.

'Don't try for things that are out of your reach
And that's what the girl told the soldier.'

Between verses the singer broke into a little routine, prancing about so that the large brass spurs at his heels jingled. Making fun of the Lifeguard with his fine uniform and his ambitions.

'My idea, that,' Rud called into her ear.

She turned to smile back at him and saw his face was blazing, triumphant.

With the final stanza she saw, the song was a story, a simple moral tale and this audience liked it for that. It was all about courting and finding a match. Trying for the well-paid undercook was too ambitious, so the soldier had to make do with a housemaid.

Aha, that's what 'mashing a tart', must mean, that strange phrase early on that baffled her. Rud had picked up a whole new language, learned to see the world from a different angle. And no cheap glamour – that was what some complained of in his Indian stories – no cheap glamour about it. She regarded his glow of pleasure with respect.

But the song wasn't over. Again and again, four times in all, she counted, the audience howled out the final chorus. What he'd written had spoken to them. He could reach anyone. It was uncanny.

Dazed, dim, she found herself out on the pavement, at his side. Pale under the streetlights, he appeared equally exhausted.

'I suppose, I mean, should I look for a cab?' he hesitated.

Whatever he could do with words, he was helpless out in the world. Like a much younger brother.

Confident all at once, 'I believe I'd prefer to walk. I know I'm incapable of sitting still,' she replied.

'Really? Would you be happy to walk back to Westminster Yard? Or perhaps Wolcott will have left the office for home. All the way to Neville St. might be rather far for you – '

'Rud, I can see you don't know me. I could walk you off your legs, given half a chance.'

She'd made him laugh.

'But I'll have to keep hold of your arm,' she added, daring. 'I'd better look respectable at least, out at this time of night, with a man. I'd better look like a wife.'

The words had passed her lips before she'd had time to think.

'You make a pretty good fist of it,' he said lightly 'though I don't know many wives with your taste for adventure.'

Stepping off into the warm darkness, linked to him, she could face anything.

*

Rud was at last settling into a congenial home-life. He had taken to staying on, talking with Carrie, on those evenings when Wolcott withdrew to work on a contract.

'I'm going to get every author worth having on my books,' he would boast. With his drive and his flair for seeing his way round difficulties, it seemed quite possible he would succeed. He was negotiating with publishing houses across Europe and was often away. Nevertheless, Rud continued to call, spending his evenings, feet up on the fender, exchanging talk and stories of past adventures with Carrie.

'When I was out West, with Wolcott,' she would counter to his, 'Up on the frontier, waiting for the Amir'.

It was a pleasure to him to be challenged.

Carrie was straightforward. Nothing flirtatious or coy about her, an independent well-informed mind. He hadn't got on so well with a woman since he'd met Mary Kingsley, back from West Africa.

'You know, Carrie, you've gone one better than Mary Kingsley,' he teased her towards the end of one evening. 'She might be a brave explorer but she was scared of the proprieties: Mary hadn't the nerve to ask me in without a chaperone. Not like you, Carrie. Look at us: here together, many an evening without Wolcott.'

'No-one can say anything. After all, Rud, you're as good as a brother.'

He surprised himself as well as Carrie with his quick, 'I don't know about that.'

There was a long pause.

A new awareness, low in his body. Did it tug at her too?

Getting up to take his leave at last, Rud hovered, uncertain. She was not to be trifled with, for all sorts of reasons. But did he dare take the plunge? He'd told the Pater he meant to marry soon, of course he had, wasn't it time? But the words had rung empty, shaming him.

To have her with him always. But the risks. This pull between them. It might spell only danger. Yet he'd seen her with Wolcott. Like his own sister, she knew how to be a friend.

He put away thought and took a step in her direction. Carrie appeared to have been waiting for his sign.

She was pressing against him.

'Carrie,' he repeated, 'Carrie,' as he fumbled to put his arms round her. A delicious shock as their lips met. Her passion – and she a white woman – was a surprise to him. And a delight.

When Wolcott Balestier finally returned, ten days later, he found his friend established as Carrie's accepted lover. He greeted the decision with his familiar lopsided smile.

'Not a word, just yet,' he agreed, in response to Rud's nervous proviso. For the present it was their secret. It would keep them all together.

From the first, Carrie'd had no scruples about teasing him. 'Rud, you have Go fever, anything but stay in one place.' But now after all that had passed between them, he did not know how to tell her that he was off again. He stuttered, faced with her direct question, her look of pain and surprise.

'You regret getting in so deep with me?' she asked. He could make no reply, though later that evening he sat down to write to her.

'My own dear girl,' he began,

'You know that I regret nothing. Not one atom of all we have become to each other. But perhaps you may not understand, even yet, what a gypsy you have joined yourself with.

Since they're not going to let us marry over a bonfire and make off in a painted wagon, I need a little time to wear out my last impulses towards the wandering life.

Bear with me.

I know that Wolcott will watch over you for me till I return.

dearest love

your Ruddy'

Quite apart from what the doctors were always telling him about taking a holiday, he was longing for sunlight. That was about as close as he could come to it. Sunlight and the dry smell of spices. In his mind's eye, as it cleared in the process of writing, a sareed figure, so close that he could all but brush the fabric, sat crouched, working a pestle. *Jeera… Haldi…* Once away on the high seas, there was no knowing how far he might go. Stevenson out in Samoa was always pressing him to come over there on a visit. The very thought of such remoteness made him quiver.

In the end, the Kamakurahe steamer schedules had been impossible. He'd failed to get beyond New Zealand. Here he was, four months after leaving London, Christmas Eve and back in his old stamping ground, Lahore. Such happiness, being served again by a rejoicing Kadir Baksh. The dear fellow had actually got leave from his new employer to attend him during his visit. Apart from that, Rud felt his return a bit flat. It wasn't the same.

How could it be? Yesterday, visiting the old office, there was scarcely a face he recognised in the print room. Still, the parents were pleased that he'd be with them for Christmas. A Punjab Christmas – he remembered the drill only too well. The pudding – one sent out from Harrods if you were lucky – if not, the sawdust flavoured version knocked up in the Club kitchens. At least there would be the Children's Party later on. The little beggars were always fun. Perhaps he could help out with that.

A step grating on the gravel outside pierced his reverie. Rud amused himself with speculation. Catching the words 'chit from the Telegraph office for the Sahib', he fancied it might be some hitch with the *Journal of Indian Arts*. Was the Pater still editing that, surely he must be going to retire before long? Wondering idly why the telegram had come to the house rather than the Museum, he took up the newspaper. He was scanning it with the critical eye of a former editor when his mother appeared.

'Ah, there you are, Rud; this seems to be for you.' It was the curse of his success, the amount of negotiating with publishers, of confirming the dispatch and receipt of manuscripts that fell to him. But surely now he'd taken on Watts to act for him, there should be less of this? Resigned, with a nod he put out his hand.

'Wolcott dead stop come back to me stop.' He had to read the words three or four times before he could begin to take them in. At his choked exclamation, his mother had stepped across to him: he saw his own bewilderment mirrored in her face.

'I… I… Wolcott? Dead? But he's supposed to be in Leipzig,' Rud babbled.

Alice raised her eyes from the telegram in order to direct a keen glance at her son.

'Who sent this?'

'Carrie, yes, Carrie, I suppose.'

'"*Come back to me*?" *Come back to Carrie Balestier*?'

Rud shivered. He had risen and was walking about the room, staring at the familiar chairs as though they held the answer to a question he could not formulate. He went back and reread the message. He wheeled round.

'There's nothing for it. I have to go.'

'What, now? You've only just got here. Rest is what you need after that awful journey. There's nothing you can do for the poor fellow that can't wait now. And Christmas is just –'

Rud looked at his mother with loathing. Did she always have to know better?

'If I leave in half an hour I can just catch the mail at Umballa. I need you to wire ahead for me to Bombay, about my passage.' He left the door swinging.

In Bombay, he found himself condemned to a wait of only twelve hours. The Mater had been efficient, he had to concede. Depositing his baggage in Watson's Hotel, where he had eaten – what, he could not recall – he set off to calm himself with a stroll in the familiar purlieus of the School of Art, through the gardens where he'd played beneath flowers tall as chimneys twenty years before. His heart stuttered. Those endless prairies had shrunk away. Absurd to be surprised, he told himself: to a child the world is vast. It did not quiet his echoing sense of loss.

But he could bring it all back. Within himself it all remained unchanged. The screens blew and flapped in the afternoon as he lay in his cot after lunch, Ayah beside him singing. Her husky voice mingled with other sounds, the occasional clatter of a plate as the kitchen boy washed up, the squabbles of birds in the mango tree. Looking around him, he saw it was the breeze off the sea that freshened the houses along the Esplanade, jerking the wooden screens. But in those days it had seemed that a single voice made itself up out of a consort of sounds and was singing him to sleep under the tent of white netting.

The blank of his initial horrified shock had given way to a sort of urgent listlessness. He knew he must get home. But he found himself utterly passive. In that condition new ideas, one after another, began to move through him, like the waters of an imperceptibly returning tide. This marked the end of India for him. There would be no more of these days of light: he was here now in Bombay for the last time.

He would, he must, find Ayah.

As if in a dream he unhurriedly made his way to the house of the Franciscans. There was no difficulty in obtaining the directions he needed. Native converts were not so many that the Fathers lost track of them.

When he turned the corner, she was standing by the entrance to her compound, one hand on a lintel, the other shading her eyes against the sun's stabbing brilliance to look along the alley away from him. Though her face was hidden, he had no doubts. This was her outline, her stance, though the saree was white. Yet he could scarcely get the words out to greet her. As though she knew, the old woman who once was Ayah turned to face him, holding out her arms.

'So fine young man,' she sighed at last, fingers smoothing his wet cheek. 'Always best, Ruddy Baba, always best.'

As he sipped luxuriously at the *nimbu pani* he had watched her make for him – 'once more, once more, Ayah, show me again' – Rud gestured towards her garments of white.

'Great sorrow, friend to my life.'

'Many years past. "To have and to hold", isn't it, the words they speak over you in your English church? If we cannot hold through all the days to come, better to have what is good, even for a little while, not so, Ruddy Sahib?'

He gestured his distaste for the term of respect but she went on.

'In my heart is always Ruddy Baba but today I see before me Ruddy Sahib. And you, Ruddy Sahib, have you yet made that choice which all must make?'

'Truly, one waits for me in my own country.'

'Then I send her many blessings. May you return in peace to her.'

Only on his way back to the docks did the proverb learned from his *munshi* come to mind:

'Lend me your child for the first three years and hear him call me mother for thirty.'

Now he knew what he wanted and knew there need be no delay. For God's sake, he was twenty-six. He would get a special licence the moment he got to London.

*

Without Henry James, it was hard to see who would have given Carrie away. Her only remaining brother, Beatty, was in the United States like the rest of her male relatives. Having been devoted to Wolcott, James was as close to family as could be mustered.

Once he'd helped her out of the hired brougham and they were standing on the pavement of Langham Place, outside the vestry door of All Souls, James paused and took breath. With the greatest hesitation he laid a gloved hand briefly on her arm, a touch so fleeting he could not be sure that it registered with her.

He was doing his utmost to fill, for this one day, the terrible breach left by poor dear Wolcott's death. Someone had to come forward to give Carrie away to that terrifyingly clever young Kipling, since he apparently insisted on laying claim to her, who could say why. There'd been not a syllable of indication.

Not that Carrie was an inconsiderable young woman, by any means. Talking with her in the big black and silver coach on the way back from the funeral, he'd come to appreciate her quality. 'Force, acuteness, capacity, courage', as he praised her to Gosse. When she described her ferocious struggle to keep Wolcott in life, the nights of watching, her eyes brimmed but she shed not a tear. All was clarity and elucidation: the emotion so channelled, she could have been a man. Wolcott had been taken ill on his way to Leipzig and diverted to Dresden. The rose spots on the chest and abdomen – James shuddered – confirmed that it was typhoid. Only when she came to speak of the end did she give way.

'He just gave up. Wolcott gave up and left me.'

Like enough, news of Kipling's wedding would be in the papers that very evening, whatever the effort to avoid public notice. What a mercy there would be no trumpery music, no vulgar straining of guests to look at them. The wedding party could hardly be smaller, or more awkwardly composed, between himself, Gosse and his family, Heinemann and a single Kipling cousin. The bride's mother and sister, so he had been told, were lying sick with the influenza in their hotel. It was true: all London was brought low in the epidemic.

In the dim light of the January afternoon, made more grey by the fog that was veiling the streets, he saw with relief that Rudyard and Ambrose Poynter, his best man, were already waiting with a surpliced figure by the altar. Carrie had caught sight of him too. James knew it by the way she thrilled at his side and he marvelled at her. Passionately as she was mourning, she was still capable of elation in this moment.

They were still several feet away from Rudyard, his tanned face inscrutable above the gleam of his collar in the church dusk, when Carrie dropped the arm that she had taken so gratefully and moved forward, drawn away towards Rudyard.

As the familiar drone of 'Dearly beloved, we are gathered here together' began, there was no mistaking the intensity with which

Rudyard clasped Carrie's hand and looked into her face.

James felt obliged to lower his gaze before such naked feeling.

So they were a match for each other, after all! He'd anticipated nothing like this. He only prayed that good might come of it: every atom of Carrie's force and courage would be needed to handle that brilliant, agitated boy.

* * *

Once back in Calcutta, Trix was beginning to feel her new status as an advantage. A married woman had a right to her views, she had seen the world without the blinkers nice girls had to wear.

When she rose at last from her desk to stretch high into the air, the seams of her yellow muslin creaked warningly under the arms. Her smile only widened. She was breaking her way out of the ugly old thing. It was only fit for writing in anyway.

She could tell she'd done enough for that day. It was like flying but she'd better stop for now. The story was beginning to hang together; she could feel it.

Now the sapping humidity began to tell on her. All around, Calcutta lay stewing in the sluggish airs of the delta: it kept the city from enjoying any breeze from the sea. Writing had made her oblivious, though she realised, fingers at her throat, that she must have instinctively undone the buttons of her high collar.

After dinner that evening, when she stepped outside, there wasn't the least movement of air. Yet in appearance, the garden lay cool as though under water, flooded by silver.

'Jack, darling, before you brought me here, you told me that everyone says it's quite splendid, the sight of the open space of the *Maidan* under moonlight.'

'Did I really? Someone must have told me. I've never actually seen it for myself.'

'Oh do let's go out there, this must be the perfect night for it,' Trix raised her eyes beseeching. She could tell from the way he hesitated that he would rather have sat reading over Survey reports. She herself had always found maps dull, if not baffling, yet Jack simply revelled – if that was quite the word for it – in everything to do with them.

She knew that if she rested a lingering touch on his sleeve, he wouldn't be able to refuse. 'You shall have your wish. Mind you, though, you may get more than you bargained for, my dear. Don't forget the native element. The Black Town. It comes alive at night.'

In the *tikka gharry* – Jack claimed his means would not run to a carriage of their own – Trix forgot her unsavoury environment, the cracked leather and the lingering, unidentifiable smells. As the great *Maidan* hove into sight, its grass stretching emerald under the moon, gold mohur trees in full burnished flower, she drew in a sharp breath.

But the *gharry* had scarcely covered another fifty yards before a wild chorus, an uneven cry of mourning, broke up the night. It appeared to be getting closer.

'What is it? What is it?' she reverberated with alarm.

'Jackals, dear, just a pack of jackals. The Old Town's full of them. They don't usually come this close to Government House.' He was patting her hand, smiling at her ignorance, when the cries grew abruptly louder and a thrusting horde of dogs poured onto the *Maidan* directly beside them. From the pack leader's mouth there dangled something at which his pursuers snapped.

'Why, what – Trix, what are you doing?' She'd thrown herself against him, eyes squeezed shut, but not before she'd made out the shape of a human arm.

There was no longer any pleasure in the night. Once home, Jack sat her down and took a chair directly in front of her.

'I know you're convinced that's what the creatures were fighting over, but Trix, I do assure you that you are mistaken. I tell you it was animal bones, probably goat that they'd scavenged from the slaughterers. The native quarters reek with every kind of refuse.'

She was obliged to subside. Of course Jack knew what he was talking about. And it was not the first time she'd been told to set aside her fears as groundless. That no-one else could see anything to prompt alarm.

*

Jack Fleming carried Trix up to Scotland to visit his family when his regular leave came due within the following year.

'Aunt Christiana, my good old godmother, has read your book and she's most anxious to meet you. You'll get on like a house on fire with her. She's a splendid old girl and, like you, a great one for the books.' Passing on the invitation, Jack didn't seem prepared for the little exclamation of pleasure that broke from Trix. At last, a positive response addressed to her herself, not merely a civil welcome to her husband's wife.

From the beginning of this her first visit to them in Scotland, the Flemings had left her stranded. A guest in Gattonside House, the home of Jack's elder sister, Moona, she had learned to raise no topic of her own. When she once volunteered 'I'm so looking forward to the next instalment of *Tess;* do you admire Mr. Hardy's novels?' she was met with nervous politeness. Instead, she now took her cues from family conversation. Country doings, a neighbour's plans to extend his estate, last Sunday's sermon, the beasts and their prices at market, planned repairs on the little footbridge over the Tweed that linked the village with Melrose, all appeared of inexhaustible interest.

There wasn't a shop for miles, not anything you could call a proper shop. She imagined that the business of selecting material and ordering a dress was a rare penance grimly endured by her new female relatives. Or perhaps there were bolts of ancestral tweed and black bombazine kept piled in a remote but orderly corner of the great grey house.

At first, it seemed to her that the world in which the Flemings conducted their sober lives was surprisingly like the hill-stations of home. Pine-clad slopes with stern stone buildings which regarded her narrowly, were confusingly reminiscent of Simla.

Only the human element failed to match. Where was all the life that pulsed in the bazaar? There the hoarse cries of vegetable women rose above the murmured enticements of silk merchants and sellers of embroideries. It was true that the bazaar's jostling wooden structures appeared makeshift and straggling when compared to the isolated, unyielding edifices put up for their occupation by the British – that is, by her own people, she quickly corrected herself. Their four-square homes of stone might be imposing but they were always a little awkward to run and inclined to damp. That was also true of most of the houses in Scotland where she'd been a guest.

Living among her new family made Trix ashamed to discover how much pretty fabrics and a graceful line in the turn of a shirtwaist meant to her. She found herself taking out an Indian shawl and burying her face in it. The faint sandalwood from the chest it lived in at home in Calcutta brought tears to her eyes.

'Quite unsuitable,' her mother-in-law dismissed it the first evening she put the shawl on to go down to dinner. 'Have you nothing less heathen?' With a rebellious heart Trix put on her sweetest smile. She wouldn't set a foot wrong if she could help it.

Aunt Christiana's house lacked even the simple charm of a setting in the Melrose countryside. A dark tower of a town house, where, Trix suspected, the air was haunted by the steam of suet puddings boiled hour after hour in sodden cloths.

The maid who'd opened the door had known Jack as a boy. 'Master Jack, it's awful guid to see you. The young imp that you were coming home with your breeks torn from the brambles and always making off with the bannocks still out on the table, cooling from the uin.'

It was evident that the woman considered herself wedded to truth so Trix would have to try to believe in this figment, a Master Jackie who had been 'a young limb of Satan but the best heart in the world on him'.

'Christiana may sound a bit fierce but she's an old pet really, you'll see,' Jack whispered as their outer clothes were whisked away.

Looking around her in the receding cavern of the drawing room, Trix could see no books lying casually about or even neatly ordered on shelves. Only as they got closer to the seated figure awaiting them at the far end of the room – its white cap, edged, she noticed, with the finest Brussels lace – did Trix register the presence of a black bible. It was slack from much handling, she saw at once from the way it sagged open on the table at Christiana's side. The filmy pages were lightly creased, like aged skin.

The old woman did not rise, and Trix was not invited to sit.

'Jack, my laddie, indeed and you're very welcome. And yon's your bride. Well, Mistress Alice Fleming, you've made your way to Scotland at last.'

The pretty courtesies drying on her lips, Trix put her shoulders back. She, who had withstood the wrath of the Vicereine, Lady Dufferin, wasn't going to allow herself to be put down. 'I am very happy to be meeting so many dear members of Jack's family,' she replied civilly, with an inclination of the head.

'Indeed. It's my own acquaintance you'll be making this day and I'm thinking, Master Jackie – why, you've not given me a kiss yet!' She put up her pale dry cheek. 'So, I'm thinking your wee wife and I should get on best if we have a little chat on our own. Away now, to the kitchen. Bessie's been beside herself ever since she heard you were coming. She's baked your favourite shortbreads.'

Jack appeared to think that this was going splendidly. He wheeled about and left without another word.

The light of afternoon was grey in the high room. The silence was only briefly interrupted by muffled exclamations as the door down to the kitchen opened and closed. Those must be greetings for the prodigal limb of Satan, Trix thought tartly.

She made as if to move towards a chair.

'Not there, if you please. I'd prefer to have your face in the light, missy.'

A seat shiny with black canvas and packed rigid with horsehair was indicated.

The old woman put the fingers of her mittened hands together. Trix could see that a hole in the crochet work of the right thumb had been exquisitely repaired. Perhaps handicrafts, needlework and so on would be possible topics for this afternoon. She was becoming accustomed to examining the prosier reaches of her experience to find common interests with the women of her new family. Before she could frame an opening, the attack was loosed.

'Have you no shame, young mistress, no shame in writing that wicked story and bringing dishonour on the head of your husband? I say nothing of the disgrace to our family name. And the sly way you went about it. Only that a dear friend, a minister who has dedicated himself in the mission field among the pagan Hindu heard our name linked with that story of yours, none of us would have been any the wiser.'

Trix felt the blood drain from her face. There'd been nothing to forewarn her. The dull light brightened to a dazzle. She grasped at the unyielding black arms of her chair.

'It's clear that you have no natural delicacy of feeling. It's no surprising that coming from your background there has been a lack of proper teaching. Writing in itself need be no bad thing, though it's not for every Tom, Dick and Harry to take it up. Improving stories have their place. But for a young woman newly married to write in such terms. "*Reading the marriage service gave her new cause for fear and hesitation. Duties from which she shrank*", indeed. Is this language to be proud of? Where is your sense of what is sacred, of what is decent?'

Remembering Jack's weight on her, the suffocation as she endured his thrusts, Trix clenched her hands.

'We all know that marriage is no bed of roses. Our Saviour never meant it to be. But how dare you, wife to that good man, how dare you give the impression of being personally acquainted with such feelings –'

Trix did hope that she was not going to faint. She felt dizzy. She wanted to interrupt. How could she be guilty of defiling the name of Fleming and of concealing it at the same time? She was confused. But she wasn't sure that she could command her voice. Perhaps it'd be best just to sit it out. She found that she could quite simply step back inside herself and watch the white face of the old woman while the mauve lips formed the words of accusation which Trix could no longer hear.

That she did not put out her hand on leaving did not seem to be observed. The moment she heard Jack's step out in the passage she was on her feet, steadied by a hand on the back of her chair. He looked surprised and gratified when she clung to his side. Trix allowed him to make the farewells, the promises of a swift return, longing only for the open air and the world of the street.

'Now, did you two have a good talk?' he asked, looking down and patting her small hand. Trix made an attempt to squeeze his arm and smile in answer but she could only tremble, filled with shame at her own weakness and confusion. As they set off along the granite terrace, she felt weightless, her head a gas-filled balloon, her feet barely making contact with the pavement.

She would have stepped directly into the path of an omnibus at the crossing, if Jack hadn't hauled her in quite roughly.

'For heaven's sake, Trix, look where you're going.'

But Trix had no idea where that might be.

* * *

Their leisurely honeymoon journey had now reached Japan, where they made Yokohama the base of modest expeditions. Rud was eager to visit nearby Kamakura. 'There's the most wonderful bronze Buddha. Forty feet tall, standing in the open air, the Pater says it's a master work.'

Four grapefruit made a pyramid in the dish placed in front of the giant statue. Rud removed his hat and stood in silence, his wife beside him, before the figure of the Buddha. After a considered moment, he cupped her elbow with his hand, steering her towards the shade of a grove of bamboo. In the light of the news she had given him the night before, he must take special care of her.

'Really, Rud, there's no need. I was a little nauseous in the morning this past week or so but I feel fit as a fiddle this afternoon. Truly.'

He relaxed. She was straight as a die; he could take her word for it. But it might be wise to cut short their travels. Stop honeymooning and settle down like grown people with responsibilities. It would mean, blast it, that he still didn't get to Samoa: was he never to meet Stevenson? They must discuss it later.

Carrie went on, 'Tell me about all this –' gesturing towards the towering statue, into whose hollow back some sniggering tourists were climbing, in defiance of the modest notice asking for respect. 'Americans,' she noted. 'It makes me ashamed.'

'It makes *me* want to thrash 'em.' She found his lurking violence rather exciting. So long as it could be contained.

'Rud, Rud, don't take it so personally. They're just –'

'Uneducated Christian bigots, not a brain between them. Do you know, I've heard one such presumed to use it as a pulpit? Chanted the doxology!'

'Don't let them spoil this day for us. Come now, you say you've brought me to the East so that my eyes can be opened. Explain what it means to these people,' nodding towards the grey-robed figures with their vivid sashes passing silently back and forth. 'I'm not sure I trust the accounts of Buddha and the Way that are printed in the guidebooks.'

'It's the stories that matter. They carry the teaching. It's all in the stories.'

'Tell me.'

Carrie straightened on the spare wooden seat and prepared herself. His beautiful voice deepened in resonance. She had told him it was his voice that had made her fall in love with him.

'First, there is the tale of Prince Gautama himself, who was the

Buddha and also' – he looked tenderly into his wife's dreaming face, now lightly filmed with sweat – 'the tale of Maya the virtuous and beautiful, his mother.'

Carrie sighed with pleasure. 'And after that?'

'After that, O most gracious and overheated one, come the Jataka tales. Which concern the beasts. Lessons about living together, really. I heard them first from my ayah but you find them all over the East.' He broke off to tickle her face with a leafy blade from the grove rustling about them. 'I think we should find someone to give us a pot of that green tea before I get going. Then when you're really comfortable, you can decide: shall I begin with the tale of Brahmadatta, King of Benares, and the noble monkey who taught him to rule with love? Or with the tale of the wild dog who brought the King to understand justice when the palace dogs chewed up the harness of the royal chariot?'

Enchanting alternatives hung on the air as they moved towards the small pavilion.

The following morning, Carrie was still asleep when he slipped out of bed. He was about due to send off another of his Travel Letters to *The Times*. The obligation could be tedious: they weren't travelling about much so there wasn't a lot of colour to charge his brush but at £25 a column it was worth the effort. And with this new responsibility to come, keeping his name before the public, was more important than ever now that cursed New Oriental Bank had failed with all his savings. Some honeymoon. He was still not sure that this success could last – it was too rash, too unadvised, too sudden. It might kiss and consume, like the lightning in *Romeo and Juliet*.

Today, though, he felt the squirm of excitement deep in his belly. There was a poem on the way.

Carrie was sleepily fishing for the end of her shawl as she came into their sitting room to find him.

'I've been up for hours.' He was exuberant. 'Just listen to this:
"Oh ye who tread the Narrow Way

By Tophet flare to Judgement Day –'"

He broke off. 'That's those Christian bigots who destroy childhood with their threats of Hell fire. I'll give you a story of mine about that to read some day.' He went on:

"'Be gentle when the heathen pray
To Buddha at Kamakura!
To him the Way, the Law, Apart,
Whom Maya held beneath her heart
Ananda's Lord, the Bodhisat
The Buddha of Kamakura."

You see, a quite different tradition: closer to the mother, to that human love.'

Carrie laid her cheek against his. Her husband went on:

"'For though he neither burns nor sees,
Nor hears ye thank your Deities
Ye have not sinned with such as these,
His children at Kamakura;"

The blind arrogance. Worship for any but their own god a sin, imagine! And they'd be amazed and put out to be told that the Trinity sounds rather close to polytheism.

"Yet spare us still the Western joke
When joss-sticks turn to scented smoke
The little sins of little folk
That worship at Kamakura."

If they can't find it in the Prayer Book, it must be ludicrous, if not actually sinful. All that Christian focus on sin is simply deathly. There's more but I'm still working on the rest of it. What do you think?'

Wide awake now, Carrie hesitated. 'It's beautiful, Rud.' She kissed him lightly. 'But is it safe to publish? Won't it give offence?' This was no time to put their income in jeopardy.

'I wager that it will pass over people's heads – all Eastern exotica. Except for those who share my sentiments. You'll see.'

* * *

Trix had now been married to Jack, stationed with him in Calcutta, for almost four years and her writing was not going as well as she'd hoped. She used to imagine she'd never look back if only she could get work of her own into print. Not as Rud's sister, the junior partner. That's how it'd felt when they'd published *Echoes* together. Nor as one corner of that blessed 'family square' that the parents were so fond of. All working together to write a Christmas number for the *CMG* had been fun but once was enough.

She was no longer a girl living under her father's roof but a married woman, a woman of experience. Surely now her work deserved to stand on its own.

She'd thought that was really going to happen, a year or so back, when her novel was accepted for publication, with the title she had chosen for herself, *The Heart of a Maid*. Jack had raised no objections, once she'd explained that it would not be coming out under her own name. It had felt like the start of a new life. She'd begun to feel confident that she was indeed a writer. So she hadn't been prepared for the way that confidence could drain away.

It was no good blaming Jack's aunt. She'd resolved not to complain; besides, she would've died rather than relive the scene with that horrid woman. She'd spoken of it to no-one. Yet she didn't seem able to write as fluently as before. After a morning spent at her desk Trix was constantly dissatisfied nowadays. There was often so little to show for all her labour. She would stare in dismay at a sheet heavily marked with crossings-out.

She used to be so eager to get people to pay attention, to make them see what she saw, hear what she couldn't help hearing. There were things that you knew that you couldn't always account for even though you could put them into words. Like Mama taking one look at that little Carrie Balestier, one look, and declaring, 'That woman's going to marry our Ruddy.'

Papa had laughed at the time. 'Alice, you are incorrigible. Spare the poor girl – there's no need to take fright at every young American woman Rud meets. Do give the boy credit. He's perfectly capable of making these decisions for himself when the time comes.'

But Mama was proved right. And now Ruddy was married and a father, settled in Vermont, oceans apart from them all. He was having a new adventure. When he wrote of being lapped to the tip of his nose in robes of fur, of driving a sleigh between sparkling pines, of roads banked high with snowdrifts blue and green in their depths, she had shivered, even as black kites screamed above her in a sky of brass. With a certain effort she could enter into her brother's joy in his new world. But she wept to see him beaming over the head of baby Josephine, in the photographs.

'What about me?' she wanted to cry aloud.

Her head was aching, as it did most days, once into the Calcutta Hot Weather. Trix gave herself a little shake. Better to admit that she wasn't going to be able to write today. She'd spent another morning at her desk staring blankly.

'What *is* the point of trying?' She laid her head down on the desk. She'd had the little desk inlaid with mother of pearl sent on to her, when she left her parents' house in Lahore.

'Other women seem happy enough,' Jack had expostulated, baffled, when he found her silently weeping over it one afternoon.

Ruddy meant to be helpful, she knew. '*Don't waste time wondering whether you're a writer, just get down to it. That's what a writer is, someone with a pen in their hand getting sheets of paper covered,*' he wrote.

He had as good as promised to get her next story published.

'I can't understand why it's so difficult to get started. Wives out here are supposed to be dying of boredom; time ought to be hanging heavy on my hands,' she scrawled on the glaring empty page.

It was a relief to be able to find some words, even words for her failure, and to set them down on paper.

The servants were a constant worry and interruption. Amit Khan, the *khitmatgar*, was supposed to oversee all the others but she couldn't feel confident in him. Seeing an unfamiliar *dhobi* leaving from the back gate one morning, his back bent under the load of the household washing, Trix paused in confusion. What had happened to one-eyed Abu, with the crimson rag tied round his head?

'Madam, madam, this man was an evil-doer,' Amit Khan had insisted, head shaking in reproof.

Determined to stand her ground, Trix looked him in the eye.

'But Amit Khan, did the Colonel Sahib give orders? Did he ask you to send Abu away?

'The Lord Sahib requires many clean shirts, multitudes of clean shirts.'

She was immediately distracted. 'Did we get back all of the Sahib's shirts last week? Have you counted them?' She brushed a damp wisp of hair back off her face.

'I will check Madam. Correct number one English dozen,' and he was out of the room.

Game, set and match to Amit Khan, she conceded.

Yet it was really no laughing matter, living with a man you couldn't quite trust. She insisted on seeing their silver counted back into the velvet slots of the canteen each evening before Amit Khan was dismissed for the night. Jack himself wasn't observant. That was one thing to be thankful for. But it meant that stupid details, housekeeping and the required social visits seemed to have taken over her life.

Before she could stop herself, she was rubbing at a mark she hadn't seen before on the polished table

No, she admitted painfully, she allowed herself to be distracted. There was after all some trace of sweetness in keeping order, in doing what was expected of her. Whereas when she sat down to write, she came up hard against something she could not name.

It wasn't as though she had nothing to say. So often she longed to argue with pieces in the journals that Papa sent on to her every month. And it wasn't only ideas that made her want to write. People had such extraordinary ways of behaving towards each other. Not enough attention was paid to that.

Later that very day, at the Babacombes', Trix saw something she'd have liked to write about, if she dared. Changing the names, of course.

'Oh, I've cut myself,' Edith Plowright cried. Trix had been hurrying to her side when she was forestalled.

'How can you be so stupid, Edith? It's always the same.' Mrs. Plowright threw down her own sewing to stride across to her daughter. The other women, gathered for their weekly morning of conversation over their sewing, hesitated uncertain. Trix knew what they were thinking: another scene from Agnes Plowright. The less attention they paid, perhaps the less embarrassment for all of them.

Edith's habitually mousy look gave way to one of terror.

'Oh it's nothing,' she babbled, 'nothing at all. I was just unpicking some stitches when I must have –'

'Let me see.' Pause. 'Oh, you've ruined that shirt you were supposed to be finishing off for me. Just look at the blood! Heaven knows whether I'll be able to get it out.' Her temper was definitely rising. With a look at Trix, Major Babacombe's wife rose to intervene. They were in her drawing room; the responsibility was hers.

'Agnes, my dear, I have a perfectly infallible method for removing bloodstains, tried and tested through several campaigns.' The little joke broke through the tension. 'Why don't you come with me and we'll have it out in a jiffy?'

Once Edith's mother was out of the room, Trix took the white-faced girl by the hand, to examine the welling slash in the ball of her thumb. She slid Edith's cuff back, to keep it clear of the blood. 'You poor thing, Edith,' she murmured. 'It does look rather deep. Perhaps we should get the doctor to look at it –'

'Oh no, please not, I'm sure it will stop bleeding directly,' Edith pleaded, her voice sharp with fear. Trix could imagine that the suggestion of a doctor's visit would be tinder to Agnes Plowright's rage. But what about the risk of infection?

Stuck with so much to write about. Yet the words, even when they came to her, looked wrong. That evening, Trix was restless. Dinner over, she stood picking at dead blooms amongst the bouquet in her yellow Liberty vase, then opened an old magazine and put it down again.

Even Jack noticed: 'You're too pale y'know. Better see the quack.'

Planning to argue, she carried a lamp over to the looking-glass and was frightened by the wan, tight-lipped image thrown back at her. Where had she gone, 'Rose in June', the Grecian beauty who had once been the toast of Simla? If that girl's smile had been tremulous, the narrow lips parting only hesitantly, Trix did not recall it now.

Her hand quivered as she replaced the lamp. Turning back to her husband, she resolved to make more of an effort. Jack was a fair-minded, decent man, who didn't run after other women, she was lucky to have him. It wasn't his fault that he saw the world differently. When she tried to talk to him, her thoughts did seem to fray apart into nothing as she spoke. But perhaps if she persevered...

'I do wonder why Mrs. Plowright is so hard on her daughter. Could she be angry with her for not being more attractive? Edith's a sweet girl but I've noticed that she doesn't get many partners when we have a dance at the Club.'

'Can't say I've paid much attention. I expect you're exaggerating.'

'No, really, Jack. Round her wrist there were scars. Like cuts. Some were quite fresh. There's something wrong there, I can't help wondering...' In the face of his blank silence, she felt her voice die away. But she had taken those nursing classes. She knew what a scar from a cut looked like.

Her fingers danced an angry tattoo.

Jack did like to listen to her singing. 'Ah, there's nothing like the old songs,' he would exclaim, evening after evening, as she rose from the piano. But it was the 'How about a kiss for me, Mrs. Fleming?' that she really dreaded.

It was months now since Trix had written anything, without crossing it out or tearing it up that same day.

'Being married to Jack is driving me mad.'

Horrified, she stared at what she'd written. She looked round, quickly. Silly, stupid girl, there was no-one watching. Not here in her dressing room, where she'd moved her desk so she could write when she couldn't sleep, nor in the deserted drawing room at the other end of the house. Probably not in the kitchen either, she thought with a hysterical giggle, for the cook would slip out for a smoke and a chat by the gate with the *chowkidar* even through the rain. His small assistant would be deep in the garden hunting the huge mottled wet-weather frogs. The wooden bungalow heaved and settled round her under a brief period of sun. It would rain again by afternoon.

'I want to kill myself.'

Who had made those marks on the page?

Recently she'd taken to writing in pencil. Then gone over to rubbing out. When she'd asked Jack to bring home one of the large official erasers from his office he'd been pleased. She could tell that he was glad that she'd asked for something he was able to provide.

Trix was afraid to look at the sheet of paper, now. What other words would have escaped to confront her there? Best to burn it.

Head averted, she turned the enemy witness face down. Somewhere in the tall *almirah* there were her curling tongs and the little spirit stove she used for heating them. But she couldn't delay, couldn't send for her maid. Kneeling, careless of her skirts on the unswept floor, she rummaged with increasing agitation. By the time she had her hands on the familiar metal box overprinted in blue, her breath was coming in sobs.

But she couldn't remember how to go about lighting the lamp. Trix sat staring at the tufty charred wick, then played for a while with the fretted metal of the surround.

'Eeny meeny miny mo…' she was counting the patterns aloud.

A huge blind effort and she was back on her feet, pushing the scramble of boxes back into the woody darkness and leaning against the doors.

Perhaps Mama would be able to advise her, once they got home leave. But that might not be till '95. At the thought of opening her heart to Mama, however, Trix found she couldn't imagine how she could explain. What would be the right words? Mama could be so sharp, so dismissive.

There was only Mama. Papa was never going to be fair to Jack. He would blame Jack for everything and she knew that wouldn't be just.

As for Rud. She flinched. It was savage, the things he'd said. He'd had no business telling her she wasn't fit to marry. If she was now beginning to feel that he might have been correct, the fear remained buried. She would keep her distance from him. But she couldn't dispel the lingering sense of shame.

'Anyway, you've let them all leave you behind,' she said aloud.

The best thing was to occupy herself. That'd been Ruddy's salvation, he'd told her so himself, having to work and work, ten or more hours a day when he was second in command at the *CMG*. That was when he began on his stories.

She too could find a way to be useful, surely? She didn't have to be left out; there must be something that Jack needed copying. Or maybe there was something in the journals she could take up and explore. Develop new interests. Forgotten, the incriminating sheet lay on her desk. Finding it later that day, she shuddered. Snatching it up, she hastened to the window, holding the paper out below the eaves until it turned to pulp in her fingers, washed in the streams that poured down without remission.

* * *

For the moment, Rud and Carrie were renting a small house, Bliss Cottage, outside Brattleboro, Carrie's home town. They were preparing to build a house of their own.

From the window of the tiny space he called his study, Rud noticed the mailman plodding up the path. That morning he had dug out the snow again, gleefully throwing spadefuls right and left.

It was something new to feel himself so fit. He could work outside for hours here. The sharp dry cold of these winters just set him up.

'There's so much work to do on it. Bliss Cottage? "The Blizzard" would be a better name,' he grumbled. 'Are you sure it's worth it for the few months we're going to be living here?'

'Rud, how can you ask? With Baby coming. And the new house – heaven knows when it will be ready to move in. The joiners and carpenters won't come down from Quebec to start work before the snow's gone.'

Carrie would never allow Brattleboro gossips to say they were inhabiting a shack. Though the word 'respect' hadn't passed her lips, he knew that she was desperately sensitive about her standing in the eyes of local people. Had she really meant that about having uniforms for the servants? He had no wish to attract unnecessary attention, himself. It had been a mistake, driving into town with the tiger-skin over the back of the sleigh. And the newspapermen were already after him, even out here.

'When the house is finally ready – they do say July – do you know what I'm most looking forward to?'

'Don't tell me, Rud. A proper bathroom? You fuss every night over that tin tub.'

'You have no poetry in you, Carrie. It's all the fun of making the garden. Finding what will grow here, what suits, what will flourish.'

Now that his daughter was a living, breathing reality, however, he found himself instead planning a path lined with flowers, with hollyhocks and sunflowers, for the Joss to trot down to play with her small cousin, Beatty's daughter, Marjorie.

'The Joss?' He grinned to recall how Carrie's mother had raised an eyebrow, registering the pet-name for the first time. You could all but hear the words: *The Lord alone knows what that boy Rud will think of next.* She knew that the Baby had been named Josephine for her aunt, Carrie's sister. Nevertheless, she was positively suspicious of 'the Joss'.

Carrie was not dismayed. 'Come on Ma, it's a kind of pun. And a remembrance. That's what they call an idol in the East, like that

giant Buddha I showed you in the photograph. You're not going
to say we don't worship the little duck –'

Somewhat placated, her mother appeared to subside.

And when the Joss could set off by herself down that path,
what sort of little girl would she turn out? Carrie shook her head
at him but he couldn't stop his imagination hurrying ahead. Baby
would take her own time growing up, Carrie was right, of course.

But the foundations for the new house were already in, grey
stone with the moss still on it. Once it thawed, the lumber mills
would be starting up and the timber would arrive. And he could
pay for every inch of it, make all this happen, just by writing!

He took a few waltz steps on his way to the door, to take charge
of the bundle of letters and papers. There was another possibility:
dances in the barn, once they had got one of their own built.
The only thing he missed about Simla was all the waltzing. He
ruffled through the bills and correspondence to see if there were
something from Trix buried amongst them. Business matters he
could safely hand over to Carrie – or would be able to again, in a
month or so. For the moment she was lost in a new heaven.

'I had no idea that a baby – that the Joss – would have an effect on
me too, on my work, that is,' he had admitted to their neighbour,
Molly Cabot, when she dropped by at teatime one afternoon.

'You mean it's a surprise that she keeps you awake nights?'
Molly'd made it clear she had no illusions about his grasp
of practical affairs. 'No, do go on, I didn't mean it,' she cried
as he made a feint of throwing a cushion at her. 'I do want to
understand, really.'

'It all happened on the one day,' Carrie put in, from her deep
armchair. 'Rud wrote and finished this new story, about the baby
and the wolves, and the Joss came into the world.'

'But it was the feel of writing it. I've had it before, the sense
that I was almost taken over as I wrote, acting under direction –'
gesturing, he knocked the spoon from his saucer and bent to pick
it up.

'Like Socrates with his daemon?' he could tell Molly was serious, in spite of her mocking tone. 'Or would it be more up-to-date to say like spiritualism and automatic writing?'

Carrie sat upright. 'Not at all, Molly. Rud's perfectly in command of himself when he writes. He just feels… stronger,' she finished, lame even to his ears.

'No, really, Carrie,' Molly was clearly not convinced. 'It's an important question. I don't see what's so different about automatic writing. Surely you don't believe in some kind of outside force that takes people over?'

He got to his feet and moved over to perch on the arm of Carrie's chair.

'If Rud can sometimes draw on energy he can't find every day, mightn't automatic writing work the same way? I mean, come from somewhere inside the individual, too?'

He was still brooding over that comparison. He didn't care for it at all. For one thing, he didn't *invite* that sense of being taken over; most of the time he wrote with no such sense of direction from outside. He was content not to understand what it was that drove him when those moments came. He just knew it by the working deep within his guts.

He wandered into the living room, where his daughter lay on a pillow placed across a wide chair, her mother at her side. Carrie was turning out a trump. Not a tremor out of her when they found the bank had failed, taking all their savings, right in the middle of her honeymoon. She had just set to with him and made a plan.

Carrie looked up from retying a ribbon on her daughter's jacket.

'This satin is way too slippery to be practical. And how are you going to keep your wife and child in proper comfort, Mr. Rudyard Kipling, if you don't peg away at that desk in there? We won't come by and visit if you don't keep your side of the bargain.'

She was joking. They'd both been astonished. He'd been able to retrieve their fortunes so fast. And all by means of his writing, what with royalties from *Barrack-Room Ballads* on top of all the stories he had in hand. The new house was going to be a stunner, and good value at $25,000. It might be more, of course, by the time they were through.

Rud bent to kiss the hands the sleeping baby had thrown above her head. He took the mother's hand then, tracing the palm slowly with the tips of his own fingers.

'I have threats of my own, Miz Carrie. One more word and no massage for you tonight.' His wife's colour deepened as she looked up at him. 'I'll get down to work if you both promise to come in to me as soon as she's awake.'

He turned back to his mail. A little whoop of pleasure escaped him as he caught sight of the stamp on a well-stuffed envelope. It was not the Mater's hand, though it was hard to tell the two apart.

Trix had sent him a chapter for his approval; *'written some time since, alas'*, she must be in need of support. Her letter admitted as much, poor kid. He did not really see why, after getting that little ghost story of hers into the Christmas number of *Black and White*. And under her own name that time. 'Mrs. Fleming' could take the credit due to her. It was slight enough, and not exactly new, the dead lover who shows up at the ball, but that fancy was well taken, her bouquet turning up far away on the grave of the dead man. He had shuddered briefly at her account of the heroine *'who was seen walking across the room alone, head a little inclined to the left as though she were talking to someone'*.

When he thought about it, though, wasn't that story she had written for the Christmas number of the *CMG,* years and years ago, a ghost story too? About a small girl who'd died and kept reappearing to another child? He pushed away the thought that Trix was just repeating herself, going for what was safe. Difficulties, thrashing about to find your own line, were inevitable at the start.

She appeared to have no intention of giving up the struggle. He knew only too well what *not* writing did to a fellow. Trix was quite correct: *'suspended'*, *'brought to a halt'*, those were the words. He must find a way to keep her going. *'Thrice-honoured daughter of my mother,'* began his reply. '*I've been wondering whether you are being too hard on yourself. Trying to be good, you know, get it right the first time. Only William could do that. But we don't happen to go by the name of Shakespeare. I have to work on draft after draft.*'

Would that help? He thought he knew the terror of getting it wrong, which might be haunting Trix.

No wonder she was falling back on repetition.

All the same, though he hated to admit this, he did not much care for her new device of sticking scraps from the poets at the chapter head. They drowned out her voice, instead of amplifying it. He did make use of epigraphs himself but they were ones of his own making. They worked like a lens through which to read the stories, at least he hoped that was the effect. Striving to imagine how it was for her, writing, he did see that these literary insertions would make her feel safer. A link with writers who were recognised, with other poets. With himself too, of course.

She was losing her nerve, afraid that if she let go of him she'd sink on her own. How could he be sufficiently tactful? There was no-one like Trix, no-one so acute, so fine. And so in need of him and his support, he would have added, but the Joss now made her entrance in Carrie's arms, her head turning, he swore it, in search of him.

'*I'm not sure that it's working yet, Infant,*' his new paragraph opened, once he got back to his letter. '*Why don't you lay the novel aside for a while? That often helps. Come back to it later. Think how many years I've been working on* Mother Maturin. *The end's still not in sight and I'd already been struggling with it for years before Wolcott and I wrote* The Naulahka.

(That spelling's all wrong, by the way. It should have the 'h' after the 'k': didn't spot it on the proofs and the Pater won't let me forget it. But did I tell you that's what we've decided to call the new house "Naulakha"? In memory of Wolcott)

Novels really can take forever. Who knows whether I'll ever manage to finish another? But stories are a different matter. What's more, there's a solid public for them out there. How about another story for the magazines? That's the public I write for – all my stuff comes out first in the magazines.'

The new house outside Brattleboro was almost ready. While it was building, they'd paid Beatty, Carrie's brother, to oversee the work. It had seemed such a good idea, Beatty honestly employed for once but she'd come to dread the sight of him. Every encounter led to a fight.

'Carrie, will you quit lording it over me?'

Beatty had always been a bully, Carrie reminded herself, stiffening. She didn't care to imagine the way he spoke to Mai, his wife, when nobody was by. No wonder Baby Marjorie had such an anxious little face.

Now he stood blocking the doorway of her sitting room, his raised voice threatening to disturb Rud, at work on the other side of the wall.

'We're not going to talk about it in here,' she led him back through the narrow hallway, out into the sun.

When they fixed on building a house for themselves in Brattleboro, it seemed obvious to make brother Beatty a kind of clerk of works. While he was alive, Wolcott had struggled to keep Beatty on the straight, to counter his recklessness and ruthless greed. Even on his deathbed, delirious, Wolcott moaned Beatty's name. Since Beatty was now their responsibility, they'd decided the best thing would be to employ him. As a farmer Beatty was supposed to be practical and used to managing men. But she should have guessed, should have remembered…

No wonder Mother was so taken with the idea. 'The dear boy needs something to absorb his energies and he's so full of notions and fun it will work out perfectly for all of you.' Yet she must have known that Beatty had never stopped drinking.

This was not the first time Carrie'd had to challenge him about the accounts. A load of wood that had never made its way up to the site. Hire for two men for a week: they hadn't been seen either. There was more. Documents that she didn't recall seeing, that had been signed in her name.

'I suppose you want everyone in town to hear you bawling me out.'

Carrie thought she caught the smell of liquor, though it was ten in the morning.

'Beatty, this is a country road, for heaven's sake, who's to hear?'

'Me for one.' Rud emerged from Bliss Cottage, exasperated.

He took in Carrie's shame and irritation. The man was as good as a family curse, dammit.

'Your wife's been giving me a real hard time, Rud.' Beatty sent an arc of brown tobacco juice into the flower border. 'I was just asking her about a small loan.'

Registering Carrie's look of amazement, Rud guessed that nothing about a loan had been said. Trust Beatty to switch the conversation, to throw off pursuit. He breathed deeply.

'I thought we'd agreed that your last advance would be paid back by the end of June?'

It was now August. Next week they would move into the new house.

'Well, Mr. Rudyard Kipling, if you're going to be as tarnation small-minded as your dear wife, my high and mighty sister, I'm not going to hang around for you folks to insult me further.'

He was off, climbing heavily onto his mare and trotting fast away towards town, and the friends who expected him in the bar of the Brooks House hotel.

Once in Naulakha, the little family could expand into wide-panelled spaces. Carrie had a study all to herself, on the ground floor, right next to Rud's. Baby Jo took possession of the suite designed entirely for her, a bright airy day nursery standing above her father's study and a night nursery behind, without the view. No sooner had she learned to walk, though, than the thudding of her triumphant feet overhead was too much for Rud.

'I just can't think straight,' he fretted.

'It's fine, Rud, we'll just switch them over. The day nursery can be at the back. Calm down.'

*

'You do understand that if Mr. Kipling goes, Baby and I will have to leave too,' Carrie observed slowly. 'I won't let any of them leave me again,' she added more firmly.

Hearing her mistress speak of going away, Evelyn, the nursemaid, took no particular account of it at the time, as she explained later. Her employers were always full of plans. She just went on with washing out Baby's things. Only when she went downstairs with her basket of wet clothes and out of the side door in the basement to the washing line did she grasp that Mrs. Kipling's words were not a plan but a threat.

Stealing a moment by the flower garden, shading her eyes, Evelyn happened to glance aloft. There, up on the first floor was her mistress, standing out on the very edge of the wide sun porch outside the night nursery, Baby in her arms. The sun porch that stood over a drop onto broken stone. As Evelyn watched, she drew back and began to pace up and down.

Panting with effort, stumbling, Rud left the road and ploughed uphill through the meadow's ragged golden rod. The long stand of Naulakha, backed by pines, rose ahead on the crest. Out on the open sun porch up on the first floor, Rud made out the figure of his wife, Baby Jo in her arms, standing in the corner, at bay.

A few feet from them stood Jim Conland, who had delivered Jo. Approaching below, Rud could make out the doctor was speaking quietly, his voice low and steady. Carrie did not appear to be listening, her fingers did not cease plucking at the baby's shawl. Yet as he drew closer, Rud saw her raise her eyes briefly to Conland's, if only for a moment. As Rud came within reach of the stone steps, the doctor, sensing his approach, motioned him to be still. The quiet voice never paused in its unhurried speech.

'It's getting a little cooler now and I was wondering whether we ought to take Baby inside. What do you think, Carrie?'

The plucking fingers paused. The mother's head turned back, withdrawing her gaze from its determined stare across the distant hillside to look in surprise at her own hands. 'Why Jim,' she exclaimed, 'I believe you are right.'

His arm under her elbow, the doctor steered Carrie with her little hostage back through the open door into the nursery.

Should he follow? Rud was shaking. The baby, the baby was safe. In the exquisite relief of the moment he felt giddy. The silent shriek vibrating against his ribs softened away. Fury rose in him. What had he ever done, that Carrie should be capable of this? A disagreement, that was all that had come between them that afternoon. Didn't he have a right to go out on his own without a crisis like this? Surely, other men did?

Still fixed in place below the sun porch, he didn't notice the continuing drop in temperature but a change in the light, a suffusing colour, roused him. He was about to make his way round to the side door on the lower level, when Jim emerged, surprising him. He seemed unruffled though his tone was sober.

'That wife of yours is altogether too hard on herself.'

This was so unexpected that Rud thought he had misheard. Apparently registering his surprise, Conland smiled. 'I know Rud, I know. She's just put you through as severe a fright as she could manage. Other people too. I can't say I enjoyed it myself but I do usually manage to talk them down.'

'Them?'

'The desperate ones who want you to understand but don't know why. If it won't offend you, I'm going to play host in your house, Rud, and call for some whisky. We can talk more easily about this if we sit and take things quietly for a while. Evelyn's taken charge of Baby and I've left Carrie sleeping. I think we'll stay down here, out of the way.'

Rud was too shaken to offer any lead of his own but mutely followed Conland as he led the way to the study. The English maid who finally brought the tray with its decanter and siphon and the two heavy glasses was subdued, darting her eyes at each of them in turn, furtively looking for an explanation for the trouble of the afternoon. Conland's smile was wry.

'I guess the kitchen's not recovered from the sight of Evelyn in hysterics. It was your cook's quick thinking located me and sent the boy running for you, Rud. But all's well now.'

In spite of his friend's attempts to calm him, Rud could not remain seated. When he paused in front of the bay window to stare out, it took both hands to steady his glass.

'She'll be her old self in the morning, you'll see,' Jim encouraged him. 'And I've seen no other sign of instability in Carrie. Rather too much steady determination for her own good. But let me ask you –'

'How much of it do you think she took in? I mean the Joss. The Baby. Baby Jo.'

Jim Conland was startled. It was the child Rud was panicking about, not the mother. Stroking his hair back off his forehead, he paused to consider.

'I truly believe that Baby Jo slept through most everything: she only cried a little when I handed her over to Evelyn – I think that woke her.'

Rud came to a halt. 'Are you sure of that?'

Conland showed his surprise.

'Why would I tell you so, otherwise?'

Rud's face changed and he looked embarrassed. A healthy sign.

'And I haven't even thanked you, or begun to thank you –' his voice wasn't quite steady.

'Come now, Rud, do sit down, or I'll feel I have to join you in this march around your property.'

At last Rud subsided, sinking into an armchair.

'Do you think it would be useful if you told me a little about what happened today, anything that might have made Carrie act that way this particular afternoon?'

Conland trod delicately, not wanting to suggest any hint of blame – no blame of any person or act. That would get them all nowhere. And it was no good just jumping in with his own ideas: of course, he had plenty of those, he hadn't lived in Brattleboro as a doctor these twelve years without knowing something about the family histories that were still astir in present lives.

And once Carrie Balestier had come back to town as Mrs. Rudyard Kipling it had revived people's memories concerning the Balestiers of Beechwood and the orphan children of that failed lawyer, the no-account Henry Balestier:

'Dying young, let alone leaving a widow and three young children, was just his final and most tiresome way of acting feckless,' Conland had heard Mrs. Goodenough declare to her particular friends, as they sat with their sewing out on the porch of her house on Main St.

That afternoon all the windows had been standing open against the heat. He couldn't avoid overhearing, in the ground floor bedroom where he was dressing the ulcers on old Ma Goodenough's leg. Taking it as his professional duty to know all he could of these walking chronicles, his patients, he'd lingered over his task.

'It beats me why that eight-year-old child should have set so much store by him,' another voice – Mrs. Harrison's? – took up. 'They say Carrie shrieked and screamed when they told her he was gone. She made out as she wanted to sit up with the body because she believed she could make him come back.'

'Oh, my stars' – several rockers creaked violently under agitated movement.

'They didn't let her?'

'Never in the world. They got the doctor to give her a sleeping draught so she was out of the way until the funeral was over.'

'I believe Mr. Balestier was real attached to that little girl,' a different voice interposed.

There it was, the individual detail, the critical one that betrayed the inner shape of things. So that was Carrie Kipling.

'No good doctoring if you were only interested in bones,' he always said. 'They're not all that shape us from inside.'

Now the doctor in him waited for Rud to respond to the cautious investigation he'd set in train. An angry flush was already darkening

Rud's face.

'Perhaps you can understand it, Jim, but I'm blowed if I do. I simply told Carrie that I would be out for some time. I just wanted to go out. And suddenly she was crying and pleading with me not to go. It was the same this morning, now I think of it, when I showed her the invitation from Norton. A few days away, that's all it would have meant. It's all very well for her to say she can't leave the baby but there are men I need to talk to over here, men like Twain and Norton down in Harvard. Not to say Henry Adams and all those Washington folk. Over here they're the ones with their hands on the tiller and there are things they need to hear.'

The doctor looked on, encouragingly but in silence, somewhat taken aback by Rud's presumption, his confidence in the universal value of his opinions.

'I have a little experience of these things – my mother's highly strung, you know – it was all quite out of proportion and I told Carrie as much. I was coming back for dinner...' Indignation raised his voice half a tone.

'Does she usually offer objections?'

Conland raised the decanter enquiringly but Rud shook his head.

'Not like today. Of course she does get lonely. I'm awful busy, but I can't live her life for her. She needs to make friends; this is her home town, for heaven's sake.'

'I guess that you may have put your finger on it, Rud. It is Carrie's home town, in a way. But I'm not sure that's to her advantage. Her family, the Balestiers of Beechwood, are big folks round here. Yet Carrie didn't necessarily get much appreciation or respect herself, the summers when her mother brought them down from New York. No father, no cash, her brother Beatty the favoured one.'

'Heaven knows why. Dear old Wolcott was worth ten of him. But Beatty's still the blue-eyed boy round here; the family won't hear a word against him.'

Conland poured himself a finger of whisky. He had heard there was trouble in that quarter. When the young Kiplings appointed Beatty to act as a kind of clerk of works for them, locals knew it was only a matter of time before they fell out. Beatty wasn't exactly crooked but you wouldn't call him straight.

'From the start, there was way too much spirit in Carrie for Brattleboro – the spirit that took her off West with her brother, even before she shipped to London to keep house for him. Your wife's a very high strung woman. There are advantages to that as well as the disadvantages you've seen today.'

His listener was on his feet again. Two of a kind.

'Do you mean the child isn't safe with her?'

'Good God, no. Carrie lives for that baby, same as she lives for you. Today, I'm ready to wager, was an exception. She's been under a certain amount of strain – I believe she had sole responsibility for your move into Naulakha, in your absence? And of course, business dealings with family can bring their own problems.' He didn't care to make more explicit reference to Beatty's loud and public complaints about Carrie and her tight control over the petty cash.

'No, it's my belief that there are cues – perhaps triggers you need to avoid or work round, that's all.' He put down his glass and fixed Rud with his gaze.

'Carrie lost her father at a young age. Then, as you told me yourself, Wolcott, the brother she was close to, died, in spite of all her efforts to save him. That leaves its mark. All I would say is, think carefully, talk it over quietly with Carrie, when you have to leave her yourself.'

Rud continued standing, now looking depressed. 'Carrie used to be game for every kind of lark. Now she doesn't dance that dance any more –'

The doctor rose to face him and putting his hand on the younger man's shoulder said quietly:

'We all have to make these accommodations, you know, me included. We're all just a mite crazy, in parts.'

Riding home, Conland recalled that Rud's father would be back at Naulakha to continue the visit he was making in a day or two. From the moment he had chanced on Lockwood Kipling, sitting across from Baby Jo on the nursery floor, drawing animals for her, with sound accompaniment, Conland had recognised a benevolent presence. Lockwood Kipling would steady the ship.

*

Life in Naulakha did pick up its even tenor, soothed by Lockwood's presence. Eighteen months later, however, long-standing tensions flared up once more.

'Beatty is way too much for me,' Carrie finally complained to her mother. 'You know we give him fifty cents bonus on every man he hires for us? Well, I've just found out that he takes the bonus then sets them to work on his own farm. But that's not the worst of it. We're not the only ones he cheats. He's bringing shame on the whole family between that and his drinking.'

'Drunk or sober, Beatty is a gentleman,' was the response. Carrie might have known Anna Smith Balestier would countenance no criticism of the son who remained to her.

Controlling her rage at this betrayal she pressed on.

'Mother, surely you agree we ought to help him to go straight. A shock might do it. We both hold mortgages on that farm of his. What if we foreclosed on them?'

The stare of affronted withdrawal told her she had gone too far.

Rud attempted to reason with Beatty more than once, making his way up to Beechwood, Beatty's place, hoping for a serious talk.

'If you could see your way to give up the bottle, old chap, for a while, and get yourself really dug in at work – that farm of yours could be a wonderful asset if you put your back into it –'

Beatty continued to regard him with an amiable smile.

'Of course it won't pay at first but that need not be a difficulty. I'd see that Mai and little Marjorie have all they need.'

'Sounds a swell offer, Rud.'

'You think you might?'

'I guess the right time to start would be the beginning of next season. I'm thinking of going into hogs.'

And so it went on, from one month, one year, to the next.

There was something unknowable, something that wouldn't, couldn't, play fair in Beatty, that looked to do harm. Impossible to complain to Mother of more private, more disturbing evidence. They would have to deal with it themselves. Rud hated being interrupted when he was his writing, so Carrie put off sharing her concerns till he emerged from his study for lunch. Sitting at her desk, she looked up at him.

'Jo's malted milk has started disappearing from the icebox. It's not you, is it, Rud? I thought not. It must be Janet. Though I did think she was more reliable.'

His cheerful, 'end of a well-spent morning' smile faded.

'Come on, Carrie, you don't know that. Better get the girl in and ask her about it.'

But the local girl who was employed to help the cook seemed angry. 'No, sir, I ain't had nothing out of the icebox. If you're *sure* you want to know,' she looked hard at Carrie, 'best keep watch first thing.' She would not be drawn further.

At daybreak next morning, Rud was standing guard, bleary-eyed, in the kitchen. While the sky was still pale, hearing the tap of the latch of the basement door, he drew back into the shadows of the hall.

A cautious step on the stairs and Beatty emerged into the kitchen and reached for the icebox.

'Can I help you, Beatty?'

Before the usual charming smile fixed itself, the look of a trapped animal rearranged the intruder's features.

'His excuses were so fluent, if I hadn't begun to know his depths, I might have been tempted to believe him,' Rud told Carrie unhappily, sitting on her bed as he waited for his bath to fill.

After that, Carrie could never feel quite as safe at home. Beatty had always had to have the best and always, as Wolcott used to say, at the expense of someone else.

* * *

Calcutta remained stifling, in every sense, but Trix had found a solution to her difficulties. A new outlet. No more tears and exclamations over Jack and over her writing. She was more at peace than she'd been for some time. Also, more hopeful, even exultant. Experimenting with the 'automatic writing' that everyone was talking about, seemed to have released something in her. And it came to her so easily. Of course, Mama had always prided herself on having 'the sight', but as a daughter she'd looked on the claim with scepticism. Be that as it might, here she was, picking up messages and scraps of poetry from who knew where and passing them on, as directed, by who knew whom.

But here lay the great joy of it. Discovering this unsuspected gift had somehow freed her to write stories again. When her new one, 'The Little Pink House', came out in the *Pall Mall Magazine* she felt she was really back to her old self. She had even dared to sign her own name to it this time: 'Trix Kipling'. It was tiresome that the editor had thought 'Trix' too undignified and had corrected it – as he thought – to 'Beatrice Kipling'.

Never mind. She'd started another novel. In such good heart she could even face with equanimity the prospect of going back to Scotland when they were on home leave later in the year. It would have been more than a little sad, if it'd not been so comical, the clash of taste between Jack's family and her own. She could laugh at it here at home in Calcutta where the menace of the approaching Hot Weather was already to be felt. The skies had lost any depth of blue and were paling day by day, a reminder of the white glare that was to come. Lying awake at night, she fancied that she caught the snarl of tigers, carried on the stifling airs from the mangroves of the delta.

In Simla, the early arrivals would be bracing themselves for a different challenge. Turning their experienced gaze around the cottages they'd rented for the season, making sure before the world started arriving that they had their full quota of chairs.

Better to get their order in early, well in advance of the rush on light cane armchairs that was certain to come. Charm had to be imported forcibly by those who could not do without it; the *darzies* would be sitting out on the verandahs of the sensitive, one foot at the wheel of their little Singers. Both hands feeding through the printed muslins at three rupees the length, for the curtains that would make such a difference. It was a pity that Mama took so little interest. Some people had their muslins specially dyed. 'A hue between apricot and shrimp-pink' as she dreamily recalled, was particularly flattering to the complexion, day or night.

Another year when she wouldn't be lingering among the wild white roses along the Mall at Simla. Perhaps it was as well to give up all that their frail moonlit scent brought back. To forget Ian Hamilton – really no more than a boy then – and the look of worship on his face when he asked if he might show her his poems.

How brief that moment had been. At the first sight of Miss Muir, after one dance with her, Trix Kipling, had been forgotten.

Once more she saw the trails of flickering light that marked the evening of a party. Flaring cotton seeds in saucers of oil laid out ceremoniously in welcome. Yet the points of light started guttering, threatening to die. With a shake of her head, Trix fought to clear her blurred vision. Lucky to have been young and reasonably pretty, lucky now to be safely married to a good man like Jack. You couldn't expect to keep them, those sharp-edged feelings forever. For a moment they might return, with the memory of a flaring lamp outdoors. A night touched with delicious chill.

Her heart sank at the thought of the chill that awaited them in Scotland. In fact, chill was too mild a term for the fierce damp that prowled through most of the houses she'd visited in Scotland. But before she had to face all that again in September she was going to see Rud. True, she wouldn't have him to herself. They would all, Carrie and Rud, Jack and herself, be expected to gather at Tisbury – wherever that was – she imagined, summoned together at the ancestral altars. 'Not very kind,' she admonished herself quickly. Only the meanest spirit could grudge her mother the relief of having left India for good, though Trix was less sure that Papa was quite ready for the life of retirement.

Rud had never brought Carrie out to India. Trix had known he wouldn't. He'd never come back, never be allowed, or more likely, never take the risk. A few years back, he'd described finding Ayah, still alive and living in Bombay. She herself really couldn't bring back any memory of Ayah yet Trix envied how much that had meant to him. He'd drawn a line under that meeting, she was sure. India was over, for him. But not for her. It made her feel rather lost.

Well, before the close of July, Rud and Carrie would at least be joining them all in Tisbury. Maybe not staying at 'The Gables'– couldn't they change that name? – certainly not, when she thought about it. Not only was there no room but she was sure Carrie would arrange things so that she had Rud entirely to herself for part of the time. Trix knew he wouldn't resist but she did wonder how long this attempt to graft himself onto the Balestiers could last. Loyal as he was to Carrie, his letters hinted that relations with Carrie's brother Beatty were becoming strained. Rud always hated the feeling that he was being cheated.

Trix didn't like to admit it but she was secretly glad, on the whole, that she wouldn't be meeting baby Josephine. It was surely wise, the plan to leave her with her Balestier grandmother. Mama hadn't a talent for babies.

Rud wanted to see what she was writing, now that she had managed to get started again. She wondered whether to tell him about the automatic writing when she saw him next month at Home. He ought to be interested and approve; heaven knew he was convinced that at times he found himself writing in a sort of trance.

Alice and Lockwood did succeed in gathering their children to them at Tisbury in their detached grey stone house on Hindon Lane. Trix and Jack Fleming were to stay with them at The Gables, while Rud and Carrie put up at a nearby hotel. Struggling to find her feet in the silent, unacknowledged tussle with Alice, Carrie was careful to keep her mother's counsel in mind.

'You'll never win, Carrie, if you try to get a man away from his mother.'

It took all her self-discipline but she usually managed to swallow her resentment and look pleasant when Alice appealed to 'Ruddy darling' for his opinion. She never wanted to know what Carrie thought.

'Of course, I'm only the little American wife,' Carrie would mutter as she brushed out her hair at the end of another evening when only Lockwood engaged her in conversation. She kept to herself the dawning confidence that she was again pregnant.

If she was, would that make matters worse, between herself and Trix? No sign of any children in that quarter and everything so chilly, so stiff between the Flemings. Perhaps that was why Trix acted so difficult with her, contradicting everything she said while always making a ridiculous fuss of Rud.

Carrie recalled an evening when Alice and Lockwood had retired early, both with colds coming on. They were barely out of the drawing room before Trix was on her feet:

'Ruddy, you do remember Ian Hamilton? I've had *such* a letter from him, he's been up on the Frontier and ran into Dunsterville. If you're very good I'll let you read it.'

She tripped across the room towards him, two or three sheets of paper held fluttering above her head.

Rud pretended to snap at them, like a terrier. They fell laughing onto the sofa.

And they were off, heads together, talking India. As they went on, their voices increasing in pitch, she'd picked up phrases she took to be Hindustani.

'No, you're wrong, Trix, you've forgotten. You've never had a head for topography. The Kashmir Bazaar is closer to the Delhi Gate.'

Rud was enjoying himself.

Carrie believed Trix cast a glance of triumph in her direction as she bore her brother off to the Pater's study, in search of the books that would settle their argument.

For the moment she had to stomach Trix's behaviour. It was a mercy that Trix would be going back to India with her long streak of a husband, while she herself would be returning to Brattleboro with Rud in tow. She liked being indispensable. He entrusted her with organising every detail of their travels.

* * *

Jack Fleming didn't care for automatic writing and all the flummery that went with it from sitting in dark rooms, to table-tapping and calling on spirits of the dead. He'd made his views very clear and imagined that would be the end of it. Yet it seemed Trix wasn't prepared to give it up.

Solar topee still in his hand, unregarded for a moment, Jack was trembling with rage. 'I cannot believe that you would so defy me. My own wife.'

Trix shuddered as she came back to herself. With a bruised look about the eyes she registered the fact of his presence.

She was wan but when she responded her voice had an edge.

'I can't give it up. It's made me sure that what I'm writing in my stories is true. I can believe in myself again. Without it I'd never have finished my novel.' Her tone softened a little. 'You seemed so pleased that Heinemann are going to bring out *The Pinchbeck Goddess* and with my own name, "Mrs. J.M. Fleming", on the cover.'

For some moments he didn't know how to continue.

He'd returned from camp some days before he was expected. The Survey's planning had been unusually ineffective and there was nothing for it but to return to Calcutta, the job half done. They'd intended to finish mapping that remote district before the monsoon. Striding into the drawing room unannounced, he'd found it empty.

The *khamsamah* had assured him that the Memsahib had spent the morning at home 'Writing, writing, Colonel Sahib' and had not yet left for her usual game of tennis at the Saturday Club.

Glancing at the row of invitations on the mantelpiece, he'd

made for his study, to put down the map cases he was carrying. Far too valuable to leave in the office, he preferred to keep his current work under his hand. But it was the expression on his wife's face as he'd glimpsed it through the open door of her dressing room that brought him to a halt. Rapt, eyelids lowered, he'd known even before he'd taken a step closer that her right hand would be stretched out quivering before her.

He'd thrown the door wide open.

Now his anger, unassuaged, lent him words.

'Good God, Trix. You promised there'd be no more of these damned trances. I cannot believe that you would deceive me in this fashion.'

The colour returning to her cheeks, Trix rose to her feet. 'Deceive, Jack? What can you mean? You know very well that I have never given you any such promise. You've indicated that you mistrust the world of psychical research but –'

'Mistrust – it's a lot of foolery, dangerous foolery and I'll not have my wife mixed up in it.'

With that he slammed his fist down on her desk.

'Then you should have taken a different wife,' she glared back at him. 'I can't *choose* to keep apart from that world, it's part of me. Whether I like it or not. And I don't always enjoy these powers I seem to have been born with – I can't shake them off or suppress them. They will have their way.'

He hated hearing this. Hated the way it took her away from him into a world from which he recoiled.

There was nowhere to put the topee down in here.

'Could you not stop cultivating them? I'm sure it does you no good. Undermines your health, which is a thing none of us can afford out here.'

Sweat was trickling down inside his collar.

'Oh Jack, just the reverse is true.' Trix was clasping her hands now. 'I've found that I get dreadful headaches and pains in my arms if I resist when the impulse comes over me.' He was frowning, uncertain. 'Besides, it's explained so much to me. About my own writing, my stories. I've been really afraid. What if I was describing in them might be just fancy. No better than lies, really...'

At sea now, he looked at her helplessly. He turned towards the door.

At once her voice took on that familiar conciliatory tone.

'But you're tired, my dear. Let me give orders. What would you like?'

He put her aside with a gesture.

'*Nimbu pani*? Tea? It's a little early for a peg.'

Stiffly. 'I'll take the lime juice. With salt.' He wished she would not use the native lingo with him.

Seated in a long chair, the drink in his hand, he began again, methodically.

'Tell me what you mean. I don't understand how it helps you. I find it very implausible.'

'Jack, automatic writing isn't something I invented. I only gave it a try after reading about it in the *Review of Reviews*. It's a form of research, into energies, invisible forces, like electricity. We're only starting to tap the world of the unseen. Clever, eminent people take it very seriously.'

She took a sip from her glass.

'I know that's what they tell you. It doesn't make it any better.'

'How can I explain if you will interrupt? I can't tell you how surprised I was when my hand began to write – real messages – to transmit them, actually. At first it was just scribble, nonsense rhymes. But then there came words that made sense.'

It wasn't going to work, Jack's face was stony.

'Looking them over, afterwards, I found I'd written a whole poem. And I realised, all of a sudden, that it was about a painting of St. George I once saw. One by Papa's old friend, William de Morgan.'

She'd only made him look dazed.

'De Morgan the tile maker? What has he to do with all this?'

How to explain? It all seemed so simple when William had encouraged her. Her poem made sense to him and to Evelyn his wife. 'We have a duty to explore these things,' he'd told her, in response to her shy but excited letter.

Trix braced herself.

'I knew Mr. de Morgan would want to read my poem and I was right. He said it had a political meaning that it referred to our policy in the Transvaal.'

She attempted to stand tall, defiant, before him.

'Our policy in the Transvaal? What utter nonsense. De Morgan, forsooth. I've never heard the man was blessed with any common sense.'

He pushed his glass away.

She would not be silenced.

'I do believe this special writing has meaning for the world beyond myself. Since then it's happened again many times. Real messages come through. That's how I've come to think it's all real. It's out there. Not just in my own head.'

She'd so often repeated the arguments comparing spiritualism with the telegraph for his benefit. She could tell he was no more convinced this time.

Wearily, he rose to his feet. But Trix hadn't finished.

'It's a gift – I have it and so do many other people. You might be able to do it yourself if you only gave it a chance.'

His face reflected such alarm that she broke into nervous laughter.

'I think you're playing with fire. While you are under my roof, I'll not have it if I can help it. I'll away to my bath.'

She knew he would say no more on this or any other topic for many days.

* * *

It was early in February, and Jo had just turned three, when Carrie gave birth to a second daughter. Elsie, they'd called her, a name his mother sometimes used. What with the monthly nurse, for a while there'd been too many women in the house for Rud's taste. By May, though, all anxiety and disruption around the birth, together with the long Vermont winter, were at an end. Full plumes of white lilac leaned over the fences.

Sweat was running into Rud's eyes as he pushed his bicycle up the hill, pausing every now and then to suck at his grazed wrist. Falling off made him no better than a kid. He should have worn a lighter jacket: spring was rushing into summer faster than he'd thought. Perhaps he'd rest once he got to the stretch of road they called The Pines on the way past dear old Bliss Cottage.

Beatty was level with him, in his buckboard, before he knew it. Rud no sooner put up a hand in salute than he was obliged to drop it in order to clutch the handlebars and brake sharply. What the devil? Beatty was turning round and coming back to overtake him. He was blocking the road.

'I've a bone to pick with you, Rud Kipling. That is if you can spare me some of your precious time.'

A breath then he stood silent. He wasn't going to reply to abuse.

'I happen to know that you've been spreading lies about me. Goddamned lies, all over this town,' Beatty slurred.

He wanted to wipe the sweat off but he didn't dare let go of the bicycle.

'If you have any message for me, speak to my lawyers.'

'Going about town boasting that it's you and your cash that's the only thing keeping me from bankruptcy. I'm going to whip the goddamned soul out of you for it.'

Beatty loomed over him, from his seat in the buckboard, a big man red in the face, swaying and waving his hands.

Rud caught the familiar taint of whisky: he could see himself being swatted like a fly. No-one around, nothing to get in Beatty's way.

Keep talking, keep looking into his eyes. Grip those handlebars, then the trembling won't show. Keep the voice steady.

'Do you mean personal violence?'

His words sounded thin and abstract, out there on the road.

'This is what I mean, Mr. Famous Kipling. I'm going to blow

your goddamned brains out if you haven't publicly retracted your lies within a week.'

Beatty jerked at the reins and was off.

Rud sank to the dusty road, shaking all over. Hearing the rattle of approaching wheels he tried to get up, ready to defend himself, but his legs wouldn't hold him. Tears of relief started to his eyes, as Matt Howard, their own coachman jumped down from his seat in the buggy with a cry of concern. He allowed himself to be taken home.

Beatty Balestier taken to court by his own brother-in-law! Laughter filled the upper floors of the Town Hall, as men in dusty overalls and women in gingham sun hats crowded along the benches.

'It's good as a comic show.'

'Just as well they've moved it out of Justice Newton's office. Blamed newspapermen're almost crowding out real Brattleboro folk.'

'It's way overdue, putting that young whippersnapper, Rudyard Kipling, in his place. Asked for a private post office to be set up, just for hisself, a while back. Can you credit that?'

'Fool writer-fellow's bringing a case against his own brother -in-law for threatening his life. I guess that high and mighty Carrie put him up to it. There's no love lost there.'

'You mind your mouth, young man!' a woman's voice broke in. 'That Beatty Balestier may sound like a fine fellow when he's got a glass in his hand, but he surely is a torment to his family. This is a black day for his sister, however you look at it.'

The men turned their attention back to the attorney for the defence, George B. Hitt. Sharp as a whip. He was going to run rings around that little British prig of a writer.

There was no formal court setting. Rud just sat where he'd been told to, at the front of the room. He kept twisting his hat between his hands, putting it down, then picking it up again. The world had gone mad around him. When he went to his lawyer about Beatty he was in fear of his life. Carrie'd insisted on it: Beatty had to be brought to heel somehow. He never imagined that before he knew it, the State's Attorney would file a complaint and Beatty would be arrested.

The blasted fellow knew what that meant to Carrie. He'd taken a positive pleasure in refusing to let them go bail for him. Beatty meant to rub Carrie's nose in it. Make her watch her brother being marched off to the lock-up.

But apparently that was the process here: take the evidence, in a 'hearing on probable cause' in a 'justice court' then decide whether to proceed to trial. It was all out of his hands. Even worse. He still couldn't quite believe it. He himself, the injured party, had to be cross-examined in public.

Wiping his spectacles, replacing them, he came to. George B. Hitt with his mean little mouth was standing in front of him. The fellow was evidently waiting for a response. But what was the question?

'Can you confirm the date of your marriage?' Hitt repeated.

Years, dates danced wildly in his head. He stuttered.

'In '92, I think. Summer of '92.' That couldn't be right. When was Jo born? 'Or spring.'

The first murmurs of laughter began.
One question followed another, relentless. Hitt's tone was hatefully familiar.

'I'll give you "forgot". I'll give you "thought", you little liar.'

The voice of That Woman in Southsea, her very tone, waking sensations that just unmanned him.

He hadn't meant to throw her beastly book away, he just forgot.

Brattleboro, the Town Hall, were dissolving round him: he stood trembling, dizzy under her anger, helpless. Would he never, never escape?

Once more he fought to hang on to what was true, what had really happened. But what if no-one believed him here either? His head throbbed.

'Mr. Balestier seemed not in his right senses, crazy. He yelled, sort of.'

It didn't sound convincing, even to him.

'You felt your business dealings with Mr. Balestier were too complicated, I believe?'

Now that vile, pushy little attorney was demanding that he expose their private financial affairs.

Sweat broke out on him again and again as he forced the words out.

'He would send up and get all the ready cash he wanted for his own affairs and pay us back when he felt like it, in kind. Work it out months afterwards, that kind of thing. Get advances all along the line.'

Was there no respect at all for privacy? Hitt was pressing him to reveal his most intimate motives.

'You claim that you had been "holding Mr. Balestier up by the slack of his pants". Has that been your mission?'

He thought he might be sick. No sign of a glass of water.

The pledge made in Wolcott's memory: that he and Carrie would look after Beatty, keep the wild younger brother on the straight. Must that too be dragged out of him?

'I have done my best. I came here to Brattleboro for that purpose, to help the boy if I could.'

The words came out awkwardly. Throat too dry.

'This has been your main object?'

He managed to force the word out.

'Yes.'

Laughter broke out all round him as Hitt drawled, 'And incidentally you have written some, I suppose?'

The old dizziness claimed him. He couldn't get his head clear. Yet he must, there was no-one else to stand up for him.

Hitt had stuck his thumbs in his waistcoat. Mountebank.

'When did you last see Mr. Balestier before this incident?'

'Not since the end of April, I believe.'

'Is it not the case that you encountered him at least three times during that period, on May 1st in passing on the road and twice on the day following in town?'

It came back to him now. Nothing for it but to agree. Through clenched teeth:

'I believe that is correct.'

Hitt only wanted to undercut him. He tried to be honest: he agreed that he chose to avoid some people. Immediately Hitt was in there with, 'I didn't suppose you were prepared to speak to reporters.'

Laughter. Were those shouts of applause? He knew he'd become notorious for turning reporters away. People didn't like him.

Hitt tripped him up again; nothing he said was allowed to carry any weight. He couldn't make them see how mad and dangerous Beatty had been.

He tried once more, his voice squeaking dangerously.

'He looked perfectly crazy. I swear I think he was raving.'

'Shouldn't you have got him examined for insanity, then, rather than accusing him of violence?'

Was this really happening, this public mockery? Not just a dream?

'I mean, his face was actually blue.' How could he make them see?

'Do you believe that colour to be a sign of insanity?'

Feet were stamping as if at a show.

His left eyelid wouldn't stop twitching. He shook his head.

'Have you ever at any time seen Mr. Balestier out with a gun?' Hitt demanded.

'No.' But wait, that's wrong. 'I mean, yes. No, I have seen him with one, out gunning.'

'Then he was gunning for game, not gunning for Kiplings?'

He was utterly powerless but he *would not* surrender.

A pause. Hitt was pretending to consult his papers.

'What was the reason you didn't stay to hear out Mr. Balestier's complaint?' he shot out.

Rud summoned himself. 'It was the first time I'd had my life threatened and I didn't know the etiquette.'

The room fell still around him.

Even as some composure returned to him, he hesitated: that wasn't true. In Southsea, when there was no-one to hear him, he'd felt as though he were going to die.

'Can you explain why you didn't just agree to take back whatever language of yours had offended Mr. Balestier, in order to calm him down?'

Rud was ready now: 'I wouldn't retract a word for fear of death from any living man.'

For a second he caught Beatty's eye where he stood apart, hands on hips, hat tipped over his eyes, a cigar in his mouth. Beatty sneered.

The State's Attorney seemed appalled by the morning's work. When the court resumed at two o'clock and it was his turn to put questions, he spoke softly.

'Now Mr. Kipling can you explain to us what had made Mr. Balestier so angry, in your own opinion?'

The relief. Being addressed civilly. An intelligent face.

'I believe he was incensed at some offers of help I had made him, instead of dropping him altogether as I ought to have done. Because I suggested that under certain conditions I would pay his creditors.'

He had his voice under control now.

'Why did such an offer seem appropriate to you?'

A reasonable question. Looking the State's Attorney straight in the eye:

'He always seemed on the edge of financial break-up, always in deep water.'

'Can you describe the course of your business relations with Mr. Balestier?'

'There was a period of about six months that he worked beautifully at overseeing the construction of our new house then he tailed off and didn't do much. Some while back we had to stop using him.'

He'd never felt so tired.

'Can you say why?'

It was unpleasant but he'd better come out with it.

'He was not altogether sober generally. In fact,' feeling a spurt of energy, 'he was just plain ugly in the morning.'

He turned to look across the room. Beatty was making an attempt to swagger then he pulled his hat low and made for the door.

Rud was too worn out to take it in at the close of the afternoon, when Justice William S. Newton placed Beatty Balestier under bonds to appear at the County Court at its September term, to face charges yet to be drawn up.

At home once more, Rud was sitting on the floor of his study, down by the bookshelves. Though the volume on his knees lay open, the pages swung back and forth, unmarked. At least now he was shaved. It was the first day they had not spent in court.

'Rud, won't you see Doctor Conland? He's got Mr. Childs with him and another friend.' The effort to dredge up the name was just too much for her.

He came to, as she'd hoped, at the sound of Jim Conland's name.

'Where is he?' and Rud shambled after her, through her study and into the middle room.

It was a deputation. They wanted him to know that he was held in undiminished respect. 'And to keep honouring us by your presence here, where you have so many friends who love you and hold you in high regard.'

The three figures swam before her. Carrie steadied herself.

Rud was slowly shaking his head.

'I don't know. I don't know. But I appreciate – I am grateful –' he turned away, his hands waving helplessly, and left the room.

The men lowered their eyes then turned to Carrie. Each took her by the hand. As from a distance she heard the kindly meant phrases: 'soon himself again, sensitive temperament, Hitt no gentleman'.

Their steps were heavy on the porch as they went away.

The following morning there was no question of shaving. Rud slept on through the afternoon. It was all she could do to persuade him to take a bath before he stumbled back into bed. For a fortnight or more Rud retreated into sleep, either in bed or on the sofa in his study. Nothing roused him, not even Jo, when she begged him to play with her.

'Dadda, be my tiger for me again, my tiger that I ride.'

Rud looked through her. Carrie hurried the child away.

Carrie did her utmost to hide the reports in the press. Rud asked for the newspapers almost feverishly but she put him off. 'Nothing come through from the city, problems at the railhead.' She trusted that he would never see the cruel parody of his poem *Danny Deever'* in the *Boston Post*.

What's that a-lopin down the lane? asked copper ready-made
It's Rudyard running for his life the first selectman said.'

Stanza after stanza, mocking her too.

What makes his wife look down so glum? asked copper ready-made.
It's family pride, it's family pride...'

They could endure no repeat of those days in court. They must be out of Brattleboro before the hearing in September. The case against Beatty would be allowed to drop.

Meanwhile, what was to be done about Rud?

She thanked God for Jim Conland, their own doctor, who finally pulled him round, by means of company and fishing trips as much as his bottles of tonic. That nerve specialist in Boston with his advice to give up tobacco was no help at all. But Jim, having been a seaman in his youth, had more at his command than medicine.

'What do you say to a little trip into Massachusetts, maybe to the port of Gloucester, since you're always at me for information about life on the cod banks for that book you're working on?' he asked, casually.

The light was coming back to Rud's eyes on his return.

'By Jove, those fellows are tough.' He could hardly wait to get inside the house to begin telling her what he had learned.

It set him off on a new tack: always what he needed. Not that she herself greatly enjoyed *Captains Courageous*. The tale of a spoiled boy saved by spending time before the mast didn't mean much to her, though it seemed there were readers enough for that kind of yarn. It was a trap, really, Rud's versatility. There were things he got involved in writing that weren't worthy of him.

'We both know it, Carrie,' Rud said soon after his return. 'Our life over here has been poisoned. There's nothing for it but to make our retreat, go back to England.'

She could only agree. Leave the country, at least for a while.

She wanted to believe that they would come back home, in time. Celebrate Thanksgiving, tap their maples for sugar once more. The barn was so handsome: they would have dancing out there after dinner again, with cider and sandwiches, kerosene lamps and simple stuff gowns. They would. Her fists clenched: Brattleboro was not going to drive her out for good.

On the morning of their departure, their old friend Molly Cabot found them both overwhelmed, Carrie for once weeping openly, Rud quite frozen. Sad enough herself, Molly was astonished to hear him choke out:

'It's the hardest thing I have ever had to do.'

She hadn't been prepared for such an unqualified statement.

Before handing over the key to Matt Howard, who would be acting as caretaker, Molly wandered back through the wood-panelled hall into the deserted space of Naulakha.

In the kitchen, wood still burned in the great black range. Absently she put up a hand to close a cupboard door that stood ajar, as she passed on and into the dining room with its blank oval table, its dozen empty chairs. The Tiffany lamps on the sideboard stood drab, unlit.

With the folding doors standing open, she could see right through the middle room into Carrie's study beyond, and even further into the study that had been Rud's. In the afternoons they'd gather for tea in there, served from the brass tray that came from Benares. A wedding present from his sister, Carrie had told her.

That wasn't the only sign of India. Those printed cottons that hung at the windows came from Lahore, sent by Lockwood following a request from Rud. He'd found the embroidered wall-hangings for them out there, too.

Molly recalled now how Lockwood had laughed at Rud.

'Vermont won't ever turn into India, if that's what you want.'

She pictured Rud, defensive in his reply.

'I like the feel of these stuffs hanging about. They remind me. I want Jo – and Elsie too, of course – to be as happy here as I was then.'

Remembering his words she shivered as she stood alone in the newly-abandoned house.

Surveying the painted screens, the tiger-skin that still hung over the back of a wicker chair, Molly saw India, anxiously reassembled on that rocky outcrop, camouflaged by those outer walls of bland green Vermont shingles.

'Of course,' she said aloud, glimpsing a child's intent fantasy.

Molly ceased to wonder that it cost so much to give it up.

* * *

Impossible to get back to sleep. Since arriving here in England, Carrie lay awake most nights, unlike Rud. It was reassuring to hear him breathing so regularly over there in the other bed. It was also frustrating. He retreated into oblivion whenever he could. That was not her way. She'd put up a bold front. Fortifications, even. She smiled wryly to herself in the dark. Rock House, the new home she'd leased for them in England, had battlements, and stood in imposing acres above the cliffs.

She lay dwarfed under the vault of its master bedroom, unsure in the darkness how long she could keep it all up. As a girl, visits to Brattleboro had always made her conscious of the whiff of humiliation and misfortune that clung to her family. Once she was ensconced in Naulakha, though, a married woman with a famous husband, and living in real English style, she'd felt able to look anyone in the eye. Sitting up in her own phaeton, driving the matched pair Rud had bought for her, she knew herself skilful, daring, poised as a queen.

All that was behind her now.

Maybe she'd be more comfortable if she turned the pillow? A moment's struggle and it was done, the smooth chill soothing under her cheek.

She was sliding away into unconsciousness, when a distant shriek made her sit upright.

Was that Baby Elsie, crying, away in the nursery?

It might be just a seagull. As the sound died away, Carrie relaxed and lay back down, drawing up the covers. Nurse must be dealing with her.

'I don't know how I got through those early weeks, last February, with all the worry of Beatty on top of the exhaustion after Elsie's birth,' she'd admitted to Rud, once they were back in England.

'It was very different when Jo was born,' he'd said heavily. 'Then we both had no thought for anything but the child.'

She'd been surprised to hear him say that. Had he forgotten? At the time his immediate concern had been her own safety. It'd taken a day or two before he'd fallen in love with the baby.

Jo was so like him, she'd always been too easily excited. Elsie seemed a calmer child altogether. Just as well, now that another baby was on the way.

As if in response to that thought, a faint fluttering came, deep inside her. She laid a hand low on her belly.

'Yes,' she whispered, 'yes, little creature, I'm awake too.'

And felt the blood rise in her cheek at her own foolishness.

Less than five months to go. Maybe this one would be a boy. Rud would like that.

A grayish light was already leaking round the curtains. Contemplating the inert form in the bed across from her own, Carrie's smile died. Rud lay turned away from her, curled tightly into himself.

Her hands clenched, watching him.

Rud was still refusing to speak of Naulakha. He could not bring himself to read so much as a newspaper article about America. Let alone any letter arriving from Brattleboro since they'd fled. That handsome Theodor Dunham had proposed to her sister Josephine and had been accepted but Carrie hadn't dared to break Rud's embargo. She'd contained herself.

She stirred, impatient, against the coil of the sheets.

It wasn't just to lay all the blame at Beatty's door, much as she'd like to. Rud had become restless even before the court case, at a time when Carrie, for one, had no thought of leaving Brattleboro. Absurdly, to her mind at least, he began to take conflicts between nations to heart, take them quite personally, as though it were about himself, not the interests of whole peoples. This seemed to get worse as relations with Beatty went downhill. When it looked for a while as though the United States might go to war with England over some crazy border dispute in Venezuela, Rud confided that he was not going to be safe in America.

'I could be killed,' he insisted, baffling her.

'Really, Rud, it's nothing to do with you, as an individual. Why should you imagine it is?' she'd asked.

He'd ignored her.

That same week he'd turned on Molly Cabot, a woman he was really fond of, and Carrie's unwilling suspicions were confirmed. He was lost to the real world and was at war with phantoms.

'If we wanted to, the naval power of England could wipe out your three largest cities; it would be good bye to New York, Boston and Philadelphia,' he'd threatened.

Molly's calm, 'I don't see the end of the United States coming just yet,' sent him stalking out of the house, too angry to speak further.

A tiny disturbance to the room's silence. It carried on. Rud was grinding his teeth again.

Carrie'd always known there was violence in him. He usually kept it under wraps, though shows of Evangelical piety brought it out. But this aggression, these unwarranted intimations of danger, continued to trouble her. And once Beatty threatened him, of course, it was as though all his fantasies were confirmed.

She'd imagined that being back in England would restore Rud to common sense. Yet the tone of his concern over international affairs continued to disturb her. Endless ranting on the topic of Imperial Federation: it made her angry being obliged to listen to him. There was a strain of unreason, an investment of emotion, that she couldn't fathom. As though Rud himself were in need of being federated and held together by law.

Since they'd been back in England, she'd done what she could to pre-empt his outbursts, to get him to speak about it coolly. As they waited for guests from London to arrive, late one morning, she'd asked him straight out 'Why does it matter so much, I don't understand what Imperial Federation means to *you*, Rud?'

Again he'd dismissed her.

Perhaps worrying about Imperial Federation took his mind away from dwelling on what they'd given up. Just as long as others didn't find it as off key as she did herself.

The tooth grinding had stopped. Rud had rolled over, he'd soon be awake.

The raw daylight was catching his spectacles, where they lay on the bedside table. Without them his face was exposed, offered to her open and free of guile as one of the children.

On the instant, Carrie's heart quickened.

All she wanted now was for Rud to get back to writing. It wasn't simply the contracts that might not be honoured. In that sense his position – and their income – were pretty much secure. It was dangerous for Rud himself not to be writing. She'd seen what happened when his friend Stevenson died and Rud couldn't write for weeks. Every day that he didn't write he sank deeper into himself and away from her. He seemed to give up, to let go of life. As though, like Wolcott before him, he were drifting away and leaving her. Like Father.

If Rud left her too, she couldn't go on living.

He would never be allowed to enter that realm of shadow again, not if Carrie had anything to do with it. From now on she must be vigilant, alert at all times to signs of danger.

'Stand still a moment.' Carrie bent over in order to settle the heavy folds of her small daughter's dress. Josephine was particularly attached to the navy serge with the big square white collar.

'Do I really look like a little English sailor-girl?' Jo asked in fascination. 'But I am still American, aren't I?' It made her parents laugh, the way she would turn off her slow Vermont drawl at will and speak instead in the clipped tones that she heard used by her father and his English friends.

'Guess I'm real British today,' she announced at breakfast, arms out from her sides, inviting them to admire her outfit once her mother had done fussing.

As an experiment, she had been promoted from the nursery meal.

'It will be calmer for her,' Carrie decided. 'She does get so easily worked up. If only she were a better sleeper.'

'And what fun for us, Carrie. We don't want to waste her company on Nurse Holder any more than we have to.'

Carrie ate slowly, not properly hungry but at least no longer nauseous. Breakfast was a protracted affair as Carrie preferred to settle plans for the day ahead in detail with her husband. Once Jo had finished her boiled egg and drunk most of her milk, a friendly wave from all parties would see her depart, so long as she'd wiped her mouth. Today she clambered down from her grown-up dining chair and went cheerfully off to her governess while Rud and Carrie were still opening their mail.

'Another one for you, my dear.' Rud flipped it across to her. The pile by Carrie's plate grew yet more threatening. The business correspondence she could trust to no-one but herself. There was also the problem of the cook. The woman's manner was truly unfortunate, so over familiar. Carrie was not completely satisfied with any of the servants; she'd not been able to vet them herself, setting up house in England at such short notice. She'd had to rely on a London agency. There would be barely time enough to get a moment with Baby Elsie.

It was some time after lunch, which Jo took with her governess, when she reappeared to tug at Carrie's hand. Her mother was wearing a distracted frown after an agitating encounter below stairs. The woman would have to go.

'Come on, Mummy, come on and see the game we're playing, Father and me.' Reluctantly, Carrie allowed herself to be drawn along in Jo's wake. To her surprise, for she imagined they'd be making for the study up on the first floor, Carrie found herself led instead along a remote tiled passage towards the boot-room, a cheerless unheated space situated at the end of a wing, close to a back door.

Jo's grip on her hand was growing tighter as sounds that she could not identify began to reach them. A sort of rhythmic chanting, as she would describe it later to Rud's Aunt Georgie. From their first meeting Carrie had sensed that confidences would be safe with Georgie. Throwing open the door, she feared that Rud was teaching Jo to play at Hindu festivals again. It was so hard to explain away to the other mothers. He never thought of that.

But no, at first she could not make out where Rud was, though his voice seemed to emerge from every corner. Boot racks and umbrella stands had been moved together while the garden rug was draped between folding chairs to make a tent. Or was it a wall? On the far side of it crouched her husband, cross-legged on the livid tiles, rocking himself as he chanted.

'I think Daddy's sad,' the child whispered to her mother.

Opening his eyes, her father looked startled. 'I thought you were still in here with me, Infant.' Registering Carrie's presence and her look of alarm, Rud struggled to his feet.

'I suppose you want all this tidied up.' Before she could reply, he had set about restoring the room, with an air of sullen obedience.

Before they'd left Naulakha, when she was trying to find them a suitable place over in England, Rud insisted that they must find one by the sea. She went along with that without questioning, especially when they were offered such a fine handsome place as Rock House and relatively close to his old school. For her part, the principal consideration was to settle at a distance from her mother-in-law. Perhaps she should have paid more attention, had been too hasty. Could she have made a mistake?

The day they first set foot in it, Rock House had seemed so inviting, even reminiscent of Naulakha in its own way, though so much grander. The wide rooms were flooded with light, sunshine bringing to life the gaudy birds that hopped among the curling flower designs of the drawing room wallpaper. Yet within ten days, a week, of their moving in, she unwillingly found herself remarking on a sense of darkening, of deterioration beneath its roof. The air was chill with a damp that drained the colour from the brightest day. Her sensitive nose picked up a suspicion of drains. Surely it hadn't been like this when they first arrived?

'So you see,' she concluded in the letter sent off to Aunt Georgie, at home in North End House in Rottingdean, 'even though we lose money by it I've decided to give up the lease.' She held back from speaking of the black mood which seemed to have settled over Rud there, a darkness that was beginning to seep into her own life.

* * *

'Together again for Christmas, Ruddy!' Trix was standing by the drawing room window, looking out. 'And it's almost like when we were small, with Aunt Georgie and Uncle Ned only just across the green!'

She watched as her parents emerged from the porch of The Elms, the house Ruddy'd taken in Rottingdean. Arm-in-arm, they were on their way to spend the afternoon with Georgie and Ned over at North End House. Both were wrapped about with scarves over their topcoats, her mother stooping a little.

A dull sinking in her chest. They were growing old.

It would be a good thing if she could come Home like this more often.

She'd been about to remind Ruddy of the first Christmas they'd spent at the Grange, how he'd lifted her up to reach the bell-pull. But turning back to the drawing room, she realised that he wasn't listening, had no attention to spare for her. Instead he was down on the carpet, snarling and pawing the air menacingly over little Jo, where she lay hiccupping with delicious terror.

Stung to anger, at the same time Trix was embarrassed. Absurd to put herself in competition with a child. Yet she felt a vacuum open inside her. She used to be the one he turned to first.

From the sofa across the room, Carrie caught her eye.

Worse and worse. Carrie had seen it all.

Trix was still shocked by Carrie's appearance. On first sight of her, the day Trix had arrived in Rottingdean, she'd felt the smile freeze on her lips. Blowsy was the word that came to mind. Also shapeless. Overflowing. Carrie sat now, her baby beside her, asleep where she'd laid him down. She did look worn. Of course it was only four months since Baby John was born but if that was what having babies did to you... maybe it wouldn't be an *absolute* disaster if she herself was never to be a mother. She would make an effort to believe that.

'Would you like to hold him?' Carrie offered, startling her. 'I really ought to go up to the nursery and see how Elsie's getting on with Nurse. All day in bed with a cold is hard when you're barely two.' Despite her words, Carrie remained leaning back wearily against the tasselled upholstery. 'It's almost time for Baby's feed, so you mustn't mind if he wakes, it'll be nothing you've done.'

The kind thought, the wish to compensate her for Rud's default, brought tears to Trix's eyes. Then it hit her: perhaps Carrie understood because she too now played second fiddle.

'Don't move, I'll come to you,' Trix replied. In a moment she was across the room and bending to take possession of Baby John, swathed in his Shetland. Trix had held other babies but the warm delicious weight, the delicate powdery smell of Rud's baby's scalp sent a shiver through her. When the time came to give him up her arms were left cold and empty.

The others had already gone up, 'I think I'll just lie down for an hour,' Mama and Carrie had each murmured. Papa was poking about in the library. And here she was, alone with Ruddy in the drawing room. At last. There was still half an hour before they must dress for dinner. She moved closer to the fire, settling down on a low chair, its tapestry cover not quite so ugly in the dimness.

'It's quite strange you know, meeting you as paterfamilias. So grand too, in this great house. And seeing what kind of home you and Carrie make together.'

Oh no. That sounded scratchy.

'Don't judge us by the furnishings, that's all. Three guineas a week – yes, that's our rent – buys you everything but beauty.'

He got up and stirred the fire, then cursed and brushed flying sparks from his trousers.

Why couldn't he be more natural? All that success was coming between them. It was a relief when he turned back to her, saying,

'You would have loved Naulakha, Trix. My word, we made that beautiful. But we just locked the door and left. It's still there, waiting.'

Forgetting all she had meant to tell him, everything but his sadness, she stretched out her hand. Without looking at her he seized it and clung on tightly.

'Forgive me, you've had a horrible time, one way and another,' she said. 'That business with Carrie's brother –'

'The court case? It was hideous. The interrogation. Worse than … than The House of Desolation.' He spoke hoarsely. 'I didn't think I could ever feel like that again. But time only seems to have made it worse. Strange, isn't it?'

He didn't want a reply. She dared to stroke the back of his hand.

It was as close as he'd ever come to speaking about their life as children in Southsea.

The effort had left him struggling for composure.

Trix waited. Here and there light pooled steadily from the heavy lamps.

'Living close to Georgie has been the best medicine. For both of us', he said more calmly. 'The baby was born in their house, you know. Carrie will never forget her kindness.'

What to reply? In the long pause the silence began to weigh on her.

'Will you excuse me,' he added, after a few moments, releasing her hand. 'The girl hasn't drawn it properly and it fidgets me.'

Stepping across the room, he straightened a curtain before returning to pull up a chair next to her own.

'Tell me, O famous author of *A Pinchbeck Goddess,* are you beavering away on another novel? Or is it single stories?'

She let out a slow breath.

'Ruddy, I don't know what to do. I've been just longing for the chance to talk. My writing –'

'We all get in difficulties from time to time, you know that, Trix.' His voice steadied her at once. 'Nothing like talking it out with another workman. Go on, tell me.'

He moved a nearby lamp so they could see each other.

'I have started stories, more than one, but I haven't managed to finish them. They just hang there. It's as if I've forgotten how.'

'Is that all? I've got notes, notebooks full of unfinished stories. They're not stalled, they're waiting. And by Jove don't they make you wait too. No alternative. When they're ready the way forward will open and they'll allow themselves to be written At least, that's what I've found.'

She reflected, staring deep into the burned out logs as they slowly collapsed. Seeing the fire low, rather than ring for a servant, he bent and made it up himself.

'I think it might feel different if I had more behind me, if I'd managed to finish more. I know I had some positive notices for *Pinchbeck* but others were dreadfully dispiriting. The *Daily Telegraph* called it '*a budget of inane chatter serving no artistic purpose*''.

Echoing on her own voice, the words made her angry.

'That's what you get if you try to write about women and their lives,' she realised.

But he failed to take it up.

'Come on, Trix. You had a good spread of notices, there must have been a dozen. And I saw *The Scotsman* used words like 'original' and even 'brilliance'.

'But what about "*trifling incidents and vapid dialogue*" or my "*very ordinary love affairs and commonplace colonels?*"'

As she repeated the insults, she felt anger rising till it threatened to choke her.

'You simply can't let yourself be subject to these people, Trix. You know what they said about *Barrack-Room Ballads*: "*coarseness, insufficiently redeemed by humour.*" Pretty crushing.'

'That was years ago. They don't say anything like that now.'

'Look Trix, you'll always have some readers who pick holes.'

His reasonable tone made her feel like a child and she looked away.

'You have to be prepared to listen. It's a question of trust: whether you value the other person's judgment.'

He waited. After a pause she met his eyes again.

'Believe me, I was hauled over the coals with the greatest publicity only a year ago. The man who did it was a friend, and he was writing in the *Atlantic.*'

She'd missed that. She sat up.

'I was "*too ready to be distracted into work that was unworthy of me.*" Try that on for size.'

She couldn't forbear laughing.

'Oh Ruddy, that man's got your measure. He could be your brother.'

'That's better, Trix. You see, all is not lost.'

His spectacles glinted in the firelight.

He was always good to her. It would be safe talking to Rud about the automatic writing. He'd see its possibilities. Not like Jack.

'You win. It's true, my news isn't all negative,' she nodded, settling back comfortably in the chair. The bell still hadn't rung. 'You must've noticed that interesting piece in *Review of Reviews*. About automatism? I've become tremendously interested in it. Spirit writing, I mean. There really seems to be something in it and it turns out I have a sort of gift, it comes to me completely naturally. I –'

She stopped. He'd gone rigid beside her.

'Don't tell me you believe all that dangerous nonsense. Trix, do you know what you're getting involved in? I suppose you sit and wait for the spirit to take over your pen?'

A flush rose from her collarbone, mounting her face. She sank further into shadow.

'Have you read about what happens to the people who lay themselves open by doing that? Myers doesn't tell you that, does he?'

She made herself sit up and face him, though her voice wavered.

'Rud, I thought you of all people would understand. You're the one who talks about being taken over when you're writing. Taken over by something almost like an outside force.'

'That's just where you're wrong, Trix. It's not outside. It's *my* daemon, something in me that speaks through me, when I get in tune with myself. Nothing external at all.'

She gave up, humiliated. He refused to accept what she had learned.

Rud was against her.

Her ears were ringing.

'Besides, what you're doing is known to be downright dangerous. There've been cases of mental collapse, you do realise that? Living in India, you are in no place to trifle with the unseen. Trix, do have a care.'

Whatever he said, she wasn't going to stop.

The sound of the bell brought her escape.

*

'Home again in Calcutta.' Trix sighed, resigned, on their return. Two 'homes' were rather hard to live with. Could she manage here on just the amusements proper to an army wife? Dinners with the same couples, tea parties and tennis with the same women friends. Tiffin at the Saturday Club. In spite of Rud, she thought she'd have to keep up her experiments. She had a duty to follow them through, having this gift that let her see what others couldn't.

So the words ran in her head.

But this was too much.

'I can't tell them. No, it's too awful. They couldn't bear it. It can't be true. It must not be true.'

But she had seen it, passing before her eyes. The crystal had shown it to her. In her panic, Trix had stepped away from the table on which the crystal sphere, small as a hen's egg, still lay on its mat of black velvet. Alongside, the precious lacquered box Papa had made for her stood open. She liked to keep her crystal safe in there. She stared at the tabletop now, breathing heavily.

'What shall I do, oh, what shall I do?'

Her first step, the automatic writing, had come so easily. Almost as a relief too – no need to make any decisions. Just be patient and wait. Yet in spite of all the arguments she had so determinedly advanced, in defending herself against Jack, Trix's confidence had begun to waver. She wasn't sure that she really liked it when she held out her writing hand and something powerful that she could not control took possession of it.

The crystal-gazing hadn't seemed like such a big step, after all, Mama dabbled from time to time. It was just the sort of party trick any of the station wives might perform for charity. Even some of the Fleming relations looked favourably on reading fortunes from the cards. Trix knew that as a child she had seen things that nobody else seemed able to and it had frightened her but she put that knowledge behind her.

It was more difficult to ignore her brother's hostility. Rud had been so absolute in his dismissal. He'd meant well, of course, with his 'Trix, do have a care'.

Care. She would be bringing him something worse than care if she let him into the secret. Her mind went back, flinching, to the images that had swelled into life once the crystal had darkened and cleared: tiny but vivid and clearly focused she had watched them in growing dread. At once she had recognised her niece, the six-year-old Josephine. Mama thought her the picture of Trix herself as a child. But in the crystal, Josephine was grey-faced and struggling for breath. She was being carried down a flight of steps in the arms of a man Trix did not recognize. The sphere had clouded then; it might have been with snow. It cleared to reveal only a white coffin.

Trix attempted to choke back the wailing that was coming from her without her volition. Conquering it, she remained fixed, clasping and unclasping her hands. It was in this state that her friend Mabel Hastings found her. Sailing into the room, already in spate with details of the absurd outfit that Mrs. James was proposing for her daughter's wedding, Mabel stopped herself abruptly. At the sight of the stricken figure she instinctively stretched out her arms.

'Trix, dearest! Tell me what has happened.'

To her dismay she saw her friend draw back, as a look that could only be described as crafty came over her.

'It was as though her face had become, I don't know, warped,' Mabel wept later, as she struggled to give an account of her visit to a mutual friend.

'No, there's no telling anybody. I mustn't tell what I've seen today. You mustn't ask me.'

'Why, Trix, whatever can you mean? Explain. Stop making mysteries.' She must have hoped that the touch of wholesome asperity in her voice would help to restore the conversation to a tone that was more normal. But Trix was backing away from her, putting a chair and then the table between them. Mabel took in the lacquered box and the crystal.

'Trix, you haven't been upsetting yourself with those messages? It's very draining, you know. You told me so yourself.' Met with silence, Mabel longed, with an alarm that was new to her, for someone else to take charge of this situation. She and Trix had been going to lunch together at the Club but that was clearly out of the question.

Was there any request for information, she wondered, that she could safely put to Trix? Could it be a touch of the sun? For a moment she almost persuaded herself that was all it was. No, what she was watching felt too intimate, too exposed. It made her horribly uncomfortable. Should she send for Trix's husband, Colonel Fleming? Common sense told her at once that his wooden Scottish uprightness would be utterly at a loss. Only a doctor could be asked to face this.

Standing out on the verandah, the Medical Officer shook his head.

'We all know that Trix, Mrs. Fleming, has a highly wrought constitution. She's overdone it in some way. That wretched writing, I shouldn't wonder.' He left it unclear whether he knew about the special writing, or was merely deploring the wish to write fiction.

'I have to get back to the hospital. I've got three surgical cases I daren't leave for long. Can you make sure she takes two of these?' He held out a wad of small packets that looked like *cachets fièvres* to Mabel's sceptical eye.

'Frankly, Major Gilchrist, I don't think I can. She shies away whenever I get near.'

His response took her aback. 'Her maid, perhaps? Mrs. Fleming was native born, or as good as, she told me herself. She does have an Indian maidservant, I believe.' He was not wrong. Whatever it was that the wrinkled woman in the blue saree murmured, for Mabel herself could not follow the Hindustani, the words calmed Trix and she allowed herself to be led away.

When Jack Fleming returned, summoned from his office by a hastily scribbled chit, he found Mabel, head on hand, seated in the drawing room, and learned from her that his wife was safely asleep, as she remained all night.

Clattering up the steps of the bungalow at an early hour the doctor was not looking forward to his interview with the husband. Always worried about his own health, was Fleming; how was he going to cope with this? A fortnight had passed, with Trix kept in a kind of *purdah*, visited by women friends, their voices lowered and their smiles uncertain as they left.

'Well, Gilchrist, she's no better. Your potions don't seem to be doing the trick at all. And I'm off on a three-month camp next week. She's supposed to be coming with me. I've told Trix she needs to pull herself together in time for it, but I've had no effect.'

Major Gilchrist cleared his throat. He felt no reason to be optimistic about this case. The pretty, girlish Mrs. Fleming he had known had been replaced by a tousle-haired figure, her once delicate features somehow blurred. He foresaw, at best, a long haul.

'Would you consider sending your wife home to her family? A mother's care and all that – calm and home is what she needs, I'm convinced. As it happens, I know a very experienced and reliable nurse, a Mrs. Bonnington, who could travel with her and take charge of the case. By good fortune she's free, just at the moment and looking about for employment that will take her back to London. Mrs. B. could accompany your wife on the voyage home.'

Fleming startled the doctor by the speed with which he acquiesced. With only a brief farewell he had hurried away to make the necessary bookings.

'Not a quibble about cost, though I thought he had rather a name for being close with money. Poor chap,' the doctor thought, 'he's completely out of his depth.'

THE KARELA,

THE BITTER KARELA,

SHALL SEED WHERE

YE LOVED

1899–1902

Carrie allowed herself to sink into the sofa's full velvet cushions. She even stretched out her toes to the fire. Life at The Elms in Rottingdean was easier for her now that Rud's spirits were improving. He was less irritable with her too, so long as he didn't dwell on the sins of his American publishers. It made such a difference to him, having Aunt Georgie living close at hand. A difference to her, also, having an ally. A woman who cared for Rud without wanting always to be first with him.

She was drifting deliciously, almost dozing, when a shiver woke her. A long breath of icy air sighed in from the hall. Rud was back from his walk.

'What a way to live. No wonder there's such a dead dull look on all the faces.' He left his coat in the hall to be put away, forgetting the heavy knitted scarf which still hung round his neck. 'How can a man think or feel when all his force is occupied in fighting cold and wind?'

His anger, coming without warning, struck her full in the chest. It wasn't just the weather, his rage was turned on her. Even when he was obviously angry he'd always been slow to admit the fact. She'd been fearing something like this. Ever since they'd had to leave Naulakha. No point in avoiding the issue any longer.

'Are you blaming me? You never minded the cold in Brattleboro. Do you feel it was my fault, that I should have made a better hand of managing Beatty? Just remember how busy I was with the children.'

To her alarm, her voice trembled. For all her fierceness, she couldn't shake off the sense that she had indeed failed.

'No-one's blaming you, Carrie,' he was gentle at once – 'it's the general cussedness of things, not to mention Scribners and their delays with the new edition. I do just long for the sun. It's what I need to feel alive. I dream of India. Even of the glare. I want the blessed touch of the sun on my back, riding out before breakfast.'

Carrie grew still. It was not the first time that she'd heard this.

'What are you telling me? You're going out there? And what about the children, you can't –'

Rud held up both hands.

'No, that's not what I meant. I'm not going to go off and leave you, you should know that by now, my foolish girl. There're other things I long for besides heat. That new-minted world of India, ablaze and waiting to be explored. I was twenty then. But that's all over. I'm too damned recognisable these days.'

Carrie took up the little shirt she'd been hemming. She sensed an opening. She would go slowly. 'You know, Rud, what you say about new worlds reminds me. I've had an idea. All these problems with Scribners and their delays. I think you'll end by taking Putnams to court for jumping the gun and bringing out that unauthorised edition. Wouldn't it be simpler if you were to go over and deal with both of them on the spot? New York in winter's not like Sussex – the skies are blue, the snow sparkles – '

'And it would be a chance for you to see your mother. I see through you, Carrie. No, don't look crushed, I didn't mean anything by it. It's hard for you not being able to live near her.'

The catch in her throat stopped her when she was going to reply.

'Well, the curse of Beatty has fallen upon us and we must both abide it. Your mother and Naulakha, our beautiful boat of a house – everything had to be surrendered.'

'But we can still visit New York. And take the children. Mother's never seen Baby John except in photographs.'

He straightened in his chair and looked across at her.

'That really might be an idea. I don't want Jo to lose her American ways. She's such a straight little creature – none of those affectations I see developing in her cousins. I'll tell you what, it's a bit late in the day to think of going for Christmas but I'll look into sailings in the New Year.'

She pushed the sewing-box aside.

'I can't believe how excited that makes me. Or how quickly you've taken up the idea.'

He grinned back at her, relieved as she was to find a plan that made them both happy.

'It does appeal to me – there's young Doubleday for instance – remember, he came out to us at Naulakha. Now he's started up on his own, I'd like to see him. There's only so much you can do with letters.'

Carrie caught at his sleeve. 'Rud, don't let your people know you think badly about Jo's cousins – above all don't say anything in front of Jo.' But he was already out on the stairs and half way to his study.

The following day over in Tisbury, Lockwood was peacefully absorbed in his studio. At the smooth click of the door handle, he looked up from the clay he was working while his hands continued their patient persuasion.

'Come in, come in,' he called but no encouragement was needed.

Alice swept past him, with scarcely a look, her own eyes fixed on a corner of the ceiling. 'How long has that damp stain been there, Jack?'

'Where? Where?' He followed her pointing finger. 'To tell you the truth...'

'Don't tell me you never noticed it. You really are too bad. I knew I should have insisted on having the man Lady Mowbray recommended but you would overrule me.'

'Be reasonable, my dear, overruling isn't usually seen as my forte.'

She wasn't listening. 'I'll just have to get him back.'

'If you're not satisfied with his work, let me deal with him. He's a good sort of chap.'

'Jack, you are so soft-hearted, I imagine he spun you a tale about his poor old mother –'

He raised a hand, in protest.

'Nothing of the kind. He asked me about firing pots.'

His wife sighed. 'Very well. I leave it all to you. But don't blame me if you find your treasures green with mould and the paper tearing apart under your pencil.'

He laughed aloud: 'However much rain comes in you know it's not going to create effects on the scale of the Bombay monsoon, you fearful exaggerating woman.'

Alice glanced over at the clock. 'It's the day for Rud's letter. The second post should be here by now – let me go and see.'

In the quiet she had left behind, Lockwood returned to his methodical shaping until the door flew open again, this time without warning. He sighed.

'Jack, did you know about this? Ruddy says they are taking those three tiny children across the Atlantic in January.'

Straightening, Lockwood slowly wiped his hands on his linen apron, 'That does seem rather odd. Are you quite sure?'

She waved the pages dense with black ink scrawl at him. 'Here, on the second page, towards the end. Read it for yourself.'

Lockwood brought the sheets up to his eyes. 'Yes,' he said reluctantly. 'That appears to be the plan.'

'We can't let him do it. It's quite irresponsible; they can't have thought it through.'

'Let him? I have no control over him and nor do you. He's thirty-three years old, not thirteen.'

'It's that woman behind it, I know. First she tries to get him living near her own disreputable family, so they can sponge off him. Then when that doesn't answer, she requires him to carry her over to America just when the fancy takes her.'

'Alice, Alice, no. Calm down. I'm afraid you're quite unjust to poor Carrie – the letter speaks of business dealings and sorting out Rud's copyrights over there.'

'But the children? Can it be wise to uproot them and expose them to that journey in the depths of winter?'

Uproot the children? 'It's not as far from Sussex to New York as it is from Bombay to Southsea', he was tempted to retort. Unlike Alice, he'd not been able to set aside *Baa Baa Black Sheep*, that terrible story of Rud's about those two children.

'I don't know about uprooting. Those children are excellent travellers. Little Jo told Rud that 'the best way to study geography was to go about in ships until you've seen all the countries.'

Alice threw him a look of scorn.

'Jack, I believe you've told me that story before. Taking them all out to Cape Town last January to get some sunshine once they'd left that gloomy house was one thing – but it's hard to see how a trip to New York in the depths of winter can be good for anyone.'

With a reluctant nod, he conceded.

'I can't pretend that I feel happy about this proposal. Yet what can we do?'

'What can we do? I shall write myself this instant and tell them we think it most unwise. I shall write to Carrie.'

He sighed. This didn't sound wise.

'Perhaps we could offer to take charge of the children while they're away? I've been feeling that we don't see enough of those babies.'

'In a house this size? Three babies and their nursemaids? To say nothing of the burden on the kitchen. And what about Trix? You know she refuses to see anyone, even Ruddy.'

An ache in his chest, remembering Rud's shock and distress. He'd arrived alone, without Carrie, but Trix would have nothing to do with him. The scene she'd made! That was when they'd agreed that a nursing home might be the best place for a while. A day he didn't care to remember.

'I thought we'd agreed that it was for the doctors to look after Trix, poor darling, until she feels calmer. It doesn't seem at all likely that she's going to be coming home before the spring. I was thinking that we'd move into The Elms and manage things there, just for a few weeks, you know.'

'You'd give up your workshop?' She stared at him then moved away towards the window. 'I suppose we could move in there, just for a limited time, though I must be free to leave at a moment's notice. I have to be here for Trix. When she needs me.' She was looking deep into the gloomy little garden as she spoke.

Less than a week elapsed before a letter from Alice, addressed for once to Carrie, arrived in Rottingdean.

Caroline Balestier Kipling could not believe what she was reading. Angry pleasure made her glow. Mrs. Kipling had excelled herself. Offering advice on the care of children, proposing to move into Carrie's home and take over her place in it.

Rud was late down to breakfast – junketing in the nursery again, she thought grimly, working Jo up before the day was even started.

'What do you think of this?'

She threw the letter down at his place almost before he could seat himself.

His face darkened as he read: *'incautious, thoughtless, responsibility as a parent, idle gratification'.*

'That she – of all women – should accuse me of indifference to the welfare of children!'

He got up and marched about the room, the letter still in his hand.

Carrie felt a thrill of satisfaction. 'Unwarrantable intrusion on your mother's part, don't you think?'

He could barely get the words out: 'Whatever her views on the matter, she's not going to stop us. And she's not coming here.'

'I couldn't think of it. The children hardly know her – and anyway we've always said that we're not going to be separated from them. Where we go, they go.'

At her words, Rud stopped his pacing. 'Thanks be to Allah we are of one mind in that, my dear,' and he bent to kiss her. She beamed back at him.

'Now suppose you sit down again with me and eat your breakfast. There's a whole heap of mail to be got through and we don't want to leave a backlog. It'll be bad enough, all we'll find waiting when we get back.'

* * *

Frank Doubleday had known in advance that the Kiplings were taking a suite at the Hotel Grenoble on West 56th St. Later he heard that the children were feverish on arrival and that Carrie too had fallen ill. Apparently she recovered quickly but by the third week of February Kipling himself had become sick.

Frank really didn't want to intrude. He was on good terms, very good terms, with Kipling and he got along well enough with the lady, too. Nevertheless, they were so careful of their privacy that he hesitated to present himself at the hotel. It was no secret that Kipling had been taken ill; he'd be betraying no confidence. And yet it didn't feel right to leave the family in the solitude of their hotel suite, when there was sickness. Dammit, he had a right, a duty as Kipling's publisher, to enquire after his health. If they didn't like it, he need not feel personally snubbed.

Arguing with himself in this way, Frank dismounted from the streetcar and began to trudge, head bent against the wind that sliced down Grenoble Street. God knew what had possessed them to choose the hotel, he thought, glancing round in the twilight of the foyer. Who could have recommended such a morgue? There were flakes of snow on his moustache, still unmelted, he noted, as he reached into his breast pocket for a card.

Fully expecting it to be returned with a scribbled note, a polite acknowledgement of his concern, he was taken aback to hear the desk clerk announce 'Mrs. Kipling's compliments and would he be kind enough to go up to the suite.' He gestured towards the brass cage of the elevator: 'Third floor.' Before Frank had time to explore the shift in his sense of the occasion, he found himself face-to-face with Caroline Kipling. He hesitated, as yet, to think of her in more familiar terms. She was already standing waiting for him in the corridor.

Her face was set and pale: he knew that he had done right to come, even before she began to speak.

'It is so good to see a friend, Mr. Doubleday. I hope you won't mind talking out here but I don't want to worry Rud and if Baby hears my voice he'll start calling out for me.'

He began a gesture of impatience – this was no time for the niceties of etiquette – but thinking better of it, simply took her hand. Carrie Kipling let it lie in his heavy clasp for a moment, as though she did not want to take it back.

'The doctor's just gone: his second visit since noon. Earlier he suspected it was pneumonia but now he told me he's certain that both lungs are affected. "Involved", I think, was the word he used.'

Frank admired her control yet wondered with a part of his mind whether it wasn't close to a form of hysteria. Before he could respond she went on with a kind of dogged calm, though he noticed that her voice was taking on a higher pitch:

'Jo, too: she has pneumonia but at present it's only in one lung.'

'Your eldest child?' he asked, pointlessly, his mind beginning to take in the scale of the threat.

'So far, Elsie only has a bad cough. But Baby isn't well either: I can tell that because he's not eating.' The almost comic note drew a giggle, despite herself.

Frank felt laughter rising in him too, impossible and inappropriate. What he had just heard was too alarming to contemplate directly. 'No,' he exclaimed, as much to himself as to Carrie, whose attention was turned, anyway, for sounds coming from the door which she had left ajar. The whiff of disinfectant which he caught sobered him in a moment.

'What can I do to help you and your family?' His voice was deliberately slow and steady. 'Where do you want me to concentrate my attention?'

She replied only with another question: 'How long can you stay?'

Frank considered. He had told his wife he would be home early that evening: they were crossing town to have dinner with her sister. He looked down at the taut figure in her high-necked dress. He removed his overcoat before he answered. 'Why, I guess I'll be staying here with you until your husband's well again.'

If he caught the sound of a single dry sob, that was the last sign of weakness that escaped from Carrie Kipling. 'That woman is one of the greatest organisers I have ever met,' he would later exclaim, remembering. She saw with fearful clarity what had to, what could be done. Within the day, relays of nurses had been found and engaged, the best nurses, for extremity sharpened her judgment to brilliance. She was ruthless, now she had him for support: other friends in the city, Jim Conland, their doctor from Brattleboro, all were summoned, every pair of hands to whom the care of an invalid or a potential invalid could be trusted. Every form of support.

And her forethought! 'We're going to need stimulants: it will have to be whisky, the best we can get, Rud hates brandy.'

Her subdued urgency was like a well-ordered military response.

It gave Frank the confidence of delegated authority. 'I would be honoured to supply Mrs. Kipling with the blend I keep for myself,' Andrew Carnegie had responded, in person over the telephone. Indeed, people wanted to help and not just because the fellow was so well-known.

It seemed Mrs. Kipling was speaking no more than the truth when she exclaimed, 'Everyone he has ever spoken to loves him and wants to do what they can.' More touching still was the invalid's patience and his hoarse thanks.

Setting up supply lines and medical support at the start was one thing. That involved challenges that could be triumphantly overcome. Over the days and the nights that followed, however, as the patient weakened and rallied, sweated and struggled for breath, the watchers too began to be worn down. It must have been during that time that she insisted, 'Carrie, please, just Carrie. That's enough.'

He'd made his bed on the floor outside the sickroom, in order to be ready to answer need as it arose. Twice a day he was dealing with the importunate press: Rudyard Kipling's illness was making headlines across the world. Under different circumstances he'd have been astonished to find himself dealing with personal telegrams from the Kaiser, but in those days at the Hotel Grenoble he was too exhausted for wonder.

In later years he could scarcely bear to look back, dreading to be lost again in the subdued horror surrounding the long wait for the pneumonia to reach its crisis. It wasn't clear whether the little girl, Josephine, was keeping step with her father. Though his own attention was centred on Rud, as he now tenderly thought of the gasping figure propped up among pillows, there was a morning when Frank realised that the doctors were taking longer in the nursery than on other days. Elsie, the three-year-old and John, who could only just walk, had been sent in the care of their nurse to stay with friends in the first days after his arrival. Josephine had lain alone in the darkened room, attended by nurses from the hospital and visited hourly day and night by her mother.

Nearly a week of that and Carrie came to him, her face bleached.

'I've made up my mind. Jo's not getting enough attention and the doctor says the crisis is getting close for her. I want you to ask Julia de Forrest if she will take her for me. She's one of my oldest and closest friends. Jo simply must have undivided attention: I can't do it.'

It made sense what he was hearing but what about the journey? The address Carrie named was twenty-one blocks away. The bitter weather, the draughts… Seeing his hesitation, Carrie spoke harshly. 'Please. Allow me to know what I'm doing. It's for her good. She needs someone who can't think of anything but her welfare. I can't be that person. Look at me,' she ended simply.

When the time came he took the bundle swathed with shawls in his arms and carried Josephine out through the dim lobby folding his own body round her to shield her from the cutting winds as he put her into the arms of Julia de Forrest, waiting in the carriage. The small face pressed into his shoulder was frighteningly hot. 'Mummy is coming to visit me later,' she told him, wheezing.

Living at such close quarters, he was forced to observe Carrie's agony of self-discipline, though it felt barely decent to do so. Her choice was more than she could bear. Later he thought she began to age from the moment she took the decision to send Josephine away, though he could never be sure when it was he first noticed her hair had lost all its colour.

For the first twenty-four hours, reports were fairly good. The next day though, Carrie hurried out of the hotel early, leaving him in charge: she went back again to the de Forrests' in the early afternoon. When she slipped out again shortly before ten, even through his own exhaustion he picked up a piercing sense of dread.

The following morning he found her crouched against the wall in the public corridor, no longer caring to hide herself or her racked weeping, only desperate to keep the sound of grief from the sickroom. There was nothing he could do for her, only wait.

'Josephine has left us,' Carrie said when she could speak.

Rud was coming through his crisis, though the days and nights of delirium seemed endless. He would not give up. Those who watched him trembled to see how his dreams wrung him.

'Lie down now, Rud, and try not to struggle. It's all for your own good we're doing this,' his old friend Jim Conland would implore.

But Rud wouldn't stop fighting the nurses: 'How dare you accuse me? I don't cheat, I've never lied to anyone,' he repeated. Tears ran from the corners of his eyes. The men round him looked at each other, uncomfortable. And what had made him so terrified of losing Carrie and the children? They were always disappearing in these nightmares. He croaked of endless journeying, terrifying confusions. Just to witness such helpless distress left observers disturbed.

But what would be his distress on waking? How to keep the news from Rud? Frank watched as that became Carrie's obsession. The doctors agreed, he must be securely on the mend before he had to take that blow. Days passed. Nothing was said to hurry Carrie, for no-one wanted to give up the glow of relief as the patient passed out of danger.

'The strain on you is too much, Carrie,' Jim Conland said at last, watching her cast off the scarlet shawl she had been wearing over her mourning as she left the sickroom. She had shown exactly the steadfast courage he had anticipated, though even with all his experience he had shuddered to see what this cost her. 'You've done your best to temper the wind to Rud but it can't go on. He'll notice your own tension, and sooner rather than later.' For the first time, Frank saw Carrie show fear. The next moment she sent a glance of appeal across to him.

In all the stress of the last weeks he had never failed her. Now Frank knew what he must do. 'If you think he's ready to take it, Jim, then I'll be the one to tell him.'

Conland who had likely been hoping as much, nodded. 'Tomorrow, after my morning visit, if all continues well.'

Rud was definitely getting back to his old self. 'They've been pummelling me fearfully old chap, to make sure that I'm getting rid of the congestion. It makes me cough something dreadful.'

Frank forced a smile and sat down. Rud was so quick, he'd guess something was up if he didn't get on with it..

'Rud,' he began, laying a hand on the other's forearm where it lay, alarmingly insubstantial, above the sheet. 'While you were ill, something very bad happened.' After a pause: 'Josephine was ill too and we couldn't save her. Josephine died.'

Out of the aching silence came a choked, 'When?'

'March 6th.'

Rud was too weak still to roll over unaided; after a moment's futile effort, he gave up and turned away only his ravaged face.

It was kind of appalling to live beside them through their struggle. They knew they had to go on, so that's what they did. Frank had no notion of what they said to each other. After the first week of shock, Rud had thrown himself like a trooper into recovery, demanding that his doctors let him spend an hour every day just talking to 'my friend Frank'. Carrying him into the next room for a change of scene in the mornings, Frank found him no heavier than a child.

He always felt he had been right to try and stay at their side until they were safe back home in Rottingdean.

He did not guess what took place when Carrie slipped off to pick up some papers from Naulakha, their old home.

Stepping through the echoing shell of the chill house, Carrie climbed to the second floor.

She threw the light switch.

They'd planned to put playrooms up here one day when the girls were older.

There was Rud's billiard table still, a scarlet ball standing alone out on the green baize, forgotten.

And there was his old roll-top desk, stored up here when he chose a more convenient model.

Carrie walked across to stand beside it. Her mouth twisting, she stared into the words Rud had carved into the frame.

'Oft was I weary when I worked at thee.'

At last, she turned and trod heavily, step by step, down into the basement. There, up on the wall, hung all their tools, pliers, saws, hammers, screwdrivers, in orderly rows. She reached up and made her selection.

Her step was lighter, going back up the two flights of stairs. Once in front of the desk, without a second glance, she brought the largest hammer crashing down on its closed lid.

Sobs shook her as she gazed down at the splintered wreck.

What was it all for, all that effort?

'Jo!' the child's name came out on a long moan. The empty space absorbed her voice.

Slowly Carrie returned to herself. She'd done her utmost for each of them, child and husband, exerted herself beyond any effort she'd ever known – and met only loss. How could she believe, whatever Rud said, that he didn't blame her? There was nothing to be done.

Retracing her steps, she made her way down to their old room with its neat twin beds. They would never come back to live in Naulakha, she knew that now. She passed through into the bathroom. But the taps were dry. A handkerchief and her own spit must make her respectable for the journey to the station and onwards to New York.

* * *

Lockwood was tired. He looked round his studio, at the sacks of clay, the pots of pencils lying ready, and sighed. He hadn't had a day to himself in here for he didn't know how long. With both children in trouble, his time wasn't his own. He'd snatched a few weeks to go out to New York to be with Rud and Carrie, during those dreadful weeks after Jo died. It had meant leaving Alice on her own to take care of Trix, who'd been able to leave the nursing home by then but what else could he do? Now October had come and Trix was showing no sign of further improvement.

Following a vain attempt at a civilised breakfast, they led Trix to a seat by the window in the drawing room. Alice had never had much of a gift for making a place comfortable. Now her daughter sat inert, her gaze turned obediently on the decaying garden. From time to time the index finger of her right hand picked at the line of brass studs that ran along the arm of her chair.

'It is at least quiet in the house, after yesterday,' Lockwood reminded his wife. They stood indecisive, already exhausted, in the cramped hallway.

'I don't know.' Alice shook her head. 'I don't know whether this silence – it's like a death, a suicide almost.' He looked up sharply, putting out a protesting hand, but she went on, 'I don't know whether this isn't worse than the screaming.'

He shuddered, remembering the previous afternoon.

He'd made his approach to Trix cautiously, once the postman had got well clear of the house.

'Now dearest, shall I come and sit by you? Would you like that?'

Not finding himself rebuffed, he'd seated himself at her side under the little arbour to the right of the front door. It was a place that caught the sun even in winter and they'd persuaded Trix into trying it for half an hour.

She was still not looking at him but he'd persevered. 'Something for you today in the post, Trixie. Tell me if I'm right, I think I recognise Jack's hand –'

'Jack's hand,' Father said.

It was a message. Secret but she had the code. Trix smiled knowingly to herself. They would not take her in this time. They meant she had to go back and let Jack touch her again.

Night after night, touch her in that place. No excuses.

Never. She would never.

But they must not suspect that.

'He is the Lord High Executioner,' she said aloud, 'Master of the Survey. Look, there's the official warrant, there in that envelope.'

Lockwood had seen her husband's name break into her consciousness like a rifle shot. He'd wondered she had the breath for all that shrieking, even as he fought to get her, arms flailing and face suffused, back inside the house.

Once in the entrance hall, the front door firmly shut behind her, Trix had snarled in his face, her narrow lips drawn back. She'd thrown herself about, heedless of the bruises that would surely disfigure her for weeks to come. They could only wait, indifferent for once to the horrified curiosity of the maid whose head had bobbed into view round a door from time to time. It was Alice who'd managed to calm Trix in the end, speaking in repeated phrases, stroking her hand, refusing to give way to her own terror.

The doctor hadn't been able to get near her, of course. Observing her head raised in renewed alert on his approach, the wild eye she'd turned, he'd retreated, leaving Alice to continue her soothing.

Stupor had succeeded the mania, this morning. Alice, for whom the doctor had also prescribed a sleeping draught, was haggard. For his part, Lockwood was grateful that nothing ever kept him awake. But he feared that he was going to fail at the task in front of him. Should he begin? He decided to wait a little, perhaps till they had seen how things went with Trix during the morning.

'Leave her to me,' Alice said, picking up his thought. Seeing him hesitate, she pushed him not altogether gently in the direction of his workshop. 'I'll know where you are.' He made his escape.

Emerging with reddened eyes later in the morning, he found Alice pacing directly outside his door. 'I've been with Trix all this time and I think we may have made a little progress.'

He would have liked to believe it.

She went on: 'I was trying, you know, to find some easy, happy things to turn her mind to. I talked and talked – about the garden in Bombay and the drive where she used to dig up the sand and carry it over to the clay pots along the driveway, about the walks in her big red and green perambulator with Ruddy trotting along beside. It took simply ages but in the end Trix herself began to speak.'

'"She wasn't so bad, you know, Mother," she said. At first I thought she meant Ayah – you know how I used to complain about her slack ways – but that wasn't it at all. She'd gone straight to Mrs. Holloway. That was who she meant.'

'The woman at Southsea?'

They eyed each other in silence. This was not going to be easy. It was more than ten years since Rud had published his revelations concerning life in Southsea. Never a word to them directly and then that story, published for all the world to read. Whenever *Baa Baa Black Sheep* came back to haunt her, Alice always tried to insist that much of it was fantasy, Ruddy's imagination, that they couldn't have guessed – Lockwood still shrank from the subject.

'But how strange. What's she got to do with anything, that woman?'

'Jack, don't you see, she's telling us, telling me, not to worry about all that – that time in Southsea.'

It was something if Alice could find a degree of comfort for herself, he supposed.

'Well, I know she did choose to go back and spend time with Mrs. Holloway. I've never been able to make it out. If there was any truth at all in what Rud claimed…'

'It's wonderful that she's really talking to me again.' Alice wasn't listening. 'I've always known how to handle her and now it's really going to matter. Keeping her here with me, she agrees, is much the best thing for her.'

He didn't know what to say. Loving his wife, yet appalled by her capacity for self-deception, he was paralysed. He did know, though, that he could not go on living like this. He had the doctor's professional opinion behind him as he finally spoke.

'Alice, dearest, we can't care properly for Trix, not in this state.'

'I won't give her up, I won't,' his wife wept, even as he knew, his arms around her, that he was going to prevail.

Once doctors had taken over the care of Trix, Lockwood made his way across to Rottingdean as often as he could. He longed to take down his linen apron from where it hung on the back of the door and wrap himself in it ready for a day's work. Instead he had to be off, over to The Elms. The burden of Rud and his terrible mourning couldn't be shouldered entirely by Carrie. Besides, she had grief enough of her own.

Finding Carrie out on his arrival but expected home shortly, he dropped his overnight bag in the hall and went straight up to the nursery. He peeped in at Elsie and John, oblivious in their afternoon nap. So perfect, so defenceless, he shivered. The duck he'd carved for John and the rabbit Elsie had requested he propped by their pillows and went back downstairs. He'd scarcely settled into a highbacked chair in the drawing room when he caught Carrie's rapid tread in the hall beyond.

'This beautiful afternoon, I thought we might have tea in the garden,' she began. 'It may be the last time this year.'

She was pale still, in spite of that brisk manner, he observed as he kissed her. It would be no bad thing for her to get away to the sun. The doctors had forbidden Rud to spend another winter in England.

'There's a nip in the air these mornings' he agreed. 'Have you two made up your minds and fixed your travel plans?'

He wound a scarf about his neck before leaving the house. It was touching, the way Carrie took his arm as they stepped outside. Like him, she sniffed with pleasure at the faint taint of bonfires in the air. Then she turned a troubled face towards him.

'It looks as though we're going to South Africa. Rud's mad for it, though I'm not so sure.'

'South Africa? Now? But we're at war there – what can Rud be thinking of?' he stood staring. What was the poor fellow up to now?

'I don't know. Though he does say we'd be quite safe at Cape Town, the fighting's all further north,' Carrie answered quickly.

'Still defending him,' Lockwood thought, and patted her square, practical hand where it lay on his sleeve.

'I'm glad to see him showing enthusiasm for anything, frankly. We could have gone to India, you know, but he shied away when the Viceroy invited him. Drooped and said there was no-one he knew there any more and Viceroys weren't really his thing. "I've no interest in their monkey chatter."'

Lockwood allowed her to see his surprise.

'Don't you have any interest in the country yourself?'

She looked embarrassed.

'Of course I do. But I've never felt I could compete with India. It wouldn't answer our troubles, going there together. He'd forget me in all that blaze of colour and light, the temples, the fascination. I'd sink out of sight.'

That couldn't be right. He gave a dissenting grunt then walked her up and down the path again in silence.

'Why South Africa, though? The South of France'd be more convenient, surely.'

'You can't have missed the way Rud roused up, came to life, as the situation with the Boers worsened?'

He hadn't put two and two together. The whole business of fighting the Boers bothered him. England laying down the law to two independent republics on the other side of the world.

'When war was declared, just now, he was positively elated,' she went on, growing pink.

In his concern Lockwood stood stock still.

'Carrie, that sounds quite morbid. Are you sure?'

'Perfectly sure. I wish I wasn't. He's fretful now that things aren't going better for our side. "I've got to go down there to see for myself what's going on," that's what he keeps saying.'

A soft whistle from Lockwood. He stamped his feet, they were going to sleep.

'Rud pores over the reports in *The Times*. The gazetteer's kept on the breakfast table these days. He really intends us to go out there.'

Lockwood shook his head.

'What sort of life could you have there?' was all he could say.

Her reply seemed reluctant.

'We have got friends in Cape Town. From last year, when we went out to warm up after Rock House. And Mr. Rhodes did make an enormous fuss of Rud – special trains to see the diamond mines, a visit to his own country, Rhodesia – it could be a useful distraction.' Then, in a rush, 'But I don't want the children mixed up…'

She was close to tears, he could tell.

Looking up, he saw Rud coming in the gate.

After tea, Carrie left them together and they went off to the study. Once the door was closed behind him Rud immediately asked, 'Trix?'

Lockwood was unable to prevent his despair from showing.

His son's face fell.

'Don't make me go into detail.' Lockwood managed, flapping his hands. 'It's doing me good to get away for a few hours.'

'Isn't there anything that seems to help her? I can't bear knowing she's so unhappy and so – like this…' Rud's voice trailed off. 'I wish you'd let me come over to talk to her, I might –'

'Don't think of it,' Lockwood interrupted. 'Not till we've got her a good deal calmer.' Catching a look of hurt in Rud's eyes, he added 'I know how much she means to you. But you've no idea how agitated she gets, even the stir of a curtain against the sill can upset her. Be patient for a little while, do.'

They sat in silence. Lockwood was beginning to relax once more when he realised that Rud was not at ease. He'd be about to speak then turn away in silence.

From his seat near the desk, Lockwood watched and waited as he paced back and forth.

At last, 'Don't think I'm off my head too. I'm afraid I'm seeing things again.'

Lockwood shrank inwardly – what now? – but attempted to appear unperturbed.

Apparently encouraged by this placid response, Rud went on.

'I see a little girl with long fair hair –' Rud's voice caught in his throat.

So that was it. Lockwood's alarm abated.

'You mean you seem to see Jo,' his father prompted.

'I tell you I do see her. I don't seem to see anything. I see Jo when I look out, without thinking, into the garden.'

Coming to a halt he faced his father.

Silence. Lockwood looked at him doubtfully. But there was none of the frantic quality that Lockwood dreaded when he saw it surfacing in Trix. Rud wasn't ill. He seemed if anything doomed or resigned. 'Every time?'

'Unless I remember to brace myself, to shut it out, to shut her out. I did try that once but not again. I've failed her too badly already. I was her father. What sort of father lets a child die without even knowing it's happening?' he asked, his voice hoarse. Turning away sharply he blew his nose.

Lockwood went rigid. If the cap fits. That story, *Baa Baa Black Sheep*. What if…

Then he gathered his wits, came back to the present and shook his head. 'No, Rud, no. You were ill.' They had gone over this ground before.

Lockwood bit down on the stem of his pipe. 'Let me get this straight. Jo is… for you Jo is' – he didn't want to yield too much ground – 'she appears to be playing in the garden here at The Elms, just as she used to.'

'Under the cherry tree, most often but sometimes on the swing.' Rud took a chair, speaking more slowly now. 'It's like a drug. Before we got home, when I was still recruiting in New Jersey and then away fishing with Frank, I kept coming back, underneath, to the fact that she'd gone. I could not take it in. And then when at last I did – just to see her again, just – and then we got back to The Elms and I found that I could. It's tearing me to pieces. At first, you know, the relief, I thought that I'd die of joy. But now, I'm beginning to be afraid.'

Lockwood cleared his throat.

'Carrie doesn't see... her?' Remembering his little dead granddaughter, he couldn't get out the word 'it'.

'No. As we came through the gate, that first day in October when you were there to meet us – I had a feeling she was waiting for us – and when I first looked out from inside the house, there she was. Carrie heard me exclaim. I didn't say anything, just pointed. And she – well, she thought that I was simply admiring the colour in the parthenocissus. She decided I seemed overexcited and might be getting a fever. I was sent off to lie down.'

For all his dismay, Lockwood couldn't help laughing. 'My boy, I think it's a good thing that you've got round to telling someone about this.'

'I've kept putting it off. You know how I feel about spirit-writing, getting in touch with the dead. It's done for Trix, I'm sure. Half-lit rooms and dreadful women preying on decay and despair. And this – Jo – I couldn't bear –'

He was gripping the arms of his chair.

'No, Rud, no. Little Jo out in the garden, it's a million miles away from all that.' In spite of himself he longed to know more. 'Does she always look the same?'

Rud seemed surprised. 'No, I don't think she does. I haven't questioned it but her clothes do change. I believe, come to think of it, that her hair sometimes looks different. Ribbons and so on.'

Lockwood nodded. He allowed the silence to grow as he slowly relit his pipe.

'You know, I don't see that you can go on like this. For one thing, I think you might be hurting Jo.'

Rud's fingers, which had been picking at some loose threads on his waistcoat, became still. 'Hurting her? Hurting Jo?'

'You know, I don't much like what I've seen of how these things are managed here at Home. The English and their ghosts, their heaven and hell. There's something altogether cleaner about the Oriental way. They'd just accept that the individual life doesn't come to an end but moves on to take different forms.'

'You think I'm stopping her, preventing Jo from moving on?'

His gaze was intense.

'Stopping each other maybe? But think it over, Rud. See if it seems to fit. It might be time – might be wise – for you to leave The Elms.'

'I see. I'd never thought of it like that. I see.' The words came out slowly.

Again Lockwood waited, puffing away.

'And meanwhile, have you told Carrie about this?'

'I haven't said anything to Carrie. It would only make her agitated – she quite evidently doesn't see Jo – and why me and not her? And I can't anyway.' A smothered sigh.

'Can't? You don't like to in case she doesn't believe you?'

'Or worse – thinks I'm heading towards a breakdown – poor girl, she's constantly on the watch for signs of anything in that direction. No, it's not just that. We don't speak of Jo. Carrie decided it was better so.'

His father was slow to respond.

'And is that what you think too?' he wanted to ask. But glancing up, he caught Rud's mouth working. Lockwood kept his peace.

Instead, lowering his head and poking away at his lowered pipe as though he couldn't get it to draw, he began,

'Do you remember when I was staying with you in Naulakha when Jo was still quite tiny? Those little rabbit fur slippers someone sent her – she was so pleased with herself when she learned how to pull them off? I can see her now, sitting up on that big cloth with the animals on I painted for her – laughing away when we pretended to scold her, just waiting for you to put them back on then tearing them off with a shriek?'

It had worked. Rud interrupted.

'Yes. And did you ever see how once she could get about she used to crawl round with one of them in her mouth? It looked so like a cat with a mouse dangling from its jaws.'

'Mouse?' repeated Carrie in alarm, as she entered the room, her son in her arms. 'Don't say the word. We've only just got rid of the last one. Oh, this fug of smoke,' waving in protest.

She crossed the room to open a window.

Turning, she continued 'I've brought John in to see his grandfather. I thought he'd like a little masculine company.'

But the little wretch pressed his face against her shoulder and wouldn't look up. Lockwood had to woo him with sly tickles before he consented to be handed over. After that he settled down to tugging at his grandfather's woolly white beard.

She moved back to stand beside her husband. Looking up at her, he announced, 'The Pater thinks we should move out of The Elms. We've been very happy here –' he appeared to have difficulty in going on – 'but we should be thinking of finding somewhere else, that is, somewhere of our own.'

He was sweating. She knew the windows should have been opened earlier.

'Why that's just exactly what I've been telling you.'

She hadn't meant to sound shrill. Her resentment was already giving way to elation. A house of their own again! She grew cautious. It would all fall on her, as usual, you could be sure.

'Still, we can't do anything about finding a house right now. My hands are full with all the planning for South Africa.'

She stood by Rud's shoulder, watching as Lockwood coaxed Rud into playing with his son.

Carrie had no intention of wasting Lockwood's prompt. That evening she returned to the subject.

'Next spring, after South Africa, we can get down to a serious search. Maybe that would provide some use for that automobile you insisted on ordering.'

'The Lanchester? A test of it, rather. They haven't got the engineering quite worked out yet on these machines. Endless mechanical failures. But don't you go pretending you weren't intoxicated by that spin Harmsworth gave us in his Mercedes. I can't wait, myself. They've promised me that the driver they're sending us is one of their most experienced men. He can take us about the country, once we get back from South Africa. The hunt is up –'

Carrie was pleased, even delighted, by her own ingenuity.

* * *

Rud stretched his legs right out under the cool sheet, hugging the knowledge that outside, Cape Town was already heating up under a blazing February sun. Apart from Carrie's even breathing in the other bed, the room was remarkably quiet. The gardens of this new hotel, the Mount Nelson, were successfully insulating it from the noisy streets. Gardens, pink walls and balconies. Not Africa at all, what could they be after, the proprietors? A Mediterranean flavour, perhaps. Set up for tourists, not men with work to do. Remembering the officers lounging about the hotel, when the family arrived some days earlier, he was surprised all over again. You'd have thought they might have business elsewhere.

He was just able to make out the bold stripes of shadow on the nearest column beyond the window. As he watched, they moved the least little bit. Turning his head against the pillow he reached for his spectacles. Was it a creature making the tree move? The shadowy branches sprang bouncing together and he laughed aloud. Her eyes still shut, Carrie murmured, 'That's the way to wake up, you laughing beside me.'

But he was already out of bed, hoisting at his pyjamas. Carrie still hadn't completed the supervision of the unpacking. 'Not in the wardrobe,' she advised as he flung open doors. 'You'll find what you need for today laid out in the dressing room.' The bedroom door closing behind him, in a moment through the wood came the sound of splashing.

She held her breath. Would he sing?

By such minute calibrations she was tracing his recovery.

Out of the question, to let him see her own despair. Nothing was to be gained by that, though Jim Conland, who was so good to them in New York last year, disagreed. When she'd laid out her plan. 'It may do more harm than good in the long run,' he'd responded, walking beside her in Central Park where he sent her to get some fresh air. It was disappointing. She'd hoped for one moment of appreciation, even, as she bound herself to silence. She could admit as much, looking back. She'd not been able to make him budge. But for all Jim Conland was a medical man, Carrie felt that she was the one who knew what was best for Rud.

When Jim had gently attempted to warn her about trying herself beyond her strength, she'd flashed out at him: 'In my family, we don't allow misfortune to break us. I'm not the first mother to lose a child.'

She had to fight against remembering Josephine here in Cape Town. Jo'd been with them, when they were here before. Only two years ago. It felt like a century. On her first afternoon she'd been attacked – any other word would have been too weak – by the memory of her daughter, five years old, laughing as she ran barefoot towards the sea. But today when Jo turned, it was not to wave but to stretch out her arms, full of longing.

A groan broke from Carrie's lips. She should never have let Jo go.

The housekeeper had been passing along the terrace on her rounds. 'My heavens, that woman's about to fall,' and she'd stepped forward with a supporting arm. 'Mrs. Kipling, ma'am', would you care to sit down? Come ma'am, lean on me, here we are,' and Carrie had sunk onto a convenient bench.

She'd been mortified. 'Thank you so much. The heat, you know, I'm not accustomed to it. In a day or two…'

A knock on the door: round it came the dimpled brown elbow of the maid, braced against the weight of a tray. Heaven, to be putting up in this delightful place with no servants of her own to plague her. Carrie gathered herself, reaching for the light shawl on the nightstand, before raising herself to sitting. A few minutes later, when Rud appeared, fully dressed, she was smiling up at him as she sipped her tea.

He bent to kiss her cheek. 'What a pretty little woman it is this morning.' It might be a good day. Even as the tentative hope formed, she felt his hand move to her shoulder, stroking slowly. Her head tilted back, eyelids fluttering. 'Well, well, old girl, perhaps later,' and the hand was withdrawn. 'I'll take my tea on the verandah; it's so beautiful out there.'

Biting her lip, she watched the light curtain he had drawn blowing behind him. She pushed the tray out of the way and swung her feet down to the smooth cool floor.

An undercurrent of woodsmoke in the air, a bright edge to the morning: Rud felt something in himself settle. He looked round with delight in his eyes. Weaverbirds were building in that mango tree. He must tell Trix how it brought back their garden in Bombay. Then a weight sank him. The Trix who'd played with him, the girl he'd grown up with, had vanished, leaving a pitiful creature in her place. He swallowed. With grim concentration he turned back to the weaver birds and their nests.

Those festoons of dusty gourds had entranced the kids when they came out on holiday last year. He checked himself. Not last year, two years ago. Before. Hurriedly he stepped forward into the benevolence of the sun.

Wandering, he passed beyond the gardens which lay glistening from their early watering and made his way round by the service quarters of the hotel. As he passed the kitchens he could hear a discreet clattering. Squeals of laughter or a deep-voiced exclamation broke through now and then. If this were really India, instead of seeming so close to it, bringing back sensations that ran soothing and sharpening through his veins like a pipe of opium, then he would have understood the speech in the background.

How good to look up and see solid blue, to have left behind those pallid streets overhung with grey skies, the world that could slow the wheels of his being almost to a stop. Allah be praised, he had escaped from England. The words echoed in his head with such passion that he did not notice his own treachery.

But what was he going to do here, what was the point? The question slipped out, taking him aback. Absurd. He was here to learn what-was-what from the men who knew.

He could hear raised voices followed by cries of, 'No stop, you're hurting me!' from the suite he had just left. Nothing would make Elsie resigned to accept the miseries of her morning toilette. It was hard for little girls, all that long hair that a brush had to drag through. He winced in sympathy at the thought. If it were up to him he'd let her have it all cut off but Carrie put her foot down. He'd better see if she was ready for breakfast.

Struggling to peel a guava, Carrie was aware that Rud was itching to get away. The very day of their arrival, when she'd still been checking off the last of their trunks and baggage to be carried into the panelled entrance hall of the hotel, Rud had stepped away across the lobby to join a knot of newspapermen. Today, before he put down his cup he was already rising from the chair. Her relief at seeing him in spirits, at a glimpse of the old eagerness, made her generous.

Lord Roberts, whom Rud had known back in India, 'Bobs' as he was popularly known, had just arrived to take over command of the South African campaign. She wasn't sure how eager Sir Alfred Milner, the High Commissioner, would be to hear Rud's advice but she was certain Rud meant to offer it. This war had him in a fever.

She put down her fruit-knife and wiped her fingers.

'Rud, you'll need to be off to meet Lord Roberts. And he won't be the only old friend from India that's about. Who knows who else you may run into – you'll be away most of the day, I should imagine. There's so much going on, I won't expect you for lunch – I'll take mine with the children.'

Transparent as ever to her, he seized on this cue for escape. Dropping his napkin, 'I should look Bobs up, you're right. And Milner did ask me to be sure to get to the High Commission before too long. Seems to think that I could have a few ideas to contribute: these damned Boers, they're wiping the floor with us.

I can scarcely credit our losses. But things will look up now, you'll see, with Bobs running the show.'

'I don't understand about Mr. Rhodes, though. He's such a big man over here. What good does it do for him to be cooped up in Kimberley, trapped in the siege? With his weak heart, I'd have thought they'd make sure to get him out.'

'It's his vision, Carrie, his tremendous vision. He thinks only of the country and its destiny, never considers his own safety as he should. I know it worries Milner terribly.'

She remained doubtful. It looked like posturing to her. But the arrival of the children, led by their nurse, put an end to conversation. Elsie exploded into giggles as Rud pretended to salaam: blowing kisses to them, he bustled out.

Field Marshal Lord Roberts of Kandahar stumped over to the large-scale map on the wall of his temporary office, with its pins and flags showing military positions, and squinted. On the voyage out he'd kept up with dispatches but he must make sure to be absolutely up-to-date before he set off upcountry. As a young officer, he'd served in the Indian Rebellion, while twenty years later in Afghanistan, he'd taken Kabul and relieved Kandahar. Now, just turned seventy, he was supposed to retrieve the British position in South Africa.

It didn't help that young Fred, his only son, had just been killed in battle. From the day his father had taken over supreme command of this failing campaign he'd been struggling against constant weary misery. Fred. Gone down at Colenso. A drumbeat. This very morning, sitting down on the bed of the wounded officer who'd been riding beside his son the day he died, Lord Roberts had broken down and wept.

He must put all that out of his mind. He checked a place-name in his generals' reports against the map. He really had enough on his plate without worrying about young Kipling. However famous he was, these days.

But Milner, the High Commissioner, had made a great point of his seeing Kipling, asking it as a personal favour:

'We need to involve him, you know, make him feel he's part of the whole enterprise. And you'd be the one to do it. He has the power to get the country – or more of it – behind this war and we desperately need that. Think of the weight his voice carries. His sales are enormous, and better than that, he is really respected because he doesn't appear to toady. Think of *Recessional*.'

Remembering Milner's advice, Roberts snorted: he was not at all sure himself about the meaning of that poem or where its sympathies lay. He knew that he for one was not drunk with sight of power and loosing wild tongues. Where did these writer johnnies get their ideas?

Judge of the nations, spare us yet,
Lest we forget – lest we forget!'

Indeed. And as for asking for an humble and a contrite heart, that seemed to suggest that the home of Empire had something to be sorry about: it wasn't how he himself saw things at all. Did the fellow believe in England's mission or didn't he?

Nevertheless, he would do what he could to forward Milner's plans. It wouldn't do to be fighting with the country at home so divided. But who would have thought that the young sprig who was so full of himself a dozen years or so past at Simla would have come to play such a part in the calculations of the men who really counted?

'Do be sure to say something about The Absent-Minded Beggar Fund when you meet Kipling,' Milner had urged. Fred Roberts planned to make it his opening move.

When, shortly before lunch, an aide-de-camp announced 'Mr. Rudyard Kipling to see you, Sir', he was prepared.

Roberts chose to have no chairs in the room where he worked, so there was no question of inviting visitors to sit. It kept conversation brief. After shaking hands:

'They tell me you've raised an extraordinary amount with that poem of yours, Kipling: quite extraordinary. Getting on for a quarter of a million, no? But I believe it's for the women and children at home, is that correct? Not coming our way out here...' he allowed himself a tight smile.

The fellow looked a bit thin but face-to-face, he recognised the direct gaze, though it wasn't as bright as he remembered.

'Very kind of you, Lord Roberts, remembering those verses of mine.' Rud bowed. 'In fact, that's just what I wanted to talk to you about: I do have access to some of the funds, to be used over here. I was hoping to ask your advice.'

Roberts tapped his riding boots with the papers he was holding.

'I suppose you want me to give you permission to run about all over the shop, deciding where to spend it, don't you? You're not the first young fellow I've met over here determined to get to the fighting by hook or by crook. Very well: I can give you a pass that will get you through the lines and into the hospitals.'

Looking up from the desk where he seated himself to scribble, '*The bearer of this, Mr. Rudyard Kipling, has my permission to proceed wherever he may desire in South Africa and may visit any of the Army Hospitals,*' he raised a hand in warning: 'I hope you've a strong stomach on you, Kipling. It won't be pretty. But I suppose you have become hardened –' he came to a halt, embarrassed. It was India and its filth he meant but perhaps Kipling would take it too personally, think he meant the fellow's own illness and the child's death.

Apparently not. Kipling stowed the pass in his inside pocket, and put out his hand, saying quietly: 'I hope you will accept our sympathy.'

Roberts was careful not to speak but bowed and the interview was over.

Alone once more, he turned to the telegrams from Kimberley, under siege since October. The commander of the garrison, Kekewich, was doing a fine job. Excellent man. Precise estimates of food and forage. Probable length of time they could withstand the siege. Numbers of sick: a thousand cases of scurvy among the natives, but thank God only a hundred and twenty of our people with typhoid.

But this Rhodes fellow. A mountebank. Trying to run the show, dictate the military strategy, put pressure on him, Fred Roberts, with his messages. Who did he think he was? Dammit, being rich as Croesus and king of the diamond mines meant nothing, nothing. Authority belonged to Kekewich. Kimberley was under martial law. And rations were dangerously low; look at the health report. Why wasn't Rhodes turning over the De Beers stores of food and wines?

'If threat to stability of town arrest Rhodes and imprison,' he telegraphed Kekewich.

The reply was swift:

'I will do my best but fear will have great difficulty in restraining Rhodes. Demands definite information on plans for relief column given him. He is quite unreasonable. Rhodes key to the military situation here as large majority of the Town Guardsmen, the Kimberley Light Horse and the volunteers are De Beers employees. He is grossly insulting to myself and British Army: "Your signallers sending out damned rot. You low damned mean cur Kekewich you deny me at your peril." Then took a swing at me.'

Roberts didn't need telling that this egotism, this rank treachery, had better not be made public. Keep quiet about division in the ranks. Above all, no word to that boy Kipling. First thing you knew it would be a choice scandal all over the papers. Like the old days.

He had not entirely forgotten ancient scores.

Beneath his affable manner, Rud had been agonisingly aware that Roberts too had just lost a child. The image of the stiff Spartan little figure haunted him.

'How does the man keep going?' he marvelled. But then, it wasn't his fault.

There's not the guilt with a grown son, dying in battle.

The following day he presented himself early at Government House to see Sir Alfred Milner. In the cool tiled vestibule a waiting secretary hurried forward.

'Mr. Kipling, good morning to you. Sir Alfred has given orders that you should be sent in to him directly you arrived. I know he is most anxious to see you. If you would care to follow?'

Rud didn't wait but darted ahead of him and only paused when the stooping figure of Milner, High Commissioner for South Africa and Lieutenant-Governor of the Cape Colony, stepped forward from a doorway further down the hall.

'My dear Kipling!' The voice was languid but he assumed that was a matter of habit. Not every visitor, as Rud knew, would have been met in the hallway.

'Sir Alfred! Tremendously good of you to make time for me.'

A limp hand slithered through his own.

'On the contrary, my dear fellow, I've been on tenterhooks till you arrived.' The secretary, panting slightly, had caught up with them but was waved away. Rud waited until he was out of sight.

'Capable?' he raised an eyebrow inquisitively. 'Doesn't strike me so.'

Milner appeared taken aback. Not used to having a man he could talk to on equal terms out here, probably. Clearly, he was going to appreciate all the advice Rud could offer him.

Once the tray of softly chinking glasses was deposited on the magnificent stinkwood table, Milner dismissed the Malay servant in his white uniform, crossing the room to check that the door was closed. He gestured towards the cool jug with its beads of moisture but Rud shook his head. Iced drinks made his teeth hurt.

'In a little while, perhaps.'

They moved by silent consent over to the desk where a sheaf of papers was held down by an ammonite paperweight. Milner moved it aside, spreading them out, as he began to explain.

'Rhodes is still able to use the telegraph to keep in touch, so we have a pretty good idea of the state of things in Kimberley. His reports are confidential, of course, but I'd be extremely obliged if you would cast your eye over them. Tell me what you think – I'm less sure about what's going on in Mafeking and Ladysmith.'

Milner coughed.

'Not happy with the military interpretation?' Rud asked, confidentially. He picked up a sheet to peer more closely. 'It's not always the pick of the army that finds itself in command. Well, thank God for Rhodes: there's one man we can trust for information from upcountry. But everything I've heard at home makes me puzzled.'

It was getting warmer, even inside with these high ceilings. Between his shoulders his shirt was sticking.

Milner was nodding thoughtfully but he remained silent.

'We outnumber these Boers, our troops are disciplined, while they're a mere rabble, we've even got better weapons, and yet we're still not making headway. What's Buller been doing? He's been out in the field for months without anything to show for it but losses. You do know that the papers have taken to calling him Sir Reverse Buller?'

'All that will change now,' Milner's voice was smooth, confident. He began gathering the scattered papers together. Rud hadn't quite finished.

'When I heard Bobs was being sent out here, I thought, "At last we mean business. The Boer's got to be put firmly in his place." It's absurd for us to let a backward race with its primitive ways stand in our path. The country's magnificent, it lies waiting to be developed and made fruitful. What a climate – we could grow anything – we've both heard Rhodes on his plans for fruit exports. The economy would be transformed.'

When Rud finally paused, Milner agreed with a brief 'Indeed.'

Motioning his guest to a seat at the desk, from a locked drawer he took out a file and laid it before him.

Rud leaned forward, at the centre of affairs at last.

* * *

Word from Rud was eagerly awaited in Tisbury.

A pass. Lockwood Kipling sighed quietly, as he sat at the breakfast table, reading the letter. On the one hand, anything that could bring some life back into Ruddy's eyes must be a good thing. But time was when the boy didn't rely on passes from great personages nor rejoice in them.

He'd reached for the envelope eagerly at the sight of his son's writing, the more pleased that Alice was late down to breakfast. She would have had it out of his hand before he could reach for the paperknife. Made of yellow jade with a pattern deeply incised, it was one he used to keep on his desk at the Museum in Lahore. Now he fingered it nervously and returned to his reading.

He laid the blue envelope down beside his plate and was staring out into the garden when his wife entered. 'You're upset and it's something to do with that letter' – it was already between her fingers. 'But it's from Ruddy, he's not well –'

'Nonsense, my dear. At times you can be much too quick off the mark for your own good. He's not ill. Sit down now and read it quietly.'

Alice allowed herself to be calmed, though not without directing a meaningful glance at his fingers, still toying with the old jade knife. She poured herself a cup of tea before beginning to read.

There was a smile on her face as she looked up.

'Dear old chap, he's really getting carried away. He forgets that it's no recommendation to me to tell me how much like India it is in Cape Town. But he does sound happy – almost like a boy again. It goes to my heart.'

The grave look he sent across the table silenced her.

'He's deceiving himself, you know, comparing it with India.'

'Deceiving himself?' She put her cup down. 'To what end?'

'Heaven alone knows. But think, Alice. We're administering India in the interests of the weakest, or at least that used to be Rud's view: protecting them from the higher castes. But whatever we pretend, it's gold and diamonds that took us out to the Cape and keep us out there now. India! A pass from Lord Roberts, indeed!' He pushed his plate away.

'What possible objection can you have to a pass from Lord Roberts?' She stiffened.

Her husband reached across and took her hand: 'Just try to remember how the boy was when he was with us in Lahore. Little friend of all the world.'

'But most of those people you call his friends weren't even English and none of them had the least education. They were just – picturesque.' Her gesture was dismissive.

'That's not my point. When the boy would slip through the back streets and bazaars, reporting some of what he saw but by no means all of it in the old *CMG*, he was doing something useful. I liked him for it.'

'And you don't like him now? Working alongside Lord Roberts and Sir Alfred Milner isn't useful?'

The tea in his cup had gone cold but he drained it anyway.

'Alice, do try to understand. I don't like the way he's lining himself up with the big men. He always used to keep his distance, hold them to account. Don't you remember?'

'I remember the times I had to apologise for him and what he wrote.'

'In those days he wasn't afraid to disturb, to rock the boat –'

'I'd say he enjoyed it. If you're accusing Rud of being some kind of camp-follower, cosying up to the politicians in South Africa, I think you're quite mistaken.'

Folding her napkin, she rose. 'It may be true that it's unlikely he'll meet many of the native people or get a chance to explore how they live or learn their language – if they have anything more than a system of grunts – but I'm not sure that matters.'

Lockwood shook his head, smiling. It was wrong of him to insist. Poor girl, with all she was still going through with Trix, no wonder she wanted to believe the best with regard to Ruddy. Trix might be well enough to live at home but you couldn't say she was herself.

Away up in her bedroom, Trix was still in her nightgown. The relief, these last few weeks, not being marched through washing and dressing before she'd got her breath. According to Them, Miss Green had been appointed as her companion but Trix knew better. She was a jailer. Not even a nurse. At last They had agreed Green was no longer needed. Good riddance.

But she didn't like what she saw when she crossed over to the glass.

Eyes too large, too dark all round them.

Still, she felt strong enough today for The Plan.

She tested the water in the ewer. Quite warm still. If she scrubbed her cheeks till they had some colour first, then she could wash and get dressed. Opening the wardrobe, she took out the grey shirtwaist.

Unbearable, remaining cooped up here, away from the friends she needed to talk to about her work. With Maud Diver and Tom back from India for good, instead of relying on letters she and Maud could work on their novels side by side again.

Where was her purse?

She took it out from behind her pillow.

Plenty of cash.

With no Miss Green eyeing her she'd been slipping her hand into jackets and pockets around the house, even into other purses. Building up funds.

Was her hair perfectly tidy? There must be nothing to draw unfavourable attention, nothing to criticise.

First the train to London, then a cab to the de Morgans'.

Rud was no use to her any more, from all she heard Downstairs. All out for war. How could he take up with these ideas? Any child could see that war was not the way forward for the world.

And no respect from him for the spirit-writing.

She thrust hard at a last hairpin.

Without the dear, dear de Morgans where would she be? They at least were really convinced of its importance for the world. That it could bring fresh understanding of our lives here. Lead to a new understanding of women. Find the way to keep peace between nations.

Some finishing touch. She scanned her dressing table. A ribbon?

The very thought of speaking with the de Morgans, even perhaps of sitting down to join them in some trance-writing, brought tears of relief to her eyes.

But she must be sure not to let Them know what she had in mind.

Hearing Trix's step in the hallway, Lockwood, still at the table, braced himself for her entrance. Though she was wan she was neatly dressed, a crimson ribbon round her throat the only jarring feature. She gave a tense smile, bright and placating.

'I thought I'd just slip up to town to see my publisher, later this morning, take the midday train.'

Lockwood's head dropped forward. He couldn't bear to watch, she was so transparent. That Trix should make such a sad little bid to deceive them. He could have wept.

'I am going up to town, Father,' she repeated. 'Did you hear what I said?'

It was Alice who broke the silence: 'Trix, my darling, I'm not sure this is the day for it, you're not well enough yet, we can send a little note to your publisher –'

Lockwood could not let this pass. All three of them knew that Trix was really after time with the de Morgans. And with those paintings of theirs that she'd been writing poems about. Of all people, she must be kept from them. No more of their encouragement for those trance experiments.

'Alice, no, you'll have us as mad, that is as confused, as Trix. There is no publisher, no appointment.'

At once the pale lips opened startlingly wide, in a high thin cry. When it stopped Trix stood braced before them, glittering-eyed.

'You won't let me have any friends. How can you be so cruel?'

Lockwood made his escape. Since Alice insisted that she alone knew the secret of calming Trix, there was no place for him.

Once in his workshop, slowly wrapping himself in his old studio apron, he revolved the possibilities. He had some clay that was ready for wedging. As he steadily rocked the heavy mass preparing to knead it, his mind cleared. They would have to think of getting the nurse-companion back. But Alice was so intent on keeping the care of Trix within her own control, so ready to declare a fixed improvement. To his eyes, each apparent period of stability merely turned out to have been a deception, a disappointment, like the healing over an ulcer that breaks down yet again.

* * *

At Milner's invitation, Rud was dropping by every morning to see him at Government House. That left only the afternoons to fill. Today, after lunch, it was his day for visiting the General Military Hospital. He had a regular routine between hospitals going now. At the entrance he collared an orderly and handed over a pack of tobacco for distribution round the wards. The Absent Minded Beggar Fund, had supplied it but he didn't have to deliver every single tin himself. He'd found a better way of helping out here.

It disturbed him, though, not being able to help Trix. He'd tried writing to her more than once, brief notes, meant to steady her.

> *'My very dear Trix*
> *It makes me sad to think of your unhappiness.*
> *Please remember how much you mean to me always.*
> *Your devoted*
> *Brother.'*

But he'd had to stop. He'd been told she refused even to touch the envelopes.

The reek of Jeyes' Fluid brought him to a halt. Like a punch on the nose. But comforting too, a smell from childhood, Bombay, wet floors after the sweepers had been through.

'I thought I'd make myself useful by writing, taking down letters, today. D'you think that would be an idea, Sister?' he asked, catching a tall woman in dark uniform dress as she hurried past.

'Just what they could do with. We're all rushed off our feet, not a moment to sit down with anyone unless, you know, at the very end. Thank you, Mr. Kipling.' She was off.

A young nurse, emerging from behind a screen, suggested he should go first to the patient at the end on the right. She sketched the background.

'His arm had to come off, this morning. The bullet had absolutely shattered it,' she whispered finally, pushing back tendrils of hair under her white cap, 'we've done what we can about the pain but he's anxious and very restless.'

Rud nodded. He felt inside his jacket for pen and notebook before he made his way down the row of beds. All casualties in here, of course, the fever patients – such numbers of them, a disgrace – were cared for elsewhere.

The man he'd been directed to was youngish, about his own age. Shock-headed, his hair still full of the dirt from the fall he must have taken when his scouting party was ambushed. The tight bandages strapping the stump of his right arm oozed.

He was croaking, his voice altered by shock.

'What use am I going to be after this? What about the children? Lizzie's not strong, she'll never be able to manage,' he repeated obsessively once Rud sat down.

'Don't you think your wife might like to hear from you? That would be something we could manage,' he began.

The fretting continued as though he hadn't spoken. Poor fellow, how to distract him?

'Really, look it's no trouble,' Rud insisted, 'my notebook's here, never without one and Sister will make sure it gets sent out with the mails.'

'My dear wife,' Rud's pen raced over the paper, following the halting dictation *'do not be worried getting this, I am getting on well, though in the hospital. Who knows, they may send me home after this. My love to little Betty and the baby, your loving husband Fred Sawbridge.'* He added his own name with a note to explain that the letter was dictated: it

was too early to add any honest word of encouragement.

He liked it when he could do that. '*The details above are entirely correct*,' he'd learned to add, together with his signature. He thought that would be believed, even read by an anxious wife or mother at home.

At the end of the hour he handed over three or four such letters to Sister Vellacott for dispatch and was fifty yards down the street, the sun blistering his unprotected head through his thinning crown, before he realised that he'd left his hat behind. No need to trouble Sister, he thought he knew exactly by which bed he'd left it. As he passed the door to her office he saw it was almost shut. Good, she must be snatching a moment's rest.

Then he stood rooted with embarrassment on hearing her voice.

'It is wonderful, the way he never fails us,' she seemed to be agreeing with someone. 'There's nothing he wouldn't try to get for the men if we said they needed it. But he's a driven man, can't you see that?'

It must have been young Nurse Gibbons, he knew that voice too: 'I wonder you don't hang on to one or two of those letters, Sister. With Rudyard Kipling's signature they'd be worth something at home.'

He wanted to hit her. Cheap little bitch.

'A driven man'. He wanted to hide. His failure was written all over him. His knees were trembling as he moved away to pick up his straw hat.

He had to force himself to go back after that. No letting those fellows down, whatever he was feeling. Sometimes it was pretty fierce, the sense of pointlessness. What was he good for, after all?

'Taking down their words quite unaltered may be useful but it takes no skill,' he grumbled to Carrie, more than once. 'A child could do it.'

'You must know it means a lot to them. Especially when they find out who you are,' she told him in the end.

'I'm not proud of myself for enjoying that,' he returned, flatly.

Yet he managed to keep up the hospital visits.

'Stocks of pyjamas are desperately low, Mr. Kipling, or I wouldn't ask you,' Sister Vellacott approached him awkwardly. 'I don't know where I'm going to find the next pair. And there's another hospital train due in this evening.'

'Leave it to me,' he replied with mechanical confidence. The Absent-Minded Beggar Fund was raising enough to subsidise any number of pairs.

But once at the General Stores, the bristling little Welsh quartermaster he approached, one man at least who clearly did not recognise him, thought otherwise.

'Any dispensing of goods requires a chit, followed by an invoice from a company officer. Two days notice is usual and delivery will take place the following week,' he rattled off.

The resistance, all unexpected, jolted him to life.

What next? He could easily obtain a note from Staff and blast the man with authority. Yet something in him recoiled. Besides, there might be a little fun to be had in remaining unofficial. He cast a thoughtful eye about him as he wandered off, all apparent submission. Sure enough, he caught sight of turbaned figures slipping between the tents, a folded stretcher carried between them.

Calling out a greeting in Hindustani, he hurried to catch up with them. There was intense pleasure in feeling the words come alive in his mouth. Incredulous and delighted, 'Who would think to hear the tongue of Hind in this country where there are no gods?' one exclaimed, laying down his burden. In two minutes they were his accomplices.

Of a certainty they would find what the Sahib desired. But not pyjamas only? Was there nothing more they could obtain for him quietly, quietly from the *godown*?

Rud restrained himself. No need to load up with spare tobacco for the men. The supplies ordered out from England were nowhere near exhausted.

'Pyjamas only, brothers. Who are we to rob the poor?'

The stretcher-bearers were still grinning when they returned under a load of striped flannel bound up with broad tapes.

'One half gross, counted,' they told him proudly.

Handing them over to Sister Vellacott was a moment of triumph. He scarcely knew when he'd felt so pleased at what he'd pulled off. School, maybe, with the fellows in Number Five Study?

He got a laugh out of the men as well, going up to her in the middle of them all and declaring, 'Sister, I've got your pyjamas.'

She looked almost pretty, blushing.

'The difference, Carrie, the difference,' he exclaimed. They were taking a stroll after tea, among the palms and strelitzias of the Company's Garden, a short distance away from their hotel. 'A few minutes with those stretcher-bearers and I was reminded. The local people here can't hold a candle to them.'

Carrie had been reading the labels on an unfamiliar shrub, so hadn't been paying attention.

'Local people? The Boers?'

'Not at all. I meant the natives, the blacks. The Boers are all too like what we have at home – I mean , what I knew as a child and hated – smug piety, Biblical texts with all the time an eye for the main chance. And ugly!' Under his vicious kick a pebble shot away down the path.

'I've lost the thread,' Carrie murmured, puzzled, 'Can we go back? You were telling me about Lord Milner and what he had to say.'

These sessions with Milner, a man who was worth talking to, invigorated him, though he suspected she failed to see their importance. She just wanted him occupied, not moping.

'Tell me again,' she repeated. Nothing pleased him better. It helped to arrange his ideas.

'As I was saying, Milner thinks we can get through this – always assumed the damned War Office sends through the funds and they get the hospitals sorted out. We can get a local government in place on terms that suit both sides. We just have to leave out the question of the blacks.'

'The blacks?' she asked with transparent caution. He was sure she'd heard him the first time.

'Yes, yes, naturally, the blacks,' he nodded, trying not to sound irritable. 'In theory, of course, we should think about enfranchising them, land rights and so on. That's certainly what those airy intellectuals, the Liberals, want. Opinion out here would never hear of it. And if we want a united southern Africa, to create a union here, one in which we are acknowledged as the Mother Country, we have to find common ground. It's the union of the two races, those of Dutch inheritance and ourselves, that must be the goal.'

Carrie kept tugging at the lace on her cuff as he was explaining.

He could see her struggle to contain herself, hear the effort behind her even voice. 'But Rud,' she began, 'Rud, have you forgotten Vermont? In Brattleboro you seemed red hot for anti-slavery, like the rest of us.'

'Well, so I am but we're not talking about slavery here. We're talking about governing natives, blacks with no more tradition or culture than a tent and a blanket. Not fit by a mile to hold land, certainly not to vote –'

She came in before he'd finished speaking

'How do you know that, Rud? What do we know of these people? It's the Malays we see most of and the woman who does our washing is sharp as a knife. Have you ever exchanged two words with one of those black people you're so quick to write off?'

She was walking so fast he had to hurry to keep up with her.

'Carrie, you really are absurd. I'm perfectly aware that some of them can read and write. We couldn't use them as interpreters else. But exceptions are neither here nor there.' Before she could speak again he went on. 'Believe me, this is out of your ken. We're talking about political life as it is carried on between nations, the governance of the empire. Small things must give way to greater.'

She stopped in the middle of the path.

'And I to you? You'll never convince me, Rud. If you'd heard those views uttered on an upcountry railway platform rather than in Government House you'd have been appalled.'

How well she looked, all at once, alive with energy. He was conscious of warmth in his own cheek, too. In the silence, however, a strain in his breathing could be heard. It was a sign they both recognised. Time to draw back.

'It's a beautiful afternoon, Rud. Won't you come with me down to Muizenberg and surprise the children? They've been spending the day on the beach with Nurse Lucy.'

He might as well. Get a sight of the kids down on the sand, earnestly digging away and happy. Anything to replace those images of a wan and haunted Trix that every letter from his father reinforced.

* * *

At home in Tisbury, it was a damp, cool late summer, with mould taking over the borders. In spite of this, Alice was in good spirits, for Trix appeared much less agitated recently.

She sat quietly beside Alice in the breakfast room, for more than an hour that afternoon, looking through old photographs together, without a sign of restlessness. Alice felt the need for change though. She began to hope that the weather would clear, so they could go outside.

'It's really too miserable for the garden, even for the sake of some air. Every branch and stem out there is dripping with wet,' she acknowledged reluctantly at last.

Slowly she reached for her sewing. How long was it since she'd dared to put a pair of scissors within her daughter's reach?

'I don't know whether you'd care to help me with this? You're such a needlewoman, Trix. But it does take concentration and you may not feel up to it.'

There, she had taken the risk.

But Trix was fingering a corner of the voluminous white linen tablecloth almost eagerly.

'It's very pretty, the design you've been working, Mama. And the single faggot stitch along the borders, I've always been fond of that.'

Deftly threading a needle, Trix began sewing, pausing only to hold up the hem to check she was keeping her stitch even.

'What good progress we've made together,' Alice ventured, smiling, as the clock struck for tea.

Trix looked back at her.

'I wish we could do some writing together, Mama.'

'Wouldn't that be fun, darling? Poems? Just as you and Ruddy used to?' Alice trod gingerly.

'Ruddy and I? No, I meant spirit-writing. You know I did. You were always boasting about having "the sight", Mother. Well, let's put it to the test. Let's plan to do some trance-writing together, find out what comes through –'

Alice stopped breathing for a moment, then spoke carefully.

'Now Trix, you know that wouldn't be wise. Everyone agrees –'

'Everyone: you mean Jack and Rud and Father. They hate me. You all hate me.'

And Trix was standing, the billowing folds dropped, forgotten crushed beneath her feet. Her hands at her temples, she was dragging and tearing at her own hair.

By the time Lockwood rushed in, drawn from the other end of the house by her cries, Trix had succeeded in ripping out a real tuft and blood was trickling onto her forehead.

* * *

The war was going better at last: Kimberley and Ladysmith relieved, Bloemfontein captured. Having caught up with Rhodes, when he was still fresh out of Kimberley, Rud was late for dinner when he got back to the Mount Nelson. But he couldn't wait to pass on news of the great man's intentions.

He was struggling into his dress-shirt as he spoke.

'Do you know, Carrie, he's got a scheme to build a house for us out near his own place, near Groote Schuur.'

To his astonishment, she looked cross.

Without speaking, she turned back to her dressing table and put in an extra hairpin.

Facing him once more 'I don't have any wish to form part of Mr. Rhodes' plan for South Africa, myself,' she began.

'You don't understand,' he hurried. 'It's my fault, I haven't explained properly. You know he's planned Groote Schuur with an eye to the years to come. British and Dutch traditions meeting in harmony and all that. A suitable residence for future leaders. Now he wants to create a place for men of the arts, a house they can come out to and live here for part of the year.'

Picking up her evening bag, Carrie got to her feet.

'And you're to be his first pet writer?'

'What's got into you, Carrie?' He felt crestfallen as a child. 'With a regular base we could spend winter out here every year in a home of our own. He made a particular point of saying you must have the final say in everything. It's dashed generous. Typical of the man.'

He could tell Carrie was merely holding herself in check.

He couldn't make out what she had to object to.

'Perhaps we'd better see exactly what Mr. Rhodes has in mind,' she said at last, taking his arm.

Such misplaced suspicion, she was bound to come round.

Rud even managed to run into Bobs when he made a brief return to Cape Town. The little man, full of renewed energy was striding up and down Milner's office as he gave the High Commissioner more details of the victory at Bloemfontein.

'Ah, Kipling, just the man I want to see,' he exclaimed as Rud was shown in. 'We need to make the men feel civilised again. A newspaper for them, that's what I've in mind. Gwynne of Reuters and Landon of *The Times* with one or two others have agreed to set it up. You know how much your name would mean to the men, Kipling. Would you consider joining the team for a week or two up in Bloemfontein?'

He didn't needed asking twice. That night he took the rattling train north.

The next morning, however, leaning out of the window to breathe in the dry scents of the veld, as they approached Bloemfontein he drew back, catching the stink of typhoid. His heart beat faster. India had taught him what that meant.

Later, after a bath and a change of clothing, he walked about town exploring and asking questions. Bobs had taken over the parliament, the Raadzaal, as a hospital, but even that wasn't going to suffice. From the hastily painted signs outside them, it looked as though many houses had also been commandeered.

'Three hundred and fifty patients lying almost directly on the bare ground with only three doctors and not a single nurse to be seen: that damned Surgeon-General didn't fancy the idea of ladies in the wards,' Gwynne told him, when he arrived at the paper's little makeshift office.

'It's a confounded disgrace,' Rud agreed. Odd that Milner hadn't spoken of it as a problem. Rud didn't feel like pursuing that, so he pushed the thought away.

Why was there something to make him angry everywhere he turned? Better angry than sad, though. He was crushed that Trix still didn't want to hear from him.

'What shall I do, set up type, read proof, write a poem?' Rud called out to the other men. He was full of go, ready for anything. This was like stepping back into the familiar office, the *duftar* at the *CMG*.

Together they plotted to get past the censors, how to coax copy out of the Tommies and their officers.

'We've got to sniff out any chap whose friends suspect him of scribbling in private. It'll be good for morale to get work from the men into print,' urged Banjo Paterson.

'Go on, Kipling, you'd better hunt them up.'

It was exactly what he used to enjoy, getting the soldiers talking. It came so easily to him. He felt no older than the youngest of them.

Back in the office, with Gwynne and the others, he fought with the ancient printing press.

'How the dickens this was ever made to function defeats me,' Landon growled cheerfully, ink to his elbows.

'Never such larks,' Rud exclaimed, then more softly, 'not for years and years.'

Once up near the front, he'd meant to get closer to the fighting, though somehow after a week he still hadn't seen action. Maybe in a day or two. It hardly seemed to matter, nothing did, working with the others on the paper they'd named *The Friend*.

The riot of laughter in their dusty little cubby-hole put him in mind of Number Five Study more than once. He was starting to feel something like his old self. *I'm glad I didn't die last year in New York*,' he found himself writing.

The hideous dreams that he was back in court had stopped. Writing back to Carrie in Cape Town he must remember to let her know. He'd seen how she fed upon these signs of health. He was coming back to life, or was it his old life, all his old life that was coming back to him and clicking into place?

'I'm joining up all my ideas with the others of many years ago,' he told her.

The evenings in the Club – more accurately a makeshift mess, set up in the Free State Hotel – were the time for listening to the stories of the men returned from that day's skirmishing on the veld.

Rud's heart kicked with pleasure as he stepped over the threshold into the irregular shadows of the lamplight. The mess servants had set up a long table: the choice of drinks was limited but the room would fill up with talk and men. Tobacco smoke was bad for him, he'd been warned. Conland had frowned when he'd refused to give up his own pipe. Now each evening the warning tightness in his chest after half an hour amid the deepening blue haze told him that it was time to leave.

His breathing was already turning scratchy when Gwynne, who

had been out of the office with a scouting column, came in and was waved over to the table. Rud had been listening to the chaplain argue with a young officer who was outraged by the way his men had been punished for stealing horses.

'It's not as if they were doing it for private gain,' he kept protesting. 'Without a mount they're no use to anyone.' Perfectly true: against a mounted guerrilla enemy what use was a man on foot? The lads were joyfully unscrupulous. Every day *The Friend* carried notices of horses missing or ones discovered riderless, now to be enquired after '*down by the cricket field*'. The schoolboy note entertained him, though the fighting men didn't seem to notice it.

Gwynne's arrival caused a pause: all heads turned his way, ears cocked.

He was slow to begin. 'It's a bad business,' he managed finally.

Attention shifted into edginess. A voice to his left was raised cautiously. 'Many casualties?'

'Not so bad. No. It's this business of clearing the farms. Well, we don't clear them, do we, we burn them. It's the finish for these people, they're all farmers, the Boers – they're just sent off packing into the veld.'

A sombre agreement.

'It cost me something, I can tell you, to watch this afternoon. The thatch had already caught and the husband, sullen enough, was turning away from the sight. All for getting off – but the woman –' After a pause, 'The mother, I should say. Have you ever noticed those little headstones out on the farms? Sometimes two or three of them together? I'd never thought of what they meant before today. That woman would not leave with her husband: instead she went over and knelt, she tried to put her arms round them, round them all at the same time.'

'And then?' A voice from the back of the room.

'She got up without speaking a word so far as I could hear. I had turned away – it didn't seem right –'

Rud was growing hot. He broke in. 'It's a modest enough return for treachery. Once they've sworn allegiance, and on the Bible.

what can they expect if they're caught signalling to the other side? Quite apart from the betrayal of that Christian faith they're always preaching, it's treason. They're lucky not to be hanged for it.'

Gwynne appeared astonished to hear him.

But Rud knew about treachery and women in unclean black garments with the Bible language always in their mouths. He remembered how many of his friends from the old days had already met their death out on the hideous emptiness of the veld.

In the uneasy silence that followed his outburst, he became conscious of a faint whistling in his chest. He carefully got to his feet. 'Doctor's orders,' he muttered for anyone who was listening, hand over his sternum, as he made for the door.

Behind him, muted voices rose into new conversations. In a corner, a tall moustached figure nudged his neighbour: 'Fancy going down to that house off Douglas Street after dinner? Some of those black bitches are stunners, wonderful shape. I've asked Landon and he's definitely on.'

Someone was calling for another round.

'Anyone ready to take me on at four-to-one that Kitchener will take over as C-in-C before Christmas?' A red-faced young cavalry officer in field dress was trying to make a book. Meanwhile, a silent figure, a horseman from the Cape Colony sat on blank with dismay.

'I used to worship Kipling and his writing,' he'd repeat for the rest of his life, 'but once I'd actually met the fellow out here during the war and heard what he had to say, I wanted no more to do with him.'

Catching his breath as he stood out in the beaten earth of the street, Rud turned his face up to the immense field of the sky, searching among these southern constellations, once so familiar. It calmed him, tracing over their patterns.

Only a few more days before he must go back to Cape Town. If only he didn't have to give up the talk and the work in that confounded little office he had grown so fond of. Still, needs must.

He drew his hand across his mouth and turned back to the hotel,
to go to bed. Carrie couldn't be expected to cope on her own
indefinitely and besides, he was beginning to get a glimmering of
something new.

When he got back to London, how he would work, how he
would use his voice! His step rang beneath him as he marched up
the wooden steps of the hotel. Everything the country had should
be thrown into protecting South Africa from these filthy Boers
with their hypocrisy and their damned readiness to go back on
what they'd promised.

And surely, once he could get over to Tisbury, he'd be able to
coax Trix into seeing him.

Back in Cape Town, in the hotel gardens, beneath the shade of a
broad parasol, Carrie sat alone.

The sheets of Rud's letter loose on her lap in the windless noon
– she must remember to get no more of that striped cotton, it didn't
wash well – she did not know whether to rejoice or weep: thank
goodness that something could put an end to the terrible visitations,
when a kind of waking sleep turned Rud into a tossing fever patient.
The terror she had known at that time, sleepless herself beside the
frantic dreamer, came back and took hold of her again.

The glass beside her was empty. She signaled to the waiting
figure in the background.

The dreams were over. But – was it a good sign that he should
get this respite only in her absence? Her heart shrank.

The Tommies adored him, she was told, and that must be doing
him good. He didn't seem to mind at all so long as it was soldiers
who mobbed him. How different from Brattleboro days.

Stirring more sugar into her lemonade, she took a sip.

Here it actually helped that you could identify him on sight.
Yet she herself scarcely recognised the reports that described his
'sturdy figure', 'energetically hauling away' at cases of supplies
to distribute to a train-load of wounded soldiers. It was like the

cinematograph, images from the past, moving images of the man she had married. She had thought that man was gone for ever.

But if Rud really were now setting to 'with a flourish' – some might say showing off – then that proved her wrong.

She knew she ought to be happy.

* * *

'Of course, we'll have to improve the road,' Cecil Rhodes squeaked in his thin voice.

Carrie looked at Rud in relief. They'd been invited to look at a house Mr. Rhodes had in mind for them at Rondebosch, this village outside Cape Town and the journey up from the main road, brief though it had been, had thrown them about more than she liked. Rather stiffly, she prepared to get down from the open carriage. It wasn't the first time they'd borrowed it. Light and highly polished, it bore the arms of Sir Alfred Milner on the side, though today they lay under a fresh powdering of pink dust. The footman too had a decidedly pinkish tone.

Mr. Rhodes moved clumsily to hand her down.

'It is a very great pleasure to have this opportunity,' he bowed. With a slight struggle she regained her balance and shaped a cautious smile.

It all depended on what Mr. Rhodes meant by the phrase 'building a house for them'. The old Dutch farmhouse they had come out from Cape Town to inspect was picturesque enough from the outside, though sadly run down. Brilliant creepers trailed down the shuttered windows and mould was growing over the plastered wall by a leaking water butt.

She stirred the sodden earth with her toe.

'The Woolsack seems such an odd name for a house. But I'm sure there's a reason,' she added hastily, conscious of sounding ungrateful.

'A little joke on the part of the last owner. Nearby there was a much bigger place known as The Woolpack,' Baker chipped in.

Carrie's smile was merely civil. She enjoyed living in the Mount Nelson. Only the servants flitting silently in their red fezzes disturbed the European scene. She could imagine herself among the Italian lakes, looking up from the terrace to the tall balconied buildings. Taking up housekeeping in Africa, for goodness' sake, surely Rud wasn't asking that now?

And if they were to make do with an inconvenient layout, shabbily finished, she feared that she would have to draw a line.

Rud, of course, was all excitement, as he had been when he first told her of the offer. She was still surprised by that. Here he was, a man who had turned down the Prime Minister's offer of a knighthood only months back, eager now to embrace special honours from Cecil Rhodes. But maybe it was the offer of intimacy he couldn't resist.

'That way we'll be able to see all we like of each other, without the trouble of setting up dinners and dates,' Mr. Rhodes enthused.

Carrie wondered what this favoured intimacy would cost. It wasn't even clear that she herself would gain. It was always Rud that people wanted to please.

With no need of his own for anxiety, Rud was already mounting the long stoep that lay along the front of the building, pausing to kick inquiringly at the edge of crumbling brick.

Rhodes was quick to take the cue: 'I've asked Baker to accompany us this morning because I want him to hear from you yourself and from Mrs. Kipling exactly what works and improvements you require. Mrs. Kipling, I imagine most of the ideas about what is needed will come from yourself.'

She had caught up with them before he had finished, feeling a surge of interest. Rud smiled back at her fondly: 'She's the best and most thoughtful woman in the world for planning and contriving, my wife.'

'I'm going to leave you then, if you'll allow me,' Rhodes fumbled a bow and was away on his horse.

Laying her misgivings to one side, Carrie accepted the large iron key Baker offered and put both hands to the task of turning the lock. With a little gasp she felt the two halves of the door part as they swung open.

'A stable door, at the front! Just as we had at Naulakha! Our house in Vermont,' she added flushing, embarrassed by the emotion in her voice. She didn't like revealing so much of herself to a stranger.

'As a matter of fact, they're very often to be found out here. Mr. Rhodes likes to keep the original character of these old places: I imagine you won't object to keeping that style of door?'

'On the contrary.' She was looking about her, charmed to find, once inside, that the house was built around an open atrium. 'It's not like anything I've ever lived in, though now I think of it I believe there's something like this open courtyard over at Groote Schuur.'

'There I have the advantage of you, Carrie,' Rud excited, was pacing out the space. 'This layout speaks to me of sun and heat, speaks of Bombay, too, in its setting. Even on the hottest day, that marvellous freshness coming up off the sea, over those green plains below us will keep us cool. Relatively, at least, that is,' he finished.

She too observed Baker's flitting discomfiture.

She stiffened for a moment in apprehension: were they to stay through into the hot season? Surely not. 'Rud, darling, you can't possibly think –'

He turned to her, eyes snapping. She fell silent.

Herbert Baker was trying to attract her attention: 'I have a few preliminary suggestions, just notes and sketches, but I thought you might like to look at them, here on the spot.' He cleared the dust from a worn bench that stood along the wall by the side door. 'We are going to find whether our tastes coincide: these are the lines, rather Arts and Crafts – the place is generous but not grand – I've been thinking along.'

It did take her back to Naulakha. In her growing involvement, Carrie didn't lose her presence of mind.

'Rud, let me have your handkerchief,' she called, and spread it out with some care before sitting down. Architect and client looked together down the length of the house.

'How many bedrooms do you think we could get out of this? And what about somewhere to put the servants? We couldn't think of living here without the children's nurses and our own maids.'

Was it going to be worth all the effort, moving the lives of an entire household out here for months every year? That's what it would mean.

She sat back, staring up at the cobwebs among the rafters.

But then she thought of the children. John was sleeping better. She hadn't realised how wan Elsie had become these last months, till she saw her brighten and pick up here in the bold sunshine. That settled it. She had to admit Rud was only just when he'd promised her eagerly,

'It's got everything, same as Bombay. South Africa's a paradise for kids.'

* * *

Once back in Rottingdean, Carrie was still determined to start looking for a home of their own. They were lingering at the breakfast table when she decided to tackle him.

'We have to find a place we can buy, Rud. I'm convinced our landlord here wants to sell. It makes me unsettled.'

She paused to nibble a last corner of toast.

'The children need to have somewhere to come home to, a place that we can't be put out of, not one we're renting. Rushing off to South Africa in the winter is all very well. I'm prepared to agree that Mr. Rhodes and his Woolsack are delightful but I want something of our own.'

'You're right, of course.' Rud was turned away, looking out at the garden. His shoulders slumped. 'It's hard, though to feel much enthusiasm when you think what happened last time. Naulakha was perfect. Our very own house and we had to let it go.'

'For heaven's sakes,' for once she allowed herself to lose patience with him. 'That was five years ago.' She refused to go over it again, all the trouble with Beatty. The nightmare of the court case. What was the good?

Shamefaced, he began to apologise. 'It's this,' he jabbed at an envelope by his plate. 'It just makes me feel useless.'

He'd glanced over his father's letter but stuffed it back inside almost at once.

'The Pater tries to soften it – "*put off visiting for a week or two*" – but the long and short of it is, Trix won't have me.'

'Can I see the letter?'

It was quite possible he'd jumped to the gloomiest conclusion.

'"*General overexcitement*" on her part's what they're frightened of, there's not a word about what Trix wants or doesn't want.'

'Are you sure?' He took the letter back and studied it. Raising his eyes with an embarrassed smile. 'You may be right.'

'I do think a nurse would know better than your mother how to keep Trix calm,' she said, irritated despite herself.

'I wish to blazes they'd get one. We could always pay for it. All this useless cash sitting in our account. I'll suggest it.'

That wasn't what she'd intended at all. A place of their own would cost money. But the idea had made him look much brighter.

'How wise you are, Carrie. I should always listen to your advice.'

He got up from his chair and dropped a kiss on the top of her head.

'I can tell that you're in earnest about finding a house. Very well, this afternoon as ever is. Of course the blessed motor car is still suffering from gastritis. But we could take the pony and trap. Get it sent round immediately after luncheon.'

'Luncheon?'

She hid a smile. Every move he made, linguistic or otherwise, registered with her. He was echoing the patrician Alfred Milner. The mild passing embarrassment of acknowledging that they were now moving in a more exclusive world than ever before, that it was changing them, made her briefly sad.

'Let's just have a sandwich. We can set off all the sooner. You pacify Cook: tell her we'll eat it all this evening.'

She was about to object. Cook was touchy enough as it was and she herself had been to some trouble in ordering the menu for that day. Then she thought better of it. This was her chance. Glancing outside, she saw that the morning drizzle had ceased. Faint shadows on the lawn gave way to weak pledges of sun.

She folded her napkin.

'While I set about getting something sent up on a tray why don't you get out your county maps and we'll plot over them as we eat.'

It became a new pastime, driving out in the afternoons, that summer, after Rud had done his day's stint on *Kim*, the story of the boy who was half-Indian, half-British. Almost like a spiritual autobiography, she thought, though she kept quiet.

Were they in the motor or the station fly, when they first saw Bateman's? They would argue over it happily afterwards. It could have been either, the Locomobile was so often out of action.

Seen from the road, as they drove past, the glimpse of a Jacobean house, discreet in its grey stone, fired them both.

Each turned to the other.

'Can we go back?'

There was some difficulty in turning in that rabbit hole of a lane. They alighted, all impatience, and walked back up the steep incline. That they both remembered. That and the utter quiet but for the lowing of cows.

A sweep of woods away to the south.

Peering through the gate, 'Can you make it out, Carrie, is that a date carved over the door?'

'I'd have to get closer. Sixteen something?'

They stood taking in the sober lines of the place, its rough-mown lawns.

'Over there to the right, that's a dovecote, above that brick building.'

'How ancient and settled it feels. Such dignity,' Carrie whispered. 'And yet no grandeur. Only a stone-paved path laid in the turf from here to the front door. A home.'

Rud pushed tentatively at the gate, which dragged on its hinges. The place wasn't being cared for as it deserved: there were other signs.

'I do believe it's rented out to a farmer, not lived in by a family,' she exclaimed.

There was no need for her to say more.

Gripping her by the elbow, he turned back down the lane.

'We can find all that out. Let me mark it on my map then we can make enquiries.'

They discovered that the Jacobean house was known as Bateman's. Though they'd fallen under its spell, Rock House had taught them to be cautious.

'The past wells and gathers in these old places,' they told each other. 'Better take soundings.'

Stepping inside over the black and white tiles of the hall, however, exploring about the panelled rooms, Rud and Carrie found no shadow of old miseries, only calm and welcome.

'It's never been meddled with; it's untouched, intact.' Rud surprised her by the depth of his relief.

But Bateman's had just been let for a year. They weren't sure if they could wait.

They kept looking.

Meanwhile they remained near Georgie in Rottingdean.

Rud did miss having a garden of his own to plan for. He was making do by pottering among the flowerbeds of The Elms when he heard a cry of fury. At three years old, Baby John had developed a mind of his own.

'No naughty. No.' He stamped his feet and threw a handful of gravel across the lawn.

'Johnny,' his nurse began to plead. His mother, stepping across the garden on her way over to see Georgie, had overheard and now came sailing over.

'John, do as you are told immediately. A big boy like you! Come here.'

But it appeared there was no going back.

'No, no, no!' throwing up his arms, he slipped through the women's grasp and disappeared among the overhanging bushes.

Carrie turned on the nurse a look of ice.

'This is not how I expect you to handle his tempers.'

Later, with Rud, she was tearful.

'I really don't know what I am to do with him. I just don't seem to have the energy. Nurse is hopeless, she lets him ride roughshod. Oh, what is to be done with him?'

He had a jolt of alarm. Ridiculous. He knew what to do. First, he rang the bell to summon tea.

'Would you prefer honey or will the raspberry jam do?' he asked. Leaving Carrie settled, with the ample tray before her and her book at hand, he set off for the nursery.

He paused outside, attentive. Elsie's voice rose in fury.

'Give it back to me, it's mine.'

A wail. When he opened the door, the first thing he saw was the tuft of blond hair in John's fist. Scarlet with tears, Elsie was clutching a drooping rag doll to her chest. Nurse Lucy, her arms full of neatly folded clothes, was standing by an open cupboard, helpless but innocent.

Elsie threw herself against him, sobbing. 'My hair, my hair!' and looked smugly across at her brother from the shelter of her father's arms. He stroked her soothingly for a moment, before handing her over to her nurse.

Then he got up from his knees and looked across the room at the little boy, who had moved behind the table. John had taken up his position for a fight. He wasn't hiding, his father noted.

Promising. He was going to make a good man out of John.

Would he respond to a command? Chasing him would turn into a game; there would be confusion and he didn't want that. No laughing and giggling his way to forgiveness: the boy needed discipline.

'Come here, my son.'

The small mouth pursed, 'No, Daddy.' But there was a look of alarm.

Again. 'John, come over here to me, please.'

Clinging to a chair, then a table leg, the small figure moved round towards him, then stopped. He began to play with a set of tassels, before glancing quickly back up at the familiar face, exploring. Nurse had taken Elsie away, ostensibly to bathe her head but evidently not eager for either of them to witness the scene which was in the making.

Rud wavered: the kid was pretty small. But he couldn't have Carrie upset every day like that. It was hard enough for her to keep in spirits without that.

'You've made Mummy very sad by behaving so badly,' he spoke, reaching out to take the unresisting hand where it dangled. 'It's no good you know, Johnny, I can't let you grow up to be a bad boy. You're going to have to have a spanking.'

Johnny looked up in surprise and interest. That sounded hopeful. He had heard older children talking about spankings. Now he was big enough to have one of his own. When his father pulled a chair out from the table and sat down it seemed that a spanking might turn out to be a new kind of story. But in a moment he found himself staring at the carpet as he lay across his father's knee: and his father was hitting him. It hurt.

He was set back on his feet.

'Why, Daddy?' he demanded. 'Hitting is very horrible and naughty.'

* * *

Over in Tisbury, by the year's end, there were grounds for hoping that this time Trix was not going to relapse.

'What an ear you have, Trix,' Alice regarded her daughter with fresh wonder. 'Do go on.'

They were upstairs in Alice's tiny sitting room. Trix was reading aloud from a piece she had just started, a monologue spoken by a wife out golfing with her husband. 'I'm thinking of calling it *On the Ladies' Links*,' she explained. She appeared to be enjoying herself enormously.

'*Wasn't that a good drive of mine? I'll pace it. It was quite twelve yards! Oh bother! My ball has stuck in a horrid little hole. George, George, come here and tell me. Ought I to play with a cleek or a niblick? There! Now it's gone into the road. Tell that bullock man to stop. I don't like walking into all that dust. Will it count against me if I send the caddy to bring it back? What a shame! Fancy, I'm eight for this hole, how dreadful! Three for you again? Well you are lucky.*'

'It's quite wicked but terribly clever, my dear,' her mother applauded. Trix was looking more relaxed that she'd seen her for years.

'I'm having such fun writing this. It was Maud's idea that I might try going back, doing a piece set in India. She's only waiting for her little boy to go to school, she said. Then we can write together seriously.'

Alice didn't respond immediately. She didn't warm to the direction Maud's sympathies were taking. She had been a faithful correspondent all through but her feeling for native life had quite warped her judgment.

Alice, shifted uneasily in her chair.

Why, in one passage that Trix read aloud, Maud had spoken of the ancient ordered law of Indian life contrasting it unfavourably with the English gospel of progress at all cost.

As for claiming that English women in India lived in a state of continual causeless irritation and suspicion that degraded them, Alice could not imagine what Maud meant. Alice was perfectly certain that repeating such stuff at the dinner tables of Calcutta, once Trix was well enough to return to them, would not be to her advantage.

Despite her qualms, Alice compelled herself to remain smiling.

If Trix could write like this about a trying wife and the silent suffering of a husband, did that mean she was getting over that dreadful animosity towards Jack?

She settled her shawl more comfortably. Meaning only to encourage, she suggested, 'Have you thought of showing this to Ruddy, next time he comes over to visit?'

It was not a good move. The look of pleasure left her daughter's face.

'Ruddy? You don't hear a word about India from him these days. All forgotten. And this new plan, living out there at the Cape half the year. Who does he think he is, Mr. Secretary for the Colonies?'

Trix put down her notebook and crossed her arms.

This anger, the fierce expression, were surely excessive. They might tip into one of the full blown scenes Alice hoped never to be exposed to again. Dreading to see her daughter's hands move up towards her hair, she intervened, swift, non-committal.

'Goodness knows. I suppose the climate's an attraction.'

It might have been too late. But instead, with a pounding heart, Alice saw Trix turn back to her notebook, pencil in hand.

'I do hope we can have a session with our poems, later on. I've got some more ideas for them. Writing together, your poem a response to one of mine, it's fun.'

* * *

For a second year Rud carried his family off to spend the English winter in South Africa. Fighting was still in progress, though far away. They were now settled in The Woolsack. Behind it reared the black triangle of Devil's Peak. You couldn't escape it, oppressive as old sorrows. Carrie tried to avoid looking back up the slope of the mountain when she was outside. Instead she gazed ahead along the paths or out over the great broad plain towards the sea.

Hearing Rud call from the garden, as she sat reading in the drawing room after dinner, Carrie put down her book. She passed quickly through the atrium and faced out into the warm darkness. Holding back her skirts she crossed over the terrace, carefully picking her way down the brick steps.

She was blinded, leaving the light.

Looking up at her uncertain figure from where he stood deep in shadow, Rud was unexpectedly moved. She was coming to find him. He was glad he'd called. Not sorry he'd given up the secret ownership of the night garden. He stepped forward, towards the halo of light streaming from the opened half-door, reached out and took her hand.

'My dear, I wanted you to see these stars.' Her face, which had been turned his way, lifted towards the sky.

They were strolling now, steered by the breaths of sweetness from the frangipani flowers, their radiance ghostly at that hour. He tucked her hand under his arm; she moved closer but almost by accident he moved further apart at a turn in the path. They quietly retraced a regular route back and forth.

Rud spoke fretfully into the silence. 'I wish I felt that I was really doing some good here.'

Dropping his arm, Carrie paused. She appeared struggling to read his face.

'Was I wrong? I thought life in Cape Town was really suiting you. It's got you writing again, you said you'd collected a heap of notions to work up here. *The Army of a Dream* is just the start. And even though Lord Milner's not here, you're always so busy, between the hospitals and Simonstown and Groote Schuur.'

'Well, there's no Groote Schuur at the moment and not likely to be any more this trip.' He couldn't keep the sadness out of his voice. 'Rhodes left two days ago. Who knows when I'll – we'll see him again.'

Carrie knew it wouldn't do to reveal how that news lifted her spirits. She tried to hide her growing resentment of Mr. Rhodes, the place he had come to take in their lives. It was complicated. When Rhodes first asked her to foster a young lion-cub from his private zoo, she'd relished the challenge, the adventure of it, the romance. She'd given Sullivan his bottle with her own hands – once she'd ransacked the Rondebosch shops for leather gauntlets. The children doted on him.

But she wasn't sure that Sullivan was really safe with children, these days. He'd grown into a daunting creature with an indolent, lordly gaze.

'Look, Sullivan can see right down through the length of Africa, just like Rhodes,' Rud would claim, leaving Carrie wincing.

Cautiously she returned to the present conversation and to Mr. Rhodes' departure.

'Do you know what his movements are, his plans?'

She felt Rud relax.

'I think I know more about them than most, I can say with some confidence, but of course they're liable to sudden change. He has the most extraordinary ability to adapt, to see ahead to consequences and adapt to the unexpected change in circumstance.'

She was murmuring agreement, wondering silently whether this would mean that Rud would spend more time with them, perhaps plan some outings for them all. The children were old enough to enjoy being taken out, being given the full attention of their parents. Or would this be – she stole a panicky glance across at her husband – the signal for a bout of paralysing gloom?

Rud was still speaking. 'You know, I sometimes feel it's Destiny itself that I'm meeting face-to-face in Rhodes.'

He didn't notice the way her arm and her whole body stiffened. She could not like the turn Rud seemed to be taking. This almost mystical language – her New England soul rose in revolt.

'There is something in the universe that is deeper than mere brute struggle. A higher order that is emerging, a spiritual order too, that we can only glimpse at certain times. In him I've felt I was seeing it blazing forth. One doesn't know why one should be so privileged… '

She couldn't let this pass.

'Rud, darling, if any man alive has earned a place in the councils of the powerful – I mean, the wise – it's you. Tell me one man whose work means more to his readers?' As an afterthought, 'And did you see the note from Effendi about the new edition? It was in this week's mail.'

'Effendi? No, I hadn't.' Ever since Frank N. Doubleday had proved himself such a friend in need, the very mention of his name, especially the pet name based on his initials, warmed Rud. Her distraction had worked for the moment.

But she wasn't easy in her own mind. They'd accepted so much from Mr. Rhodes. She herself was almost seduced when he paid her the compliment of acting on her advice. Usually he set little store by women.

He'd been speaking of encouraging young men to travel for their education. At first she'd listened without a word as he and Rud laid out their plans.

'Scholarships are what's needed. Bring the most able men from the colonies to the Mother Country and give them a chance to develop their minds in the company of the best.' That was Rud.

'English speakers, of course,' he emphasised, while Rhodes nodded vigorous agreement.

'Bring them to Oxford; give them a year or two.' Rhodes, who had studied there, was spellbound by the place.

At the name of the university a shadow'd seemed to pass over Rud's face: was he recalling how he used to envy his cousin Stan, up at Oxford, while he himself was toiling through the Hot Weather of Lahore?

She'd imagined uneasily that they had no notion of including coloured races. Only when it came to the financial arrangements, though, had she spoken out.

'Two hundred and fifty pounds won't be sufficient to cover their expenses for a year. You've forgotten. The terms may be eight weeks long but they have to live over the vacations.'

'Mrs. Kipling, I congratulate you. You've a better head on your shoulders than your husband and myself put together.'

Rud's naïve delight had been painfully transparent. Her own feelings had been more divided.

Rud was already guiding her up towards the house again. He gestured up at Devil's Peak in its looming darkness.

'That black shape used to plague me, you know. Coming between me and the sky. But now we're getting better news of Trix, somehow the threat of it has disappeared.'

She wished she didn't have to be reminded. Of course she was relieved Trix was mending but she was weary of her ghostly presence in their lives.

As they reached the steps where light fell on the heavy pots of geraniums, she paused to tidy away a broken stem. Rising with the scarlet flowers between her fingers, she called her husband back. Making for his study across the atrium, Rud turned, eyebrows raised, then his concentration gave way to a smile as he took a spray of scarlet from her hand.

'I think I'll just drop a line to Rhodes,' with these words he turned away, the door closing behind him. Biting her lip, Carrie looked round a little wildly, then rang for her maid. In a moment she thought better of it and sent the girl away, then sat down alone before the looking-glass, reaching up to take the pins out of the crown of her white hair.

'It has been terribly lonely since you left. Rather like living in a landscape with half the horizon knocked out,' her husband was writing to Cecil Rhodes. *'PS. We have been walking round the garden in the starlight and saying things about you that would be absurd in print.'*

*

Sylvia Thompson, brought out as governess to John and Elsie, had gone up to her room straight from the dinner table. If she didn't, she knew she would feel Mrs. Kipling's eyes on her. Just to place herself beyond any possible criticism, for heaven knew the woman seemed to have inexhaustible powers in that line, she ostentatiously went out of her way to look in at the nursery, at the other end of the house, where Elsie and John lay sleeping.

The door was latched ajar, as all the downstairs bedrooms could be, to catch the cool night air. She slipped the brass hook out of its catch and stepped inside. At night, in the darkness, her own poor vision ceased to trouble her. She was on a footing with everyone else. The sound of even breathing, broken by little snorts from John, who really needed his adenoids seeing to, and the stirring of the light curtain in the night breeze calmed her further.

Every evening she found herself going to bed in a rage. She would have the privilege, Mrs. Kipling had grandly told her, of dining with the parents, though during the day she was to take her meals with the children and Lucy, their nurse. But sitting at that table, her back to the dresser, placed, she knew miserably, so that Mrs. Kipling could invent the need for Sylvia to effect little transfers of objects back and forth from the table, she never for a moment lost awareness of her humble position.

Why, on evenings that the famous Mr. Rhodes was invited, she was sent to eat early supper with the children. Mr. Kipling had seemed surprised.

'I rather thought it would be an opportunity for Sylvia to be introduced to Rhodes: it's not a chance that every girl is going to get,' but his wife's mouth had settled into a line.

'I don't really think it necessary.' No more had been said.

The happiest hours she had had since leaving London had been spent with Mr. Kipling, that morning when he took her sightseeing after their ship docked in Madeira. He was like one of her young uncles, sparkling with life, interested in everything, including her own response to what they saw. The little boys diving on the quayside, the sallow men sprawled on the verandah at Reid's Hotel that he pointed out as they trotted past in the high sprung brougham, the blazing flower market, with the haunted faces of the flower sellers.

He laughed, delighted when she turned to him as they were returning towards the quayside: 'It's been the best morning I've ever, ever had.'

'My dear girl, you've no idea what a pleasure it's been to me. You've been wonderful company: it's brought me back to life and reminded me of outings I once used to take with another girl, though she was a good bit younger than you.'

He ceased as the carriage came to a halt. Only later did she come to wonder about her predecessor. Surely she, Sylvia, could not be reminding him of Mrs. Kipling?

It was impossible to make out her behaviour. It had seemed so thoughtful, so generous on her part, to be concerned over this dreadful near-blindness. Mrs. Kipling had obtained and passed on the advice of the distinguished specialist Mr. Barnard. When he declared that Sylvia must try a hot climate, she had immediately followed that by an invitation. But what had sounded perfectly acceptable terms – Sylvia would take charge of the two little children – had quickly broken down in reality to prove, as Sylvia felt, sore with the experience, a series of snubs, humiliations and exclusions.

Was it that Mrs. Kipling didn't like her receiving attention from men? Remembering the night of the dance Sylvia's eyes stung with angry tears. She had been on her way to join the distant sounds of music when Mrs. Kipling stopped her in the corridor.

Eyeing the lace on Sylvia's white dress, 'I can't think what you are planning, Sylvia. It would not be at all appropriate for you to dance. I do have to answer to your mother. I can't possibly take the responsibility.'

Silent, less docile than shocked, Sylvia had turned on her heel and locked herself into her cabin. It was nonsense. She knew her mother wouldn't have hesitated to let her go to the dance.

In her letters home from The Woolsack, she hung back from describing the quarters she had been allotted. She couldn't bear to worry her mother, who would know, however lightly she passed it off, that there was a tacit insult, one repeated every day, in giving Sylvia that tiny hot room over the kitchen. She imagined that it was meant for a black houseboy. To reach it after dinner was in itself an ordeal, for she had to make her way through the kitchen, where the maids, Lottie and Rose, sat with their guests, a couple of British Tommies. She felt herself shrink every night before their bold gaze.

Meanwhile, down on the ground floor, at the same level as the

Kiplings' bedrooms, the spare room stood empty every night.

The evenings were so long, since she couldn't read to amuse herself. She saw that Mr. Kipling had noticed this, in his thoughtful way, when he offered to read to her himself, joking that it was one of the joys of his life to make people listen to his stories. Those three nights of *The Jungle Book* had been as good as the theatre. But Mrs. Kipling had put a stop to that too.

Sylvia would be much older before she could bear to take out these memories and look at them again.

* * *

By July the family was back in Rottingdean, Rud charged for action. The war out in Africa was dragging on, an apparently unwinnable conflict, where British forces were constantly outflanked by the skill and courage of the Boers. For Georgie Burne-Jones, who thought going to war with the Boers in the first place was a disgrace, this made gratifying news. She knew that it meant something very different for her nephew. Rud was taking the setback to heart and brooding over it as though it were his own.

This afternoon he'd come over from The Elms after her rest, as usual. She saw immediately that he was armed with a sheaf of foolscap: he must be wanting her to provide an audience.

'I've been working on this story I began in Cape Town and it's got a bit stuck. You wouldn't mind if I tried it out on you, Georgie? A live audience makes such a difference…'

Setting aside a mild foreboding, she smiled, 'Of course, Ruddy dear. I'm listening, off you go.'

He straightened his spectacles and plunged in. Page after page of it and dead as a doornail. Not an atom of the life that made his best work so entrancing. Half an hour passed, according to the little clock on her worktable, though it felt longer, before he looked up.

Sitting opposite him over her sewing, Georgie struggled with herself. He was a dear, dear boy and his gifts were astonishing but no, she did not care for the direction his work appeared to be taking. Yet with those bright eyes seeking so trustingly for her approval, as they had since he was a little boy, how could she withhold it? There was no point in anything but honesty, however, when it came to matters of art. That's what her life with poor Ned had taught her.

She trod delicately.

'I'm not perfectly sure of myself when it comes to war writing, Ruddy dear.'

She winced to observe a cloud come over his face.

'Of course, your dialogue, the voices in this *Dream Army* story of yours give me pleasure. But your argument, it's so forceful, doesn't it risk… '

She hesitated, not wanting to be more specific. The story spelled out Rud's new plan for national defence, clothed in only the skimpiest disguise. She'd felt hectored.

He jumped in, 'But that's the whole point: the story's there to get my argument across. You have to exaggerate or people won't take any notice.'

Her sewing put aside, she pressed her palms together.

'But don't you have to keep them with you, your readers? Is a story the right way to persuade people that children should be trained up as soldiers?'

A matter of technique: surely that was a question he would be able to hear. She had always admired the way he would tear up and abandon work that was going wrong.

'I'm longing for a cup of tea, would you ring, darling?' She must break the silence somehow.

It was no good. She couldn't pretend. That story embodied an extraordinary and repulsive notion. She wondered whether those years he spent in the power of that dreadful woman in Southsea had anything to do with it. Fending for himself. Always on his guard. But how could he fail to anticipate reactions like her own to this… pamphlet? You couldn't really call it a story. Mixing children up with matters of national defence! Wanting to train them up as soldiers from the age of six!

But a dogged look was coming over him. He bent to collect the dropped sheets of his story from the floor.

She changed tack.

'Perhaps I'm simply too much out of sympathy with this war, Rud. I just cannot see it as you do. To my mind, our action in attacking those Boer republics is a matter of shame. Other countries despise us. But we've agreed to differ on this, my dear, remember?'

She saw that he could not resist her gentleness.

Emboldened, Georgie went on. 'But I do hope that we see eye to eye about Miss Hobhouse and the concentration camps.'

'The unspeakable Hobhouse, with her poking and prying into matters she can't begin to understand?'

'Ruddy,' she paused, 'Ruddy, I don't understand why you're so angry. I thought Miss Hobhouse had undertaken a very necessary task. If we're rounding up women and children into camps – their poor innocent black servants too, I hear – isn't it right to ask whether they're adequately cared for?'

'Cared for!' He was on his feet. 'I don't think you sense the temper of the country at all. But how could you?' He controlled himself and returned to his seat. 'I can tell you, Georgie, that there is outrage among ordinary working folk here in England at the notion that we are feeding and supporting these people while their men are off fighting against us.'

She was not intimidated. She had nursed the man before her through croup when he was a child.

'I'm sorry, Rud, but I cannot see that that justifies cruelty. The rations aren't sufficient for health. Conditions are desperately insanitary and mothers are losing their children.'

She fell silent, suddenly conscious.

'Greatly exaggerated.' His voice was staccato. 'The army has everything in hand. It's time this war was brought to a close. No doubt there'll be absurd sums paid out then, once we've defeated them, to get their wretched farms and equipment up to scratch.'

He looked at his watch. 'I really don't think you should distress yourself about the camps. Take my word for it, Georgie.'

'Do you think it will ever be forgiven, that we stood by and let their children die?' Georgie too was standing, though her hip gave a painful twinge at the sudden movement. 'It's not like you, to be indifferent to suffering, specially not in children. Just because these are Boers and their men are ranged against us – '

'Degenerates, mouthing the Bible and not shirking any treachery. Isn't that enough?'

She could taste his bitterness on her own tongue. This was as bad as the plan for an army of children. There was no arguing with him.

And now she'd forgotten to ask how Trix had seemed, still cooped up with her mother, when he last went over to visit them.

And Only the Master Shall Praise Us,

And Only the Master Shall Blame Us

'My dear Mrs. Kipling, consider the strains to which you have been subject over recent years. Nervous exhaustion is only to be expected. A fortnight of complete calm with no domestic worries, the care of a nurse and regular massage are what is required.' Sir Charles Ogilvy, the leading specialist, shook his head sympathetically.

She slumped back against the unyielding chair. Permission. The shelves of books which lined the consulting room appeared to waver and swim. She reached for a handkerchief, and tried to pay attention as Sir Charles elaborated. The doctors had finally decided that her wretched spirits were not after all caused by inflammation of the womb, their initial diagnosis. Her increasing stoutness was no cause for concern.

All the while, 'complete calm with no domestic worries' echoed in her ears.

She was too relieved at being spared an operation to ask why two weeks of isolation and tedium would put her right. Accepting a cool manicured hand from Sir Charles, along with the name of a reputable nursing agency, she made her way out into Harley St.

But what about the family, how would they manage without her? Before her taxi reached Hyde Park en route to Victoria she saw her way. Rud had been planning to go on manoeuvres with the Fleet anyway. They could arrange for the children to spend a fortnight at Crowborough at the same time. She would remain at home in peace, cared for by a nurse.

A week into her rest cure and, as she'd known it would, duty broke in. The first telegram arrived before she'd got out of bed. Nurse Todworthy had conceded that Carrie should take her meals downstairs but solely on the condition that she didn't set foot to the ground before ten.

'Our aim,' she kept reminding her patient, 'must be rest, complete rest. We must take advantage of this opportunity, with the children and their nanny off on holiday and Mr. Kipling off on business – out of the way,' she added roguishly.

Carrie finished the last of the toast on her breakfast tray. The tea in her cup had gone cold. She made a face as she pushed it away and was just wondering whether she'd like fish for dinner when her maid Ainsley arrived, bearing the orange envelope. Nurse Todworthy was radiating disapproval in the background. How tiresome, it must be Rud warning that he was going to be delayed. She'd known that would happen when he decided to fit in a visit to his parents: she clung onto all she could get of him, did Alice Kipling. Never would Carrie consent to call her 'Mother' – she knew too well what strength of will had been opposed to her from the first. Well, at least she had not given the order for the fish. Perhaps she'd just have cauliflower cheese on a tray.

Once she'd taken in the message, her lips pursed. She struggled out of bed too quickly and had to hold herself upright by the tall oak posts.

'There'll be a reply: don't let the boy go back till it's ready.'

With 'an emergency in the family' she faced down the disgruntled nurse.

She looked around her for a moment before finding the cream woollen dressing gown in its place draped over the ottoman: wrapping it tightly about her, she moved over to the little writing table and reread the telegram with its raw appeal '*Situation desperate. Unable leave. Advise. All love.*' How to reply?

'*Unable leave*' was nothing new. However, this did sound like a real crisis. Something must have set Trix off again. What horrors were implied by the discreet '*desperate*', she dreaded to think. It was only a month or two since they'd been told Trix appeared much improved. Rud had been expecting to see her this time. Looking forward to it, she could tell, though with a background of tension. Those fits of madness in Trix – she, at least, would speak plainly in the matter – distressed him beyond measure. He wouldn't be able to put pen to paper for days after this visit.

A glance at her watch, told her that time was passing. But she couldn't decide quickly. She called her maid and gave the word to let the telegraph boy go on his way. Jarvis, the gardener would have to take her reply to the Post Office.

There they all were together down in Tisbury, stewing, as only the Kiplings knew how. And so proud of the group they made, referring smugly to 'the Family Square', even now. Mrs. Kipling would see to it that not one of them could escape. But perhaps, this time, since Rud had actually asked for advice, instructions from basecamp – the image made her smile – her views might carry some weight. She'd only heard reports of these attacks, Trix's screaming, the attempts to tear out her own hair. It was enough. Though Rud refused to look facts in the face where his own family was concerned, as a straightforward American woman, she was in no doubt. It was absurd to try to contain Trix within an ordinary household: nursing care in some kind but well-regulated establishment was indicated.

She was still weighing the form of words available to her when the second telegram arrived.

'Pater acute bronchitis. Suggest join me.'

Grudgingly she registered that Trix might not be the whole problem.

This time, Carrie chose not to hurry. She had enough respect for her doctors to want the routine of her morning to be re-established: otherwise her heart would race intolerably. Bathed, fresh from having her hair put up, her grey jersey dress improved and lifted by a small sapphire pin at the shoulder, she appeased Nurse Todworthy by taking to the sofa with both telegrams.

Of course, it was out of the question that she should go to Tisbury. How could a writer so subtle in his imaginings be so obtuse among his family! He would never accept the fact that she and Mrs. Kipling paralysed any good there was in each other. It would only heighten the tension if Carrie joined the party.

'Imperative obtain professional nursing,' she wrote at last. *'Suggest return lighten household.'*

There, she could only hope that the voice of common sense would carry the day. She watched from the breakfast room window as the boy cycled off with her reply. The morning was gone.

'We're going to be late with our massage,' an aggrieved voice intoned behind her.

She was not enjoying the break from the children as much as she'd expected. On an ordinary day they would have come clattering down the stairs from the nursery, pushing each other and arguing about names for the kitten Aunt Georgie had given them.

The sun was in her eyes. She moved away from the window.

Lunch with John and Elsie might have been a pleasant distraction. For once she could have enjoyed their spirits wholeheartedly, forgetting the clamour that so often set her teeth on edge.

John seemed to pride himself on making noise.

'The little beast uses that knife and fork like percussion instruments,' his father observed.

She fancied that she could have been happy confirming that no shadow of grown-up care hung over their faces: she wouldn't even have raised an objection if John pushed away the bread-and-butter pudding and made off down the garden.

A glance at the newspaper and she let it fall, to sit idly waiting for the tray of coffee.

Before she obediently retired to lie down after lunch, still at the table, she was handed a third telegram. To her confusion, this made no reference to her father-in-law's illness.

'Eager take Willoughby Manor.'

She rapped the board in irritation. Tuts from Nurse.

Why Rud should choose this moment when she was supposed to be free of all demands to press her in this way was beyond her. Months earlier, when he'd first spoken of Willoughby Manor, she had been no more than mildly attracted by the idea of an old house with an Elizabethan wing and the ghost of one of King Arthur's knights. But she could guess what they were saying to him in Tisbury. His mother would be only too pleased to have him living near Salisbury, within easy reach.

'And what about the ghost?'

'Now, Mrs. Kipling dear, you mustn't upset yourself.'

She was mortified. She hadn't meant to speak aloud. To her alarm, tears were rolling down her cheeks as she stuttered.

'I don't want any more ghosts, any more haunting. I can't bear it as it is.'

The nurse moved to a chair at her side but wisely forbore to take her hand.

'I'm sure no-one is going to make you do anything you don't want to, my dear. And judging from my professional experience, let alone what the doctors advise, I can tell that you aren't really yourself at the moment. This will all blow over, you'll see. Now, I do want you to take a little rest and then later, if it's sunny, how about sitting in the garden and having your cup of tea out there?'

Five o'clock and the sunlight brilliant against the tall trees, as Carrie sat on by the depleted tray. She did enjoy a good seed cake. Shaky as she'd been feeling, she almost giggled to observe Nurse Todworthy advancing from the house, another tell-tale envelope in her hand. '*Excellent terms WM visiting tomorrow advise clinch.*'

He was waiting, she knew, for her approval.

She could not, would not, sign away her life, put them all at the disposal of Mrs. Kipling and the madness that had been spiralling around Trix.

Her spine straightened.

But neither could she be happy again, not for weeks, not until the children were home again and Rud had come back to her.

Rud's return a few days later was fraught. Still barely inside the house, he pushed Carrie's ready commiserations away.

'Not at all. You've got entirely the wrong end of the stick. I hardly saw her. The whole problem was the Mater. She just went to pieces with the Pater so ill. You could hardly expect me to leave, with her in that state?'

She recoiled, though he hadn't meant to be savage.

'Went to pieces? I find that hard to credit. Really, Rud, don't you find that excessive? It's just the usual pattern. Your mother can never bear to let you go.'

'I imagine she's simply exhausted herself over Trix,' he snubbed her. 'And by the way, Trix seems well on the way to recovery. She was off with a friend in the next village. When she did look in, she was mercifully calm, really almost her old self.'

He didn't insist on Willoughby Manor, though he let her see his disappointment.

'I thought you were all for it, Carrie. But if you've changed your mind, there's an end of the whole business. I can tell when it makes sense for a wife to have her own way.'

'Do try to understand. I haven't just "changed my mind" like some silly fanciful girl. There are good reasons to avoid a place that's haunted by the past. That's not what I want for John and Elsie.'

'Very well, whatever you say, my dear.'

Like any husband, he knew how to annoy a wife.

*

A few weeks later, an old friend arrived at The Gables. Ever since Maud Diver, who'd been back living in England for several years, had learned that Trix was well again, she'd been pressing Alice to let Trix pay them a visit. Now it was considered suitable, she'd come down from London specially to carry Trix home with her.

'I was so relieved when your letters started up again,' Maud confided, holding both her friend's hands as they sat on Trix's bed. 'I knew something was terribly wrong when they stopped, we've kept it up so long, this correspondence. Ever since we were girls…'

'It was your letters that kept me going when I was ill. You didn't stop, you just –'

Trix made as if to write vigorously in the air.

'Kept babbling on about Tom and about the baby,' Maud finished for her. 'Are you sure that all my stories of Cyril and his funny little ways didn't upset you? I did wonder, afterwards, looking back,' Maud searched her face.

'Not a bit. They left me full of hope and interest in the world. Reminded me that there's still time, you know.

Maud was looking doubtful.

'But there is, Maud. You'll be able to write seriously once Cyril's gone away to school.'

'Ah. I thought you meant – never mind. You're quite right. I will get time to myself, but at what price? Losing Cyril for weeks and months at a time.'

Feeling Maud droop, Trix pressed her hand.

'But we mustn't linger. It's time to be off, was that your bag in the hall?'

Maud was her brisk self again.

'I was just a bit afraid your dragon-guardian Mama wouldn't let you come, at the last moment,' she giggled, as they stood together before the mirror to put on their hats.

*

Alice and Lockwood now had The Gables to themselves, for the first time in several years.

'You'd never know that Trix ever had – difficulties', Alice observed, turning to her husband after waving the pair off.

They couldn't have hoped for better proof of her recovery: standing arm-in-arm with Maud, the happy wife and mother, Trix looked every bit as bright eyed, every bit as charming, in her new spring coat..

'Perhaps there is still time. Trix isn't really too old. Though she might not be able to stand the noise, they do make a racket –' Alice was thinking aloud.

He stared at her, incredulous.

'Hold on, Alice. You're not imagining Trix with a child? You haven't even spoken to her about going back, back to India to live with Fleming, have you?'

'Not exactly. Not yet. Before today I wasn't sufficiently confident –'

The clumsy front door, with its too-heavy fittings, groaned as he closed it behind him, before leading her into the drawing room.

'The time has come for us to face this, my dear. Trix can't stay here with us indefinitely. She isn't a child. As a married woman her place is with her husband, out in Calcutta.'

'It's rather soon. I'm really not sure she's fit enough,' Alice's words came fast.

Neither of them had paused to sit down. This air of tension was just what he'd wanted to avoid.

'I know –' he gave himself time to settle in his usual chair, 'I'm quite as troubled as you are at the prospect. There's no sign that life with Fleming has made either of them happy. But you know as well as I do what would happen if Trix stayed here.'

'No-one could say anything,' Alice argued. 'She's only just getting over a serious illness.'

'That won't wash for much longer. A woman who's well enough to go about paying visits –' he didn't need to continue.

She was silent, picking at the fringe on a cushion. Then she spoke in a rush.

'People are so cruel. Why should it matter to anyone outside her family where Trix lives?'

'In the eyes of nearly everyone you know, Alice, a woman living apart from her husband, whether it's Trix or anyone else, puts herself outside the pale.'

She murmured but he pressed on, pulling at his beard as he spoke.

'We mustn't deceive ourselves. It's seen as a scandal. Isolation follows. Foolish and unjust, but that's the case. At first there might be a trickle of visits, a few friends calling, but that'd soon die away.'

Alice bowed her head. In a muffled voice, 'I can't bear the thought. Trix left with no-one.'

'Won't you come and sit here, beside me, love?' He stretched out a hand to draw her towards him. 'We can't let that happen.' 'Not again,' a voice in him whispered. And there was another thing his wife needed to understand.

'Don't imagine that we wouldn't be affected. It's starting already. Eyebrows were raised when you let it be known that Trix was off to stay with Maud. You told me so yourself.'

For once, she appeared defeated. Her eyes closed.

'I'm so tired, Jack. I don't think I can go through –'

'It's not impossible for them to make a go of it, you know. Rub along, the same as dozens of couples. Not everyone can be as happy as we have been,' he leaned across and took her hand, to kiss it.

'Trix hasn't said anything to suggest that Fleming's a monster. I could never make out what was behind her refusal to hear his name.'

'A temporary hysteria, perhaps? She does seem perfectly calm again now.' Alice sounded more hopeful.

'He's a dull enough stick but he doesn't run after other women or beat her.'

He ignored the sharp breath she drew at his plain speech.

'I really don't see why they shouldn't make a go of it. And in the end, what's the alternative?'

Alice looked down at her hands, twisting them together.

'There isn't one,' she said, her voice barely audible. 'I know you're right. I just hope we can find the right moment to say something.'

At the end of her week's visit, Trix returned. As she ran upstairs to tidy her hair, 'Let's take our tea outside,' Lockwood called after her. 'We've waited it for you.'

She threw back over her shoulder 'We worked on our stories every morning, just for an hour, till little Teddy was ready for us to play with and again during his nap in the afternoons. Maud says that when he goes to school she's going to write all day.'

Alice and Lockwood waited, silent in the late afternoon sun. As Trix appeared, Alice stopped fiddling with the sugar tongs, to pick up the tea strainer and direct her attention to pouring.

Lockwood waited till they each had a cup in their hands.

'Trix, darling, have you started to give any thought to going back?' He hoped his tone was light.

'Back, father? Back to Maud's? Are you teasing?' Trix's smile didn't falter.

He stirred his tea.

'Back to India, I mean.'

From under lowered lids Alice fixed her eyes on Trix. Lockwood kept his own gaze turned away.

The silence filled with the cooing of wood pigeons.

'Oh.' Trix laid her cup back down in its saucer. 'No. I hadn't begun –' she broke off.

Her voice steadied and she went on.

'Silly of me, I suppose. I've just been happy to be well again. And with ideas for poems and stories. I hadn't really thought –'

She'd lost some of her colour.

'You know how much I miss you when you're away,' Alice interrupted, her voice breaking unexpectedly. 'But what life can you have, darling, a woman separated from her husband, without the excuse – the justification – of illness? No-one would agree to know you. Where would you turn for a friend?'

'Perhaps the oldest and dearest ones, like Maud, might stand by you. But otherwise you'd be alone. Your life would wither away,' he warned. There were tears in his eyes.

Trix was cutting her bread and butter into diamond shapes.

'How do you know that? Not everyone is as narrow minded as your friends down here – I mean the county people. I could go to London, stay with –'

Alice didn't allow her to continue.

'It's out of the question. What would you use for money? Your father and I haven't the means and you can hardly expect your husband to finance you.'

Coaxing, he asked 'Do you really intend to condemn two people, yourself and Fleming, to such loneliness, Trix? Would that really be for the best?'

His choice of words had its impact. Now Trix seemed about to cry.

'I don't want anyone to be lonely,' her voice shook. 'It's a shock. I should have seen this for myself. I can't think why I didn't. But give me a little time to get used to the idea. Of being a wife again, I mean. I think I can do it, if I have to.'

Later, when Trix was fastening Alice's necklace for her, before dinner, and they were alone, Alice ventured, 'If Jack does insist on your marital duties,' – she spoke carefully – 'it's always possible to pretend that it's not happening you know, dearest. Just put your mind somewhere else.'

Trix nodded thoughtfully masking the outrage that swelled and threatened to choke her. 'Put her mind somewhere else?' Didn't her mother understand by now that a mind that went off somewhere else was a terrifying liability? Anything to avoid losing herself like that again, anything.

The first thing was to stay calm, though. Nothing strident.

Looking her mother up and down in her evening dress 'I'm not sure that fabric is really your colour, have you thought of dyeing it? she advised, sweetly.

*

Weeks after their return, John and Elsie were still consulting the ragged strip of seaweed they'd brought back from their holiday, Carrie was amused to observe. That time at the sea had done them good. November and no sign of a cold from either of them, she congratulated herself as she came downstairs. The alarms of the summer were behind her. Every morning Rud was shut away writing hard.

The garden hadn't much in it at the moment but she'd have a look. A trug over her arm, she was on her way back inside with a few sprays of foliage for a vase when Perceval Landon arrived. Since Rud worked with him in Bloemfontein he'd become a family friend.

'The children will be down in a trice, they know you're coming,' she warned him, as they settled down by the drawing room fire.

'So Rud's still pegging away at that plan of his for army reform?' Perceval Landon spoke over John's head. Arms braced about the tall man's knees, he was attempting to push him over.

'Steady, Johnny, steady there, you'll have me crashing onto your mother on that sofa.'

Elsie had only just left off swinging from the elbow he'd crooked.

Carrie laughed. The children could be left to take out their affection on Mr. Landon without fear of rebuff.

'Pegging away's the word. He insists on making a short story of it but it's a struggle.'

'Surely not that same piece he'd already started on the way out to Cape Town last year?'

Landon's surprise encouraged her to go further. 'You've no idea how worked up and anxious he was about the soldiers, even before the war was properly started. And once things began to go wrong, as they did, he was in a perfect fury.'

'Against?'

'Against the government, the War Office, I suppose. That they sent men away to fight so ill-prepared. He took it so personally. He's been obsessed by the need for defence, proper defence, ever since.'

Landon was impatient: 'I don't understand but then I'm only a newspaperman – that's enough now, kids, I'm going to sit down. He seems to be taking a long time in laying out some quite straightforward propositions.'

The temptation of sharing an editorial discussion was too much. Besides, she didn't understand Rud's investment in this piece either. She mistrusted it, just as she winced at the gabble of information and plans for stories which broke from him when he was carried away by an audience.

'He's rewritten *The Army of a Dream* so many times I can recite parts by heart: '*all boys begin physical drill to music in the Board Schools when they're six; squad drill one hour a week when they're eight; company drill when they're ten –*'''

Landon put up his hand, laughing. 'Doesn't sound much like a story to me.'

'You put your finger on the problem. Rud's worked out his plan for universal defence in the most elaborate detail. It might be a government report. But of course he wants to reach all those readers of his, so he pretends it's a short story. You can imagine the work involved in trying to dramatise it.'

'Can it really be worth it?'

'We're not supposed to ask. He's nowhere near satisfied with it yet. But when Rud starts on matters of national defence, I've learned to keep my own counsel. That's where he is now, of course, up at the Rifle Club he's started. Rud's determined that all the young men hereabouts will learn to shoot: he's up there most evenings but today, in your honour, he's restricted himself to an hour in the afternoon. I think I hear him now.'

With a roar of delight, her husband advanced, throwing his hat down, hand outstretched to greet his guest.

* * *

Once Trix had left for Calcutta, Lockwood gave in to temptation. These days Alice had no interest in travelling but he'd accepted the invitation to join Rud and Carrie out at the Cape.

Back from a morning in the Malay Quarter, he eased himself into a wicker chair overlooking the garden.

Laying her work down on the low table, Carrie asked, 'Were you hoping for tea?'

'In a while perhaps, my dear. But it was for the pleasure of sitting with you that I've come out.'

'Poor girl,' he noted how her eyes had filled at his words. 'She'll never admit it's too much for her. Thank goodness I was able to come out to join them this year. At least while I'm here there is someone to pay her a little attention. Keep her company.'

'You know, I believe I am ready in fact for my cup of tea,' he said aloud. 'Shall we ask them to bring it?'

They sat companionably, Carrie nibbling at the cinnamon biscuits while he admired the view down over the great broad plain towards the sea. Rud thought it asked to be planted with orchards. What made him such an expert, all of a sudden? He ought to take him up on that.

'Tell me again, when's Rud coming back?

Carrie didn't smile.

'D'you know, I'm not entirely sure. It seems to fidget him to fix anything, so I don't press him. I only fear he'll exhaust himself. Hour after hour in the hospitals with the wounded. Concerts for them. He recited a couple of his new war poems at a concert for five hundred of them a week or two before you got here.'

He didn't reply, encouraging her to go on.

'Of course, they all adore him, the men. I sometimes wonder if all this isn't too much like a drug, the excitement of it all, what Rud calls the political side of his life. I was so glad when Henry James said it for me. He absolutely scolded Rud; I saw the letter. *"Chuck public affairs, it's an ignoble scene, base humbug,"* those were his exact words.'

He considered. 'And you, Carrie, you feel there's something actually excessive in the way he's throwing himself into affairs over here? I would have to say, my dear, that I agree with you. But I am also hopeful that it is only a stage, possibly a necessary stage, in his recovery from…' He allowed his voice to die away. A field of force around Carrie barred direct reference to Jo's death.

'If there were only this running about – you'll forgive me for speaking so plainly – this running about with famous men involved, I would be truly concerned. But you spoke of the hospitals: that's something different. He's always been good with sick people and children. As a rule young men don't care for babies but Rud was crazy about them, even at eighteen. I suspect that it's something of a lifeline for that side of him, working in the hospitals.'

Carrie nodded, reluctant recognition. She could probably have done with more of that at home.

'I can't say that winding bandages and packing kitbags, the sort of work that comes my way, makes me feel any better, but I suppose you may be right.'

Sensing they shared a train of thought, he went on: 'It's not just the physical illness, is it, that he's got to get over?'

She drew herself in, speechless.

'My dear girl, I'm so clumsy. Let me try again. He blames himself, I believe, can't help blaming himself.' He didn't need to be more explicit. 'I've come to believe that while Rud's doing his best for these sick men, he's fighting to recover his self-respect.'

'To make amends?' she asked in a voice of bitterness.

For the wrong choice that she herself had made? Would Rud ever forgive her? Lockwood couldn't escape her meaning.

'Perhaps. That might not be the best way to put it but it

will answer.'

'It is different from dining at Groote Schuur, I can see that,' she answered slowly. 'And anyway, those particular days are over. Sir Alfred's moved his headquarters out of Cape Town and Rud doesn't want to accept it, but Mr. Rhodes' heart is finally giving out. I'll think over what you've said. And I won't stand in Rud's way, whatever it costs.'

She remained silent for a while, then turning to him, 'I often say that I could never advise a girl to marry any literary man. They so live off their nerves. When they're not writing all they need is for you and everything else to be dead calm.'

He faltered, reaching for some more positive note.

'You and I can do nothing but stand by and let him fight this battle. At least it's taking place over ground that he's chosen.'

*

Cecil Rhodes had gone down to a shack above the beach to die. Trudging down from the ugly brick-built station at Muizenberg, Rud came to a halt in the narrow shade of an overhanging bougainvillea and removed his straw hat to wipe his forehead. Hanging leaves left their debris caught in his hair. Irritated, he brushed the dry traces away and felt a tiny fragment slip down inside his collar. March, a heatwave and as yet no sign of the cooler weather.

He looked out over the bay. Glass-green curled over sheets of turquoise, the heavy rhythmic crash echoing inside him. Was it for this, the sense of weight and power, that Rhodes had insisted on being nursed here?

The lanky figure of Jourdan, Rhodes' secretary, was standing out on the rickety stoep. Dapper as ever, though his face was shockingly pale, he cut an odd figure in the shabby cottage.

His voice was low as he explained, 'Not a good night. His breathing is very difficult. He gets… agitated.'

Rud had never really cared for the man but his heart softened at such evident distress.

'I'll only stay a few minutes.'

'It's quite important, the doctor says, not to let him talk; he tires so easily.'

With some irritation – what did the fellow think he was going to do, suggest a debate? – Rud nodded assent. Ushered inside, he was struck again by the violent contrast with Groote Schuur. At the thought of the big house there had been such pride in designing, the site of so many splendid dreams, Rud shook his head. Now all that Rhodes could hope and fight for was a mouthful of air.

Once in the room with Rhodes, though, he meant to make the best of it.

'Rather larks, your little camp, just by the beach.'

The jovial premeditated words were scarcely out before memory silenced him. Many photographs of Rhodes on camp were displayed in Groote Schuur, images of Rhodes seated, his black servants at his back, before a tent pitched at the side of a wagon.

'That's when he's happiest, you know. Away from home, away from his own people,' Carrie'd whispered.

They'd asked about the other photographs of the stern-faced mother, the vicar's wife, the cluster of brothers.

'I was her favourite,' Rhodes had admitted, with something like embarrassment.

Rud saw no photographs here by the invalid's bed.

The stranded hulk slowly turned its head.

'Rud, is that you?'

'Don't try to talk, old man, they don't want you to talk.'

'They never did, she would never let me – '

'Hush.'

Was he wandering? Viewing that degraded body, it was clear that the end couldn't be far off. The once baggy skin around the eyes was now puffed out, the eyes themselves hardly more than slits.

Panic swept through him a sense of sliding, a tilt in the world. He reached out and grasped the sick man's hand, convulsively, feeling a sob rising in his throat. It might be their last meeting. He would never see Rhodes again. But the hand he took was restless within his own. The sick man fretted and withdrew from his touch. Abashed, he cursed himself and his cheap, sprawling emotions.

'Is there anything that we can have sent to you?' he heard himself say.

The air of the sickroom was making him nauseous. Guiltily, he reached for his hat.

'Jourdan's promised to keep us informed. They do say that a storm's coming tonight and after that it should be a little cooler.'

He couldn't tell whether Rhodes was listening.

'She never wanted me to think and if I did she never wanted me to speak,' came the voice from the bed.

He'd have to go. There was nothing he could do.

Wait. They obviously couldn't get round it to turn Rhodes. They'd need to do that, he'd lent a hand himself in the hospitals, more than once. No space and it would take several people, his frame was vast. Yet there was a way to cool him and make him more comfortable.

Rud beckoned Jourdan down the path.

'Couldn't a couple of workmen be got to cut a hole in the roof?'

That way they could lower a block of ice into the back room where the gasping bulk lay stretched.

Jourdan stepped back, his nostrils quivering at the intrusion.

'But Mr. Kipling, the noise?'

'Muffle their boots with rags. That'll deal with most of it. Cutting a hole in this tin roof won't take five minutes: it's rotten with rust.'

Reluctantly, Jourdan agreed to look into it. The visitor clearly had no idea that he'd been a disappointment. Mr. Rhodes had often complained, 'He's written almost nothing about South Africa. After all I've done for Kipling, I did think he'd be more use.'

At the station Rud sank gratefully onto an empty bench. He was struggling against a rising anxiety. Though there were plenty of seats, when the train came he found it easier to stand, appearing to stare out at the suburbs as they bumped past. The effort of climbing the path up towards The Woolsack was welcome: he wanted it to go on, not to stop. He would climb up farther. Seeing the flash of Nurse Lucy's uniform among the garden trees, he approached. The children were making themselves a house. They had chosen a wide stretch of shade and were arranging Elsie's dolls in a circle around a small stool.

'Look, Daddy, it's a party!' John ran up to him.

'A party for dolls, old man? There might be more exciting games for you to play. Why not a game of soldiers? After all you are four'.

John's face fell. He looked at the miniature cup he'd been holding and threw it down.

'Good afternoon Nurse, I'm off on a bit of a walk. I'll take Elsie; it will do her good. Come on, child, let's race as fast as we can.'

Elsie looked up at her father, considering. At six, she was learning to take thought before she spoke. She set down the leaf plate she was carrying and got to her feet. Time on her own with Daddy, especially now when she could tell something was wrong. Daddy was sad.

*

'You're not joining us on the funeral train?' There was astonishment in Milner's voice.

For once Rud could be grateful for the prohibitions of doctors.

'They think it might be too much for me,' he offered discreetly, defying further question.

He'd escaped the interminable procession by rail out to the Matoppos hills where Rhodes had elected to be buried. They would have to pause at every blockhouse to accept a round of respectful fire. Marching down Adderley Street in Cape Town, as the body was conveyed from its lying in state was enough. He was relieved to have made his decision.

'If I go, they'll expect me to read my poem on his death, at the graveside,' he explained to a baffled Carrie.

'But it's so fine, so dignified. You're not afraid of breaking down?'

'There is that. But you know, I'm not sure I want to go so far in that direction. As it were. Those "*great spaces washed with sun*" I wrote about, they feel too exposed. I thought I'd stay here with you and the children.'

'You are a mystery,' she exclaimed, almost provoked. 'But you've made me happy.'

* * *

Only a matter of weeks after Rud and Carrie's return from Africa, Home Leave brought Jack Fleming to London and with him Trix.

Rud and Trix were reunited in Tisbury.

'I can't tell you what it means, Trix – that you're back to your old self once more –' Rud broke off, laughing shakily. 'Tell me again how the poetry got started.'

They were sitting, together with their mother, in the little breakfast room of their parents' home. All round them stood the memorials of another life, from the peacock screen, now a little battered, to the heavy pieces of embroidery that hung on the walls. Lockwood, off in his studio, was giving some little girls their weekly drawing lesson.

'Mama began it. Don't frown, Ruddy. It's no more than the truth. She suggested she and I should begin writing together. A little every day. And in the end, we found we had a whole bookful of poems.'

Rud's smile was touched with constraint. He was not sure he could display enthusiasm for the anaemic verse coming out under the title of *Hand in Hand, Poems by a Mother and Daughter.* But the project had served its purpose. Trix moved on to writing and publishing something a good deal more sinewy, a set of parodies, and, what was more, under her own name, the one she was legally entitled to, 'Alice Fleming'. Best of all, she really seemed herself again.

Alice spoke from the wooden embrace of the old Windsor chair, which she claimed was the only place she could sit in comfort.

'Your father really didn't approve at the time, but you see I was right all along. I decided it was the writing that stood at the core of the problem and I must get her going again. Poor Trixie, when she was … not herself, she kept getting so worked up about publishers, she would insist that she was… '

She stopped, picking up their rigid silence.

'Well, it's not "poor Trixie" is it any more? It's big fierce "Alice Fleming" of the *Pall Mall Magazine*, scourge of feeble-witted poets, including her hapless brother,' Rud said firmly.

Trix looked uncertain. 'I did wonder whether you'd mind my jokes about your verse from the war. But I thought it must be all right when Father decided to ask Mr. Cornford to place my comic odes as a set.'

Trix hadn't seen her father's covering letter. *Fratricidal* was the word he used, when he sent the poems off to Leslie Cope Cornford, their family friend.

'Don't sell yourself short, Trix,' Rud objected. 'They're parody and first class. You've faked up just the sort of drivel people will produce in honour of the Coronation.'

He must be generous with his encouragement. But it had given him a turn to see her publish – publish! – those mocking lines.

He reached across and took the thick May issue of the *Pall Mall Magazine* from his mother. It wasn't clear whether Alice was stroking the smooth cover or pressing it closed.

In his hands the magazine fell open at the page.

'The cream of it is the way you've brought off the voices. They're absolutely distinct. Alfred Austin and his droning pastoral –' he took up the *Magazine* and read, spluttering:

'Ah, stay, I have not mentioned roses yet
Nor verdant meads dappled with lowing herds,
I should not be Myself could I forget
The dicky-birds'.

He waved the journal about in his glee, then had to find the place again before he could go on.

'And what about Willie Yeats – timid, dreamy sort, a great hulk of a chap, living in the past – you show him no mercy in *The Pavement Stand of Westminstree*. His *Lake Isle of Innisfree* will never be the same:

> *'I will arise and go now, and go to Westminstree*
> *And a small campstool take there, that's very strongly made;*
> *My gold watch will I doff me for fear of pickpocketry,*
> *And meet with my fellows unafraid.'*

Each catching the other's eye, forgetting all that had passed, they stood together again, back in Lahore, back in his little curtained-off writing space in the house on the Mozung Road, sure of each other and laughing.

The following day, back in his own well-appointed study, Rud riffled through the heaps of unopened mail on a side table, till he came upon his own copy of the *Pall Mall Magazine*, still in its wrapper. He scrabbled, swearing, at the packaging. Beneath his pleasure in her accomplishment, he was discomfited by Trix and what she'd exposed.

Had that friend of hers, Maud Diver, had a part in this? She'd fancied herself as a writer. He'd never been happy that Trix was so thick with her.

He laid a heavy ruler flat on the opened page. Trix had gone straight for his war poems. Anyone could see that. He read over her opening:

> *'Let the trumpets sound for the Day of Coronation.*
> *(Listen all ye people in the lands beyond the sea.)*
> *Ended now and over the Year of the Probation,*
> *And the time has come appointed for the solemn Pageantry.'*

It was horribly near the knuckle. Facile. And much too close for comfort to the opening verses of *The King*, the poem he sent *The Times* back in '99 at the start of the war. He'd opened with trumpets – '*Here is nothing new nor ought unproven say the Trumpets*' – and then brought them in again at the end of every stanza: '*Trumpets round the scaffold at the dawning by Whitehall!*' He recalled he'd been rather pleased with that at the time. Well, perhaps he had over-egged that pudding.

But all he was trying to do was warn the country against the Transvaalers, make them see that President Kruger and his sense of divine right meant danger and would destroy freedom. Now Trix was making fun of him about it and in the public press. People simply couldn't mistake what she was getting at.

He had the impression that she'd been following every line he published then deftly, ruthlessly, reassembling them. He crossed to the bookcase to fetch the most recent scrapbook, where all his newspaper work was pasted up. What else had she targeted?

He peered again at the magazine:

'Then till sword be beaten to ploughshare, and Mausers to motors weld,
We will care for our own as we now care, and that which we hold shall
be held.'

'You have to hand it to her, she's caught my voice,' he said aloud.

'Well, I hope she's going to let it go again,' his Aunt Georgie broke in. He'd been too absorbed to notice that she and Carrie had joined him in the study, taking the door left open in his haste as their invitation.

'Listen to this.' He had no time for pleasantries. 'This is Trix, in the *Pall Mall Magazine*. A parody. It's me to the life.

'It behoves us to take good heed
Of the Work that is but beginning, of the Plougher who looks not back
Of the Strife and the Stress and the Sinning, and the train on the four-
foot track..'

As he put the paper down, he was grinning in reluctant admiration.

'She really has caught your … way with the Authorised Version,' Georgie murmured. She held back from saying 'trick'.

She remembered how Lockwood, who steadily refused to go to church, had challenged Ruddy on his use of Biblical language.

'Some might call it cynical, Rud.'

'It's a universal key,' the son had insisted. 'Everyone in England – myself included – possibly barring Jews and the RCs – finds themselves opening up willy-nilly to the authority of that voice. We can't help ourselves: it's been drummed into every one of us as children.'

Like Lockwood, Georgie remained doubtful. Dear Ruddy, he did want to make people sit up and take notice. And he did take his responsibility as a sort of prophet so very seriously.

Now his cry of distress brought her back to the moment.

Till the Empire, in solemn seeming, frames the perfect entity,' he read aloud.

'Am I really that fatuous?' he turned to them, wounded.

She saw that Carrie was flushed with indignation, too much put out at first to speak. Then, 'How ungenerous, how sly,' Carrie broke out.

The words were scarcely uttered before Georgie discreetly motioned her to silence. She looked across at Carrie for permission before beginning to speak.

'That's only a tease. Ruddy dear, it's such good news that Trix is entirely well again and I must find time later to read her little piece. But now I want you to make me a promise. I know how busy you've been since you got home but I want you to take up your old habit of coming over and reading your new work to me in the afternoon.'

Taking his arm, even while appearing to lean on it, she walked him off to the drawing room, where long windows lay open to the twilit garden. She inhaled with pleasure.

'I can tell that your mower's been out today. Ours too.'

Before she left she would have a word with Carrie.

Once he'd seen Georgie home across the green, Rud went back to the open scrapbook. He was disturbed. Put together, presented as Trix had, his vision of the Empire lost some of its substance, its conviction for him.

For the first time, on turning over the scrapbook pages lined with columns of newsprint, his archive, he felt that what lay before him was failure. He was losing readers, unable to carry them with him. Though *The Times* had taken one essay on treachery among the inhabitants at the Cape, they had refused a second. And they'd not really backed him on the plan to train up boys as a future army of defence.

Carrie was calling him.

'You're not still brooding over Trix?' she was yawning as she came into the room.

'It's just uncanny, the way she's taken me up, word for word. Look here –' he stabbed with a finger:

When service is never venal, for that shall be witchcraft's sin
And the playing of games shall be penal, and each shall as soldier begin.'

'Remember my essay *The Sin of Witchcraft*? I've got it here,' he pointed at the scrapbook, 'here, *The Times*, March '01. And "*the playing of games shall be penal*", that's a crack at *The Islanders* in *The Times* this January.'

She gave a weary sigh. There'd been such a fuss in response to that poem: writing of '*flannelled fools at the wicket and muddied oafs at the goal*' had not been popular. If he wanted to get the landed classes to address their responsibilities and defend the country, as he claimed, he should have been more tactful.

'Come to bed, Rud,' she said, stroking the slight shoulders, as they bent over the papers on the desk. 'You can't expect to get people to share your feelings every time.'

'They're not feelings, they're views,' he snapped, jerking upright. 'There's a difference.'

He was always like this when he was trying to convert people to his ideas about this war. Obsessed by the need to guard against treachery, the need to prepare for future defence. She despaired.

'Very well, Rud. They're views. But they're not ones I share and I'm going to bed.'

He couldn't get anyone to listen. They were all turning away. As he sat looking blankly ahead in the darkened study, he felt the psalmist's words rise up in him. *'My soul cleaveth unto the dust.'* He made a struggle to laugh at himself but failed. The pang of rejection lingered.

'I have chosen the way of truth' – was that how it went on? So he had. He couldn't pretend not to see what was right in front of him. He must speak out about politics: the fate of the world, let alone the Empire, was at stake. How were different peoples to live together in community with the least damage? How to contain the violence of greed? He could see now, at a distance, that was what Mowgli and the Jungle Law had always meant. But the fools – his readers, the world – had turned 'the law of the jungle' on its head so it meant rapine and slaughter. With a groan he repeated aloud *'Take not the word of truth utterly out of my mouth –'*

He checked himself. Onwards, enough of these wretched regrets.

There was some comfort. He noticed that Trix left his lyrics alone. There was no mocking echo of his *Bridge-Guard in the Karoo*. Tracking it down – '01, if not earlier, in the scrapbook, he began to read it over, and was lost once more among the echoing spaces of the veld:

> *'The twilight swallows the thicket,*
> *The starlight reveals the ridge;*
> *The whistle shrills to the picket –*
> *We are changing guard on the bridge.*
>
> *(Few, forgotten and lonely,*
> *Where the empty metals shine –*
> *No, not combatants – only*
> *Details guarding the line.)'*

Out in the war, there usually wasn't much time for that brand of feeling. But Trix, like himself, could recognise loneliness and respect it.

He sat up straight.

Think of it: Trix recovered, back out in Calcutta, taking up her place in the world again. A new lease on her life. And meanwhile, that low grey Jacobean house near Burwash they had liked so much was now on the market. He must keep his name out of it or they'd be rooked, but by God he'd have that house.

* * *

That June the contract was signed and at the beginning of September they moved in to Bateman's. This was the house for him, all right, more congenial even than they'd guessed. Every morning he woke in high spirits. A new start.

They'd been in less than a fortnight when the last invitation he wanted arrived through the mail. He was sorting papers on a rickety card table, in the room that was going to be his study. The long table he'd bought to write on stood downstairs in what was going to be the drawing room, waiting for the protective hessian to be removed.

Bringing a draught that fluttered every sheet, Carrie came in.

'I've wired Curzon that it's no-go. We're not trekking out to Delhi for that Durbar of his,' he announced.

'Delhi? Durbar? Whatever do you mean?' She stammered. 'It's no time since we moved here. I can't contemplate outside distractions. Workmen are swarming everywhere and the plumbers have found a fresh difficulty with the W.C.'

'I did tell you,' he reminded her, with a sigh. 'Curzon's show out in Delhi, for the coronation. One hundred native rulers invited, thirty thousand troops to be inspected and he wants us out there as part of it. Part of the show. I'm blowed if we allow ourselves to be used to grace the triumph of George Nathaniel Curzon. It sounds to me as though it's as much in honour of him as of the King.'

He made a grab to retrieve a letter that was too close to the edge of the table.

'Is wiring him enough? Hadn't you better write as well? I'd really come to discuss the estimate for the drains but you'd better finish dealing with that first.'

'I've just done that. You'd better cast your eye over it,' he held out the letter.

Putting down an armful of teacloths she reached for a chair.

I would give more than a little to be able to go to Delhi for the Durbar but as things are at present I must go down to the Cape this winter where instead of seeing India consolidated I shall have the felicity of watching South Africa being slowly but scientifically wrecked.'

'I suppose that will do, it's civil enough, but what do you mean, you must go. You make it sound as though you're under an unpleasant obligation to visit the Cape.'

'So I am. I don't want to but I feel I must. As for India, it's over for me, I tried to get Curzon to grasp that back in '99, the first time he invited us. Why he should think I'd have any interest now in this New Delhi is beyond me.'

He tapped his fingers against the rough baize of the card table.

'You really don't care for India any more?' she ventured, wistful.

'My dear, it was the old days out there I used to long for. And they'll never come back.' It was a surprise to hear himself admit that.

'I've never heard you say that before,' she exclaimed, startled.

'Somehow I can feel a different past in this place, one that's also mine in a way. Or could be, if I chose to make it so,' he finished.

'You mean – stories?'

'Ssh!' laying a finger to his lips 'not yet. But perhaps.'

Carrie hardly knew where her feet were taking her when she left the room. India firmly behind Rud at last. And she wasn't entirely sorry to hear him speak of South Africa with frustration. How else was he going to give up his passion for The Woolsack and give his loyalty to a new home?

Passing a window, she paused to gaze out over the space of the garden and beyond to the wooded slopes.

Not quite right to call this house new, with its long history in the fold of the valley. It was exasperating to hear Rud exaggerate its age in reports to their friends. But if it meant so much to him to claim that their little mill went back to the Domesday Book, so be it. At least he'd stayed with recorded history, stopped short of the Garden of Eden.

As she made her way down the wide oak staircase – she still hadn't quite got a feel for its risers – Carrie frowned to see a ladder propped carelessly against the fine old panelling. The house had kept its dignity through years when farmers made use of one or two rooms for eating and sleeping. No careless workman was going to disfigure it now. She made a note to remind the foreman about protecting the endpieces with wadding.

Considering there'd been no running water upstairs, let alone a bathroom, and no electricity in the house when they signed the contract a mere three months past, perhaps the frightful disorder was only to be expected.

The friendly chaos suited the children. Outside in the stable yard she could see John, armed with his own little pail of whitewash, 'helping', aproned to the eyes. From the landing came murmured voices, as the head housemaid counted the linen, while Elsie stood by, pencil and new notebook in hand, solemnly keeping the record.

'Confound it, the place imposes its own tone,' Rud complained. 'It's all very well buying a distinguished house but I never imagined it would set itself up as a silent critic of our taste'.

They looked sheepishly at each other and at the oak settle. Once they had it standing there in the hall at Bateman's, it looked neither genuinely old nor worth what they'd paid.

'D'you suppose they'd take it back?' she agreed. 'Never mind, that French walnut desk we bought for you fits perfectly .'

Her heart gave a thump. When she was listing items of furniture to be sent over from Naulakha, still standing deserted, she'd taken care to say nothing about any desk, battered or intact. All past ruin must be forgotten, left behind.

His high spirits on their trips together, out hunting furnishings, infected her. Opening her diary later, she found that he'd written 'A honeymoonish time', over the days they'd spent together.

'How to feed them a magic that belongs to this place?' Rud wondered aloud, as they sat together on the terrace after dinner.

Carrie raised her eyebrows encouragingly.

'The world I grew up in, my first world, I mean had so much of it. Wayside magic, threshold spells. They made the world alive to me and this new/old house has brought it all back. I'm in the middle of a poem about it. They're just pouring out of me, suddenly. Hang on, I think I can remember the bit –' He closed his eyes and began to chant:

We shall go back by the boltless doors,
To the life unaltered our childhood knew –
To the naked feet on the cool, dark floors,
And the high-celled rooms that the Trade blows through:

To the trumpet-flowers and the moon beyond,
And the tree-toad's chorus drowning all –
And the lisp of the split banana-frond
That talked us to sleep when we were small.

The wayside magic, the threshold spells –'

'Rud! It's magnificent.' She was alight. 'But it makes me want to cry, too. However can you give John and Elsie anything to match that, growing up in Sussex?'

He had to wait a year or so till they were old enough. First he told them the story at bedtime, now and then breaking into incantation:

'Ye spotted snakes with double tongue
Thorny hedge hogs be not seen
Newts and blind worms do no wrong.'

They took the bait all right. He overheard them, chanting remembered lines when they were on their own, correcting each other.

'John, no. It's not *"Wake when a violin is near"*, it's *"Wake when some vile thing is near"*. But it's very good for your age.'

Rud snorted. Elsie had her own idea of kindness.

Once they were making it theirs, he was ready to make his proposal. He chose a moment when the three of them, out together in the fields for the afternoon, had thrown themselves down beside the big hayrick.

'How would you like to act this out for yourselves? We could put on a show out here in the Quarry for Mummy.'

'Bags I be Puck,' John shrilled immediately.

His father chortled: 'I was hoping you wouldn't choose Titania, old man. That's *my* part.'

'Oh *Daddy,'* John and Elsie shrieked in unison, throwing themselves as one on him as he sat propped against the tickling wall of hay.

'And anyway, I'm the only girl, so it has to be me,' reproved Elsie, resuming her eight-year-old dignity as she got to her feet.

'Dadda, that only leaves Bottom for you.' John was six. That name always reduced him to giggles.

'We'll start practising tomorrow,' he promised, getting to his feet. 'Time to get home now for tea.'

He walked round by the Mill towards home, while the children ran off to visit a new litter of puppies in one of the cottages he'd paid so much to make weatherproof.

'It's a curse inheriting tenants from an indifferent landlord,' he complained as he took his cup of tea. Carrie'd rung once she heard his light step out on the terrace.

'What we've taken on here, though we didn't realise, is a huge project of restoration. Just as well that Naulakha and all the bother of it are going to be taken off our hands.'

She flinched but tried to keep her expression neutral. That chapter was better closed.

'I'm glad it's Molly Cabot buying it. I couldn't bear our home to go to strangers.'

'But what a loss! Five thousand dollars, including all remaining contents and to think we spent upwards of twenty-five thousand on it. Thirty thousand would've been more like a fair price.'

He drummed angrily on the arm of his chair.

Attempting to distract him, 'It is a huge project we've taken on but it doesn't seem to be making you unhappy.'

'I do like the chance to bring order, to make the land flourish and bear.'

She gave a wry smile, remembering the squirrels who'd dug up her tulips.

'But it's yourself that you've finally planted, Rud, here in England, isn't it? You and your poetry. That's flourishing.'

The thought seemed new to him.

'I suppose you're right. I hadn't thought of it like that.' An interval, while he stared out over the swimming pond they'd had dug for the children.

Flicking the crumbs from her skirt, she was just thinking of the letters she'd write before dinner when he burst out.

'If things had turned out differently in South Africa, if the party of government had been made of sane and honourable men, that would have been the place to try farming.'

That hobby horse again! Trying to distract him, 'I do regret that wonderful climate. But there'd have been no Roman horse-bit for you to find out there when you sank a well,' she teased.

He brightened immediately.

'To see the land reveal its history, it's astonishing. It feeds me. So many stories, I can't get them all down.'

Back in his study the afternoon post had arrived and among the pile of letters a long narrow parcel. At once he set about slitting the brown paper, pausing to sniff with pleasure at the sealing wax. He was right: inside the stout cardboard box lay the old open-work iron bell-pull.

'Come up and see,' he called to Carrie. 'By Jove, that fellow who bought Georgie's London house off her is a decent chap. I did wonder whether it was an imposition, asking for the old bell-pull. But here it is, by return of post.'

'So that's it, just as you described,' tracing the heavy loops of metal with a forefinger.

'Feeling the shape of it against my hand was always the beginning of happiness. All I'd learned in that other place, the House of Desolation in Southsea, melted away.'

She slipped her arm through his and squeezed it in silence.

'I'd like it if other children could feel hope like that, when they take hold of it by our own door. But before I forget,' he moved the box from his desk to a smaller table nearby, 'I've had an idea. Just one letter to write, then I thought you and I might take a stroll before dinner. It's simply divine out there.'

He saw a way to deepen the magic. Gwynne from Bloemfontein days was coming down at the weekend, together with the Permanent Secretary of State for War. The kids were fond of Gwynne: he wouldn't mind being asked a favour. Rud sat down:

'Dear Old Man,
Now this is serious.
Can you when you come down with Ward on Saturday get for me from some London toyshop a donkey's head mask, either in paper or cloth sufficiently large to go over a man's head and also a pair of gauze fairy wings.'

* * *

'You'll be taking proper care of yourself this time, Trix,' Jack said when she joined him once more in Calcutta.

'No more of that nonsense,' he repeated as she stood in the hallway the first morning, surveying her new home. 7/1 Loudon St. was the lower apartment in a handsome building on the corner with Theatre Rd. She could make it attractive.

But how to respond to him?

She knew she must live with Jack wherever his work took him. Girls didn't realise what that meant.

Smoothing down her skirt, 'Indeed, Jack, there's nothing I value like my health and strength.'

Never again, if she could possibly help it, those dizzy plunges, that tearing rage. She shuddered.

Seeing he still looked uncertain, she added quickly, 'Apart from yours, my dear. We must look out for each other.'

With a grunt, he left to collect his papers for work.

Not much but the best she could manage. She must settle to housekeeping and getting back in touch with friends.

Trix lay back in a long chair, too hot even to make an attempt at a poem. She hoped that no spirit messages would try to come through that day. When the messages from Myers started she'd taken care to hide it from Jack. She hadn't courted them. True, she'd been reading his book, *Human Personality and its Survival of Bodily Death*. And reading it knowing he was already dead himself. Surely, though, she was only one among thousands of other readers. But William de Morgan, who recommended it, had been quite correct in predicting: '*The book will mean more to you, Trix, than to most people.*'

Still as she was keeping, drops of sweat were trickling down.

It had been the most extraordinary relief to read an account which so thoroughly explained her own experience, experience that others shrank from hearing. Mother had hushed her with a look when she tried to describe what she saw in the crystal before Josephine died.

She didn't seem to have her *eau de cologne* at hand. Was it worth the effort of ringing for it?

Just reading the chapter headings, especially *Sensory Automatism*, *Phantasms of the Dead*, *Motor Automatism* had given her a sense she had at last come home. And all so closely argued, so based on experiment and observation. As she read on she'd made sense to herself as never before.

A blast of scorching wind rattled the windows. Outside scarlet petals from the gold mohur and the cassia would be flying like sparks.

She couldn't have known, wasn't responsible for what followed on reading Myers. The spirit messages, the insistence, the pressure.

'You are to be a reporter for me,' the trance-writing had instructed, claiming it came from the spirit of Myers himself. *'Pass on my messages.'*

A deep shiver ran through her at the memory of the headaches that announced them.

Hearing a servant pass, she called for a shawl, then stopped, confused.

In the end, though she'd been shrinking in fear of Jack finding out, she'd felt obliged to write to the secretary of the Society for Psychical Research. The relief, on opening her heart, on being able to ask for help: *'it puzzles me a little that with no desire to consider myself exceptional, I do sometimes see, hear, feel or otherwise become conscious of beings and influences that are not patent to all.'*

She'd covered page after page.

Flexing her fingers, she recalled how they'd ached by the time she finished.

The joy of finding the Society had a welcome for her! She hadn't realised till then how homeless she'd been feeling. And now here she was, *'one link in a chain of spirit connections'*, as Miss Johnson, the kind secretary explained.

Perhaps after all she would try a little tea. But none of that disgusting boiled milk.

Of course, in her own case, the work all had to be done under an assumed name, 'Mrs Holland'. The family were all so hostile. Now when the messages came, she sent them on to the Society in London. They said they sometimes found patterns but she'd no idea what that really meant. Miss Johnson called it *'a set of cross-correspondences, a very remarkable experiment'*.

That petticoat was clinging to her thighs so disagreeably. A cautious wriggle. Stickier than ever.

But these people were all so far away, she had no contact with them and the messages were so fragmentary. It was lonely work. At times she wondered about its value.

Abruptly, she clapped her hands together.

No brooding, she'd promised Father. Better to write to dear William de Morgan, he was always encouraging. Yes, a letter. Just put the heat aside and keep the page free of the marks of sweat.

Do you remember my automatic script? You and Evelyn are of the few I venture to talk to about it. It goes on fairly regularly, yet is dull when I read it over. But I send it – secretly – to the patient S.P.R. and they sometimes find things that seem to count. For instance – here in Calcutta on Oct, 17th 1906 my hand wrote: –

"Nor guessed what flowers would deck a grave. Downing …

Do not let A. be seriously perturbed. This will be a slight attack and a very brief one. A.T.M."

That doesn't sound very evidential – but when one learns that on Oct. 17th – Dr. A.W.V. of Cambridge went to see the Downing Professor – who was ill – finding this particular attack had been slight and brief, and that A.T.M. are the initials of a dead doctor of medicine, friend of them both – it gives one a little to think, doesn't it? Also – on the death of the poor Downing Professor two months later – there were two "coincidences" in my script. Of course, I am not told of anything evidential until long and long after...'

She read her own words through doubtfully. It did all seem rather weak. But they'd assured her that her part in the work was invaluable. It was specially important, they said, that she was so remote, away in India: there could be no question of collusion.

Besides, what else could she do with herself and her messages?

That evening, sitting at dinner, she replied with scarcely a qualm when Jack asked her how she'd spent the day.

'I was awfully lazy, I have to say. Reading mainly. Though I did compose a note to dear old William, thanking him for the copy of his last novel. It seemed a perfect disaster when the tile business went under but he's turned out to be *such* a writer. You really should try it, Jack.'

Her husband snorted, 'Let us hope he's a better novelist than he was a businessman,' before he put on his spectacles and spread out his papers to do some work on his project. *The A.B.C. of the more important battles of the Eighteenth and Nineteenth Centuries.*

*

Trix had come Home, for the English spring, on one of those regular trips 'to keep your health up to scratch', that Jack now encouraged. She was staying at Clouds, the great pile built by the Wyndhams, old friends of her parents. Accepting the invitation to join their house party meant leaving Alice and Lockwood, for her mother was becoming frail. As Lockwood put it he'd 'no intention of leaving her alone to brood'.

Now Trix stood in her bedroom, before her looking glass, a moment after hearing the bell for dinner. She knew she was looking particularly well. The fashion for jewelled collars suited her.

'Almost forty but you could pass for thirty, my dear,' she told herself.

And this evening dress, her oyster silk, was wonderfully well cut. No-one would guess it was sewn by her little *darzee* in Calcutta. Such a narrow fit, though, over the hips. It wasn't easy to walk in. Gathering up the heavy, sinuous folds in her left hand, she stepped cautiously over to the door, through a cloud of California poppy, her perfume, Eonia by Atkinson. Maud's gift.

Pausing at the head of the broad staircase, she fingered the solid carving of the newel post. From the shadows to her left came a scuffle, suppressed giggles. The children, supposed to be out of the way, if not in bed, were gazing down like her at the grown-ups gathered before dinner.

She blew a kiss in the general direction of the muffled sounds. The sight of very young children brought back a familiar pain. No nursery of her own and never would be.

Downstairs, a man she didn't know turned, looked up and caught sight of her. He bowed and raised his glass. Colouring with pleasure, Trix began to make her way down to join the party.

On her left, conversation between Madeline Wyndham and Sir Oliver Lodge was steady and animated. Her hostess had given the distinguished scientist the seat of honour on her right. Of course, they were old friends too – both of them members of the Souls.

How she longed to be part of a group of thinking people, like that. Distinguished politicians and intellectuals, meeting casually in society, linked by shared interests in new ideas, in politics and the arts.

She drew back to give the butler room to fill her glass. If she hadn't married Jack, condemned herself to exile, would she have been taken seriously like Madeline and Violet Asquith? Been counted among the Souls? Trix shook herself out of it. Her smile mustn't grow fixed. Since Madeline had chosen to seat her between Sir Oliver and George Wyndham, it would be foolish to feel despised and ignored.

She'd known George Wyndham more or less since they were both children. His sister had been at school with her cousin.

'George?' She began the work of the evening. And paused. What a handsome man he was now, with that straight nose and fine brow. 'George, I know I'm rather behind the times – you've given up being secretary of state – but I've been so much wanting to hear from you about Ireland. Your Land Act. Are the tenants making a go of things, now they've got an acre or two to call   their own?'

A delicate fragrance rose from the clear soup she'd chosen in preference over the heavier cream of lobster. The Wyndhams kept a good table. She picked up her spoon.

'Trix, I might have known you'd ask. Never anything trivial,' he teased. 'I do have to say I'm pleased with how things are shaping over there. But I've got a much more urgent topic, a request and it's rather selfish. Can I show you some Ronsard translations I'm working on? I feel certain you'd see how to iron out a few sticky bits. And I want to know what you've got coming out. Any more of those devastating parodies?'

Her shoulders relaxed: they made plans to meet after breakfast next day.

A maid leaned in and removed her plate. She had only toyed with the salmon.

'I shall argue fiercely with you about Scott,' was her parting shot as she turned gracefully towards the neighbour on her other side.

Sir Oliver Lodge, physicist. Fellow of the Royal Society. They'd been briefly introduced before dinner but it didn't make her less nervous. She mustn't seem too eager. It was such an opportunity to get him to talk about clairvoyancy. It wouldn't do, though, to rush right in.

To gain time, she took up her glass, smiling charmingly over the rim, though she had no intention of taking more than the merest sip, the wine was much too dry. She couldn't possibly discuss electromagnetism. But maybe she could ask about its relation to other forms of invisible energy.

It was as though he'd been waiting. Bending towards her, 'I'm so glad to have this opportunity, Mrs. Fleming'. His smile broadened. 'Or should I say, Mrs. Holland? I believe you spend a great deal of time overseas.'

A bolt shot through her. Her fork dropped. He knew. And was he going to betray her, let everyone hear?

'Please. Sir Oliver, don't – '

'My dear Mrs. Fleming, I had no intention – my foolish little joke.'

He paused. All round, voices were rising, conversation fuelled by the champagne. Glancing from side to side, she was satisfied no-one had overheard.

She waved away a dish loaded with bleeding slices of flesh.

'Let us talk of other things, just now,' Oliver Lodge went on kindly. 'But perhaps later, in the conservatory, over our coffee, we might take up this conversation again?'

Almost composed, able to perform as she should, once more. But no risks, no topic that might be dangerous.

'I would like that very much. Later. But at this moment, if it wouldn't bore you dreadfully, Sir Oliver, nothing would give me greater pleasure than to hear you explain how the telegraph works. I know it's to do with wave pulses and electricity. But I'm such a dunce about these matters.'

Embraced by the warm, smothering air of the conservatory, Trix shivered. It brought back Calcutta and feelings – not quite of distaste: they were almost like longing. She mustn't linger over them, though. Now was her chance to explain her earlier show of nerves. Once Sir Oliver was stirring his coffee, she launched in.

'You understand, my people, my brother Rudyard,' – she couldn't resist the boast, though she despised herself – 'they're all dead set against my work for the Society.' She simply had to get that out of the way, explain why she'd been so alarmed. He mustn't think her odd. 'Some years ago I was rather ill and they insisted on blaming it on the automatic script.'

He nodded sympathetically. Encouraged, she took a moment to reach for her cup.

'I find it quite irrational. My mother's always claimed to have "the sight" – she's a Macdonald, you know. And as for Ruddy, it's his notion that a "daemon" takes over his writing at times and that's what's behind his best work.'

'I'd no idea. Fascinating. I suppose he wouldn't be interested in describing the experience? – no, I can see by your face that he would not. Nevertheless, if you'll allow me I'll just –'

He took a small notebook from his waistcoat pocket and scribbled.

'I dare say your people don't appreciate the scientific nature of our enterprise. My study of electromagnetism reinforces the idea that there is a realm beyond the material world. So we must now apply the methods of scientific investigation to that realm. Assemble our evidence with scrupulous care, make the tests we put it through rigorous. I see these explorations as an extension of my laboratory work.'

The relief of hearing those words from a man of his standing. A Fellow of the Royal Society. A university professor, celebrated for his inventions. The blossoms on the overhanging hibiscus blazed more brightly.

She became bold.

'I have always been able to see things not apparent to others. Crystal vision is the least of it, actually, but it can all be rather a worry. The fact that these things are out of my control and can't be explained.'

'Remarkable,' he was murmuring, but she didn't pause. Her pulses were racing.

'Understanding more would be such a help to me. Those tests you speak of. Can you tell me something about them? I've never been told how they work on my scripts. I just send them in to you, to the secretary, Miss Johnson, I mean, every week with no idea of what they might mean.'

'That's exactly what keeps our experiments pure, my dear Mrs. Fleming. Much better that you know as little as possible. No contamination that way.'

Trix stared at him, brought to a halt. Against her will, anger surged through her.

'Contamination, Sir Oliver? Contamination if I knew what use my work was being put to? I'm not sure I understand.'

Her tone clearly took him by surprise.

'It's just a term we use. You see, we men of science have to question how far the scripts represent material from the automatist's, that is the writer's, own subliminal mind. That's why we have to keep you and Mrs. Verrall and the other ladies in darkness. Our whole endeavour is to create stringent tests, to establish whether souls, having survived death, are communicating with us using a network of automatists. You, I may say, are the most gifted of them.'

She sat silent, not reassured. His words had left her still more troubled. Her own subliminal mind might be behind what she wrote? She flinched, remembering the constant note of appeal in her scripts, the naked longing: '*I should die from sheer yearning to reach you ... if I could only reach you – if I could only tell you – I long for power and all that comes to me is an infinite yearning – an infinite pain.*'

The headache which had begun to threaten was making her eyes dazzle. Fortunately, nothing of her discomfort must be showing, for Sir Oliver was smiling benevolently at her and appeared to be speaking.

Trix took a deep breath and tried to listen.

'You can have no idea, Mrs. Fleming, what a pleasure this is for me. I've been keeping track of your scripts ever since the cross-correspondence experiments, as we call them, began. Dear lady, I don't think you know how exceptional you are. You can't appreciate your own gifts. They seem to come to you by nature. But let me tell you this, very few persons can learn to develop anything like your capacities and skills, and that only after extensive training.'

'I'm never sure that they're natural, Sir Oliver, or even healthy. I get all sorts of pains and symptoms with the writing. And the jolt, if I'm interrupted, is downright unbearable. My nerves are left screaming and my whole body is thrown into disarray.'

'Mrs. Fleming, we all make sacrifices in our different ways for the sake of progress. Promise me that for the sake of science you will persevere!'

She was dazed. So much more recognition than she could have hoped for. But she was all of a sudden quite used up.

'Your encouragement does mean a great deal to me, Sir Oliver. Sometimes I've felt so isolated and unsure. Indeed I will do my best for you.'

She managed to squeeze out a few more words of thanks before making her excuses. Wending her way through the leaning palm branches, she made to go back into the body of the house and from there up the stairs towards her bedroom, a haven of silence and solitude.

A hateful confusion of feelings overwhelmed her once she was on her own.

But long practice had taught her how to deal with that. An hour on her bed, *eau de cologne* on her temples, and she was able to take pleasure in Sir Oliver's praise. Even though no-one who might speak of it to her family must know, this confirmation was too thrilling to keep absolutely to herself. She swung her feet to the ground and went over to the desk, where her own morocco writing case lay open. Wait till Maud heard about this!

* * *

Rud left for Tisbury immediately on getting the wire, even though the hour was already late. Two years on, his mother's life was drawing to a close.

The Mater's health had been in decline for over a year, so he thought himself pretty well braced for the farewell to come. All the long moonlit drive across country from Bateman's to The Gables, he was able to keep his mind on the scenery.

Trix arrived there almost as soon as he did, though she was coming all the way from Edinburgh. Only lucky that she wasn't out in Calcutta but home on leave with Jack. Rud quailed as he followed Trix up the stairs. At the door of the sickroom, without speaking, they reached for each other's hand.

Their father was kneeling beside the bed, stroking his wife's forehead.

At the sight of her children, a smile hovered over the sunken face.

'Dearest ones...' Alice whispered.

Trix bent to kiss the clammy forehead.

'Oh Mama, dearest Mama, don't try to speak.'

Under the ticking silence that followed unbroken, Rud knew

that he was being addressed. That the Mater wanted something from him. Was she asking him to say that he'd never suffered left behind in Southsea? That he forgave her? He froze.

Before long she drifted off into sleep. From that moment forward, until she died on the morning of the fourth day, she gave him no further signal.

Carrie came over before the funeral, to be with Lockwood and Rud, which meant she witnessed the first signs of disturbance in Trix. At first she didn't recognise them for what they were.

'No really, I'm not at all hungry. It's always like this when I can't sleep,' Trix insisted at dinner, tugging anxiously at her fringe. Her plate untouched, she left the table.

'She's been showing tremendous composure,' Rud reassured Carrie. 'It's all the more amazing since, as ever, she was thick as thieves with the Mater, even sleeping in a bed set up in her room when she came to Tisbury on visits.'

In response to her frown, he went on, 'Yes, that did seem a bit much but it was the Mater's idea, according to Trix.'

Not wholly convinced, Carrie could only hope that she and Rud would get away before Trix started causing problems. Nothing had prepared her for the scene that she found taking place in the drawing room on the morning of the funeral.

'Now, Trix, you know you can't go upstairs to see the Mater. The men are bringing the coffin down. Listen, you can hear them.'

Rud was holding his sister's hand, straining, as Carrie saw, to keep her in the drawing room, away from their father. Lockwood was standing shrunk with grief, bareheaded by the wide space left by the open front door. Jack Fleming had taken himself away to the window where he stood with averted gaze. Impatient as she felt with Jack and all his limitations, with his constant worrying over his own health, she knew it had been an evil day for him when he married into the Kiplings.

The car was waiting for Lockwood and Rud. There was to be a quiet interment in the little churchyard: she could tell that for once both could accept and were even grateful for the ritual of religion to move them through the final necessary steps. She was tenderly helping Lockwood into his overcoat, wrapping a muffler round his neck against the November air, when Trix, who'd been left in Jack's company, burst out of the drawing room.

'You can't go without me. I won't let you,' she was panting.

Rud and Lockwood turned to Carrie.

There was only one way to save the day. Hysterical altercations at this moment would be unbearable. It was not the thing for the women to attend funerals but needs must.

'We're waiting for you, Trix, hurry and get your warm things on.'

Without pausing to call for a maid, Carrie shrugged herself into her own black coat. The men wouldn't care that Trix wasn't wearing mourning. The great thing was to preserve a sense of solemnity, for their sake. Little as she'd cared for Mrs. Kipling, the coming of death levelled all scores. She really would try to do what she could for Trix.

Carrie almost pushed Trix ahead of her into the pew, making sure that she was hemmed in against the wall. Care of the Pater she would have to leave to Rud. But within minutes Trix was turning to look behind her, with a frank curiosity more fitting to a child. Carrie picked up the uneasy stir in the small congregation.

The vicar was just inviting them to join in the hymn when Trix decided to make her own contribution to the performance. Removing her hat, with great solemnity she waved it aloft, before clasping it to her bosom and bowing deeply to the pews behind. Though Carrie clutched at her arms and whispered fiercely, this had no effect. Worse, Trix demonstrated her resentment by throwing herself round to stare at the stonework, in another theatrical gesture, presenting Carrie with an angry back.

She filed after Carrie quietly enough when the time came. But though Carrie herself tried to appear recollected, at her side Trix blew kisses right and left as she trod down the aisle. Thank heavens, walking ahead, behind the coffin, Rud and his father continued unaware.

'I want to go home now. Carrie, take me home,' Trix demanded as they passed the last pew.

It was many a day since Carrie had heard words that were so welcome.

Home. Trix picked up her skirts and ran upstairs. The bed lay stripped and empty in her parents' room.

She peered into the looking glass. So difficult to see with the blinds drawn.

'Mama hasn't gone away. She wouldn't. She promised me.'

'Look, I can see her, how alike we are; Mama's dress is awfully like mine. I'm afraid it's rather too young for her, but she never cared to admit her age. She always wanted all the admiration.'

Why did no-one answer?

Oh no. That dreadful Jack had followed her in and was trying to speak to her. She wouldn't listen, no, she would cover her ears. He never listened. Never understood.

'Go away, I shall never forgive you, you might as well know that.'

Had her voice been louder than she knew? Her hands were still over her ears. It must have been, for Carrie had come hurrying in. She was talking to Jack. Let her.

'Get him out of my sight, Carrie. Mother doesn't want him in the house.'

Such a fuss, too many people. It made her cry.

Yes, she would be a good girl for Father and drink the medicine.

Once Lockwood had led Trix away to her room, shaking his head at any move to accompany them, Carrie was left alone with Rud. He hadn't a tinge of colour. She looked about but there was nowhere to sit in comfort. The ordinary routines of housekeeping in The Gables had lapsed. Drifts of papers in the study, trays with the remnants of meals left standing about.

They took refuge in the breakfast room, where at least someone had thought to have a fire lit. Drained by her own attempts to contain Trix, she was wondering how soon the two of them could get away.

Watching Rud as he stood, stiffly by the sideboard, not taking his eyes off the door, Carrie knew that she'd need all her force of persuasion.

'It's not the slightest use our staying on, you know.'

She wasn't sure, at first, that he'd heard.

Beyond the cramped little window the winter afternoon was giving way to darkness. When he did speak, she was startled.

'I can't just abandon her,' he said, his voice flat. 'Without the Mater. She always trusted me.'

It was Trix and her distress that had struck home. Not his mother's death at all. Extraordinary, when you thought how little they saw of each other. She was never going to be free of Trix.

Carrie left her place by the hearth to stand face-to-face with Rud. She obliged him to look at her.

Without saying anything, she gently brushed back his hair.

'Darling Rud, there's nothing you can do here.'

'Do you want us to turn round and leave the Pater with this – this catastrophe on his hands?' There was a catch in his voice but it was angry now, more alive.

She took a breath then made herself speak calmly, though she was desperate to take him away, out of this house and back to their own home, back to Bateman's.

'You've seen for yourself, he's the only one Trix will take notice of. And don't you think it may help him to have something urgent to occupy him?'

Rud looked stubborn. Before he could speak she hurried on 'Think of South Africa, the hospitals. They were a lifeline to you when' – she swallowed – 'you told me so yourself.'

He blinked.

'You're right. They were.'

'It may be the kindest thing we can do at this moment, leaving him with an occupation, don't you see?'

It took a little more pressure on her part but they ate dinner that night home at Bateman's.

He was slow to get back to work in the days that followed. She was accustomed to the way he shed responsibility for practical details, the planning and arranging of their lives. He cast it all on her.

'I'm just a cork bobbing on the waters when I'm with Carrie.'

She used to love to hear him tell friends that, in the first years of their marriage. She was less enthusiastic today, as she sat at her desk.

'Carrie, I'm bored.'

She knew it. Here he was, hanging about the door of her study, hands in pockets, shoulders slumped.

She must be patient. Not ten days since the funeral, what did she expect? A son loses his mother – *this* son loses *that* mother –

With a gesture towards the papers she was studying, she explained.

'I've just got a few more things to see to, darling. Two or three letters and bills that must go off by the afternoon post and then I'll be with you.'

She could walk him over to that couple of fields she meant to make an offer for. It was a good buy, land adjoining their own.

'While you're waiting, why don't you send John a line? You know how you loved getting letters when you were away at school.'

'I wrote to John yesterday.'

It didn't seem wise to suggest a letter to Trix.

'Well, have you looked at the papers yet?' She tapped her fingers, quietly.

Usually he'd have spent an hour with the newspapers and then made straight for his desk. But all his routines were in abeyance, even if her own couldn't just be dropped.

'Nothing in the papers.' As he stood kicking grumpily at the door frame, he reminded her of John at five years old.

Her smile broadened. It was in her to enjoy the comic side. Experience had taught her that he recovered from these periods of collapse, infuriating as they were to manage.

'I'll tell you what Rud. You sit down and write a note to your father.' Forestalling all objections, 'Just news of John, what was in his last letter, Elsie and her friends, what's coming on in the garden – once you've finished that it will be time to get our waterproofs. We'll be out in the fields for at least an hour and just look at that sky,' she pointed to the window.

Wet or fine, she was going to get him out of the house and moving about. Otherwise he'd be on the sofa, eyes closed. He was not going to sleep the day away.

'You won't be long, will you?' came the plaintive reply, as he wandered off into his own study.

She shook her head, picking up her pen. The day scarcely begun and already she was falling behind.

*

Stumbling as he moved about his studio, heavy, Lockwood felt every one of his seventy-four years. He had a new plan for soothing Trix today, though in his weariness he did not anticipate much success. She was talking incessantly, brightly, even, which was at least better than her charged silence, but her chatter quickly left him feeling drained.

'Do you think we shall see Ruddy today? I do hope so, don't you, Father? I'm sure he'll bring Mama with him. But not Carrie, she's always been so difficult. Elsie is dreadfully like her, don't you think? Father, when do you think Mama will come?'

For the moment he had left her in the breakfast room leafing vigorously through the new issue of the *Review of Reviews*.

'It's the articles that begin with "J" that carry the secret,' she flung over her shoulder as he left.

Now he laid sticks of charcoal and wide sheets of drawing paper out on the long table, as he used when the children came to his drawing class.

That was Before.

Now he must look after Trix.

When he fetched her, leading her by the hand, unresisting into the studio, for a moment he thought her little cry was one of pleasure.

But dropping his hand, she ran across the room, to snatch up the sheets of paper, screwing them into balls and tossing them away. Sticks of charcoal were ground underfoot before he could stop her.

Then he knew he could never let Trix inside his studio again. But she could not be left for more than couple of minutes or she might be down the drive, away on some fantastic errand. As he locked the studio door behind him, he knew himself exiled from the place where he'd always found comfort.

Visiting Tisbury, Rud was shocked by his father's appearance.

'For heaven's sake, this is all too much for you. Let's hire a nurse or send Trix somewhere that she can be looked after.'

'Your mother would want me to care for Trix, she'd never forgive me if I left her care to strangers,' he replied.

No question of help from her husband. In view of the fits of rage which the sight of him seemed to provoke, Rud could scarcely blame Fleming for retreating to London.

'Pater, she's more deranged now than I've ever seen her. She's too much to manage at home: it's a case for professionals. There's no need to worry about the expense, I'll cover any cost –'

'Perhaps, in a week or two, if she doesn't come round a bit,' was the best he could get out of him.

Rud saw that his father was afraid. That he had put the exhausting distraction of Trix between himself and an agony of loss.

For himself, the company of Trix in such a state was the stuff of nightmare. He simply couldn't remain in the house with her. He'd have to ask Carrie what they could do to protect his father.

Rud left, intending to make himself return.

When a brief note from Tisbury told him his father had given the care of Trix over to others, he knew he'd succeeded. He hurried in to Carrie with the good news.

'He's gone to Clouds, to stay with the Wyndhams, their old friends. They've carried him of for a rest. That might be best, for the moment but let's get him over here soon.'

When a telegram arrived, ten days later, he knew it had all been too late.

For weeks he didn't seem able to get warm.

Once the funeral was over, there remained the task of clearing the house. Jack Fleming had removed Trix to a nursing home.

Carrie found Rud in his father's studio, where a steady drip from the leaking roof was keeping time. He was tying the strings of his father's old apron around himself.

'Useful to the end. He would have liked that,' she spoke quietly, subdued by the effort to reason down her own helpless sense of loss.

'Exactly. If we have to break up the little home here, let's do it as though he were directing us.' He was still dazed.

'I can't imagine a world without him,' he'd told her, choking.

Rousing himself, 'I'll get down to the books now.'

He laid her hand briefly against his cheek, before making for the door. Then, turning, 'I've been through the papers. One thing we must do before leaving is burn all those old letters. Our family life is entirely our own business. We don't want anything falling into others' hands. John will enjoy the bonfire.'

She glanced into the kitchen where Elsie was helping pack up the china. Most of it could go to charity but there were a few good pieces to be put aside. Before setting off to make her inventory of the carpets and hangings, which were of quite a different order of value and must come to Bateman's, she went out through the back door into the garden, looking for John. She found him by a carefully selected pile of stones, practising his aim, taking the white birch by the fence as his target.

'For heaven's sake, John, come in and get those hands clean. Daddy needs you to help him and you aren't fit to go near a book.'

Reluctantly, thirteen-year-old John went off in search of soap and water.

He was still brown as a nut from skating all day outside on the rink at Engelberg. The children didn't seem to miss their winters in South Africa.

'I don't mind lessons as long as they're to learn skating,' John had conceded.

Winter sports were small consolation to her for giving up those slow melting days at The Woolsack.

She pulled her jacket round her, shivering, as she went back into the house. A deadly chill had set in, now it stood empty.

There'd really been no alternative, they just had to give up South Africa, after 1908. It made Rud so angry to see how affairs out at the Cape were going.

'It's an unholy mess. Less than five years after a big war, the enemy are given control of the revenues and administration of the conquered country,' he repeated to anyone who would listen.

It was better they should not go back.

Within weeks of Lockwood's funeral, Rud got Jack Fleming to meet them both in London to discuss what should be done about Trix. They sat awkwardly together round a table in a private sitting room at Brown's hotel.

'I have the greatest faith in Dr. Williams-Freeman,' intoned Fleming. 'He intends to keep Trix in his nursing home for as long as she remains dangerously disturbed. Meanwhile, I am making out papers for the Lunacy Board, as Trix is clearly in no state to manage her own affairs.'

Rud drew in his breath sharply. It was a moment before he could speak. The Lunacy Board! Trix! He was technically powerless. The fellow was her husband.

Carrie threw him a look of alarm.

Clearing his throat, 'You're quite convinced that is necessary, Fleming? The Lunacy Board: is her case really hopeless?'

'All I know is that I cannot answer, I'll not be held responsible, for anything she may do.'

His brother-in-law sat, arms folded, stiffly upright in the high backed chair.

'Did you realise that she's been in correspondence with the Society for Psychical Research?' he continued.

Rud recoiled.

Naturally, the fellow had to deal with any letters that came for her. But he was torn between distaste for Fleming and outrage at Trix. Leaning forward, he gripped the edge of the table.

'You mean to say that Trix was a member of the Society for Psychical Research? In spite of everything? The warnings I gave her? The way that damned writing set off her first breakdown?'

'My family don't share your views. They thought it quite innocent, a form of amusement, looking in the crystal and palm reading,' Jack Fleming blustered. 'My sister Moona encourages it when we're up there on leave.' In the face of Rud's fury, he added sullenly, 'I never authorised it. Hate the whole bag of tricks.'

Carrie stayed at home the following week, when Rud went up to London on his own. Returning in the late afternoon, he came out to find her out on the lawn admiring a magnolia that spread itself against the house.

'It's almost completely out now,' she called.

His answering smile was half-hearted.

'Can we go inside?' he asked, once he got up to her.

She followed him over the terrace and into the drawing room, apprehensive.

He took the nearest chair, motioning her to one close by.

'I gritted my teeth and asked Arthur Doyle what he could tell us.'

She was taken by surprise. He'd drawn back from Mr. Doyle since he'd gone head over heels for spiritualism. 'If only the man'd stick to Holmes and Baker Street, keep his feet on the ground,' he'd complain.

'Asked him if he'd heard anything about Trix and her psychic activities?' She knew what that must have cost him.

'No wonder she can't keep things straight in her head,' he exploded. 'You'll find this difficult to credit. She's made a career out of that business' – he disdained to name automatic writing – 'a whole career. In that world Trix is famous.'

'Are they aware that she's your sister?' she returned in alarm.

'Apparently not, but that's hardly the point. However, I agree, it's a relief. Doyle only worked it out by putting two and two together and he'll keep mum.'

His irritation was infectious, she had grown taut.

'She's made a name for herself – quite literally, he continued. 'They know her as the celebrated medium "Mrs. Holland". And in a horrible backhand way, she's made a name as a writer. She's one of the *authors* of what they call the "Cross-correspondences". Awfully proud of her, that blessed Society, it seems.'

Responding to her blank look, he added, 'Sets of messages, apparently transmitted by telepathy between England and India etcetera. Don't ask me. A Mrs. Verrall, one of those female professors at Cambridge, is involved in it too, I believe. According to Doyle, that college for advanced women, Newnham, is riddled with it.'

They sat in silence for some time, taking this in. The sunshine was beckoning to her from outside and she longed to suggest a stroll in the garden before dinner but it was no moment for interruptions.

'Do you think we should tackle her?' she began, then corrected herself. 'I'm sorry, that's nonsense, what would be the point?'

'Remembering the last go, it could be years before anyone gets sense out of Trix again,' he nodded miserably. 'There's nothing we can do for her now, except to be kind. And encourage that idiot Fleming to keep away from her, if possible.'

*

The voice said 'It's a year you've been here, stupid. Andover, don't you remember? I told you the last time I came on duty.'

terrifying   so helpless

shut down
this rage
sweeping

weak after attacks weak   the fear

she had no idea what she might have said.
or done

people frightened of her
        No-one came close

she liked that
she woke up crying
        Some days it was quieter inside her head.
        More and more days.
Now they let her wear her own clothes once more.

*

'But I feel I will never be the same again,' she told Dr. Williams-Freeman, as he sat at his heavy desk behind a bowl of artificial flowers. Her husband had entrusted her to this man's care.

'My dear Mrs. Fleming, you sound like a good child who has once fallen into naughtiness and now believes they will never be good again.'

The man was a perfect fool. She was not a child.

But she was being treated like one, like a naughty child who must be sent away till they have learned to be good.

*

Three years on and Trix was still without a proper home. She and her current nurse had just moved to Scarborough.

'Lovely views, dear, and wonderful air,' declared Nurse Tomkins, inspecting the rooms that had been taken for them up on Castle Road, poised above the great double scoop of the bay.

'I believe one of the Brontë sisters is buried in that churchyard along the street,' Trix offered.

Nurse offered clucks of sympathy in reply.

Brisk fingers of that wonderful air made their way into the sitting room even when the sash windows were firmly closed, moving Trix to clutch her Shetland shawls close round her. The gaunt mahogany furniture crowded in. Fretting, she took herself to the windows, but she had to grip the frames as she gazed out, for fear of falling into the vast emptiness that lay between her and the wash of the sea.

'I know you don't like me to bother with the newspaper, Nurse, but I'd love just five minutes with it again today,' Trix asked, folding her napkin carefully as she finished breakfast.

Nurse Tomkins hesitated. Delaying her reply, she moved over to the window to consult the weather.

'I really think we might get a walk in before the rain if we don't put it off,' she observed.

Mrs. Fleming could give her a tiring hour or two if she became excited. On the other hand, refusing might produce as much rumpus as overstimulation. She had strict orders to allow this patient pen and paper only under close supervision. None of that automatic writing. In view of her professional experience of similar cases, she'd had no trouble in agreeing. It was like a drug to them and afterwards they were not themselves, not at all. A pity, though, that they mustn't even read the tea leaves, let alone the cards, together.

'I dare say, dear, by and by,' she offered, adjusting her cap.

Now and again she did let Mrs. Fleming have a glimpse of the newspaper, just for a treat. She really preferred her patients to read only knitting patterns. Then they were learning to amuse themselves and be useful while keeping calm.

She scrutinised her patient again.

Mrs. Fleming hadn't had a bad day in all the past fortnight, not since Colonel Fleming's last letter. And she was such a sweet lady, you did want to bring a smile to those large mournful eyes.

'You don't believe me, Nurse, do you?' She'd exclaimed sadly one afternoon. 'I really did write novels and stories and have them published before I moved on to higher things. Maud Diver, you know who I mean, don't you? The famous novelist, we've been friends ever since we were girls.' And rummaging along her little bookcase, Mrs. Fleming picked out a copy of Maud Diver's *The Amulet*. It opened at the printed inscription, '*This book is dedicated to Trix Fleming in memory of Dalhousie days.*'

It'd been a shame to see her dab her eyes.

Delving into her bag where the paper lay folded, waiting to be read after lunch while her patient slept, Nurse Tomkins decided to risk it. At least it was the *Morning Post,* something respectable, not one of those rags some went in for.

Trix picked at a hangnail. All Jack wanted was to be rid of her, hide her away. Between them Jack and the doctors had cut her off, trapped her and kept her from knowing what was going on in the world. She did hear regularly from Rud, but he only told her about his new dog or the home farm at Bateman's, safe topics designed not to upset her. Nothing about the war.

She really needed a file for this. It would do later.

She'd been wondering a good deal about him with this war. In its second year now. Those repeated warnings, his emphasis on being ready to defend ourselves, they'd been justified. She longed to know what he was publishing these days. It was a bit of luck that Nurse Tomkins ran to the *Morning Post*. He often wrote for it.

She turned swiftly past the advertisements and the dreadful close-printed lists of the Roll of Honour. So many dead, where was the honour in that? Ah, here was the international news on page seven, alongside the Court Circular. As she held the sheets out wide, preparing to concentrate, one name leapt to her eye.

'Dear God,' the words dried on her lips. 'The death of Mr. John Kipling.'

Nurse Tomkins rose to her feet but made no other move.

Trix laid the paper down and gathered herself.

'It's my brother. I mean, it's his boy,' she spoke mechanically. Then she read flinching through to the end.

'reported 'missing, believed killed' ... boy for whom Puck told the tales of the beloved land ... for which this supreme sacrifice ... barely eighteen ... indomitable courage ... nominated for the Irish Guards by Lord Roberts ....

Determined to take his share ... urgent pleas ... father ... mother also ... dearest of all possible sacrifices ... altar of their country ... only son ... sympathy of the whole Empire.'

Only son. Missing, believed killed. She looked up, stammering. 'Oh, Ruddy, Ruddy! I can't bear it.'

Nurse Tomkins was baffled to hear her sob: 'He was all I had.'

She sank to kneel at her patient's side. The wild gaze that was turned on her then showed what a mistake the newspaper had been.

'You won't leave me, Auntie, will you? I'll be very good.'

Mrs. Fleming wasn't the first patient to call Nurse Tomkins by another's name. Auntie? She didn't argue, she joined in. 'Now, Trixie dear, you mustn't go upsetting yourself like this.'

But Trix was pawing at the white uniform of her keeper.

'Promise you won't go away. Promise.'

The nurse took the frantic hands firmly in her own.

'Of course, dear, don't you worry, I'm going to stay here with you. But it's time for our rest now, there's a good girl. I'll sit by you till you drop off.'

The flowered eiderdown drawn up round her chin, the draught swallowed, Trix lay obedient. Moment by moment a low sound came to be heard. As the humming grew stronger it gave way to unfamiliar words, perhaps those of a lullaby:

'eekre, eekre, bus re morah,
hara kha, pani pi
phir, ooran ja'.

It wasn't English, Nurse Tomkins realised, something foreign, from when her patient lived abroad perhaps, but it seemed to soothe the poor thing. After a week or two, she ventured to ask Mrs. Fleming about her song but she didn't seem able to remember.

The touch of a circling finger, brown on her own small pink palm, that once accompanied that Marathi lullaby, had passed beyond recall.

*

1920 now and the war over but Trix was still on the move, in the custody of paid companions.

The afternoon post arrived rather late that day. Trix was still reading Maud's letter when Mrs. Fotheringay, her new companion, announced a change of plan. Lodgings had been taken for them in Cheltenham.

'Cheltenham. I suppose I might as well go there as anywhere. How long have I been here in Guildford? It must be more than six months.'

'Now, Mrs Fleming, try to be more positive.' Mrs. Fotheringay, put a ridiculous value on brightness.

'Am I not permitted to complain at all?'

Trix heard her own voice turn waspish.

Mrs. Fotheringay looked back at her, prim.

'Colonel Fleming explained in his letter of instruction that he thought taking the waters might do you good, my dear.'

'Do me good?' She crumpled Maud's letter as her hand clenched into a fist. 'If he wants to do me good he might start by writing to me direct, asking for my opinion. And did he *explain* when this traipsing about the country will come to an end? Have you any idea how many sets of dreary lodgings I've moved into?'

'You're to have your photograph taken once we get to Cheltenham. Isn't that a nice surprise? Quite a little treat –'

Not to be distracted, Trix broke in.

'Whatever for? My photograph! What's Jack planning to do now?

She stood, clasping her hands together to prevent them from shaking.

'I believe it's for your passport, Mrs. Fleming,' the other replied with maddening calm.

Trix sat abruptly, feeling the blood leave her face.

'He means to really get rid of me,' she quavered. 'Some awful cheap rundown European spa, in the back of beyond, somewhere I don't know the language.'

'Well, if I may say so, Mrs. Fleming, it's all in your own hands. I'm sure the Colonel would be only too happy to have his wife at home with him, if she could behave like other ladies.'

Trix understood that a mask was being held out to her. But she was not yet so desperate that she would consent to hide herself.

'*Unduly irritable*,' Mrs. Fotheringay would write in her weekly report.

*

'According to the newspapers, the Isle of Wight is bathed in spring sunshine,' Carrie urged, laying down her knife at the end of breakfast. 'A few days there would do us all good, don't you think?'

She threw a glance of appeal at her daughter. At twenty-six, Elsie was still living at home.

Rud remained silent, preoccupied. He'd hardly touched his egg.

'Absolutely, do let's, you will come too, won't you?' Elsie responded loyally, looking beseechingly at her cousin Lorna, who was staying with them.

'You see it's because of Great-Aunt Georgie dying,' Elsie interpreted, once she was alone with Lorna in the old schoolroom at Bateman's. She'd taken it over for entertaining her own visitors.

Her cousin appeared confused.

'Mummy's trying to outrun death, or at least its effect on Dadda. He hasn't picked up in the weeks since Georgie's funeral. The plan will be to distract him by arranging to go away and then to set him down in the sun. It's not a bad idea; he's always ready for the off. And I think Mummy told me her brother, the one who died, used to have a house at a place called Chale on the Isle of Wight. Before the Flood.'

The young women's laughter was good natured.

Carrie had mixed feelings embarking on the ferry back to Portsmouth at the end of that trip. She left Elsie and Lorna to stand at the bow, heads thrown back, lacquered cheeks whipped into natural colour by the wind, while she remained close to Rud, looking down over the ship's rail at the stern.

The promised sun had been slow to materialise but that was not all that had troubled her. She'd not allowed for the strength of the past. As the ferry drew slowly away from Ventnor, with its bright little harbour, Rud must have felt rather than heard her muffled sob. He tucked her hand under his arm.

'Long farewell, dear heart, isn't it? Long farewell to Wolcott and to our own young days.'

Their visit to the Isle of Wight had turned out to be a kind of pilgrimage. In 1891, one way and another, they'd spent a good part of the summer there, Carrie keeping house for Wolcott with her mother and sister, with Rud training down from London to join them every chance he could. Wolcott's last summer. And now her mother too was dead, had been dead a whole year. The past was closing up behind them, vanishing as they watched, like the pale wake sinking into the winter sea.

Vanished away too, beyond her reach, beyond her touch, her own lost children.

Rud was speaking.

'Come now, you mustn't get cold, we'll go inside.'

Once seated in the stuffy little cabin, Rud surprised her with an invitation.

'You know that when we dock at Portsmouth the girls are leaving us and going off on the London train. Johnson will be waiting with the Rolls and I could get him to drive the two of us over to Southsea. It's no distance. As a small boy I used to walk it with Uncle Pryse when he went to collect his pension at the Dockyard. We could see if we can find the House of Desolation.'

Carrie drew breath. This was the last thing she'd expected. But that eager look of his – she mustn't disappoint him. Just let this not be the start of anything too bad. 'I would like that, Rud. If you're sure you're up to it. It might be good for us to go back together, after all this time.'

Rud told the driver to stop in Outram Road.

'Let's walk from here. This was my route back from that miserable little apology for a school.'

She kept her hand in his after he'd helped her out of the car.

They moved off together along the suburban street with its grey starved gardens. His increasing tension was transmitted to her right down his arm.

'There it is. Lorne Lodge.'

He had come to an abrupt halt as Outram Road swung round and gave way to Havelock Park. The mean little detached house with its narrow brick arch over the gate would have spoken of pretension, not despair, to an outsider. Rud didn't seem to want to cross the road but eyed it from the pavement opposite.

'Our mother gone without a word. I wasn't quite six. Trix was just three. A huge gap at that age. I felt as responsible as though I were her father.'

Carrie judged it best to listen without interrupting.

Rud went on: 'I could see what it was doing to Trix, could sense it, though of course I couldn't put a name to it as a child. The devil himself was in that woman to do that to children. I came damned near losing my mind with fear, between her own cursed punishments and the threats of a God who intended us to burn in flames for our sins.'

She'd heard it all before, or something like it, even to weariness. Yet standing beside him, before the very house, for a moment she was overwhelmed with terror. Carrie found herself struggling for breath.

He hadn't finished.

'When I think how it was when our own kids were small. How we shielded them, how we'd have died –' his voice broke.

She saw that he couldn't go on, that Josephine and her memory, with their own failure to keep her safe, had come between them.

'Darling Rud, let's just walk to the end of this street, then we can turn back to the car and you can shake the dust of this place from your heels for ever.'

* * *

The first that Moona knew of Trix's return to grace was a pressing invitation from her brother, Jack, to inspect the new Edinburgh house he'd bought. 'Just a step away from Eglinton Crescent, you'll not have to come far.' Ten years his senior, at 76, Moona resented the suggestion that a ten minute walk would be too much for her.

'You've done well, Jack,' she told him as they reached the end of the tour. He had marched her room by room through the three floors of 6 West Coates.

He looked gratified.

'Have you marked the craftsmanship in the doors and fittings?' he pressed.

'The work of skilled men,' she agreed, 'It'll be a pleasure to you living here.'

But Moona was curious. She'd not been best pleased when he sold the home in Napier Road where they'd grown up, though she understood his frustration. Angry outbursts and scenes of distress had marked the brief periods some years earlier when he'd tried to bring Trix there to live with him. He'd taken to bachelor's lodgings after that.

What was young Jack up to, buying a large detached house at this stage?

She was longing for a cup of tea but there was no chance of being offered one in this echoing unfurnished shell. She'd have to wait till she got home. Jack never gave any thought to making life comfortable for himself or anyone else.

At that moment a new idea struck her. Perhaps she was wrong. Perhaps comfort was precisely what he had in mind. Was that why she'd been subjected to this tour?

Silent under her umbrella, Jack tall beside her as they trod towards Eglinton Crescent, Moona became increasingly sure that she was correct. That was no house for a bachelor. Jack wanted her help.

He was feeling his age, she suspected smugly. He wanted a home of his own again and companionship. But he meant to learn how the land lay before he made any overtures.

'Do you not think you might be lonely in that fine mansion?' she asked, holding out a full cup to him, as they sat by her fireside, facing each other over the tea tray. 'Would you like me to go and see how things stand nowadays with Trix?'

Moona liked the thought of getting things back on a decent footing. Jack used to bring Trix up to Scotland every leave before Mrs. Kipling died and Moona'd grown fond of her, flighty as she was. She'd be in her fifties now. The family had all wondered at Jack and the way he'd sent her off. He'd never been a patient man. It was no way to treat a sick woman. But there'd been no talking to him.

A visit from Moona? Trix was almost more frightened than pleased, as she sat reading the note from her sister-in-law. The egg congealed on her plate unnoticed. Did this mean some new scheme of Jack's was afoot? Over the hours that followed she struggled to think of a way to protect herself.

On the day itself she summoned her dignity and insisted on receiving her visitor alone.

'I'll ring if I need you, Mrs. Postle,' she promised.

She could tell at once that her appearance shocked Moona. Trix knew that she'd aged quite dreadfully. But there was no hesitation, no sisterly peck. Stepping forward, Moona folded Trix into her embrace.

Trix felt her eyes fill with tears. Oh no, she was going to look weak and silly. As they moved apart, however, she realised that Moona was dabbing her own eyes.

'My dear,' Moona said, a catch in her voice, 'it's more than time. Jack wants me to ask you to – to make your home with him once more.'

In the silence that followed Trix tried to remain calm. Before she was ready to reply, Moona spoke again.

'I won't deny that he's stiff and a difficult man but he does try to do his best, according to his lights. It will never be easy living with him. But 6 West Coates is a large house.' She paused before adding simply 'You would have your own separate bedroom.'

Trix's heart was beating fast. She nodded.

'I'm not a child. I do know what it's like, living with Jack.'

Hands clutched at her breast, she hesitated.

'But I don't think I could bear … if it wasn't to be permanent … I couldn't join him on notice, like a housemaid.'

Moona looked horrified.

'I'll be making it quite clear to him that *if* you are generous enough to return to his home there'll be no going back.'

As Trix blinked, uncertain, Moona added, 'I wouldn't expect you to decide all in a moment, my dear. This has been hard on you. Sleep on it.'

'I'm not sure I have any choice,' Trix said slowly. 'At least it will be better than this – ' and she waved her hand around at the dingy rented sitting room with its limp, sun-shrunk curtains.

* * *

6, West Coates, which Jack had bought at an advantageous price, as Trix came to discover, was a little too close to Haymarket Station. With its heavy baronial decoration the place radiated a prosperous security, which she both welcomed and detested. Yet she *had* succeeded in making a life for herself in Edinburgh, she acknowledged, stepping briskly out in the fine morning. She'd put those twelve years spent in the wilderness behind her.

'I do find these shops a great comfort,' she murmured aloud, once inside Mademoiselle Zephirine's atelier, as she hovered over the enticing display of new millinery for spring.

Knowing where to lay hands on a good dress or a becoming hat kept her spirits up. These light colours certainly were flattering. Or was she deceiving herself? She tilted her head towards the shop mirror, wanting to see the effect of the mauve cloche from a different angle. Yes, it was decidedly pleasing.

'Thank you so much, I'll take this one, Maisie.' The girls in the shops were so pleasant and friendly, she'd got to know every one of them by name and they always had a smile for her.

As she waited, tissue rustled deliciously.

What a relief that her looks had definitely come back. Those hollow eyes in the glass used to give her the shivers. It did make a difference, being established here, at the centre of a family again, with Moona, living virtually on the doorstep. A very kind woman, if sometimes almost too bracing.

With the striped hatbox over her arm, Trix set off on her favourite outing, to visit the Zoo. She was meeting a young cousin there. Finding herself popular with the next generation had come as a delightful surprise: they positively vied for time with her. 'You're so amusing, so witty and entertaining Aunt Trix,' Betty Macdonald had insisted. 'There's never a dull moment with you.'

Did they really enjoy those tales of her young days, she wondered anxiously as she crossed over Prince's Street. She knew she did embroider, just a scrap. It was innocent enough, just like the odds and ends she scribbled now and then for her own amusement.

She was afraid that sometimes she talked too much, but she did love company.

Next day, coming down to breakfast, Trix was still pleased with herself at finding that hat. Her eyes brightened further, as she glanced over the pile of mail. She took her time in opening the envelope. Just the sight of Rud's hand had made her heart lift. She would stretch out the pleasure of feeling him close. The same excitement sparked in her every week when she found his letter. It had arrived early this time; she hadn't been expecting one till Thursday.

Across the breakfast table her husband was absorbed in laying out his pills for the day. She wanted to let no sign of her pleasure escape, for Jack was sure to growl something disparaging on hearing Rud's name.

'Oh dear, this one is rather short.' She couldn't help herself, after all.

Jack, however, made no response. She thought he'd been growing deaf, though she couldn't be sure. Was it that he just didn't want to hear what she said?

Relieved by his silence, she returned to the page.

Dear Trix

I'm sure you will be interested to know that our Elsie is engaged to a man who was in the Irish Guards (Captain George Bambridge M.C.) and who is now attaché at the Madrid Embassy.

They have known each other for five years; he is a man whom we thoroughly like; and I hope they'll be very happy. They expect to be married in the autumn.

Ever your loving

Brother.'

With great deliberation Jack was unfolding *The Scotsman*. She knew he didn't care to be interrupted in his task, or even spoken to before he had sipped his way through a tepid glass of boiled water. But she had to speak.

'Can you imagine, Jack, Elsie's engaged. It's a man who was in the Irish Guards with John. So terribly sad, I don't like to think of it but one can't help it, can one, when one is reminded like this?'

Her husband grunted. He did not put down his glass.

'I do hope he's the right man for her. Rud's often told me that Elsie reminds him of me. The same profile, perhaps; in snaps she has a quite distinguished air.'

She put her head on one side, appealing.

'But Jack, can you remember reading anything about this man in Rud's book about the Irish Guards?'

'What man, can you not give me a name, Trix. You go babbling on –'

She hadn't waited for him but continued, 'That *History of the Irish Guards in the Great War*, it took him years, you know. Step by step, company by company. The detail. I simply don't know how he did it; Rud's never been one for facts. Father used to twit him about it. Check your sources, my boy, he'd say when Rud was on the old *CMG*. Don't you remember?'

'I can't say that I do. But then I was never in on your family games with the writing. I'll tell you one thing, though, woman. Your brother drove himself to write that book for his son. Now are you going to give me the name of this young fellow of Elsie's or not?'

'I can understand his writing those *Epitaphs of the War*, though. They were based on classical models, you know, Jack. Rud and I used to write parodies together, when I was seventeen, it was one of our favourites. Such happy times, I sometimes wonder whether he's been really happy since. Did you ever read any of them I can't remember whether I showed you?'

Jack Fleming, who had endured the *Greek Elegies* as a schoolboy, threw down his napkin and placed both hands flat on the table. He rose, taking up his newspaper.

'If I cannot take my breakfast in peace, Trix, I'll be off.'

Trix's hands began to shake. 'Oh no, Jack, please – I'll just read the rest of my letters, I won't speak another word.'

She was only pretending to read. Married next October. Would they let her go to the wedding? She had a right to be there. Rud would want it, surely. But Carrie? She was always ready to make difficulties.

The weeks passed.

'Carrie's leaving it very late sending out the invitations. It's not a bit like her: she can't bear not to be on top of everything,' Trix wondered aloud one evening, as they sat putting in the hours till it was time to go to bed.

Without raising his eyes from the *Journal of the Royal Geographic Society*, Jack Fleming responded.

'Not at all, Trix. Our invitation came last week.'

She let her book fall.

'What do you mean? I never saw it.'

'I opened it. You were out shopping. The invitation was addressed to both of us and I answered for us both.'

'Oh Jack, do say we can make a real trip of it, have a whole week in London,' she cried.

'Surely you don't imagine you're fit to travel and see all those people. I declined – civilly, of course. I explained that your health would not permit it.'

Drawing the band from her thin finger, Trix hurled it at her husband and swept from the room.

*

At Bateman's, Carrie was still in two minds about Elsie's wedding clothes.

'We have to think, too, of how it will read in the newspaper. *"The bride's sole ornament was a single string of pearls"* or something of the sort strikes a note of sobriety,' she advised, as she sat, notebook in hand, on her daughter's bed.

Elsie, who had been leaning back on her heels, searching among empty shoe boxes and drifts of tissue paper, turned to scrutinize her.

'Don't tell me you're losing your nerve, Mother. Not after egging me on all this while. I've never seen you so enraptured as you were with the effect of that satin, once they laid the silver lace over it. "Day-lilies under frost," that's what you said.'

'And so I am, enraptured. But it's those colours. We don't want to give the impression we're striving for effect. Restricting yourself to Peggy Leigh, a single bridesmaid, is bold enough these days, when eight seems to be the fashion. But dressing Peggy in yellow velvet, without a wreath but a brown velvet hat instead – I just don't want us to have gone too far.'

'My sheaf of lilies will be chaste enough,' looking sideways at her mother.

'If that's a joke, my dear, it's not a very nice one.'

Elsie scrambled to her feet.

'Come on, Mother, I'm not a blushing ingénue, I'm pushing thirty.'

That was rather harsh. Carrie made a deprecatory gesture.

'How different, from the time when your father and I married, all in a rush, in the middle of winter. I barely had a chance to comb my hair, let alone order wedding clothes.'

Elsie gave an indulgent smile.

'You know you're just in love with that orange brocaded coat shot with blue that we chose to wear over the orange *crêpe de chine* I'm going away in. I've watched you stroking the nutria trim.'

'It really is the height of style. And no more than your father's daughter should be able to carry off – '

'And what about my mother's daughter?'

Carrie didn't hesitate.

'Your mother, Elsie dearest, is the one who insisted that the hat to wear with that coat had to be in mole-coloured *crêpe georgette*. The orange velvet one you wanted would have made the whole effect look like something out of the Ballets Russes.'

'I do hope George is going to appreciate the lovely things we've chosen,' Elsie ventured at last.

There was a perceptible silence.

'You never know with men. George is such a man's man, I wouldn't pin my hopes on it.'

'I told Peggy I'd telephone her before lunch,' Elsie excused herself, moving towards the door. We need to talk about stockings. She's found a marvellous little place.'

*

The morning after the wedding Rud and Carrie were sitting over a late breakfast in Brown's hotel. Ever since they passed the first nights of their honeymoon under its roof, Brown's had served them as a London home.

Now they sat, each contemplating the fact that the previous day had seen them waving their only child goodbye. A bride with her new husband.

Partnered by a single forlorn glove of Carrie's, Rud's top hat still lay on the desk over by the window, where he had dropped it the night before. He was seated, newspaper in hand, across the table from her.

Though he'd drafted the notice for *The Times* himself, he still quailed at the remorseless description, *Elsie, only child of Mr. and Mrs. Rudyard Kipling.* But he must make an effort for Carrie's sake. Mothers losing a daughter to marriage – the turmoil was considerable. To say nothing of the work Carrie had put in. Efficient though she was, organising always left her exhausted. Thank the Lord he hadn't had the planning for five hundred guests.

'I never felt more equal to being looked at, going up the aisle at St. Margaret's with that vision on my arm.' With the same classical profile and in certain gestures, the Child had grown to remind him so much of Trix. It had almost felt as though he were giving Trix away, instead.

There had been no question of Trix being present, even though she was able to live at home these days. They all agreed that keeping house for her husband in Edinburgh was quite enough excitement.

Carrie's strained face relaxed. She took a sip of coffee.

'She did look happy, didn't she? And I was so relieved that there were no accidents with that long train –'

'Yes, she did. Happy and beautiful. But, oh, did I tell you? You remember the little girl who works the lift here?'

'The one you've been feeding books to, you with your soft heart?'

'What else could I do? Leave the little thing adrift among the penny dreadfuls? Anyway, the girl looked at Elsie in all her glory

with such big eyes when she was taking us down yesterday, that I
picked out a bud from the Child's bouquet and gave it her.'

He chewed at his toast cautiously, mindful of his dentures.

'But what a performance,' he continued, swallowing. 'I still think
a country wedding might have been easier.'

'With a maypole, I suppose, and jousting?' she snapped, evidently
not yet ready to be teased.

'Rud, you can be such a child. We went over this so many times:
with five hundred guests to accommodate and the weather not to
be relied on this late in October. Cousin Stan's house in Eaton
Square was the perfect solution. There were double that number in
St. Margaret's. Where would they have been put in the little church
at Burwash?'

'I don't grudge the expense, you know that,' he attempted to
calm her.

'No, but you did try us dreadfully about all the fittings and
changing our minds.'

'I don't see what all the excitement's about. A new pair of
trousers doesn't seem to lift my spirits in the same way.'

At last, he'd made her laugh.

As she poured herself a second cup, Carrie wondered whether
she would ever plan another shopping campaign with Elsie.
Married and living in Brussels, with a husband newly posted to the
Embassy, Elsie would be looking to Paris rather than London. But
would she want her mother's company there?

'I hope we don't live to regret that generous settlement you
made on her. It would be a pity if it encouraged George to be less
active in finding his place in the world. Being honorary attaché in
Brussels won't do for ever.'

Rud didn't answer directly. She'd watched him put aside his
better judgment, in order to accept Elsie's choice of husband. When
they first met him, years before, they'd taken George Bambridge
for a decent enough fellow, and so he appeared, now they knew
him better. But was he up to Elsie's standards, worthy of her?

A wasp, come in through the open window, was circling the

marmalade. Rud flicked at it with his napkin.

As she'd expected, he dismissed her and made excuses for his new son-in-law.

'Plenty of good men in worse case than Bambridge, after this war. Not just the officers employed on commission in motor car showrooms. It's a scandal. Men who fought in the trenches selling boot-laces in the street.'

She shivered. Those haunted men on every corner. She had to hurry past.

And what would John have come back to? Her jaw tightened. The question hung unspoken between them. Both of them would have given up all his radiant prospects, taken even a crippled, blinded son back with thankful hearts.

Sorrow had made them selfish.

'We kept Elsie with us far too long, I blame myself,' she grieved.

His face was sombre as he nodded.

'When I saw how she sparkled at the prospect of a house of her own, my heart did smite me.'

No question of admitting any qualms about Elsie's husband. She might have known. Perhaps after all that was for the best.

'George was extremely dashing in his uniform. He makes a fine figure,' she conceded.

'Sound chap, very straight. Not up to our Elsie in matters of intellect of course but I've always found a clever wife a great advantage, myself.'

Coming round the table, he bent over her where she sat and kissed her.

Now they had only to brace themselves for the afternoon, with its homecoming, for the entrance into a house from which the only child had departed.

*

Trix and Jack Fleming were in London for the week and were coming down to Bateman's for the day. It was only one day. Carrie could perfectly tolerate it. Besides, any visitor, even Trix Fleming, brought some life back into the house.

Between them, she and Rud made sure there were many visitors.

She stood indecisive in the hall. Perhaps the white tulips she'd intended for the centre of the table would be better in a different vase. Setting it down, she stood back to consider the effect.

The echoes of her steps on the black and white chequers died away.

Always so still in here, where there'd been such bustle in the first year of the War. Before John died and all her energy went with him. Parcels piled all over the hall, giant bundles of old linen for bandages, sent from the States, wool in hundred pound packs waiting to be given out and knitted up. A mitten a day, that's what she and Elsie had set themselves. On Thursdays a pair.

Her hands were chilled after doing the flowers, she rubbed them together.

And now Elsie was mistress of her own house, or should be, if only that husband of hers could settle to some occupation. George Bambridge was turning out every bit as unsatisfactory as she'd feared.

Eight years married and no sign of children. Carrie was well aware of what remained unspoken when her own friends asked after Elsie.

She poked at the tulips, which kept flopping tiresomely. Perhaps it wasn't the vase that was the problem.

There'd been so little choice for any girl after the War.

'Soon I'll only know people who are dead,' the poor girl had said.

They'd known the telegram would come, of course, all their friends had lost sons. Telling Elsie John was missing had been an agony in itself. Waiting and waiting to tell her, until the friend who was visiting had left, then bracing for the moment when understanding would wipe the light out of Elsie's face.

Carrie's throat tightened again at the memory.

Without John, they'd fallen into a silence that they didn't know how to break. The house was still too dispiriting for a young person. Even the little under-housemaids refused to stay. 'Too desolate' according to the last one.

The flowers would have to do, it was only the Flemings. Raising the vase in both hands, to keep the improved arrangement steady, she continued into the dining room and set it down.

On the sideboard in its silver frame stood a photograph of John in uniform, cap at an angle, small new moustache. Just as she'd seen him for the last time. Twenty years ago, almost. Her glance lingered, dangerously.

She could still be overcome by that paralysing mood of the first months after he went missing, a sense that she was only miming, that none of her actions had any force behind. Then determination to find the facts, to discover anything at all about what happened to him, had taken over.

From the very start Rud only kept the enquiries going for her sake. He'd never believed there was the slightest chance. She'd raged when she realised that. If they gave up hoping it would be letting John go.

She drew out her cambric handkerchief and passed it gently over the glass covered face.

While she still lived here in Bateman's, he wasn't utterly lost to her. She could conjure him among the early mists, a boy urging his dog away from the ditches beyond the lawns.

Brother and sister were pacing the grey-flagged terrace, out in the sunshine, lifting their faces now and then to the drifting scent of lilac. Mike, the black Aberdeen terrier playfully nipping at their heels, begged in vain for a walk.

'Later, old chap, I promise,' Rud bent to look into his eyes.

'Did I tell you, Ruddy dear, that I'd been back in touch with my old beau Ian Hamilton?' He *was* her beau really, or would have been, if only that Muir girl had not come between them. 'What a year that was, '86, I had my choice of offers from the peerage, you know.'

'You've kept your looks, Trix, my dear. I'd never put you down as sixty-four. More of a dishonest forty.' Beneath the hedge of his eyebrows, Rud's eyes were dancing with the old mischief.

'Isn't this the terrace you call the quarter-deck? That is *so* like you, so amusing.'

In answer, Rud drew her arm through his.

'There's a fine show of blossom on our little crab apple over in the orchard. It's one I planted myself, come and see.'

They were standing together gazing up into a canopy of crimson, when Rud clapped his hand down on hers where it lay on his arm and exclaimed,

'What does this remind you of, Trix?'

'With you under the table. The red covering,' she flashed.

Gazing back at him, Trix could tell that she had made him happy. He was the same dear boy. Yet it made her sad, to see him so altered, so thin and worn in the face. As for Carrie, the word 'stout' did not begin to do her solid figure justice. Trix smoothed the becoming 'old rose' of her well-fitted skirt over her own neat hips.

'Not much,' he'd responded when she asked whether he was any better. Having all his teeth out was meant to put an end to his stomach trouble. It must be almost twenty years that he'd been suffering these fearful bouts of pain. The operations. The diets – he'd eaten only plain boiled potatoes at lunch. Poor darling. Carrie'd said it all began just when John was killed.

Useless doctors, the whole tribe of them. But that was one of the things she wasn't allowed to say.

Her last nurse, Mrs. Turney, had been very firm. 'No, really dear, I wouldn't go saying that to people, not if I were you.'

And old Turney's advice, which put the lid on many topics, had been good. It had worked. Jack had agreed that she was well enough to join him in Edinburgh. Granted, he still threatened to leave her from time to time. But better their fights than those miserable years spent wandering between watering-places in the company of nurses. Fifteen years of that and she was prepared to hold her tongue.

What was he saying?

'We've had all our fruit trees treated against twig blight.'

She smiled back.

But she still knew what she really believed. Rud and Carrie had cheated her, they'd carried off treasures from The Gables when her back was turned. He must have destroyed Father's will in that bonfire. She'd never had her fair share. Why, the Bokhara rug in the hall here at Bateman's came from Tisbury.

Her fingers twitched against the rough tweed of his arm.

Rud himself was gazing again into the tent of blossom, lost in thought.

'On the day I put this tree into the earth, John held it for me to shovel soil round it.'

Squeezing his arm was all she could manage.

He burst out, 'I used to think I'd spend the rest of my life here in this house but I don't care where I live now.'

'What, "go *sannyasin*", take your advanced age as a cue to become a mendicant, like some ancient Hindu?'

But he wasn't laughing.

In half an hour they'd be gone. Trix had gone in 'to powder her nose'. Rather than risk having to face time with Fleming, Rud was strolling round by the place where they buried their dogs. One sadness he could just about cope with.

Talking to Trix had stirred things up. Here, away from India, there was no form for expressing humility, for stepping aside from the world and the life one had lived in it. He'd gone as far as he could when he published those *Epitaphs of the War*. Written in his own heart's blood:

'If any question why we died
Tell them, because our fathers lied.'

There it was, out on the page, but to what avail? No-one seemed to recognise just how much he was admitting, how much his interpretation, his understanding had fallen short. Publishing that did nothing to mitigate his sense of shame. He had failed to grasp something larger, something had escaped him, though he was blowed if he could unravel the business now.

Keep walking. That's the way.

Carrie, bless her, tried to bring him comfort.

'Whose voice has been more truthful, more honest?' she always asked.

The left shoe seemed to be pinching a bit. Ignore.

From the first she swore that she would never blame him about John.

'How can we keep our son when everyone else is sending their own boys off to war?' had been her line all through.

She was right, of course. She was right. And John himself was wild to get to the Front. But they weren't taking men with weak eyesight like John's at that point in the war. If he hadn't known Bobs, if he hadn't been in a position to pull strings and get John in, would he be alive now?

No good, he must have picked up a bit of gravel from the path. Taking the shoe off, he shook it then laced it up again.

Time to turn back.

He'd never wanted to imagine Josephine growing older. With John it was different. He'd have been getting on for thirty-five now. Astonishing to envisage that boy careering about the lanes in his little Singer as a solid citizen. John, with his father's own taste for the low world of music-hall. Thirty-five and a father? There might have been grandchildren…

Oh no, not back into that groove again.

There they all were, out by the magnolia, waiting for him. He must pay attention to Trix. She'd be off any moment, back to London, after that to Edinburgh. How she stood life up there with the weather, let alone in the company of Jack Fleming, he'd never know.

Husband and wife stood together outside the gate, to wave the Flemings off to their train. In the hired car, Colonel Fleming inclined his head while Trix fluttered gloved fingers as she left her brother's company, all unwitting, for the last time.

'Dear Love,' Rud was speaking, his hand on Carrie's shoulder, as they turned back to the old house together, 'we've not done so badly, you and I.'

* * *

The dim January day left Westminster Abbey in near darkness. Elsie at her side, George Bambridge behind, Carrie was led to her place under the lantern of the great cathedral church. Above her, the roof soared into impenetrable dusk. Seated, she stared out at the platform of dark wood, surrounded by six tall candles. They pooled the area with soft light. Everything ready, set up for Rud, to receive him.

But not Rud. His ashes.

They were to lie by those of Hardy and Dickens. He was being taken away from her all over again.

Through her heavy veil, she looked steadily ahead, ignoring the twinges in her hips. Aware that Elsie was glancing at her anxiously, she straightened her shoulders. This was not the time to give way.

She'd managed to appear composed in the photographs taken as she left the Middlesex Hospital the morning after he died. There was no privacy for them of course. The papers carried all the details: at first the haemorrhage, the burst ulcer, the emergency operation. Later, the daily bulletins of rallying and relapse, the weakening heart. Just as with Rud's pneumonia in New York, long ago.

But this time he was seventy years old. She could only hold his hand and wait for an end they both knew was coming.

As his grip relaxed, 'I'm sorry. I am a bit tired,' he'd whispered.

Carrie closed her eyes, not to see that sunken face.

The organ's groan came to a stop. Everyone stood. In the silence, treble voices rose from the approaching choir. She turned, as Rud had turned to her when she came up the aisle towards him for their wedding.

The gold cross of the Abbey. The choir. Slowly the eight distinguished pall-bearers advanced at last. A spasm in her throat as the hidden body, all that was left of it, neared. A white marble urn, under that Union Jack.

Resistance stirred in her, it was absurd. A procession. A show. He'd have hated it. But there was no avoiding prominence, since he wanted to be a guide, a voice of truth for the world.

And the King had heard him. 'The late King,' she corrected herself.

The King has gone and taken his trumpeter with him,' the papers said. As though he'd been a kind of Poet Laureate. Yet he'd turned the post down when it was offered.

And what did they know or understand of the friendship between those two men? All his life Rud could talk to anyone. The King knew that when he got Rud to write the speech for that first Christmas broadcast.

At the memory her lips trembled, Rud had wept, that afternoon, hearing the King speak the words he'd chosen for him.

They were lifting the flag away, ready to move across to Poets' Corner for the interment. Now she could see it, the urn she'd chosen for him, white marble to hold him. At last it hit her. She would have to go away, leave him behind in this cold, dark place. In spite of all her resolve, her shoulders rose in sobs she could no longer master.

EPILOGUE

The summer before the second war, three years since her brother's death, Trix was an invited guest at a Discussion Meeting of the Kipling Society. The May sunshine had brought out the women in flowered *crêpe de chine*. They sat, smiling agreeably from beneath fashionable hats, round the depleted tables. A few waitresses, crowned with stiff pleats of white linen, were still gathering up the odd untouched knife or spoon. It had been an excellent lunch but then, the Secretary always made sure of that.

'Damned fine organisation, the Kipling Society,' one man murmured to another.

At the top table, the Hon. Secretary was on his feet, ready to introduce 'our distinguished speaker'. The elderly lady at his right leaned forward, her large, slightly protruberant eyes bright, as his talk on the subject of Kipling's early stories got under way.

'Oh, but forgive me, I think that's not quite correct. "The Strange Ride *of Morrowbie Jukes C.E.*" was already being worked on quite early in 1885.'

Checked, startled, but supported by the discipline of his training, the retired General paused, inclining his head in affable enquiry.

The Hon. Secretary stepped in.

'I should explain, for the benefit of those members and their guests who are seated further away, that Mrs. Fleming, the lady who was speaking, is none other than the sister of Rudyard Kipling and our guest of honour.'

The unease occasioned by the interruption was soothed, as the old General, with perfect command, turned to Trix.

'How very fascinating, Mrs. Fleming. Do tell us more.'

'It first appeared in *Quartette,* a Christmas number for the *Civil and Military Gazette* – the *CMG,* you know, as we used to call it – put together by our whole family, my parents and myself as well.'

'Indeed. You wrote for it too?'

'Oh yes, my story, 'The Haunted Cabin' was in there too. My first prose to reach print, though of course my brother and I had published verse together, in *Echoes.* Parodies, you know.'

It was as well that the General was experienced in tactical adjustment. He'd mapped out his talk with some care but now he saw that he must save the occasion. Mrs. Fleming was not going to relapse into silence. The next time she spoke, he was prepared. With every appearance of pleasure, he invited her to elaborate, taking the cues for his own remarks from hers. By the end of the twenty minutes he'd been allotted, the scheduled talk had been recast as a dialogue.

'Well done, old thing,' Irene, the General's wife whispered, patting the creased back of his freckled hand. His wink was almost imperceptible.

'I hope you'll consent to let us make a record of this auspicious day,' one of the members, up from Devon, was asking. 'I've always felt it a matter for regret that during his lifetime your brother never felt able to join us in our celebrations.'

A gracious assent. Together they stood, the Hon. Secretary, shoulder to shoulder with the guests of honour, Trix, black straw hat charmingly atilt and Florence Macdonald, her cousin, fox fur over her arm, while the camera shutter fell.

*

There was a little crowd behind Trix, now in her eighties, as she made her slow progress through the Edinburgh Zoo. One or two of them knew her as old Colonel Fleming's widow, though to most she was just the lady who made so much of the animals.

She paused to speak at every enclosure.

'These are some of my greatest friends,' she laughed over her shoulder to those who followed, well aware of the entertainment she was offering.

At her approach, the macaws flew shrieking to greet her from the other end of their cage, in a blaze of scarlet. She seemed just as well known to the hippo. Finding no sign of it when she reached its pool, Trix summoned it in her clear high voice.

'Mabel, my dear, do come over and have a word with me.'

The heavy beast came lumbering, its little eyes eager and bright. Once Trix had made her farewell, it trotted quietly away again.

When she addressed the aloof camel as 'James', he lowered his long nose, ready to accept the tidbits Trix had hidden for him in her bag. It was forbidden to feed the animals: she looked round with a pleasantly conspiratorial air.

But it was the elephant they were all waiting for.

From some way off, the creature recognised her and gave a shrill trumpet.

'Oh dear, he does get so excited,' she exclaimed.

'*Dhat. Biri. Dhat,*' she said severely, as soon as she got close.

'There, there my dear, I'm just as pleased to see *you.* Now show me you haven't forgotten your tricks.'

'*Billai,*' she said distinctly.

A foreleg was heaved up.

'*Tul.*' This time a back leg.

She clapped her hands, looking round at their delighted audience.

'And now I'll ask him to sit down.'

'*Phulai baith.*'

And the great wrinkled hindquarters sank to the ground.

Trix nodded encouragement as all round her the murmur of wonder and pleasure broke out.

Other fiction titles from

AURORA METRO BOOKS

POMEGRANATE SKY

Louise Soraya Black

Winner of The Virginia Prize For Fiction 2009

Living in post-revolutionary Tehran, Layla refuses to bow to the ayatollah's rules, resisting her mother's relentless attempts to find her a suitable husband. Instead, she embarks on an illicit affair with her art teacher Keyvan, and they tentatively imagine a future together.

But the sudden death of her uncle, an outspoken journalist, raises many unanswered questions and when Layla's cousin, who is visiting from America, is arrested by the morality police, the Komiteh, Layla's plans for the future begin to unravel.

Beneath the polished surface of upper-class Iranian life lies pain, fear and dark, dark secrets.

'a bittersweet tale of betrayed trust and ruptured innocence... the feel for colour and language is vibrant' *The Guardian* first novel choice

'Vividly written, fresh and eloquent, a girl's poignant tale of love and menace in contemporary Iran.'
Fay Weldon

£8.99

ISBN 9781906582104

THE SCREAM

Laurent Graff

Translated by Cheryl Robson and Claire Allejo

The narrator is a solitary soul living at the end of the world, continuing his daily routine of going to work in a toll booth on the highway. A terrible, mysterious sound that seems to come from nowhere is wiping out the population and every day fewer and fewer people come by. But not everyone can hear the sound and very soon the only survivors will be those 'silent ones' left unharmed.

What peculiar power does Munch's painting of *The Scream* exert? Why does reality become stranger than fiction? *The Scream* begins in the twilight zone of science fiction, taking the reader on a hallucinatory road trip where emotions shape the world to the point where it becomes unrecognisable.

'Laurent Graff's books are crazy, weird and outlandish, which makes them totally indispensable' *www.event.fr*

'There is no doubt about it, the writer of *The Scream* is an extravagant and profound storyteller.' *Le Mondes de livres*

£7.99

ISBN 9781906582258

MOSAIC DECEPTIONS

Patrick Gooch

When Matt Clements meets an enigmatic prophet on the Kurdistan border, he is set on the trail of ancient relics that have profound consequences for our time. Assembling his team, he travels to the most remote desert regions of the Middle East, unaware that the search for evidence endangers all their lives.

In a race against time, Matt must outwit his adversaries to present his discoveries publicly in New York – discoveries that will send shockwaves throughout the Western world and rewrite history as we know it.

'Thought provoking and intelligent thriller' *Metro*

'…A real page-turner that jolts us out of complacency with a bold and clever plot…' *Dazed & Confused*

£8.99

ISBN 9781906582142

Coming soon....

DAFNE & THE DOVE

Jonathan Falla

When Silke Khan and her husband Theo come crashing into Dr Mattieu Macanan's carefully constructed life as a medic in Patagonia, his world is irrevocably altered...

An avid pilot, Theo wishes to run an airmail service to the area, one of the remotest parts of South America, and Mattieu must face intrusion and change. But what has he been hiding from? Should his way of life – and that of the local tribe he seeks to protect – be preserved at any cost?

A beautifully written and absorbing story of violence, addiction and repressed desire, exploring the human psyche from a remote part of Chile around 1915…

Reviews of Falla's previous work:

'A book saturated with loving detail, unpredictable and opulent.'
The Sunday Times

'Refreshing, unapologetically subjective and original.'
The New Statesman

£9.99

ISBN: 9781906582388

THE VIRGINIA PRIZE
FOR FICTION

Virginia Woolf (1882–1941)Virginia Woolf completed and published her first novel *The Voyage Out* while living in Paradise Road in Richmond-upon-Thames, England.

In 1917, Virginia and her husband Leonard founded the Hogarth Press to publish work by fellow writers.

Named in memory of Virginia Woolf, the Virginia Prize for Fiction celebrates her significant contribution to modernist literature and her enduring inspiration to women writers everywhere.

The Prize is held biennially and is open to any woman over eighteen years of age who has written a full-length unpublished novel in English. Authors who have had other work published previously are eligible to apply.

For more information:
www.aurorametro.com

To find out about other titles from
Aurora Metro Books please visit our website

www.aurorametro.com